The Lady of the Red Moon

ANN WALLAND-MOORE

Pen Press Publishers Ltd

First published in Great Britain by
Pen Press Publishers Ltd
39-41, North Road
Islington
London N7 9DP

ISBN 1-905203-57-8

Printed and bound in the UK

A catalogue record of this book is available from
the British Library

Cover design by Jacqueline Abromeit

Disclaimer

The world of imagination in which the events related in this book take place was originally a shared invention of Joy Chant and myself. She has already published in RED MOON AND BLACK MOUNTAIN and THE GREY MANE OF MORNING, books that have developed and explored her part of this world.

Inevitably, because I have been slower to bring my part into print, and as the inexorabilities of our lives have drawn us apart, discrepancies of fundamental importance to our once unified concept have arisen.

We feel it best, therefore, whilst happily acknowledging the common origins of our myth to let it develop separately. A careful comparison between the cosmology of our two worlds would consequently be unprofitable, but we each hope that we have been true to the inner consistencies of our own variant inventions.

About the Author

Ann Walland-Moore was born in Peterborough in 1944, due to the war, but prefers to think of herself as a Londoner, where her father's family have lived and worked in printing for generations and where she herself grew up and started work in the early sixties. She is the oldest of seven children.

When her parents moved to Norfolk in the seventies she followed them, working for Norwich City Hall and then a local newspaper.

She married Peter Moore in 1973, but kept her maiden name as well since she bred Burmese cats under this name, and Peter got fed up with people calling him Mr Walland.

In 1974 they moved to North Walsham and have lived in the same house ever since. Before her husband left local government to start his own Town Planning Consultancy, she worked a cook in a hotel and then for the local printer, but is now a partner her husband's business. She is much involved in politics and does the printing for her local party at election time. She is a town councillor.

They have three children and two grandchildren who live next door. Her hobbies are, when she has time, patchwork, bead jewellery and gardening.

This book is dedicated to the late Rayner Unwin with thanks for all the encouragement and help he gave me over the years; whose hand so strangely reached beyond the grave and sent me once again to record the history of the Lords of the House of Abard.

THE AVENYA PLAINS

NEROS ERINYOS

1500 metre line

To Kaeyama

500 metres l

Yakré'a
North Gate
of the Mines

R. Yaval

R. Telga

Mara-set

R. Quereïa

R. Quantor

R. Tréanda

Quantos

NEROS YANNYOS

R. Randa

R. Safel

Irterian

Vadré Dru

To Irranya

Ebrinen   Mara-mer

R.Telga

Furah

Banéros

R. Wyre

Pleorine Hills

500 metres

East Gate
of the Mines

R. Lee'ma Ra

WARNY LANDS

Grey Halls

Mara-lei

Nenaterian

Belia

500 metres

1500 metre

ERUETH KINGDOM

Elen   Runi

Lake
Vanda   Eloruna

Tal-elen

R. Elda

R. Evénfel

Hordé

High Aré'las Pass

1500 metre

NEROS ARE'LAS

PELELORNE

MUNDRA

Mundra

South Gate
of the Mines

Hélans Dru   The Gate

500 metres line

NEROS ARE'LAS

1500 metre line

500 metres line

KINDATH

MORDATA

The Sea Kingdoms
of André'as

Loré'as

PROLOGUE

The night was dark without the moons, but a red glow from the earth reflected on the low clouds. The burning mountains made smokes and reeks in the unquiet sky. The air was foul with sulphurous fumes. Occasionally, a great flare would suddenly light the black range red and orange and then die back to a sullen glow. These were the Neros Yannyos, the Mountains of Fire, which marched the length of Avenya keeping the western sea from the eastern plains. Here, where the Neros Erinyos sprang from their eastern flank, they burned their strongest, creating a barren landscape alive only with fire.

There was a road that led up the Yarval valley to the mightiest of all the mountains of fire, Yakré'a. On this path rode the Lord Eldest Malcarious on his black beast, which men called a horse (although that was not his name for it). Presently the path ended in a sheer mountainside. Two great pillars of black stone were set into the mountain and on them hung the northern gates of the mines under the mountains. These gates were full five times the height of a man, their gilded copper cladding reflecting the lurid light. Patterns of topaz, carnelian and garnet shone on them and on each gate was the copper disc symbol of the red moon.

Malcarious smiled grimly at this. He dismounted and there came the hard sound of metal on metal as he drew his sword, Yadra, from the scabbard slung over his shoulder. Then he spoke the password and the gates opened to him.

He stepped into the high domed hall behind the gates. The white light was dazzling for a moment. The gates rolled shut behind him, but he was not afraid and his sword was in his hand.

Waiting for him in the hall was a Daline, one of the small, swart creatures of the mines. The Lord Youngest Mildur he was called. Once he had been lord of the Dalines and ruled all the dwellers in the mountains from André'as to Kaeyama, but the Lords Eldest had taken all he had and now he was but a servant to them and steward of Yakré'a.

"Where is she?" demanded the Lord Eldest, sounding each word.

Mildur did not reply instantly, instead he looked the man up and down, noting the shabby garments, the new hardness in the dark face and the beard, which did not hide the stern line of the jaw. If he took pleasure in anything it was Yadra, the jewel in the cunningly wrought hilt and the gleaming bronze blade. He had forged it himself in these very mountains and knew its temper well.

The Lord Eldest took a step forward.

"I said, where is she?"

"Lord Eldest Malcarious, the Great Lady Yannya is in her room of seeing. Doubtless she is aware that you are here. I shall see if she will speak with you."

He took another step forwards, Mildur stepped hastily back. Then another voice spoke, a low and melodious woman's voice. "I am here and I shall speak with you, but not if you bully my people. Any quarrel you have is with me, not them."

He looked up and beyond Mildur to the speaker and the sight of her was a physical blow. He had forgotten that she was so fair. In the ages of his imprisonment, he had forgotten the substance and remembered only her shadow. When his kinsmen had spoken to him of her at his trial, he had not remembered the half of her beauty. On his long journey to Yakré'a he had forgotten her face, but not his anger. Now she stood before him. A woman, tall, with a copper skin and stormy dark copper hair. A perfect face, a perfect figure. Beautiful and fierce. As still and terrible as the eye of a storm. She was as strong as the mountains yet a woman, full and immeasurably fair. For a moment he remembered his old love, but it drowned in the bitterness of her betrayal. "I would speak to you alone, woman."

She motioned him to follow her and together they passed through the corridors of the mountain. How well he remembered them, the variety of the patterned mosaic walls, the odd stone of gold glinting in the overhead lights, some great panoramas, some scenes of myths from before the time of the coming of the Lords Eldest, some just patterns repeated endlessly interspersed by undecorated living rock. Presently they came to an arch closed by a curtain of fine white linen sequinned with gold flowers. She held the curtain back for him to enter and followed him.

This was her room of seeing. A great circular room, the walls of which were pierced by three arches, each closed with a curtain. Facing the entrance through which they had come was a throne of grey stone set hard against the wall centrally between the other arches. Behind the throne, a great mosaic spread showing the red moon rising over fields of corn, full of rich reds, oranges and gold. The cream marble floor of the room fell in three wide steps, each edged in dark basalt, to a circle at the very centre of which stood

3

a copper brazier full of hot coals. On one wall hung a full-length copper mirror, its surface not bright, but misty.

She stepped across the room and sat in her throne to face him. He was forced to stand lower than her, as a plaintive. He clenched his right fist and held hard to the sword in his left, but she feared no sword of power. Only one thing could unmake her. She had watched him in her mirror on the way up the Yarvel valley, so his arrival was no surprise to her. She did not know why he had been sent to her, but knew it must concern his trial and subsequent punishment, and doubtless her own punishment. So like the Eldest to make him come to her again. Such petty spite. They could have sent anyone else.

"Will you have a cup of wine with me?" she asked, not entirely seriously. "I had not thought to welcome you again to Yakré'a."

"You will have no thought of welcome when I am done, woman." Even to his own ears his voice grated.

"Then speak your business and have done." Poor man, she thought, what have your kinsmen done to you? And you trust them, not me? And if I tease you for my own amusement I hurt only you, not them. What am I to do?

"Hear me, woman, the Lords Eldest have taken council and this they have decreed: that for your part in my failure to defeat my brother Yatior and force him to return the Diadem of the Eldest, you are to be imprisoned. From this time forth you will be confined to Yakré'a. Never again will you see the sun rise or set, never again will you smell the forests nor the grasslands, never again will you hear any sound save the tread of your Dalines through the mountains. And it will be death for mortal man to look you in the eyes."

Interesting, she thought, refusing to be impressed by this. I wonder what the Lords Eldest are up to now? Whose hand is misdirecting whose eye? It all sounds very easy to me. I thought they wanted me dead?

He thought the punishment would have dismayed her, for he knew how much she loved the mortal realm, but her face showed him nothing save a mild curiosity.

"Tell me," she asked, "is that all?"

"Is that not enough?"

"My Lord Eldest Malcarious, do your kinsmen really think they have enough power to confine me here for ever? Have you forgotten that my power waxes and wanes with the red moon and on the night it is full not one of you, nor all of your Lords Eldest shall prevent me from walking where I will. And shall the Quarenyos Queens be unable to endure my gaze? They are my friends and servants amongst mortal men."

"The Queens are dead. The Quaren are slaves of the Alliance of the Free Peoples of Avenya. Your temples are burned and your priestesses scattered."

Then she understood: this was true Eldest revenge. "You sanctioned this, High Lord of the Eldest?"

"As you of all people know, I was imprisoned in the mines under the mountains until the very end, Madam."

She leaned back in her throne and looked hard at him, trying to puzzle out what the Lords Eldest's real purpose in this was. She had not dared look closely at him before, but now she thought she might do so without betraying her true feelings. She saw how old and tired was his well beloved face, how shabby his clothes, how cold and bitter his anger. He was hard now. His Eldest brightness had gone. He would never need or want her help again. But she had known what she was doing. Better he lived hating her than died loving her.

He took this pause as his dismissal and bowed. "Goodbye, fell sorceress. I do not say farewell for I wish you ill in all you do and hope never to have reason to see you more." He turned to go but she spoke again.

"Stay!" she commanded and he obeyed. "Lord, you are by birth the High Lord of the Eldest, but you come to me in clothes so travel-stained and worn that a man would not wear them. You have told me of my fate at the hands of the Eldest, but I know them of old. Tell me, you failed them through no fault of your own. What punishment have they laid on you?"

"That is between me and my kin and no business of yours, woman!"

Her yellow eyes looked into his green eyes and found to her horror that they were those of a mortal. She was more powerful than he, who should be the High Lord of the Eldest. "Tell me!" she commanded and held him in her gaze.

He tore himself away from her eyes and looked to the floor and this action hurt her more than any other, for he had been a proud prince and the son of a queen, the greatest lord amongst all his kin.

He said slowly, "For my failure, unwitting as it was, the Lords Eldest have taken my name away. No longer am I the Lord Eldest Malcarious, but the lord of darkness, for out of the dark I came and of darkness only am I the lord. And here in the mortal realm I must dwell with mortal men as a man until, being mortal, I die. My uncle Mérior is High Lord of the Eldest." He took courage and glanced at her face, expecting to see vengeful pleasure there, and was surprised to see only pain and compassion.

"Terrible indeed is the justice of the Lords Eldest."

He said, "I am a fool, tried, condemned and now punished."

She stood up and walked down to him, holding out a hand, but he thrust it away.

"Touch me not, woman, your love has brought me low, but your pity will destroy me. It is too late now for regret." He turned on his heel and walked away from her, intending never to return.

CHAPTER ONE

The lord of darkness left Yakré'a and travelled south to the Elta city of Mara Set. Thence he rode south and east, across the wide plains of Avenya, through forest and rich corn land, crossing the great rivers, the Telga and the Lee'ma Ra and after many days he reached the Warny lands. He took the old driftway which led to the upper plains and where the Aré'las Mountains marched in a great wall eastward to the sea he came to the Grey Halls, city and fortress of Warany, prince of the Warny.

Although night had fallen, the gate-wards let him pass into the fortress town. He left his horse at the main stables just within the gates and climbed the narrow cobbled streets to the castle that towered over the rest of the town. This was Warany's home, the prince of the Warny. Here he entered unchallenged, for Warany had no need to set a watch on his own doors, and found his way through the sprawling castle to the private apartments of the mortal who had befriended him.

Warany sat by the fire, his little daughter Anya on his lap and his eldest son Derany, full five years old, on a stool at his feet. He was a tall man with curling dark hair, weather beaten skin and brilliant blue eyes. Nanenethen, his wife of six years, sat with her head bent over her sewing. Her hair tumbled to her waist in great waves and was gold as autumn leaves. Her eyes were as green as beech trees in the spring. She was exceedingly beautiful.

When he saw that it was the dark Lord Eldest, whom he had taken under his wing after his escape from the mines under the mountains, who entered, Warany sprang to his feet and, handing Anya to her mother, embraced him. "Lord! It has been so long! I last saw you when you were arrested by your kinsmen after the battle at Nenaterian. I thought perhaps you had returned to your proper place as High Lord of the Eldest, and I should not see you again!"

The Dark Lord shook his head, "No, my uncle Mérior has taken the Lordship of the Eldest. On me they laid the doom of mortal man and took away my name." His voice was full of sadness.

Warany was horrified. He had wondered why his friend had looked so haggard, travel stained and so old. "How can they do this?" he asked. "Is there nothing that can be done?"

The fallen Lord Eldest shrugged and with half a smile said, "I never desired the Diadem. If my uncle wants it so much, let him have joy of it. I am, at least, free of my imprisonment in the mines. I have you, old friend."

Yes, thought Warany, me but no other. He remembered how bright, how shining, the Lord Eldest Malcarious had been. Now there was no brightness. His clothes were shabby; there was mud on his boots and no Eldest would ever wear a beard. "And what of your brother the Lord Eldest Yatior and the..." He hesitated to speak Yannya's name, knowing it could be dangerous, "...the red witch?"

"I was held to account by a jury of my peers. Yatior's exile was continued in his absence, half my brother Gawen's power was taken away and the sorceress is bound under her mountain."

"Bound?"

"She is as hard to hold as a handful of water, but I have delivered to her the decree of my kinsfolk. Whether they can hold her prisoner is a different matter, but for good or ill I have done my part and she lies under Yakré'a now and forever a forgotten thing behind me. The moons have waxed and waned many times since last we loved and gone is all that ever passed between us." He sighed, "Hé, Warany, do all men feel the weariness that is on me?"

Warany put a hand on his friend's shoulder, "Come Lord, rest now with me. Join my family by the fire and forget that you ever had other kin. You shall be as my brother." He escorted the Dark Lord to a chair and took his tattered cloak away from him. "You know my wife, Nanenethen, lady of the Erueth?"

The Dark Lord smiled at the lady. Aeons before it had been suggested by his father that he might take her as his wife, but he had seen his brother's concubine, the Lady Yannya, and fallen in love with her instead.

"We know each other well," said the lady, "our kinsmen hoped we would marry, but we both found our pleasures elsewhere." She looked covertly at her husband, her strong, beautiful husband and thought again how much she loved him and how seldom she saw him. She wished he would have nothing to do with the Alliance but now the Dark Lord might share the burden, and perhaps she would see Warany more.

A servant brought cakes and wine. The Dark Lord sat by the fire sipping, from a silver goblet. "The wine seems to have improved," he said.

"Only the best Mundran now," said Warany with a smile. "Darké'us has a shipload of it sent up every year."

"Darké'us?"

"You don't know what happened after that last battle when we defeated the Quaren, do you? Your kinsmen took you prisoner in our moment of triumph. Oh I needed your common sense. It seems that only you and I in the whole of Avenya have any."

"But the Alliance defeated the Quarenyos Queens. You had won. What was the problem?"

"Foolishly I had not realised that it would be one thing to lead the Alliance to a great victory and quite another to apportion the spoils. The moment everyone realised we had won it was like being at a family funeral where there was no will, with everybody out for what they could get and some out for what they could stop others from getting. To be frank, I am beginning to think the Quaren were welcome to Avenya and the Queens made a pretty decent job of ruling it."

"At last," said Nanenethen quietly.

"Sounds rather heretical."

Warany made a face at his wife before continuing. "There we were: no rulers, no one to tax the peasants, which seems to be the only incentive they recognise to grow more food than they need, banditry springing up everywhere, and war lords settling old scores. The whole of Avenya was in danger of falling apart. So I had to decide who should rule what. Where the Quaren had recently conquered a country and there was still the remnants of a royal family fighting on our side, I gave them the country. Trouble was deciding who had the greatest right. Does a king's sister's son have more right to the throne than a king's daughter's son? I don't know. I had to knock a few heads together I can tell you. Your brother Gawen's mortal son Ruén took over the Sea Kingdoms of André'as as overlord and I left him to sort out the petty kingdoms, except for Loré'as which I had to give to Herumanus, because he had been such a loyal member of the Alliance. Deranin is king of Kindath, Terué is king of Mordata, which was fair and for Pelélorné, I chose Verne, not that I like him but I liked Branden less."

"And Mundra?" asked the Dark Lord, the thought bringing a smile to his lips.

"Ah, Mundra," said Warany also smiling, "well, I saved the best until last. I knew there would be real problems there. Darké'us was going to make the best job of it, I knew that and Darké'us knew that, but his claim to the throne was non-existent. He was only lord of hosts and a Banérothen to boot. I couldn't see how I was to pull it off. I put off the decision for as long as I could. I mean, the man had virtually saved us, getting the city lords to change sides when he did. We owed him a lot."

"Being Darké'us, he probably took it, too."

"What's a little gold here and there?"

"That depends on your definition of a little."

"All right, so he stole the temple treasure of Nenaterian, but he did win that last battle for us. Anyway, by the time I came to see who was eligible to be king, there was no one left but him. Everyone else had either died or left Mundra for their health. So the problem was solved. And we are delivered a ship full of decent wine every year."

"You have to admire Darké'us," said the Dark Lord. "His ability to change sides at the right moment is breath taking. His grasp of politics amazing. I wished I had had him with me when I was on trial before my kinsmen, but then I would always have had the uncomfortable suspicion that my uncle Mérior had already bought him off. And that brings me to the girl. The daughter of the High Queen, the Andra they called her. What of her?"

"Curious thing that," said Warany reflectively. "Her

mother thrust her at Darké'us although he was only her traitor lord of hosts at the time. She has settled down in Mundra to be his fourth or fifth concubine and got herself pregnant to ensure her pension. All the rest of the Quaren royal family are dead now, except that sister who is hiding in the Pleorine hills. She is less trouble than the Alliance."

"Issue?" The Dark Lord's voice was hard. He remembered the day when the Alliance had held the High Queen at bay in the temple of Yannya at Nenaterian, when the High Queen had cursed him. Not Warany, who had engineered her fall, nor the other mortals, but him. He remembered her words, *And you, Lord Eldest Malcarious, you shall regret this day, for my daughter goes with Darké'us and she shall bear a son and that son I now bestow on you, for he shall be your servant and your friend and he shall destroy all that you hold dear. Then shall you remember the High Queen of the Quaren, and her people whom you have destroyed, and shed bitter tears.*

"I had arranged with Darké'us that if it was a girl she should die an early death," said Warany, "the Alliance cannot afford a daughter to the Quarenyos Queens."

Nanenethen looked at him and sighed, not understanding how a man who loved his little daughter as much as Warany loved Anya could speak so unemotionally of robbing another woman of hers. She remembered her uncle's words, *Mortal men bring pain,* and it was true. For all the joy Warany had brought her, he had also brought much pain.

"But as the High Queen said, it was a boy. Keré'us he was called, which means light in Quarin. He must be about the same age as Derany here." He smiled at his little son.

Nanenethen stood up, "You men will talk all night," she said, "but the children need sleep and Terany needs feeding.

I must go." She kissed Warany, her beautiful hair sweeping his face and shoulders, then she gathered up her children and left the room.

In her absence, Warany dared ask the question that was burning in his mind, "So tell me Lord, are you as mortal man in the number of your days?"

"I do not know, Warany. All my Eldest magic is gone, but I still have the wild magic from my mother, which they could not take from me. But it is hard, so hard not to be able to travel by the High Roads. To walk or to ride everywhere. No wonder you mortals tire so soon.

"Mind you, I had an interesting time of it crossing the plains, although there seemed to be some order emerging." He smiled at the memory of the occasional bandit who had been foolish enough to cross his path.

"I had an interesting time of it sorting out the plains," said Warany indignantly. "If you remember, the Quaren had nine cities on the plains. Those whom you and Darké'us persuaded to remain neutral when it was obvious we were going to win we left alone. I let the city lords carry on – I had no one who could do the job. I didn't even have anyone who knew what the job was. Most of the cities that stood against us we razed. To destroy the memory of the people who once lived in them we have taken away their names and given them numbers. Only Mara Malac, which we now call Mara-lei, the ninth city, we had to keep running. Without the warriors who served there we had no police force. I've changed the uniforms to a serviceable dark green and put them all in trousers, so they look like men and left Herany in charge, creating the title Maren-Ra for him. He embraced the chastity, discipline and poverty of the old order with both hands and is now running an interestingly fanatical organisation of which I am a little terrified, but which is bringing back order to the chaos of the plains. He demands that all our sons are sent to school there, to be educated in the art of the chivalrous warrior and makes the rest of the lords of the Alliance meet there once a year for a council. He calls his new organisation the Wanderers, the Trumarei, the warrior brotherhood, who bring law and order. They are keeping the Alliance together by keeping us all in touch with each other and they spend a lot of time killing bandits. They worry me, but I can't do it all."

"So that is the cities. I was at Mara-set recently, so I know Warond the Elta took it over with his people."

"His brother Arno is building a new city to the north west of lake Vanda, using the old stones from the destroyed city there."

"I was going to ask you about that," said the Dark Lord, "I left his new city well to the west when I crossed the Lee'ma Ra, but it made me feel uneasy. Does Arno still have the hilt of the sacrificial knife, Hiruéven, that he took from the Queen?"

"Yes, the copper blade was broken and he had a new blade forged on the hilt and renamed it Aren, meaning iron blade. Some wandering Daline fell into his clutches and was forced to do it. He's up to something there."

Warany sensed the Dark Lord becoming suddenly more interested.

"My uncle escorted me back to Avenya personally to begin my exile. When he did so, he mentioned the sacrificial knife to me. He told me that it had in its hilt some stone of power, which that red witch Yannya had stolen from him long ago. Apparently, she had left it with the Quarenyos Queens for safety. A clear stone, like a diamond, he said. It had a platinum collar round it so it could be removed from the hilt."

Warany looked puzzled, "I had heard a rumour that the stone in the hilts of Hiruéven was more than that."

"Then my uncle suggested to me that should I manage to lay my hands on this, this minor stone of power, he might, after a decent interval, use his supreme powers to quash my exile."

"But…," began Warany.

"Yes, I know which stone is set in the hilts of Hiruéven, because I was there when it was taken from my brother Yatior by the red witch, and I stood behind her, with Hara, Gawen and Amunrhoieneth all bearing the swords of power and making a great magic to defeat him. I was there, too, when she had Mildur set it into the hilts of Hiruéven, which she wore as her sword in the wars of the Diadem. Until she betrayed us all.

"I did not know what had happened to it until, in the moment that the Queen used it to curse me, I saw it and recognised it. I tried to stop Arno, but then my kinsmen came for me. But I know Arno knew what it was.

"Now, I know Arno is a sorcerer. He might have guessed the significance of Hiruéven, or someone might have told him. My brother Yatior springs to mind. The appearance of a wandering Daline makes me wonder as well. Any species less likely to wander than a Daline would be hard to find. But I know that the red witch has an interest and there are many others as well. Any of my kin could have commanded a Daline."

Warany frowned, "Yet others say that stone is set into the throne of the Lord Most High Eldest and it lost all its power when the Lord Eldest Yatior used it to turn Yannya from a copper statue into a woman." His frown turned to a laugh. "I can see that if your brother deceived your uncle, when Yannya took it, he could hardly complain to anyone."

"I am troubled, Warany, that stone has so much power.

A great number of other creatures will be trying to take it from Arno. Wandering Daline indeed? Both my brother and the red witch knew it was out of their hands and into those of a mortal, and my uncle obviously knows as well. I should be rather anxious if I were Arno."

"Old friend," said Warany clapping him on the shoulder, "I shall let Arno be your special concern. The Star-stone is no business of us mere mortals."

The Dark Lord looked grave, "Mortal men will fare ill if it falls into the wrong hands. A man holding the Elorianen could enslave the world. An immortal holding it could enslave the universe."

"Yet the Queens did not use its powers, nor yet the Lady Yannya."

"The Queens did not need to use it and for all that has fared between me and the red witch, I must say that she did not want to rule the world. Would she have not done so else?"

CHAPTER TWO

The Dark Lord over-wintered in the Grey Halls and in the spring, he and Warany set out for the meeting of the Trumarei at Mara-lei. Nanenethen watched them go with foreboding and, although Warany promised to be back within three months, she did not believe him. She had seen before how the Alliance took all his time and hated it for this. He had won the war for these people. Why would they not let him spend the peace at home with her and their family?

"Make no rash promises my lord," she told him, "for you will regret them."

At Mara–lei they met with all the lords of the Alliance and Warany was again expected to settle disputes, but this time with the Dark Lord's knowledge to call upon. Order was slowly emerging out of the chaos of the victory over the Quaren and the Trumarei were becoming acknowledged as a force for justice. Local bandits became scarcer and farming more productive when a Trumaré, clad in his uniform of dark green, occupied the empty house of the displaced Quarin priest in a village. Staging posts had been organised and communications improved vastly.

The fanatical Herany said to Warany, "Give me a few more years and they will remember the rule of the Queens as the bad old days. If only we could subdue the Gate, we would control the whole of Avenya."

The Gate was a thorn in Warany's side too. It was the only pass through the Aré'las mountains low enough to be crossed in winter. There was a small, but enthusiastic Quaren garrison stationed there and during the wars they had built a wall across the road for ease of defence. They had thus managed to keep the André'ans in the south from joining Warany's forces in the north. Ultimately, Arno had been sent with his Elta army to destroy the Gate, which they did by sheer force of numbers and not a little high magic, but the fortress on the mountainside above the Gate was not destroyed and many of the defeated Quaren soldiers escaped thither. Once the Alliance armies had passed through the Gate and gone about their legitimate business of destroying the Quarenyos Queens, the soldiers on the Gate, under their enterprising captain called Melin, rebuilt the wall rather more substantially and were now operating it as a toll-gate. The Alliance found it humiliating to pay a toll to the Quaren and their lack of control of the pass irritated them. Many of the sea kingdoms of André'as had switched to using ships to transport cargo, but the city of Banéros controlled the confluence of the three main rivers of Avenya and they charged harbour dues, and the distance to some of the cities was doubled travelling by water. When everything else was running so well it was most unsatisfactory.

"I can't do everything," said Warany, and Herany was forced to leave it at that.

The Dark Lord embraced the dark green uniform of the Trumarei together with their wandering lifestyle, but no one dared ask him to make the Trumarei vows. Although, as one of the Eldest he was not permitted to take human life, few miscreants, on seeing him riding into a previously lawless town, waited to find out if this were really true. He and Warany mostly travelled together from dispute to dispute, only returning to the Grey Halls for Warany to supervise the harvest. It was then that Nanenethen told Warany that she was expecting his fourth child, which would be due just after the year-turning. She seemed particularly concerned about this child and begged him to be there when it was born.

"I shall be back for the year-turning, I give you my word." he said, taking her hand.

"As you were all those other times? Lord, since I wedded you seven years ago, I have spent barely a year with you. Do you know what that one year has cost me?"

Warany looked at her sad face and kissed away the warm tears that sprung unbidden from her unhappiness. "Nanu, you knew when you married me how life would be with me. I did not choose to be first lord of the Alliance. That destiny your uncle chose for me when he put the sword of power, Erindra, in my hand. I had hoped to be back with you by now, but life is not so. Avenya will not run itself. Be patient my dear, and do not chide me like this. You know I shall return to you as soon as I may and that my heart is ever here with you."

And she knew what he said was fair, yet she loved him so much she could not find the words to tell him of the promise she had been obliged to make to her uncle before he had agreed to her wedding a mortal. So she kissed him and forgave him, as always.

When Warany and the Dark Lord left the Grey Halls, Nanenethen took her children and went south to the forests of D'Erueth to be with her own people for a space. The Erueth were not immortal, but were Lords Youngest, with lives far outreaching those of mortal man and many more powers. Nanenethen's father had been their lord, but when he died at Malcarious' side during the battles for the Diadem, her uncle had become lord of the Erueth.

Nanenethen stayed with her brother, Kaerhoieneth, until the leaves of the forest turned gold, then she bade him goodbye forever and returned to the Grey Halls.

Warany was firm at Mara-lei. He bade farewell to his friends and turned south in good time to reach the Grey Halls. He had a gold necklace made, set with peridots, the colour of Nanenethen's eyes, as her gift for the year-turning and he was looking forward to the pleasure it would give her.

"This time," he said to the Dark Lord, "they will have to come to the Grey Halls if they want Warany. I'll not break my word to her again."

They took the Quarin road south, pausing at the site of Arno's new city of Elen, which he was building on the headwaters of the river Lee'ma Ra, since they were interested to see how Arno fared. However, Arno was not a sorcerer for nothing and prudently absented himself on a visit to his brother Warond in the north. Only Hraldor, his chief of staff, was there to offer them hospitality. He had been Arno's lord of hosts during the Alliance wars and they were old friends.

"How goes it?" Warany cheerfully asked him over dinner, which, having been cooked by Quaren slaves, was far superior to anything the Elta could produce.

"Slowly," Hraldor gloomed into his wine. "These Quaren are enough to drive anyone insane. They are organised by master masons from the old Mara Keltior. All enslaved now, but privileged craftsmen. You'd think they would be pleased to be working at their old trade. I keep telling them that if they don't like it there are always the copper mines in the Yannyos mountains, but it doesn't stop them. This, that and the other, if we don't do it a certain way it's unlucky...you can't build when the red moon's dark, it's unlucky...I had enough, but then the Lord Arno was there one day when they were moaning and he stood no nonsense, ran the chief mason through with that new sword of his. That speeded the rest of them up a bit. We are doing better with the fields. Our people are clearing them and we had our first real harvest last year." He paused. There was very little the other two could say in response, so he continued, "I hear you are still having problems with the Gate?"

Warany sighed, "Perhaps I should send Arno down there again."

"The trouble is, they've seen what he can do once. They'll have some Yana priestess waiting for him, the old Queen's sister from the Pleorine hills or one of the Five from Banéros. That would make things interesting."

"Remind me," Warany said to the Dark Lord, "to sort out the priestesses of the Pleorine hills."

"On your own, or will you need some help?" asked the Dark Lord.

Hraldor laughed. Warany's prowess with the ladies was legendary.

Warany changed the subject back to the Gate, "I am sure that if Melin and I could talk man to man, I could get him to see sense, but he refuses to talk to me. He has forgotten that he is the last remnant of the Quarin Empire and if he continues to be recalcitrant, I shall be obliged to remember this and deal with him accordingly."

"Did you know that there is more trouble down there?"

asked Hraldor. "Verne of Pelélorné has tried to take some soldiers through the Gate. The man's an idiot. He should have waited until spring and taken them through the High Pass, but oh no, he's king of Pelélorné and Melin has to do as he says."

The Dark Lord smiled. "I can imagine what Melin's response was to that."

"It doesn't help the Sea Kingdoms. Melin has shut the Gate and refuses to speak to anyone. Can't get supplies through. The Sea Kingdoms are going to be in a real muddle without supplies of corn from Hordé. Bad harvest down there this year and winter is no time to be moving grain by sea."

"They'll have to get some from Mundra instead," said Warany tired of the demands made on him.

"Mundra will require paying in advance," said Hraldor.

The weather turned suddenly and they set off the next morning through driving rain along the muddied track Quaren slaves were slowly turning into a paved road. The road ran alongside Lake Vanda, the waters of which were swollen by the unusually high rainfall that autumn. They stayed that night in a new inn, half built, which would serve the new road. After a supper of Elta soup and unleavened bread, Warany sat on the bed and morosely watched the rain drip through the unfinished thatched roof into a pot originally supplied for a slightly different purpose.

"At least it will be snowing in the Grey Halls."

"And if it is, we must make haste," said the Dark Lord, "for by the time we get there the roads will be closing."

The next day they reached Runi, the town that had grown up around the bridge Arno had lately built over the river

Lee'ma Ra, where it flows from Lake Vanda. They went to stay at the Trumarei post there. The warrior in charge welcomed them eagerly.

"Lord Warany, I have a message for you from the Gate, just arrived. We were hoping that you would break your journey here." He led Warany to a travel-stained party of fellow warriors who were eating in the refectory.

The leader sprang to his feet and saluted sharply. "Lord Warany, it is the greatest good fortune that we find you here!"

"Maybe for you."

"Lord, Melin of the Gate has agreed to parley with you."

"Not me, I have promises to keep. I have to be at my halls by year-turning."

"I will go," said the Dark Lord.

"Nay, Lords, Melin said he would speak to Warany and none other."

Warany looked grim, "Can Melin not wait until after the year has turned?"

"Lord, Melin cares not how long he waits, but the snow is already thick on the high pass. Unless the Gate is opened soon, we shall not get supplies to the Sea Kingdoms before the spring."

Warany looked at the Dark Lord, his blue eyes troubled, "Eight or nine days if I go by road, six or seven if I go cross country and hope to find better weather on the west of the hills the far side of Hordé. A day or two talking, then eight or nine days to the Grey Halls, if the high Aré'las road is passable. I could just make it if all goes well. Otherwise it will be three weeks after the year-turning before I can get to Melin, longer if the roads are bad. Will you go to her and explain? Tell her I shall be there for the year-turning though all hell should bar my way. She will understand I cannot abandon my friends."

From her window on the west Nanenethen saw the Dark Lord on his black horse riding alone to the Grey Halls and guessed what news he brought. She sent word down to the gate wards that he was not to be admitted and she saw him ride back across the snow before the sun set that day.

The Dark Lord rode south west, up into the Aré'las mountains and took the track which led along the north side of the great range. The snow was already deep and still falling. It was well for him that neither he nor S'elrashen, the great black beast he called his horse, were much affected by the cold, but he feared for Warany on the same path. By the third day even he could go no further and was forced to wait out a storm in a cave. Then, as evening fell, the snow died away and the frosty skies cleared, the last shred of the silver moon shone pale and he could go on, S'elrashen breaking through the freezing surface of the snow. As the first fingering rays of morning made long blue shadows on the desert of snow, he found Warany, still walking, more dead than alive.

"I had almost given up hope, Lord."

"Horse?"

"Dead a day back. I have known these mountains all my life and have never seen so much snow as early as this. Did you tell her?"

"She would not let me in. You must make haste. Take my cloak and horse. I shall make my way as best I can." He wrapped Warany in his thick cloak and set him on S'elrashen's back. The dry cloak and fresh horse put new heart into Warany. He set off home with new hope in his heart and S'elrashen, glad of the lighter weight of a mortal, bore him easily.

Nanenethen, daughter of the Erueth Lord Youngest Amunrhoieneth, lay in child-bed, knowing that this child was not mortal as her other children, but like her own people and that it would take her place amongst them. She knew, too, that she would die at its birth, for such was the agreement she had been forced to make with her uncle before she was permitted to marry Warany. She had never told Warany this, for she loved him so much she could not hold such a threat over him, to bind his actions. Now in her last hours, as the child fought for life within her, she looked out onto the west, hoping in vain to see her lord riding out of the dying sun. But out of the west came no Warny lord. Then, as the last limb of the burning sun sank behind the hills, she saw a man riding a black horse hard, to come to the gates of the city before nightfall. Full of hope, she and her women waited until the man was close enough to be recognised, but they saw only the Dark Lord's horse and his hooded cloak. So, heavy of heart, Nanenethen gave up hope of ever seeing her dear lord again and as her last child, Nareth, was born, she closed her eyes and gave herself up to the mortal lot of her chosen lord.

Warany left S'elrashen at the gates and ran through the snowy streets to his palace, but he came too late, by moments, even to bid Nanenethen farewell on the long road she had chosen.

Then great was his grief, and the grief of his people, for even as the leaves fall gold from the beeches in autumn, so Nanenethen, princess of the Erueth, fell into the shadows.

When the Dark Lord came to the Grey Halls, he and Warany

went up into the hills behind the city and there, on the edge of the forests that overlooked the sea, they buried Nanenethen. And Warany set a beech tree at her head, for among the Erueth she was Lady of the Beeches and next to the beech he planted a young oak tree, the symbol of his house and his promise that he would lie next to her again, be it only in the cold earth.

And Warany said, "Best beloved of women, I kept my word, but you lost faith in me. I give you another promise now, that I shall rest here at your side when my life is done." He turned to the Dark Lord and said, "You will give me your word on it?"

The Dark Lord clasped his hand and his green eyes gazed into the blue. "I give you my word," he said and Warany knew it was sooth.

Warany had seen fifty eight years when she died, for the Warny are a long lived folk, but Nanenethen's years could be measured in mortal generations. She had dwelt in Naru before the Lords Eldest came and forced their rule. Those of her people who had loved her and her father mourned her bitterly, but her uncle, who had given her to Warany in exchange for the defeat of the Queens, saw yet more power coming to his own hand.

Then Warany forsook the Grey Halls, appointing his brother as steward to govern the Warny, and, side by side with the Dark Lord, he rode with the Trumarei to bring the law of the Alliance to all Avenya.

CHAPTER THREE

In the twenty seventh year after the fall of the Queens, the Lords of the Alliance met on the first day of spring at Mara-lei. The Trumarei had made this a yearly custom, which helped to bind the disparate countries of the Alliance together. A quarter of a century had made the Trumarei a people without a country but with laws, customs and land that crossed the boundaries of every country. Their law bound everything save the individual statutes of the members of the Alliance.

Warany led the Council. No one had ever tried to take that task from him, however hard he had tried to give it away. Although he was now in his seventies, this was no age at all for the Warny, who were a long lived people. His hair was grizzled with white and his weather-beaten face was aged by his lifetime of making decisions for other people, but his blue eyes were still as merry as those of a boy in spring. Round his neck he wore the magical blue stone on a chain of silver, which Nanenethen had given him when they plighted their troth and he twisted it between his fingers as he looked around him at those who had also attended the council.

He sat at the head of a great table. Before him on the table, to mark his rank, lay the sword that the Erueth had given him: Erindra, Death Bringer. Mildur the Daline had fashioned it of bronze long years ago in the mines under the mountains. In the hilt, the blue stone shone faintly. Whether the sword served him or he served the sword, Warany was not sure, but the older he got, the heavier it seemed at his side and the less he chose to wear it. Being mortal, he had never been able to loose all the magic bound in it, but its edge had served him well enough.

He glanced to his right where sat the Maren-Ra, high commander of the Trumarei. Herany had died some years before but the new man was quite as fanatical. A dangerous man to cross, thought Warany. On his left sat the Dark Lord, his face more aged by that quarter of a century now passed than by all the aeons of his previous existence. Before him lay his sword, Yadra, Fire Bringer.

We are a pair, thought Warany. Life has treated neither of us well and how old we are. Look at the rest of them around this table, where are my old friends? All gone. Only these fresh faced lads, their children, standing in the places where proper men once stood. Ruén drowned and his son Ranhé'us sits here, all of thirty, thinking he's a hero like his father with a sword of power before him that I would tremble to use. Garenmegra, Storm Bringer, which Mildur made for the Lord Eldest Gawen and here it is in the hands of a boy. A boy, moreover, who managed to get himself captured on a raid and tried for piracy in Mundra. Twenty thousand bathens it cost him to go free and, fool that I was, I lent him most of it because sweet Anya begged me. What sort of a husband would he make for my daughter? I would rather see the son of Darké'us who caught him here. At least we should have some of Darké'us' native wit and cunning to liven up a very dull meeting. And Selin, well, at least he has no airs and graces and if you want a job done,

he'll do it at once and properly, but I miss Deranin. This lad
may be Hara's nephew and he may carry Hara's sword,
but he'd rather have his nose in a book than his behind on a
horse. Which reminds me, I must get to see that damned
Lord Youngest Hara again soon, if only to find out the truth
of the rumour that he is the red witch's lover. My Dark
Lord will soon pluck those fine white wings of Hara's if
that is true and he has been muttering about it for some
time. I wonder what she is like, the Lady Yannya, this
sorceress who sends immortals wild with passion. Keep
your mind off women Warany, you're in the Trumarei halls!
What would the Maren-Ra think, if he knew, which thank
the Eldest he does not.

With an effort he turned to the matters in hand. Arno is
still with us, dry as dust, and one I would not be unhappy to
lose. What are he and his brother Warond up to? Some
nonsense about the Halucias breaking their agreed bounds?
Why would they do that? There's no reason in any of it. All
right, so sometimes the Halucias break their bounds and
we escort them politely but firmly back to their lands, but it
is really only a game. Why do the Trumarei insist on these
time wasting, boring meetings?

Then the sound of movement at the back of the hall
made him instinctively reach out for his sword. He might
be old, but his reactions were faster than any of the half
mortals present. The lads were still moving when he was
standing up, the hilt of Erindra comfortably familiar under
his right hand.

A young Trumaré entered the hall, trying to combine a
respectful attitude to the high lords present whilst
maintaining the urgency of his mission. Behind him,
unhurried, magnificent in her robes of red and gold, crowned
with what could only be a copy of the terrifying mask-like

crown of the High Queens, came the high priestess of the
Quarenyos Queens in exile who dwelt in the Yana temple
under the Pleorine hills.

"I knew there was something you had forgotten to do,"
the Dark Lord said to Warany under his breath.

Undaunted by this gathering of her enemies, the priestess
walked up to the Dark Lord as she would to an equal. The
Dark Lord pushed his chair round to look her in the eye
and the legs rubbed noisily across the stone floor.

"Greetings Lord of Darkness."

The Dark Lord inclined his head.

"I come as the messenger of the Lady Yannya."

A shadow passed across the Dark Lord's face at the
mention of that name, but he spoke courteously to her. "I
do not blame the messenger for the message. You are under
my protection whilst you are within these halls."

"I thank you Lord for this courtesy," she half bowed.
"Lord, some twelve nights ago the Lady Yannya appeared
to me in dream and bade me come here to Mara-lei to
speak these words to you:

Where now is he, who in grim company,
Rides to his destiny, rides to the north?
Seek now the shattered sword,
Seek now the broken word,
'Therewith I keep my weird, Lord Eldest of Darkness.'

"The red witch must find her imprisonment most irksome
if she is reduced to composing such bad verse."

The priestess gazed into his eyes with such sorrow in
hers that he relented his harsh words. "I know her of old.
She has explained this verse to you?"

"Yes Lord, she said, *Tell my Lord of Darkness that
the curse of the High Queen whom the Alliance*

murdered is come to fruition. Before the door of the temple at Nenaterian the High Queen of the Quaren promised you her daughter's unborn son to serve you until all that you hold dear be destroyed. That son is now full grown and dwells in Mundra and he shall be your servant, he and his house forever. This destiny can neither you, nor he avoid."

The Dark Lord gave a short laugh, "Does Yannya from her prison seek to scare me?"

"Lord, I know not what was in the mind of my Lady Yannya!"

"Then you and I have that much in common, madam."

The priestess gazed at him. Behind the copper crown which masked her face her yellow eyes were hard. "I have not finished yet, Lord of Darkness, so listen well to me. I have given you the Lady Yannya's message as she instructed me and thus far she cannot fault me, but there are other things I must say to you which will bring her wrath on me. I cannot be silent."

She was obviously distressed and the Dark Lord spoke more gently to her, "If you wish to speak to me privately, we can go now and talk. Have no fear, I shall deal with you fairly. Have I not said you are under my protection?"

She shook her head, "No Lord, no, I will not speak to you alone, for I am now about to betray my Goddess and my people and I will not have it said I betrayed them in secret. You shall be my witness, you and your people and the very stones of Mara Malac.

"There is another verse abroad in Avenya; have you heard it?

Why now together are four swords to make or mar And Aren the darkest far, Master of Evil?'

"I tell you, heed that verse, though it come from fell

33

Lord Eldest Yatior himself. Heed it, for the Andra's son shall destroy not just that which you hold dear, but our whole world. Something more terrible than even you can begin to understand will come about if you take this man as your servant. I beg you, have him killed now and let this thing end before it is begun."

The Dark Lord heard the pain in her voice; he saw the despair in her eyes and in kindness spoke gently to her, "Weird cannot be outwitted nor fate outrun. It is not for me to appoint the death of a mortal. I cannot alter fate, any more than your mistress can."

"Little you know then," cried the woman, "for she will alter fate. One day you will stand at the side of the Andra's son or his line, and he will destroy the thing you love before your own life and you will weep bitter tears. In that day, remember me!"

"There is nothing in this world I love," said the Dark Lord with the firm quiet of truth.

The priestess shouted angrily, "Beware of hope, for hope is false. Light casts shadows but a flame has no shadow!" She turned and hastily left the hall and all those present saw her tears.

CHAPTER FOUR

In sea-girt Mundra, the morning sun shone bright pale gold on the grey stone castle that watched over the small city state. The wide ocean swell broke gently against the harbour walls; sea birds swooped and cried over the unloading fishing boats. Bulky grain ships swayed on the incoming tide. The smaller fighting ships of the Mundran navy bobbed and bowed to the sea.

It was early yet. Few were abroad in the town, only the fishermen and their buyers tied to the tides. However, in the castle, under considerable protest, Darké'us, Lord of Mundra, was awake. Called from his bed, to which he had only lately taken, to greet a dour, green clad warrior of the Trumarei.

Darké'us knew the value of ceremony and had insisted that the meeting take place in his throne room, where he sat on his gilt throne and regarded the Trumaré with sleep heavy eyes.

"For your eyes only, Lord Darké'us, from my lord the Maren-Ra, high lord of the Trumarei!"

Darké'us was unexcited, he sat wearily on his throne staring at the letter in his hand. One of his younger sons, also named Darké'us, was at his side. The youngster has been woken by the commotion caused by the advent of the

Trumaré and had arisen wondering if it was yet another palace coup. (A heavy sleeper in Mundra tended to sleep deep in a cold bed sooner than those who were roused by the first clink of steel on steel.) He was a stocky lad of about twelve with blue eyes and black hair, much favouring his father, that is to say he was already a scheming liar who would have sold his grandmother to the highest bidder had not one of his elder brothers already done this. He held out his hand for the letter. He was itching to know what it contained and he had no objections at all to reading another's mail. "I'll read it for you, father."

His father gave a grunt, which it was convenient to interpret as assent. The lad scanned the letter. He went from being amused to looking very annoyed.

"From the Maren-Ra of all the Trumarei, to Darké'us, by grace of the Alliance, Lord of Mundra, greetings!

"The matter has been discussed in high council and it has been decided by the Lords of the Alliance that in the interests of peace in Avenya and in particular the interests of our dear friend the Lord of Darkness, that the son of the Andra, the daughter of the Quarinya Queen, should not be allowed to live. You have many sons. It is but a small thing I ask you, to rid yourself of this one Quarin for such overall gain. I ask you as a friend, under my hand and seal, that you have this man killed for the good of the Alliance from whom you hold your power. And it looks like a genuine seal. Father, he asks that you kill Keré'us my brother!"

"It does rather sound like it," Darké'us considered the options for a moment. Then he stared hard at the Trumaré. The warrior stared back. He was a fighting man and thought he was a match for any lord who held his lordship from the

Alliance purely as acknowledgement of his considerable ability to change sides at the right time.

"Has to be nonsense," said Darké'us. "Keré'us is one of the few sons I trust. Well, to be fair, the one I trust most. He is a good sailor and only recently I put up his pension because he caught that fool André'an Sea-lord Ranhé'us, and the ransom had come through. He is a the most valuable member of my navy. Of all my twenty three sons," he glanced at the youngster at his side.

"Twenty one, Father, you had Misha and Ranin executed last month for treason."

"So I did, but I thought that that Kaeyaman concubine had twins the other day?"

"You weren't seriously thinking of claiming them as yours, Father? Everyone knows they were Misha's."

"Well, he won't have any more." He turned his gaze back to the Trumaré, "No, tell your Maren-Ra and the rest that they can't have Keré'us. You could have had Hen'ath or Lorin with my blessing and I would not miss Arbeth or Danhé'us, but they're not having Keré'us. I have fought beside Warany and the Dark Lord and I do not believe they would ask me to do this." He settled back on his throne and seemed to think this answered everything. "Besides, I am the only person in these enlightened years who sends people letters like that. You must have got it the wrong way round." He waved the Trumaré away. "Go to the kitchens. They'll feed you before you go back and sort this mess out."

"Lord," said the Trumaré, gritting his teeth. He had been on the road now for many, many days and borne the letter through many perils. He was tired and this was not the reception he had expected. "Lord, I beg of you, for the sake of the Alliance, do as my master instructs you."

The last thing he wanted to do was to have to kill the man himself. Trumarei were supposed to keep the peace, not go round murdering people. Only city lords could get away with doing that. "All Avenya will be set in chaos if you let this man live!"

"I never did mind a bit of chaos myself," said Darké'us.

"You cannot disobey the High Lords of the Alliance," counselled the Trumaré.

"I see only the Maren-Ra's seal, not Warany's!" said the boy.

"Difficult," mused Darké'us.

"But Father, Keré'us promised to take me out in the *Kemikae* today, to see if we can catch any more pirates. And anyway, I need Keré'us for when I'm Lord of Mundra. He doesn't care about money or position, so I know he'll be loyal. I have to have him for chancellor. My whole scheme to be lord collapses if I don't."

Darke'us was intrigued. "You are my seventeenth son, or is it now fifteenth in succession. How are you going to become Lord of Mundra?"

"By killing whichever of my brothers finally succeeds in killing you, Father, thus avenging you and profiting myself in one fell swoop."

Darké'us proudly put a parental hand on the boy's shoulder and laughed, "Well, I think you'll have to do it without Keré'us. There'll be no Mundra left if I don't please this lot." He pinched the boy's shoulder unobtrusively.

"Oh I suppose so, but you'll have to make one of the other captains take me out today!"

Darké'us turned back to the Trumaré, "Very well. On the understanding that I keep this letter and produce it if anyone argues later, I shall do as they ask. I'll send someone to kill him. Go back and tell them I did as I was told."

The Trumaré bowed and left the hall. The elder Darké'us looked at the younger. "The way I see it is this, and I hope you are learning a lesson from it all. If the Alliance want a man dead, there are at least two other factions that want him alive, and since I do not know which faction I am siding with at the moment, you will take this purse of gold and go and wake your favourite brother and tell him to get out of Mundra as fast as he may. Meanwhile I shall go back to bed for at least an hour, and when I next awake I shall instruct Lorin to pursue Keré'us and kill him."

The lad made a face, "Lorin, that's mean. He hates Keré'us!"

"Then I cannot be accused of favouritism, can I?" He stood up and put an affectionate arm around the youngster's shoulders, "After all, if who I think is on Keré'us' side *is* on Keré'us' side, he will kill Lorin, and that falls in neatly with my own plans."

"Father, did you know this was going to happen?"

The Lord of Mundra considered carefully, and smiled. "I think the answer to that is yes, and no."

Aboard the fighting ship, the *Kemikae*, the young lord Keré'us, ninth son of Darké'us and fifth or was it third surviving, woke in confusion as his young half-brother bounced on his bunk.

"Wake up, Father is sending Lorin with some of the city guard to kill you!"

Keré'us sat up, ran a hand absentmindedly through his curling dark red hair and groped around for his shirt. "Is it urgent?" he asked as he pulled the garment over his head.

"It's life or death!" cried his brother.

"It usually is if someone is trying to kill you!" said Keré'us and then heard his own words. "Oh no, not another palace coup!"

"Worse than that!"

Keré'us pulled on his trousers and boots and sought urgently for his leather tunic which young Darké'us was holding out for him.

"Are you coming?"

"No, it's only you they are after. Mind you, I bet it would be more fun, but I have to stay here to keep an eye on the place. When you hear that I am the Lord, come back and you can be chancellor."

"Who is it, then? You're much more of a threat than me."

"Apparently not. We are talking all Avenya here, not just a petty city state. The Maren-Ra sent a letter asking Father to kill you."

"The Maren-Ra – something to do with my aunt I suppose?"

"No one said, but Father wanted to keep his options open so you'll find your horse is provisioned with food and wine and blankets and things and he gave me this purse to help you on your way."

Keré'us took the heavy purse curiously. His father was not well known for parting with gold. Then he buckled on his sword and went up on deck. It was a beautiful morning. He blinked in the golden sunshine. His horse, a smallish grey mare was optimistically seeking the odd blade of grass on the cobbled quay. He climbed down the rope ladder and mounted the patient horse.

"Tell me," he called back to the boat, "it was Lorin you said he is sending after me?"

"'I'm afraid so. I think most of the Trumarei will be after you too."

"Great! How open did he think he would keep his options sending Lorin?"

"He wants Lorin killed, not you. Now will you go," cried

young Darké'us in an agony of suspense, "you've only got an hour or so start. Lorin will catch you at this rate!"

"Before I go I shall give you one piece of brotherly advice." Keré'us wagged his finger at his younger brother, "I've told you before, you think too small. Don't go for Lord of Mundra, that's a dead end. Go for some strategically placed city where you can earn all your money from tolls on other peoples' goods, Belia or Banéros or somewhere like that. Don't waste your talent on this backwater! And good luck!"

He laughed and turned the horse away from the sea to face the north, to set off on a journey that was to be longer than he could ever have imagined.

CHAPTER FIVE

Through the bright spring day Keré'us travelled north and slightly west, first on Mundran roads and then on the old Quarin road, which led to the Aré'las mountains. In the heyday of the Quarin Empire, when Mundra had been one of its most valued corn growing southern states, the road had been built to take goods and messengers to and from Banéros. Now all that was over, and the Mundrans found it faster to send their grain by sea, the paved road was neglected and overgrown. Where it ran from village to village it was still mostly clear, but once the inhabited areas had been passed, only the sound of the mare's shod hooves on stone told Keré'us he was still following the road.

As they travelled he wondered how much of his hour or so start had already been lost. Lorin and the guard would travel light and they had big strong horses, with not so much stamina as the mare but good when you were in a hurry. Young Darké'us had obviously expected him to survive and supplied him accordingly, the mare was slow under the weight of her saddlebags. Oh that he was as confident as the lad!

By late afternoon he could see an ominous dust cloud behind him on the road and hear the faint clink of shod horses.

They were now passing through the brecklands on the feet of the mountains and there was no place to hide. Keré'us could think of nothing to do to avoid them. He was loath to dismount, but the horse would not carry him much longer. The road rose and looking back he could see the distant men. Six of them! Heroic odds for a distinctly non-heroic Quarin. It was no good offering them the gold in his purse, since they would take that from his dead body. Nothing would be gained by reminding Lorin of their kinship. Lorin hated him. He did not like Lorin either, but Lorin had taken an act of generosity from their father to Keré'us as a personal insult not improved by their father pointing out that Keré'us was the most profitable of his sons. He wished he had never captured that André'an Sea-lord! Whichever immortals had kept him alive for twenty six years in the political maelstrom of the Mundran court seemed now to have abandoned him in his hour of greatest need!

Then as a final blow, he heard the sound of a horn, its golden notes rippling out in the growing twilight. His heart sank to new depths. Only the Trumarei communicated thus. He was trapped, with Lorin behind and Trumarei before. And it had been such a nice day!

The road cut through the top of a low hill and in the cutting he stood the mare over against the wall and drew his sword. The horn rang out again as the bearer rode up the far side of the hill. Lorin and his men gave tongue as they saw their quarry standing at bay. The Trumaré, for there was only one, rode into view. He was a tall, dark-haired Warny warrior on a great black horse, a symbol of doom shadowed in the now setting sun. Keré'us swore. A Warny was worse luck than most, but all he could have expected today. However, the Trumaré, having looked at the Mundran guard, raised his hand to Keré'us in greeting, whilst still keeping one eye on the pursuit. Keré'us turned to face him, his iron sword gleaming dully in his hand.

"It appears I am just in time," said the Trumaré.

"That depends," said Keré'us, "on what you have come for."

The Mundrans drew to a halt, obviously expecting this Trumaré to aid them and as hosts, allowing him the privilege of the first blow. The Trumaré, who appeared to know what was going on which was more than either of the other two parties did, said, "You have been given the wrong orders. You are not to kill this man."

Whew! thought Keré'us.

Lorin looked first disbelieving and then disappointed. "Right or wrong, my father has ordered me to kill this man and kill him I shall."

"No," said the Trumaré, "you will not!"

Keré'us thought, shall I just slip away while they are arguing. But he felt obliged to await the outcome and the mare needed the rest.

"I do not take my orders from you," said Lorin. "I shall kill this man and if you get in my way I shall kill you too!"

The Trumaré looked at Keré'us and seeing that he was left handed, moved to cover his right side. Now they were close Keré'us could see his eyes were blue as the morning sky, his black hair curled down to the leather collar of his jacket and half hid the blue stone on a silver chain he wore about his neck. He was young, possibly as young as Keré'us and the Quarin was surprised. He had never met a young Warny. The race generally had a reputation for being old and sage.

The Warny drew his long bronze sword, "It is more than my life is worth to lose you now. Shall we charge?"

"Let them bunch better."

Both side hesitated, then the Trumaré made a sound of impatience and, whirling his sword about his head, shouted a Trumaré war cry and charged at the Mundrans. Keré'us ducked under the gleaming arc of bronze and feeling somewhat responsible, followed him.

The Warny was a brilliant swordsman and Keré'us could put up a good fight when cornered. They soon had the Mundrans retreating when, with a sound as of glass breaking, Keré'us' sword shattered. Lorin swung his own sword to kill, but hardly pausing in his own fight, the Trumaré brought his fist down on Lorin's neck and the Mundran fell from his horse stone dead. The rest instantly fled.

"Thanks!" said Keré'us looking ruefully at the remains of his sword.

The other grinned, "My pleasure. Their hearts were not in it." He sheathed his sword and looked Keré'us over to make sure he was not hurt. "Shall we leave this spot?"

"We'd better deal with Lorin first."

The Trumaré helped him to drag the body to the side of the road and they piled stones over it. There was nothing else they could do.

Kere'us sighed "When the guards get back I expect they'll send someone to pick him up."

"You knew him?"

"My brother, well, half brother."

"Just as well I killed him, then. Immortals can be rough on fratricides."

"Pity he did not think about that."

"I'm starving. Have you got anything to eat?"

"Oh, plenty, let's go over the hill and light a fire and make camp. I never cared for Lorin's company when he was alive and I certainly do not want it now he is dead."

The two men led their horses over the brow of the hill into

the lee and Keré'us produced bread, cold meat, cheese and red wine from the saddlebags, together with one cup. The Warny carried his own cup. For a while there was a companionable silence as they dined.

Eventually, when Keré'us had taken the edge off his hunger, he asked, "Do you know what is going on? Why did the Trumarei ask to have me killed and now are trying to keep me alive – don't get me wrong, I would rather be under their protection, but I find it all rather confusing."

The Warny laughed, "You don't know?"

"If someone says 'run' in Mundra you run, you don't waste time asking silly questions."

"So you have not heard of the words of the priestess at Mara-lei? Nor the strange verses that are supposed to speak doom for all Avenya?"

"Sorry, no."

"Oh dear. Then I had better tell you." With great enthusiasm the young man related the tale of the Yana priestess at Mara-lei, for he had been there at the time, and while he spoke Keré'us tried to guess who he was, for despite his youth the man had an air of lordliness about him and he wore the symbol of Warany's house, the blue stone on a silver chain, a copy of that which Nanenethen had given Warany when they plighted their troth.

"And when the Lord of Darkness found out that the Maren-Ra, on the advice of Arno, had sent to your father to ask that you be killed, he was angry and sent me swift on the trail of the messenger. The man was five days ahead of me and I feared I would not catch him. It was fortunate for you that we chose the same road. Even then the verses speak of a shattered sword. I had to take a chance on your red hair." With a degree of vulgar satisfaction he added, "I have never seen a prophesy fulfilled before."

Keré'us laughed and ruefully looked at the shards of his sword. "Nor yet have I. It might still be a lucky chance for me."

"Well tell me, were there runes on your sword?"

"Of course: *This iron tongue brings word of death.*"

"There you are! Broken words!" said the Trumaré triumphantly.

"I'm still not convinced."

"You are as bad as my father – but I have not introduced myself, have I? How rude, and after sharing supper with you. In the Trumarei my number is Set, lei-heim, van, but you may prefer to know that I am Derany, son of Warany."

"And I am Keré'us, son of Darké'us of Mundra, and my grandmother was the last of the Quarenyos Queens."

They looked at each other, grandson of the queen of a fallen empire and the son of the Warny prince who had brought about that fall. Two young men with only a handful of years between them and the whole world. Keré'us held out his hand and Derany clasped it and for a moment it seemed that the world stood still, for this was the first meeting between Warany's house and the young lord of the yet unnamed house which was to set all the world in chaos.

The silver moon rose away in the east, soon followed by the red, both nearly full. Derany yawned, "I'm tired. Shall we sleep now? In the morning I shall have to go on to Mundra."

Keré'us was disappointed, "I had hoped you would ride with me, since you have accomplished your task, and kept me alive."

"Nothing would give me more pleasure, but I have to go

to Mundra. I have a twofold mission and the other matter is that the Halucias have broken their bounds and the fell Lord Arno and the Maren-Ra have decreed that the Alliance will make war on them and drive them back. I bear the call to arms for your father. I do not personally think the matter very serious, but if we let the Halucias break their agreed bounds once, they will carry on doing it. Lord Arno just wants a show of strength (they *are* his lands they are over-running), but the rules of the Alliance are quite clear. Every member must send men to defend any other member who calls on them. I rather wonder if the Maren-Ra only agreed to see if the system still worked. Father is always saying how devious he is."

But not a match for my father, thought Keré'us almost fondly.

They camped that night under the two moons and in the morning after breakfast they saddled their horses and mounted up.

"Now I must bid you farewell, friend," said Derany, "may you have a safe journey. I shall return on this road and try to catch you before you reach your journey's end."

"Where is my journey's end?" asked the Quarin.

"Interesting question," grinned the Warny. "The Dark Lord said he would meet you at the bridge at Runi." He forestalled the next question and pointed west. "Which is that way. Follow this road to the turning to the Sea-kingdoms, but turn off north through the Ni-Lequar pass, that they call the Gate. You will have to pay a toll there. On the far side of the Gate take the western arm of the cross roads that indicate Banéros. It has the Trumaré star marked on it. Follow that to the Stair down by the side of the Eldraedé Falls and ford the river. The road runs on the far side of it, at the feet of the Yannyos mountains until it crosses the river again just before it reaches Lake Vanda. The road then follows the east side of the lake until it crosses the Lee'ma Ra at Runi on the great new stone bridge that the Lord Arno had built to replace the one further down stream that my father destroyed in the war. There is a Trumaré post there, but I expect he'll be in the inn. Certainly if he's with my father. You won't have any difficulty in recognising him."

"And if I choose not to?"

Derany laughed, "Friend, there is no element of choice in this. If the Dark Lord says he will meet you at Runi, there he will met you, whatever direction your feet take."

"I had a feeling you were going to say something like that," Keré'us laughed. "You have made me feel a little safer, friend Derany."

"You are not safe," said Derany anxiously, "don't get that idea. Both Trumarei and Quaren will be after you and probably others as well. I'll be back with you as soon as I can. Until then, take care!"

"And you, Derany, take care and tell my brother Darké'us I am safe, from Lorin at least!"

Then they waved farewell and set off on their separate ways.

CHAPTER SIX

So, alone, with many a backward glance, Keréus set off westward along the old road to the Gate, away from his native land, away from the comfortable life he understood to a future he could not imagine.

These lands were uninhabited. All that remained of the Quaren who had worked them were the occasional ruins of a farm or some roofless barn. No one had wanted this poor land. Only the road, built to endure the tread of armies, had withstood over a quarter of a century of neglect.

For days he travelled, the moons both waxing and growing closer together in the sky. His food supply was holding out, Darké'us had provisioned him well, and the loneliness did not trouble him. Occasionally he thought about what Derany had said, but the whole thing seemed nothing but shadows - he, illegitimate son of Darké'us to be a servant to one of the Lords Eldest? So might his brother become Lord of Belia!

Eventually he came to the crossroads where the road through the High Arélas pass crossed his own, and there was a small farmstead. The evening was growing cold and the place had obviously been an inn in more prosperous times, so he knocked at the door to see if they would give him a bed for the night.

He was answered by a woman in her fifties, a Quarinya with yellow eyes and grey in her red hair. She looked him up and down. "What do you want?"

"A bed for the night and a meal, if you can."

"I can always find a welcome for another Quarin."

"I'm afraid I'm hardly that."

"And you with your red curls and yellow eyes!" she smiled. Her husband took his horse and she led the way into their main room, where a fire burned in a huge stone fireplace and a savoury aroma of stewed pork filled the space. "Sit, and I shall bring you food. You must take pot luck, leavened bread, beer and my pig stew."

"Thank you. I am most grateful. The night was cold and I did not want to spend it on the mountainside." He sat down by the fire and luxuriated in its warmth.

The food was good. Keré'us ate his fill and afterward the woman showed him a side room with a box bed and a curtain over the door. He dropped his pack on a chair by the bed. The woman hovered, hesitating, then said, "Lord, my husband told me your horse has the Mundran royal brand."

"Yes," he admitted cautiously, wondering what was to come.

"There was a Trumaré through here a few nights ago. He wanted me to warn any Quarin from Mundra of danger."

"Was that Derany the son of Warany?"

"I thought so."

"Then I have met him and know what may befall."

"But do you?" she asked urgently. "Do you? Are you not the son of the daughter of the last Quarinya Queen?"

"I am also the bastard son of Darké'us of Mundra, and no one sets much store by that."

"Then there is hope!" she said and the accent of the vanquished Quaren was soft on her tongue. "When your mother's sister, the High Priestess, came before the Lord of Darkness at Mara-lei she spoke these words: *Eré abarten, se abartin reluin, keruin erakés santon, e ya santor ni arné*"

"I do not speak Quarin."

"In the common tongue it runs thus, *Beware of hope for hope is false, light casts shadows, but a flame has no shadow.*"

"Even in the common tongue it makes little sense."

"Your name is Keré'us, which means *light*. If light means the end of hope to the Alliance, then it must mean the beginning of hope to the Quaren."

"Should I lead a people whose tongue I do not speak?" asked Keré'us.

"Since your mother's sister drowned herself in lake Vanda to atone for the evil she did in asking the Dark Lord to have you murdered and betraying the Lady Yannya, you are the last of the Royal House of the Golden Throne. Remember that, for others will. Weird cannot be outwitted nor fate outrun." She bowed and left him. Keré'us sat on the bed and took his boots off, then lay down to sleep in comfort for the first time in many days. Her words did not concern him, he still counted himself a pawn in the affairs of men and gods and prayed he would remain so.

For the next three days Keré'us followed the road and on the third night there occurred a very rare astronomical event. First the silver moon rose, full and fair, flooding the mountains with white light. Then the black shadows she cast were slowly turned bronze as her sister red moon rose like a burnished globe of copper in the east. The red moon waxed and waned more slowly than the silver, so they were rarely full together, but now they both turned the world unreal in their strange light. The Quaren had worshipped the red moon as sign and symbol of their Lady Yannya, but the Alliance hated it for the same reason.

In the eerie light the grey mare grew uneasy. Keré'us threw more wood on his small camp fire which flared pallidly. The mare was still scared. She whickered so he went to her and put a comforting hand on her trembling flanks, but she was not comforted. He followed the direction of her eyes to see what troubled her and then he too trembled, for the mare was staring across the fire and now he saw what she saw.

Behind the fire, flames and smoke lapping about her, stood a woman. The red moon shone copper on her face and caught in a garnet ring on her hand, but her hair and garments mingled grey with the smoke and the shadow. "Who are you?" he asked.

She said nothing but held out her hand across the fire to him.

"Who are you?" he asked again.

"I am Yannya, Lady of the Red Moon, whom your foremothers served." Her voice was low and musical, but used to command. "Now take my hand and come to me through the fire. It will not hurt you if you are swift."

Keré'us stepped towards the fire, but hesitated on the brink. He could see her, but he did not know if he believed he could see her.

"Come, time is short!" The slender hand with the ring burning light from the red moon reached out and he put out his hand to touch her fingers, which were real. She gripped his hand and pulled and he fell forwards into the fire. Smoke filled his lungs. Her other hand steadied him and then he could breathe again and regained his balance. The moons had gone and in their place was a single bright light hanging from a domed ceiling in a great circular room pierced by three gauze curtained arches. The floor fell in three wide steps, to the centre where a small sweet smelling brazier burned and opposite him stood the most beautiful woman he had ever seen. She looked like a Quarinya woman, with a golden heart-shaped face and yellow eyes. Her hair was a shining copper red and it swirled to her waist in stormy waves. His eyes soaked up her beauty. Never had he imagined a woman could be so fair.

Her first words were a trifle disconcerting. "Looking at me does not seem to have killed you," she said and her lips quirked in half a smile. "I knew the Eldest were lying."

He did not know what to say and continued to gaze at her. She looked him up and down consideringly. "Sit down, we must talk." She indicated the lowest step closest to the brazier.

Keré'us sat and she sat next to him. Her perfume was heady, but although she roused pleasure in him, she did not arouse desire. She was too august a being for him to presume to think of her as a woman, so powerful that he both feared and worshipped her. Her power was that of a sleeping volcano, pent but lambent.

"You doubtless wonder what is going on?"

"Well, Derany did explain it to me, but only the what, not the why."

She smiled, pleased, "So you are one of those who recognise there has to be a why as well as a what."

"I *was* brought up in the Mundran court," Keré'us said, almost indignantly.

"Yes, I know. I put that into your grandmother's mind."

He gave her a hard stare and then realised this was probably lèse-majesté, but she only smiled again.

"But not the curse. When your grandmother promised that you would serve my Lord of Darkness until all that he holds dear is destroyed, it was without my consent. There was only the power of mortal hatred behind her words, the power of the red earth of the Quarenyos Queens. Yet as it happened, as so often happens, she spoke sooth without knowing. You shall indeed serve my Lord of Darkness until at least one thing he once held dear is destroyed and as fate would have it, I am constrained to aid you. In truth you are my servant as well, Keré'us. Your foremothers worshipped me and in return I gave them of my power. To you I shall give power, the power I gave them. The power of the Elorianen. You know of the Star-stone?"

"All I know, Lady, was that it was a stone of great power which lost its power when the Lord Eldest Yatior used it to breath life into the copper statue which became yourself."

She looked amused. "True, it was a stone of great power. It came into this world of Naru worn by Zarazinnya the Shining One, guardian of all Naru who was murdered by the Lords Eldest. Then afterwards the High Lord Eldest Alvious was murdered by his son Vallior to gain it and Vallior in turn was murdered by his son Yatior. Yatior, to make peace, gave it back to Mérior, the High Lord of the Eldest, who was the brother of Vallior, saying that the Star-stone had lost all its power when it turned me into a living being. However, the Lords Eldest are not well known for their veracity and in fact he gave Mérior, to put it bluntly, a fake. Since the magic which gave me life was that of the Star-stone, only that can unmake me. It, therefore, seemed logical to me to take it from Yatior, who could not complain since he was not supposed to have it in any case. I had Mildur set the Stone in the hilt of a sword so I might bear it in the Wars of the Diadem, and afterwards I gave it to my mortal friends, the Quarenyos Queens, for safe keeping. They called the sword Hiruéven. When Nenaterian fell Arno took it and later had a new iron blade forged onto the hilt, renaming it Aren.. However, by birth, by the power of your grandmother's curse and by my own power, the Elorianen belongs to you and your house until the curse is fulfilled. The guardianship of the iron sword, Aren, which Arno now holds is yours. I would have it safe in your hands."

"I have heard that Arno is a fell necromancer."

"Arno is probably the least of your worries. He is, at any rate, technically mortal. The Lords Eldest will try to take back the Star-stone, for they need it if they are ever to escape from Naru, but it belongs to me and through me to you. With it you shall serve my Lord of Darkness for as long as your house shall endure."

"My house?"

"The House of Abard. You have heard of the House of Wargany, of the Houses of Deranin and Ruén, who bear swords of magic power. You shall be their equal and their peer. Together with my Lord of Darkness you shall bring the rule of law to Avenya. The House of Abard, the house of hope. I promise you, you shall ride on the flood of your fate. Although your enemies will be many, your friends shall also be many and true and it is within my remit to give you the love of a faithful woman from whom shall come your only son to inherit the curse and magic of your house and keep the Elorianen from harm. Come, let us pledge our friendship - or would you rather turn your face from it? Go back whence you came?"

"I fear you are testing me," said Keré'us, "*Weird cannot be outwitted nor fate out run.* I think I have no choice."

"No, I cannot compel you, that is to say, I have the power to compel you, but not the desire. But if you did not wish to serve me, then you would not be the man I want to serve me." She stood up and clapped her hands.

The curtain moved and through it entered a Daline with a tray on which rested a flask and two goblets. Keré'us stared. The Lady Yannya just came within the scope of his imagination, but this swart dwarfish man with scaly skin and clothes of metal amazed him.

"This is the Lord Youngest Mildur my friend and steward. It may be you will meet him again. Since I am bound here I occasionally send him on errands." She stood up and took the flask, and poured a cup of wine for them both. Keré'us rose to his feet to take the proffered goblet. It was gold, set with precious stones, of marvellous workmanship. She touched her cup to his, "Keré'us, may we be friends, and as friends serve each other in trust and joy."

Keré'us desired nothing more. "Lady, so be it," but as he raised his cup to his lips Mildur sprang forwards saying, "No! Great Lady, no!"

Confused, Keré'us hesitated.

The Lady Yannya turned to Mildur with sorrow in her face, "Lord Mildur, the choice I made was mine alone to make."

"Then you have betrayed us all to the Eldest. What is he now, this fallen Lord Eldest?" Mildur said angrily and his voice took on a jeering tone. "Mortal, dying, Lord of Darkness."

She closed her eyes momentarily in pain at those words, "Enough, Mildur, I will not have this. You confuse our guest." Mildur turned on his heel and left the chamber.

"Will you trust me Keré'us?" Her voice was low and beautiful.

Keré'us raised the cup to his lips, "You said my fate was already bound with yours. If so, I can no more escape it than you, and if not, a goblet of good wine under the mountains is neither here nor there."

She laughed, "Oh ye Lords Eldest beware, for the House of Abard is hereto formed and he can twist my words, so what shall he do with thine?"

And Keré'us said, "Lady, The Lord of the House of Abard pledges you his service, through life to death, for I accept my destiny and could in no wise serve any other."

She touched her cup to his. "Keré'us son of Darké'us, Lord of the House of Abard, I pledge you and your House my protection as your liege lady, through life until death. Now kneel before me and I shall bless you."

He knelt and she put her hands on his head. The floor was hard and real under his knees but the rest of the room seemed filled with confusion. The weight of her hands was heavy. He shut his eyes but could still see light all about him. He felt her power run through him and suddenly he knew his strength. He could feel his hands, his arms, his body, more completely than ever before. He opened his eyes and somehow his sight seemed to spring into sharper focus. She took both his hands gently and pulled him to his feet.

"Now you have the power of the red earth that belonged to your foremothers. When that is allied to the ring of twisted iron and copper which my Lord of Darkness presently wears and the Star-stone, then even the Eldest will fear you.

"Now you must go." Suddenly smoke rose from the brazier and behind it Keré'us could see his camp in the strange moons' light and his horse waiting patiently.

"Fare you well, Keré'us, you shall never be far from

my thoughts." Keré'us bent and kissed her hands, then looked again into her yellow eyes, wanting to remember this moment always. "Lady, I shall never forget you."

Then he passed through the fire and returned to the bleak mountainside on the Aré'las road.

CHAPTER SEVEN

It was in the middle of the morning the next day that Keré'us reached the Ni-lequar Pass, the only point at which the Aré'las mountains could be crossed in winter. The Gate was still in Quaren hands under the agreement Warany had made with Melin in the year that Nanenethen died. It was now in fact a tiny Quarin state within the lands of the Alliance. The soldiers who guarded the pass and collected tolls still wore the orange and brown uniform of the High Queen's army, although many of them had not been born when the last Queen died. Because the Gate was Quarin it became the natural goal of all escaped slaves and rebels and Melin trod a narrow path between survival and nationalism, doing his best not to make any move which could be misinterpreted politically.

Keré'us, bemused by the events of the previous night, clung grimly to Derany's instruction to meet the Dark Lord at Runi. It was not much, but the only firm rock in very troubled waters. In any case, he knew that unless someone took him into service, he would not survive long on his own slender resources. Life at the Mundran court had fitted him only to intrigue well, fight competently and control his men on board ship. He could not farm, fish or trade and the chances of finding a city lord wanting a new chancellor were fairly remote. Well, there were always the Trumarei!

He looked up the wooden gate set into the massive stone wall which separated Avenya from André'as. It was made of hewn tree trunks and looked impressively strong. There was already a straggle of travellers, most with patient laden pack mules, waiting while the guards stopped everyone and questioned them. He feared that the words of the high priestess at Mara-lei might be taken very seriously at the Gate, but there was no way he could pass through at speed. Therefore he was going to have to submit to the questions, and he could guess what they might be. Well, he thought, *she* had said that he would ride on the flood of his fate. He would take her word for it. He joined the queue regretting that he had not taken the High Aré'las pass despite the fact that it would have taken him several days journey out of his way and likely as not been impassable.

"Where are you from, friend?" asked the guard when he reached the toll gate.

Keré'us had always found the truth was less complicated than lying. "Mundra," he said.

"Do you carry any arms?"

"Only my sword and a dagger."

"I have to ask you to show the sword to me."

Keré'us knew immediately why, and that there was no escape. He drew his broken sword and said, "*Seek now the shattered sword, seek now the broken word.*"

The guard was pleasingly taken aback. Obviously no one had expected Keré'us to go boldly through the pass. He grinned quietly to himself while the guard conferred with another. Eventually a superior officer was summoned and he led Keré'us, politely enough, to a door in the side of the pass, where, after a few words, other soldiers led him up a narrow spiral stair cut into the rock. The stone steps were well worn by generations of soldiers, and difficult to climb, lit only by narrow arrow-slit windows in the rock. After the first hundred steps there was a rest station with benches and a water stoup on a landing.

"You'd better have a rest. There's still a long way to go," said one of the soldiers, as they all sat on the benches to catch their breath.

The steps continued for a further hundred or so and then turned into a broader stair within the mountain, lit only by lamps burning unrefined rock oil which after the clean mountain air brought tears to Keré'us' eyes. Finally they traversed a straight stair of well dressed stone within the fortress which led to a small chamber. The door was unlocked and Keré'us escorted inside.

"You are to wait here while we send word to the Lord Melin," said the leader of the soldiers, then the door slammed with a resounding thud, the key turned in the lock and Keré'us was left listening to their feet as they echoed away down the stairs. He looked about him. The only comfort in the cold mountain air was a fire together with a supply of logs. There were two chests covered with rugs to sit on, but no other furniture, nothing that indicated more than a very short stay. The narrow glazed window set into the depth of the wall above his head showed nothing but the blue sky.

Keré'us sat down, looked up at the window and considered his interesting position. If not scared, he was certainly apprehensive. He thought of the Lady and flexed his fingers, feeling her power in his hands. He felt safer now remembering her. He had survived the court of Mundra, a few Quaren at the Gate should be child's play - perhaps.

Time dragged by. The quality of the light from the window slowly changed. He threw some logs on the fire to keep it going. Then as the first stars lit in the casement, he again heard steps on the stairs and the door was unlocked.

Four uniformed men had arrived to take him downstairs, this time following another route to a floor with carpeted corridors lit with lamps of sweet oil. A door was pushed open and Keré'us propelled through ahead of the soldiers. This was Melin's private suite. The walls were hung with tapestries and the floors carpeted; the woodwork was much carved and the chairs and couches as comfortable as any in the heyday of the Empire. A girl played softly on a stringed instrument. The smell of food assailed Keré'us.

Four men relaxed on couches at the end of the room. Before them on a low table stood what was obviously the remainder of a splendid meal. Keré'us was very aware that he had not eaten all day.

One of the men stood up and held out his hand, "I am Melin, Captain of the Gate." He was about sixty years old, his brown hair now grey and thin but his slight body still strong. Over his long robe of brown silk he wore a pectoral of gold set with topaz. He wore a seal ring on his right hand, but his left was, in the manner of fighting men, not hampered by any jewel.

Keré'us took the proffered hand. "I am Keré'us, son of Darké'us, Lord of the House of Abard," he said. Had she not given him that name?

Melin raised an eyebrow. "A lordship of which I am afraid I am ignorant," he said. "However, I sought a man, the Quarin son of Darké'us who bears a broken sword, and I dare say you are he." He looked at Keré'us thoughtfully. "What were the runes on your sword?"

"*This iron tongue brings word of death*'"

"I think that could be interpreted as the 'broken word', within the confines of a four line verse."

"Others have done so."

Melin began to circle round Keré'us thoughtfully. "You have, of course, heard the various prophecies in poor poetry that are going about Avenya at this time?"

"I have."

"And what do you think of them?"

"That they are very poor poetry."

Melin smiled. One of his companions, a much younger man with curly red hair like Keré'us, who wore the kilt of an officer, gave a snort of laughter.

"Yet all Avenya rings with them. I, Melin of the Gate, do not know what they mean, so I sent for two more knowledgeable friends." He indicated the two older men still reclining by the table, "And they do not know. The only interpretation I have heard is that of our High Priestess at Mara-lei and she said you should die."

"I would hesitate to take her word for it," said Keré'us.

Melin smiled, "Rumour has it that the Trumarei were trying to kill you."

"Only some of them. Others are trying to stop me being killed."

"When the Maren-Ra of the Trumarei and our High Priestess share the same object one begins to get confused."

"Not as confused as I am," said Keré'us. The officer laughed again.

Melin continued, "I have given the matter some consideration, and until someone shows their hand more plainly, I am prepared to give you sanctuary, now or ever, within the Gate."

In view of the position held by the Gate this was a magnanimous offer. Keré'us wondered how he could show his appreciation and still refuse it. "Lord Melin, I know what cost such sanctuary might be to you. Much as I thank you for the offer, it is one I must refuse at present."

"Then what are your plans? You will be safe nowhere in Avenya!"

"I am instructed to go the bridge at Runi and there meet the Dark Lord."

"The Dark Lord, a Lord Eldest, enemy of our people? Enemy of the Lady Yannya? And you are going? You are the only heir by blood of the Quarenyos Queens. Had you not considered that much of the Quarin population of Avenya would be glad to follow if you rose up against the Alliance? Long and hard I have worked to keep the Gate safe in Quaren hands. Apart from the women under the Pleorine hills we are the only free Quaren who have not submitted to the Alliance. Yet this whole wide, rich, bright land is ours. It belongs not to these Warny invaders. The Queens brought about our defeat because they would not trust a man to rule and the petty jealousies of the city lords pulled our country apart. Now the Queens are dead, but we are not. The Quaren shall return to power led by a man. You are young, and victory will take time. You have the blood royal and the red hair which signifies it, and if you have reached your majority in the courts of Darké'us, you must have some political ability."

It had never crossed Keré'us mind that any one would see him as heir to the Queens. For a wild moment he saw himself as king at the head of orange and brown clad armies marching against the Alliance to glorious triumph. It stirred his blood and he smiled as a king might smile, but then he laughed. The laugh stopped on his lips when he saw Melin was serious.

"It is your duty to free the Quaren from their oppressors," said one of the old men, a priest.

"I have other duties which I fear will have to come first." Keré'us could feel the atmosphere chilling. Refusing the offer of a throne was difficult to accomplish tactfully.

"What duties can you have more important than saving our people?" asked Melin. Keré'us sought for the words to explain and then remembered the words of the Lady the night before in a surge of warm thanks.

"I have been told that to carry out my grandmother's curse at Nenaterian, I must go to serve the Dark Lord." Keré'us looked at the Quarin, hoping that this would be enough. "To destroy what he holds most dear must aid the Quaren."

Melin thrust his face forward and looked into Keré'us' eyes. "That was not what the High Priestess said. She said you would destroy our whole world. You cannot serve the Dark Lord and the Lady Yannya. The days when they walked hand in hand are long since past. Your duty is to us, to your people."

Keré'us looked straight back into Melin's eyes. "No," he said carefully. "I know whom I serve and to whom my service is due. You may wish that I could put your long nurtured plans into action, but I know where my duty lies."

The young officer laid his hand on Melin's sleeve, "No brother," he said. "Keré'us, ignore him, as you intend to. He dreams the dreams of an old man by the fire in winter. The spring which comes is not his spring, but ours. We both know there is no hope in rebellion against the Alliance. How could we lead more of our people to death and destruction? Our future is in reconciliation."

"Felanin, half-brother you may be but I am Lord of the Gate and my will is law!" Melin's voice was even, but Keré'us was aware of his anger mounting.

"It is because I am your half-brother and stand to inherit the Gate some day that I am trying to keep this last outpost of the Empire safe," Felanin cajoled him. "So Keré'us serves the Dark Lord? Do we not want a voice that will be heard in the councils of the Alliance? Warany will not live for ever and he is all that stands between us and the Alliance!"

"And a stone wall and a few soldiers," muttered Melin.

"Look, we cannot hope to defeat the Alliance. Did we not try it five years ago with the help of the Hill, and do I not carry a lame leg, and a price on my head as a result of that disastrous campaign. And were you not glad that I took the blame and you could absolve the Gate? In the name of the Lady, let Keré'us follow his chosen path. Do not try to choose it for him. How are we to know what the Lady has in mind?"

Melin shook his head. "I cannot agree with my brother," he said. "You refuse a throne and it is of no moment to either of you. Go and play your silly games with the Alliance, and see what standing a Quarin has with them. Do you think they will treat you as any more than a slave? Do not come wailing to me then. Felanin will find you a bunk in the guardroom for the night. Go!"

Felanin took Keré'us' arm and led him out into the cold mountain air of the keep where the two moons glittered in the sky. "I can offer you more than a bunk. You will come to my quarters with me, and I shall get some food sent up. You must be starving. You must forgive Melin. He lived in the last days of the Empire and he remembers and thinks those days will return. I know things will change, but not backwards, we must look forwards to a new world…" He froze suddenly. Something had caught his eye in the sky. Keré'us looked up and saw with Felanin a great white bird, an eagle surely, stooping on the Gate.

"What in the name of the Lady?" asked Felanin.

"An eagle, at night?"

"Times are strange, Keré'us."

"You know what it is," said Keré'us.

Felanin frowned, "I know what I think it might be, but I will not talk of it."

In the morning Keré'us was awoken early by a soldier, who escorted him to see Melin again. This time the Captain of the Gate was in his study, a small room hung about with maps of old and more recent campaigns. Keré'us tried not to look at them too closely. A tray of fresh baked bread rolls and a pot of fragrant herbal tea stood on the desk. Melin motioned to them and Keré'us indulged himself with hot rolls and melting butter. The Gate Captain looked older in the morning light, older and more worried, as if he had had little sleep.

"Lord Keré'us," he said once Keré'us had taken the edge off his appetite. "Lord, I must apologise for my words last night."

Keré'us waved a buttery knife forgivingly. He liked Melin and could not hold a grudge. "Long have I sought one to take my place and become the saviour of our people. You are the obvious choice and it seemed that fate had brought you to me. I thought Felanin was supporting you because he wanted to be king in your place, not because he knew I was wrong. But now I know you came here for a reason."

"Only because the High Aré'las pass would be blocked."

Melin smiled almost grimly, "No, you came for a different reason as I found out last night. All my life I have given lip-service to the Lady Yannya. Now, when I am so old that I have forgotten her in my own ambitions, she sends me a messenger and bids me be kind to you. In her name I would have made you king. Now in her name I tell you, go forth in peace and with my blessing. I shall give you provisions and a guide to the Eldraedé falls which is as far as I can protect you. She says to tell you that the road along the mountains is dangerous, but not as dangerous as the one through Belia, for you will find friends on the far side of the river. But you had already been told to go that way?"

Keré'us nodded.

"I have spoken with Felanin and he will be happy to escort you to the Stair. Your horse has been provisioned and all is in readiness for your departure. I have been told that time is short, there are many who wish you ill and you will not be safe until you are under the protection of the Dark Lord." He looked at Keré'us hard, then slowly drew his sword.

"Lord of the House of Abard, this blade was sworn in your Grandmother's service. At her feet I knelt and offered her the blade in the name of the Lady Yannya. Take it and perhaps it will stand guardian between life and death for you. I too am left handed. See the spirals on the hilt go against the sun."

Keré'us took the sword and weighed it in his hand. It fitted snugly, but he handed it back. "By choosing me the Lady has ordained my sword. Aren is my weapon, I shall carry no other."

"Then I wish you luck in the taking of it."

Keré'us grinned, "I shall need more than luck."

"But my sword shall still serve you, if you call upon me. Five thousands I could send you should you ever have need."

"I am no king. I shall not need an army."

"But perhaps you will, and then in your need turn to the Gate, for you are the grandson of the last Quarenya Queen, last of the blood royal, and we shall serve you to the last man."

"I am the bastard son of Darké'us of Mundra and ask no man to die for me."

Melin said, "You are the chosen of the Goddess. We must all die for you if called upon."

CHAPTER EIGHT

Melin led Keré'us out to the courtyard where Felanin was waiting with two horses. The morning sun was bright and the day blue and cloudless. Guards saluted them sharply. Keré'us mounted his grey mare, noting the plumpness of the saddlebags. "Felanin, I place the Lord of the House of Abard into your care."

Felanin nodded his acknowledgement, then to Keré'us' acute embarrassment, Melin knelt before him and offered him his sword as he would to a Queen. Felanin smiled and joined him.

"Fools," hissed Keré'us, "I have no power and well you know it. Will this give you strength against the Alliance?"

"For good or ill our lot is thrown in with yours, Lord Keré'us," said Melin, smiling. "Now go, before any of those pursuers can catch you!"

Felanin stood up and mounted his horse. "Come," he said, and their shadows, long in the early morning sun, stretched before them as they turned west, "this may be fun!"

The mountains soon closed behind them as they left the pass behind and the road wound in silence between snow covered peaks. Felanin, released from some years of inactivity at the Gate, whistled cheerfully.

"You can tell me why he changed his mind," said Keré'us. "What was the white bird?"

Felanin made a face, "Well, he has not specifically instructed me not to speak of it, so I suppose I can tell you. It was Hara, Prince of the Merédur."

"The Lord Youngest Hara, the one with white wings?"

"The very same."

"I have this feeling of drowning," said Keré'us. "I only survive by not thinking about it. Two weeks ago my biggest worry was …To be frank, I didn't have any worries, not compared with the ones I have now."

"Well," said Felanin in a brotherly fashion, "you've got me here to protect you now!"

After about two hours they came to a cross roads. The main road on which they had travelled so far continued downwards, wide and relatively smooth, into the upper plains. It was marked with a standing stone inscribed *Banéros*, for all Quaren roads ran to and from that city. The road it crossed was narrow and unpaved, indicated by two slender standing stones lest it go unremarked. The eastern sides were graven with an oak leaf, sign and symbol of Warany's house; the western sides with several symbols carved and painted, all of which had been white-washed out and replaced by the green nine-pointed star of the Trumarei. This narrow stony path they took and followed until night fell.

The moons waned. For five days Felanin and Keré'us travelled, wary of every stone fall, but no harm came to them and they saw neither man nor beast, although after two days they saw the remains of recent fires and it was obvious that someone was travelling the road perhaps a day ahead of them.

The sudden appearance of the fires puzzled Kere'us. "Who do you think it might be? It cannot be someone who has passed through the Gate, or the cross roads, for we would have seen the fires sooner."

"My guess is it is someone who crossed under the Hélans Dru, either because they had need of haste, or because they did not want to pay the toll at the Gate. Probably a Trumaré."

"Or because they did not want to be seen?"

In the afternoon of the fifth day they reached the falls. The path brought them to a point just below the top of the falls where they could look across to them. They gazed in awe, for although Felanin had seen them before and Keré'us had heard tell of their beauty, that could not diminish their power; they were glorious and terrible beyond any words. In the time beyond time the side of the Hélans Dru mountain had slipped away and the river Elda fell over the side of the chasm in a terrifying cloud of spray which hid the distant ground. The whole earth shook with the drumming of the water and the air was resonant with it. Felanin pointed to the side of the falls where, protected from the spray by high walls, were the wide, worn steps of the Eldraedé Stair. In the old days Quaren merchants from the north had come to trade with the Dalines at the South Gate of the mines under the mountains. The Dalines were cunning workmen and artificers, working the precious metals and jewels they mined there into all manner of goods, both toys and weapons and iron knives. The Lord Eldest Yatior had forbidden this trade when he took the mines as his residence in exile and ultimately closed the south gate, but the Trumarei, recognising the value of this back way to the south, had kept the stair well repaired.

Felanin moved back from the falls to a place where Keré'us could hear him, "It is too late to travel the stair today. It is a difficult task with a horse and the light would be gone before you reached the bottom."

Keré'us nodded, his mind still full of the thunder of the waters and the beauty of the falls. They found a sheltered spot to make camp and settled down for the night.

When the true blue of early morning showed in the sky, Felanin, on second watch, woke Keré'us. They breakfasted, packed their gear and then Felanin made his farewell, "Friend, are you certain that you want me to come no further? It may be that you will need my help. I am prepared to risk the price on my head for the sake of a more interesting life."

"No, go back to the Gate and look after my interests there. It may be that I shall need Melin's help one day and he will not be so willing to give it if I have robbed him of his second in command."

"Then all that remains, brother, is to say farewell. Take my long knife I beg of you, for otherwise you are unarmed."

Keré'us made a face at him, "No Felanin, all I ask of you is your friendship. If the Lady tells me I must take Aren, then Aren I must take. Nothing else will do."

They clasped arms in the fashion of Quaren warriors and parted in the bright morning.

Keré'us carefully took his little mare down the wide steps of the stair to the valley floor. It was a long job, needing much patience and the sun was past noon by the time they had reached the bottom. Both man and horse were relieved to be on level ground again and so tired that he decided that they would go no further that day. He unloaded the mare, hobbling her, and she wandered off along a low shelving beach by the river's edge where the first, sparse blades of grass were green. The river here was wide and shallow and a crossing of great flat stones bore the road across to the far side, to run parallel to the river, along the slopes of the western mountains, the Neros Yannyos which formed the backbone of Avenya. Keré'us was still at a great altitude and the bright air was cold, sharp and clean. Spring had not yet reached these slopes and snow stood in sheltered corners. Asphodel and gentian were still in bud. Only the bright yellow crocus glowed in golden patches among the grey rock.

The far bank was rugged, with boulders and great outcrops of rock, giving cover to the road and Keré'us realised that he would have done better to have crossed the river. There was plenty of daylight left, so he unhobbled the horse and led her across. Then he went back to collect his saddle and pack. As he stood on the first stone of the river crossing to return he saw a man, long sword in hand, walking across the bridge towards him. The man who had been travelling ahead of them! He must have been hiding in the tumbled rocks while Keré'us traversed the Stair. Keré'us called himself every kind of fool and wondered how he could have failed to see the man. And just what he was going to do.

The man was a tall Sea-lord from the far south. His long dark hair and beard were curling and unkempt, his eyes blue and hard. He wore a quilted jacket of dark blue, embroidered, most unsuitably, with flowers over tight leather trousers whose colour could only be guessed at. His boots were long, supple, black leather sea boots. It would not have been quite so bad if Keré'us did not recognise him, or he had not recognised Keré'us. The Quarin's heart sank.

Of all the André'ans he knew, this one was the man he least wanted to see, especially with a sword in his hand.

"Well, well, well, of all the people I did not expect to meet here, you are the least expected! Have you given up piracy for banditry?" demanded the André'an.

"You were never able to understand that point in your trial, but *you* were the pirate, Lord Ranhé'us." Keré'us' mind raced through the possibilities open to him to save himself. They seemed few if not non-existent. His dinner knife paled into insignificance against nearly three feet of sharp tempered bronze that was also reputed to have magical powers. Now was the time to regret turning down Felanin's offer of company and a long knife. He continued to cross the causeway, saddlebags hanging over his shoulder and saddle in his arms.

The André'an advanced towards him. "The High King of André'as is no pirate!"

"Anyone who steals, or in your case, attempts to steal, Mundran grain ships is a pirate. We would have hung you, but you offered ransom."

Ranhé'us growled, "There was enough talking done then. No man robs me of twenty thousand bathens and lives to boast of it!"

Keré'us considered the options again, but they had not improved. His horse was on one side of the river. He was on this side with his saddle and provisions. In between was a very angry André'an Sea-lord. Think Keré'us, he told himself, what had Derany said? Ranhé'us had been at the meeting at Mara-lei. Even if he was not now a Trumaré, he must be nominally on the same side as the Dark Lord. Perhaps if he could take the edge off the Sea-lord's rage he might get him to see sense. Friends on the far side of the river, that was what Melin said the Lady had said!

Keré'us edged back across the causeway and dropped his bags and saddle on the bank, then he boldly approached Ranhé'us, who was by now in the middle of the river. Humbly offering a prayer to the Lady Yannya he spoke as if he had an unbroken sword and several men at his back.

"Very well, Lord Ranhé'us, I shall carry out that sentence of our court which you bought off!"

"Anyone can buy your father off!"

Keré'us laughed and made a feint towards the Sea-lord and then turned and ran. Ranhé'us roared and chased after him. When Keré'us considered his foe had sufficient momentum he turned again and stood his ground. Unable to stop, Ranhé'us lost his balance and with a neat wrestling throw Keré'us tipped him into the river. The Sea-lord found himself sitting in the shallow, but exceedingly icy, waters of the Elda, looking up at the Quarin.

"I wouldn't sit there all day if I were you. You'll catch your death of cold!" Keré'us bent to pick up the bronze sword from the other side of the causeway and stood there just holding it thoughtfully. This was partly because he could feel some power in it, like a great excitement building up and partly because it was too heavy for him to wield comfortably.

Ranhé'us regarded the Quarin and stood up carefully, stumbling in his water filled boots. "Damned unfair!" he said. "Why didn't you use your sword?"

In answer Keré'us threw the bronze sword back to the André'an and drew the shards of his own weapon. Ranhé'us paled. "Oh my sacred Grandfather! And to think I would have killed you! *He* would have eaten me alive!" He lovingly rubbed his sword on the only dry portion of his shirt he could find and sheathed it.

He held out his hand, "Can't remember your name, son of Darké'us, but shall we be at peace?"

"Keré'us, Lord of the House of Abard, and yes, we shall be friends." he put his hand inside the giant and still damp paw of the Sea-lord who shook it with the vigour of a man who does not know his own strength.

"What the hell is the House of Abard?"

"Me, apparently."

"Some Quarin title?"

"I think you could say that."

"What are you doing here?"

"Derany says I am going to the bridge at Runi to meet the Dark Lord. It seemed as good an idea as any."

"Then our roads lie together. I'd better help you with your things. It will be night before we know it and I shall have to hunt for my supper - unless you have provisions."

Keré'us laughed: due to the poverty of their land André'ans were notorious for their ability to invite themselves to supper. He and Ranhé'us went to the eastern bank to pick up his gear and take it across the river where the Sea-lord already had made a camp. Keré'us got a big fire going and hung Ranhé'us' clothes up to dry while the André'an huddled in a blanket and sipped Mundran wine.

"Did Derany say anything about the Halucias?"

"He said they had broken bounds again and he was taking the call to arms to Mundra, and presumably Pelélorné."

"I've just got back from the Sea-kingdoms. I've organised the muster and Danhé'us will be bringing them up. We met at the border just south of the Hélans Dru and organised it all and I had to turn straight back. The Dark Lord wants us all back at Elen as soon as possible. He has some concerns about Arno, I think."

Arno, thought Keré'us, it all comes back to Arno.

"I have heard tell that Arno is a fell sorcerer," he ventured.

77

"Very fell," said Ranhé'us, "and nasty with it. In my opinion, the Halucias are welcome to his lands, but rules are rules, and if the Alliance do not stand up for each other there is no Alliance left. It makes no odds to me. The Quaren never wanted my lands anyway, but the trading dues they charged on salt and iron were disgraceful. If they were brought back my country would be bankrupt." He went to say something else but forbore. Keré'us suspected it might have something to do with ransom. He changed the subject. "Good wine this."

"Yes, Mundran."

"Rich country, Mundra. Wine, grain and hot summers."

Keré'us said nothing. Mundra could have spared a ship-load of grain for starving André'as - so why had no one asked? Was he going to have this bear of a man's ransom on his conscience now?

"Still, it had its compensations," mused Ranhé'us, his thoughts following a path Keré'us' could not. He raised his cup, "Shall we make a toast, Keré'us, to the ladies? May they never grow any less!"

To the Lady, thought the Quarin as they touched cups, congratulations on getting me so far unscathed!

CHAPTER NINE

The road from the falls followed the river which over long years had cut out the valley through which they now travelled. The rocky sides slowly heightened until they lost sight of both the river, although they could still hear it, and the mountain peaks and were enclosed in a barren corridor of stone. Ranhé'us had a splendid bass voice and he sang as he rode, mostly bawdy sea songs, which echoed unmercifully off the stone walls and put the eagles, the only other visible living creatures around, to flight. Keré'us occasionally joined in but his native caution mostly restrained him. It was well for Ranhé'us, who, like the black bear he bore as coat of arms, was so big and strong he had no natural enemies, but the Quarin was mindful of his own more cat-like proportions and present lack of claws.

As the days passed the note of the river deepened and the valley walls began to fall away again as the Elda flowed into the Upper Plains. At last they had a view over the whole land of Avenya. To their right green grassland vanished over the edge of the world and before them river and sky mingled with the blue of lake Vanda. On their left the Neros Yannyos grew more distant as both road and river swung eastward to cut through a band of forest now putting forth slender green leaves. The spring that they had left to cross the mountains returned to them. The sun was warm again and carpets of cyclamen and hyacinths heralded the month of late spring. The road was overgrown with new grass, ferns unfurled their cautious fronds and the sweet jessamine of the mountains filled sheltered places with its heavily scented white flowers.

On the evening of the eighteenth day since the full of the red moon, when she was half waned and her silver sister new born in the north, they cleared the forest, forded the river and saw the first signs of human habitation since the Gate. Sheep had been cropping the grass, although the beasts were not visible in the deepening twilight.

"I think I can see a farm down there," said Keré'us, squinting into the gloom.

"Think you're right. Perhaps we shall have a hot meal and a comfortable bed for the night."

"Even a bath," mused Keré'us.

"That might be taking it too far. Don't forget I fell into the river a week or so ago!"

The windows of the farmhouse began to glow as candles were lit and after so long in the wild they could smell the domestic animals and the wood smoke of the fire. Both men were happy in anticipation of comfort to come, but the sudden, urgent thudding of hooves on the turf behind then soon altered that.

"Unshod ponies!" cried Ranhé'us. "Surely that can't be the Halucias? I knew Arno said he was having trouble, but I didn't think they were getting this far south!" His sword, Garenmegra, rang as he unsheathed it and the last light flashed green briefly in the stone in the hilt. He turned to face the tightly formed troop of Halucias who were bearing down on them, armed with spears and axes. "We'll not get to the farm, and if we did, I doubt they'd let us in."

"Perhaps you'll lend me your long knife then," said Keré'us philosophically.

Ranhé'us threw him the knife. "Oh well, here we go, you take the five on the left and I'll take the six on the right." Keré'us followed him down the hillside towards the tribesmen who broke over them in a surge which left one man fallen to Ranhe'us and the two friends unscathed. The Halucias wheeled and charged again but at that moment there came the note of a horn, clear as crystal in the twilight air.

"Derany!" they both cried. Ranhé'us grinned and in moments the firstborn son of Warany was at their side. And even as he joined them another came, on foot from the farmhouse, a tall Warny with a gleaming blade in his hand. Then, if it were not enough for the Halucias to find four men standing where only two had stood moments before, came the final blow. A sudden flood of light engulfed them, which made friend and foe alike shield their eyes as a creature as unbelievable as he was beautiful dropped from the skies. The Halucias fled in terror. Ranhé'us sheathed his sword. Keré'us could do no more than stare. The creature was still surrounded by a dying radiance; for the most part he looked like a man, tall and dark skinned, with white curly hair in which rested a silver circlet, but the strangeness was his wings, his glorious wings which sprang from his shoulders in a swan-like arc of white feathers and swept to his feet. This could be none other than Hara, Prince of the Merédur. The white bird at the Gate.

The man who had come on foot from the farm was speaking to the Merédur as an equal and a friend. "It was fortunate that you should see our little fight here, Hara."

"Do not pretend to be surprised," replied the Merédur in an amused voice. "When you see whom you have saved you will know my part in this and the part of others. Although had I known you were on hand, I would not have bothered. Now I must go. I like not to linger on the ground this close to the mountains."

Keré'us watched enthralled, but the other men had obviously met the Merédur before.

"Come," said Derany, "let us get to the farm before the Halucias return." They led their horses to the farm in silence, alert for any sound, but there were none, save the ordered noises of the night. The farm was surrounded by a stockade of sharpened tree trunks. The man who had come from the farm banged on the gate, calling to the inhabitants to let them in. The gate swung open. Tall fair-haired Elta, Arno's folk, stood in the light with weapons at the ready and the gate slammed shut hard on the travellers' heels.

In the blessed light and warmth of the farm they took stock of each other. Derany and Ranhé'us were old friends. They had joined the Trumarei in the same year and Ranhé'us had often stayed at the Grey Halls with Derany's family. The third man was well known to both of them. He was tall, even for a Warny, dressed in Trumaré green, but not young. His hair was grizzled, his weather beaten face was old and scarred by a lifetime of battles, and his eyes were blue, as blue as the jewel he wore on a silver chain about his neck. His kinship with Derany was obvious.

The Warny stared at Keré'us as keenly as the Quarin stared at him and in his gaze the Quarin felt uncomfortable, for it asked questions he was not sure he wanted to answer. Yet such was the power of the old man's presence Keré'us knelt before him. Grandson of the Quarinya Queen he might be, but this was the man who had destroyed his grandmother's empire. A noble and venerable man.

"Keré'us, Lord of the House of Abard, at your service, Lord Warany," he said, and offered him his broken sword.

"Nay, Keré'us, do not kneel to me. We are all equal in our service of the Dark Lord." Warany's blue eyes smiled, suddenly merry, and Keré'us smiled back knowing he had found another friend.

The Elta matron sat them out of her way at a table by the central fire of the hall that formed the main room of the farm. She found them bread and cheese and served them with beer, the Elta's staple beverage and as they ate they talked. Keré'us, as behoved the new recruit, listened and tried to look as if he understood, although a lot of what was said went over his head. First Derany spoke, for he had to tell his father how many men had been promised in the defence of Arno's land. "Mordata and Pelelorné will send all they can mount, about a thousand in total. Darké'us - well, I'm afraid he said he had done his bit for the Alliance by killing Keré'us."

"But we didn't want Keré'us killed, and anyway, he didn't!" muttered Ranhé'us.

"I did experience a degree of difficulty explaining that," said Derany, "but he was firm. No men. There was no time to waste arguing. I thought it would be more important to catch up with Keré'us."

"Had it not been for Hara, it would have been," said his father, "but as it is, someone seems to be making doubly certain of his safety." He looked at the Elta variously occupying themselves around the fire with household tasks and decided to say no more.

Ranhé'us said, "I had not realised how grave Arno's problems were with the Halucias."

"The party which attacked you and Keré'us, or should

I say Keré'us and yourself, for I am sure he was the target, were the first party I have seen across the Lee'ma Ra, but as you can see from the stockade such attacks are not unusual," said Warany.

"I still think it is a stupid time to start a war. I have spent most of this year so far riding up and down Avenya. My men will have to leave the fields when they are most needed. It will cost us dear in lost man power. Danhé'us is bringing up all I can afford to mount since men on foot will never reach Arno's lands in time."

"We shall need all you can spare." Warany shook his head, "I don't know what is going on, but it feels wrong. You know the Halucias signed an agreement with the Alliance to portion out the lands of the old empire when we jointly defeated the Quaren. I know they like to keep us on our toes with the odd border raid and we politely but firmly escort them back and nothing else happens for a year or two. But now something has changed their attitude. Arno went and spoke to them, to no avail, so the Dark Lord and I went to speak with the Gerhart, who is the ring-leader as usual. It was obvious that they are massing to attack Arno's city of Elen. They gave no reason for gathering there so far south of their traditional birthing lands. I thought perhaps Arno had offended them, but no, they said not. They just thought the land was theirs and we had robbed them through the treaty. They gave no reason for waiting twenty seven years before bringing the matter up and then not discussing it beforehand, but going straight for a fight. They have plenty of room for their herds north of the river Telga. The land is warmer and the grass grows better. It is their traditional land, with all their shrines and sacred places. It is not even a good time for them to fight. Their ponies will be foaling, their cattle calving, and they will need all the men they have to tend them. To fight now will seriously affect the whole of Avenya and only the merchants in the great cities will gain by that.

"I am sorry Ranhé'us that we have to call up your men, for I know how narrow the margin is between survival and starvation in your land. You are the only lord of the Alliance who still works the land. It is long since I, or even Derany, milked a cow. Or Anya." He smiled at the thought of his beautiful daughter.

Ranhé'us said, "I didn't know Anya ever did anything as domesticated as milking a cow. I thought she spent her time out on the plains herding the steers!"

"She does," said Derany, "and more often now since our father refused to let her join the Trumarei with me and Terany. And now Terany is married and she has to give his wife precedence she is quite unbearable."

Ranhé'us smiled, "I did not expect the Grey Halls to hold both Anya and Garnya."

"They certainly don't," said Warany, "our only hope for peace in the Grey Halls is to get the girl married to some likely king or high lord, but she has refused everyone I have suggested to her. Hérumanus wanted her, you know his wife died the other year, but when he met her she scared him silly. Terué of Mordata wanted her for one of his sons but she was so rude to them all that the boys both fell in love with her and their father took them away as quickly as he could. The Lord over Banéros sent a messenger and a very pretty diamond necklace. He was lucky the necklace had a strong chain…" He and Derany looked at each other and grinned.

Ranhé'us smiled again. "She told me about that, I thought she was exaggerating."

Warany shook his head, "Even Selin considered her -

for about a day, I think. She seemed to be waiting for the right man." He looked hard at the Sea-lord.

"The cold lands of André'as are poor and no place for Warany's daughter," mumbled Ranhé'us.

"We aren't asking much of a bride price," said Derany to no one in particular. "I mean, the girl is a liability. We'll be glad to get rid of her."

"I am already in your father and Selin's debt somewhere in the region of about fifteen thousand bathens." Ranhé'us paused to glower at Keré'us, "And I won't be able to repay any this year, not with my men all coming north."

Keré'us opened his pouch and brought out his purse and the one his father had given him. His purse contained twenty five bathens, his share of the ransom Ranhé'us had had to pay, a few copper and silver coins and an unset garnet of unusual size. He had not even looked in the purse his father had given him and was surprised to see there were a further thirty bathens in it. He put twenty of his own in that purse and threw it across the table to Ranhé'us. "You are welcome to this, in the name of friendship, but apart from these odds and ends I have no more."

As Ranhé'us great paw closed round the purse, his face changed. Keré'us could not know, but he had no money on him and had been desperately aware that as the grandson of one of the Lords Eldest and High Lord of a group of kingdoms he was going to cut a very poor figure when hospitality had to be paid for. He pretended not to be too interested in the money, transferred five of the gold bathens into his own purse, which would pay for all his wants until he got back to André'as, and passed the rest on to Warany.

Warany looked keenly at Keré'us. A man upon whom gold has no hold is, as young Darké'us had discovered before him, a rare man indeed. "Come," he said, "let's to bed. We have a long journey ahead of us in the morning."

The daughter of the house led them to a hayloft over a barn in which the cattle were bedded down for the night. She gave them blankets and left them to make beds in the hay. The others settled down, but Warany sat for a while and watched and listened to the night. The cattle mumbled and snorted. Their coats steamed and the smell was strong. Not easy for an old man to sleep.

So this is the grandson of the queens, thought Warany, well, well! Aren't Quaren small? Nice and light on his feet though, and from what I saw, not scared to fight. Think he'll be a useful addition to the team. I like him, he's clever but quiet with it. He didn't say much but he listened keenly enough. Not interested in gold! Poor Ranhé'us, we do put him through it. I didn't realise he had no money at all on him. Things must be really bad down in André'as at the moment, but still he obeys the treaty. A true Lord, even if he is poor. How are we going to make it so he can marry Anya? He's too proud for his own good!

I wonder what himself will think of the Quarin? Wonder what he'd say if he knew Hara was involved somewhere. Better not mention it, for the sake of peace. That sorceress of the red moon is up to something but what I would not presume to guess. He yawned and settled down in the hay. I'm too old for this. I miss my bed, he thought, and fell asleep.

CHAPTER TEN

In the morning the four set out for Tal Elen, a large village on the southern bank of lake Vanda. Derany and Ranhé'us rode ahead, while Warany rode with Keré'us, intending to question him.

"The day after tomorrow we should meet the Dark Lord, if he is still at Runi," said Warany. Keré'us said nothing. He was not particularly looking forward to that meeting. "I do not understand," continued the Warny, "what exactly the Lady Yannya intends that you should do."

"No more do I."

"Why then are you coming to find him?"

"Because your son suggested I should."

"Come now, what sort of reason is that?"

"It seemed like a good idea at the time. I hadn't anything else to do."

The Warny looked deep into Keré'us' eyes, "And what did the Gate think?"

Keré'us smiled. "They thought I might be better employed as a king."

Warany had the grace to flinch. "And will you take the Golden Throne?"

"I have found, over many years in my father's court, that if you have anything of importance, people are always trying to take it away from you. Why should I spend the rest of my life fighting to keep a throne I do not want?"

"A man after my own heart. I tell you Keré'us, being High Lord of the Alliance is a thankless task."

"Of course, I didn't definitely say no. I pointed out that their late queen had put on me the weird that I must serve the Dark Lord until I or my house destroy that which he holds most dear. It was rather hard to refuse Melin flatly."

The Warny laughed, "Quite dangerous too I should think, but you seem to have handled him well."

"I had practise when I lived at home."

"But tell me, you speak of your weird. Have you met the Sorceress of the Red Moon?" It was almost a throwaway line.

Keré'us gave it the answer it deserved. "Yes."

"By the Lords Eldest, this is like playing Ra-malcron in the dark. Tell me what she said. I do not ask out of idle curiosity."

Keré'us thought back to the brightness of the Lady. She had not forbidden him to speak of their meeting. "She said I must serve the Dark Lord and that my grandmother's curse served her own purposes. She did not say what they were. Yet I do not think she meant him ill."

"What is she like? I have served the Dark Lord most of my life but I have never seen her. Is she as fair as they say?"

Keré'us smiled as he replied, remembering the shining goddess. "She was in shape like a young Quarinya woman, as fair as any woman I have ever seen. Her eyes were yellow and her glorious hair copper in great waves falling about her waist. Glad, she was, filled with laughter but terrible and powerful. Too exalted for me to desire, but gentle enough for me to love. You call her a sorceress, yet she is my goddess and I shall serve her gladly until the end of my days."

"But she betrayed my Dark Lord to imprisonment in the mines under the mountains, she was his woman and she betrayed him to his deadliest enemy. He gave her all his love and trust and out of that love she branded him with her mark so all might know she had made a fool of him."

Keré'us looked hard into Warany's eyes, "Then I say this, if she chose to treat the Dark Lord so ill, the alternative must have been more terrible still." His words struck home.

Warany frowned as he tried to remember something and then his brow cleared. "Someone else once said that to me. You have taken me back over many years."

"Who?"

"Nanenethen my wife."

The sun was beginning to set as they reached the village of Tal Elen. Warany led them to the inn to find lodgings for the night and a meal. "I think they had some trouble here when I came through," he said, "but I was in too much of a hurry to listen. Now they can catch me I suppose they will expect me to do something about it. That's the trouble when you're old and famous like me. Everyone thinks you have nothing better to do than save them from a plague of red ants."

Ranhé'us grinned, "I keep asking him to save us from the plague of Mundran pirates, but he won't help us!"

Keré'us showed his teeth in a friendly fashion.

Derany asked curiously, "How would you save someone from a plague of red ants?"

"I'd cover you with honey, let the ants crawl onto you and stick and then throw you into the lake," said his father.

"Well, I just thought it might come in useful some day," muttered Derany crossly.

By the time they had made themselves comfortable at the inn, with tankards of beer to hand and dinner ordered, a number of the tall, fair-haired Elta had come to stare at them curiously. In Mundra, where the natives were basically a mixture of André'an and Quaren stock, Keré'us had seen few Elta and they looked strange to him. They were all very tall and silver fair, the men wearing their hair short. Their eyes were blue or grey, their faces long and clean shaven with pale skins, and instead of sensible trousers and tunics, the men wore tunics, with short kilts, like the city-dwelling Quaren on the hot plains, and the women had skirts which came only just below the knee. The Elta were famed for their weaving and even the poorest wore clothes with decorative woven borders, each housewife producing her own special pattern. Although they were big folk, and in the Quarin's experience big folk were more serious that the smaller Quaren, the Elta seemed very much more serious than the Warny or the André'ans.

By the time dinner had arrived so had the mayor, the town council and the local priest. Warany gave a deep sigh.

"Lord Warany," began the mayor. Warany fished a likely looking piece of meat from his stew with his spoon, regarded it, then plucked up courage and ate it.

"Lord Warany, surely the Lady Eldest Aeta has brought you here in our time of trouble, to deliver us from the terrible Worm!"

"I am happy to say," said Warany firmly, "that I have never had any dealings with the Lady Eldest Aeta in my life."

Ranhé'us laughed, the Elta worshipped the Lady Eldest Aeta in the aspect of the virgin goddess of the silver moon and Warany's reputation where women were concerned was legendary.

"However," continued the Warny Lord, "if you will tell me what your trouble is I shall do my best to help you."

Thus encouraged the mayor began his tale.

"Lord Warany, you know that these lands were once the property of the Quaren and were given to us and our Lord Arno by the Alliance. When we moved here the village had been razed and the temple which the Quaren had dedicated to the Lord Eldest Gawen had been sacked. We lived here, we fished, we farmed, we rebuilt the village and we rededicated the sacked temple not to Gawen, who has never aided us, but to the Lady Eldest Aeta, who is our Lady of the Silver Moon and bestows all blessings on us…" He paused in his narrative, awed by Warany's expression of anger.

"I expressly directed," said Warany, making an effort to keep calm, "that you were not to rededicate temples already dedicated to the Lords Eldest. I suppose you were too mean to build a new temple? I have had this trouble the length and breadth of Avenya. When will you ever learn? You do not interfere in the affairs of the Lord Eldest Gawen! Everyone knows what a temper he has. Well, what's he doing to you?"

"Oh Lord Warany, he has sent a terrible Worm. A beast bigger than our fishing boats. It has eaten my daughter, a priest of the Lady Aeta and the blacksmith. A Trumaré tried to help us and he was eaten also. None dare fish in the lake, the women cannot wash the clothes, and the children cannot play by the lake shore. Oh Lord Warany, High Lord of the Alliance. I beg you, save us!"

Warany pushed his dinner away from him (it was no great loss) and looked up into the man's pale eyes. "I am Warany, I serve the Lords Eldest, therefore I cannot help you, for if one of the Lords Eldest has passed judgement on you, who is Warany to gainsay him?"

The mayor's face fell, "But what can we do? We cannot trade. We cannot plough our lakeside fields. We shall starve!"

"Get a Gawen priest from Banéros and let him rededicate the temple and build another to your Lady."

"But that will take many months and gold, which we do not have, Lord."

"I cannot interfere with the will of the Lords Eldest."

"But who then can help us?" The mayor looked hopefully at the other lords with Warany.

"The Lord Eldest Gawen is my grandfather," said Ranhé'us, "I can in no wise help you."

"Well, I am sworn to no Lord Eldest," said Derany, "and a monster which kills women and children does not sound to me like a considered punishment but more like hot revenge. I may not have the years or wisdom of my father, but I shall try and help you!"

"My son, do not do this."

"They looked to you to save them," said Derany, "if you will not, then must I, lest the House of Wargarny be put to shame!"

The rising moons showed a group of people on the beach by the edge of the lake. Someone had lit a fire of drift wood and it burned brightly. The sightseers gathered around it, warming their hands. These included Keré'us and a very reluctant Warany. Ranhé'us had refused to come. The rest were villagers come to see the death of the Worm or the young man. Whichever it was it promised a good evening's entertainment.

The stars brightened. The lake was still and the ebbing red moon touched its slow ripples with faint fire. Keré'us was hoping for his friend's sake that the Worm would not come. He could not tell what Derany hoped, alone by the water's edge, sword in hand.

Now, either the mayor had not seen the Worm for himself, or he had deliberately understated its size so as not to discourage any would be slayer, for presently there came a terrible belling and roaring and the water whipped up into white crests that parted angrily. Keré'us had seen nothing living which could compare with the Worm in size. It was as long as the grain ships of Mundra, thin like a snake, an evil green in colour with bulging icy eyes that glittered in the fire on the beach. It opened its bearded mouth, revealing rows of long teeth and roared until the very heavens shook.

It ignored Derany and made straight for the fire. The watchers scattered save Keré'us and Warany. Derany, pale but determined, slashed at its coils but his blade bounced off the scales and the creature shook itself contemptuously. It swayed from left to right, looking and sniffing, as if it sought something. Then it lunged at Keré'us. Weaponless the Quarin snatched up a brand from the fire and with the surefootedness of a sailor, leapt back. The Worm lunged again. Keré'us thrust the brand into its face and it hesitated. He danced round it and burned its back and it screamed. Keré'us hit it again and again until all that it wanted was to get back to the lake, but the Quarin and his fiery brand stood between it and the cool water. In fury it roared again, feinted with its head and as Keré'us stepped aside, caught his legs in its coils and twisted about him. Derany slashed angrily at the beast without any effect. The Quarin struggled but could not free himself. Warany, forgetting his own warning, drew his sword and ran down the beach, but he was too slow. Already the head with its gaping mouth was bearing down on Keré'us. In desperation the Quarin found the strength to move his left arm and, as the terrible teeth came nearer, he thrust the torch up into the creature's mouth and down its throat. It screamed in agony, dropped him and writhed and groaned. Keré'us snatched the sword from Warany's hand. The Worm was still trying to regain the lake, but the Lord of the House of Abard smote it. The moonlight caught on the bronze blade and flashed blue in the stone on the hilt as Keré'us sliced through the scaly neck. The head rolled away. The body writhed and was still.

Keré'us, crushed and winded would have fallen had not Warany's arm been there to catch him. "Steady there, we'll get you to the inn," he said, as the grateful crowd bore down on them, thanking the Warny, assuming Keré'us to be his slave.

Derany took Keré'us' other arm and together they propelled him to the inn and up the stairs out of the way.

"Whew!" said Warany as he sat down on the bed. Keré'us half fell, half sat on the other side.

"Ouch," was the only contribution he was fit enough to make to the conversation.

"I'd better go downstairs," said Derany, "they'll only come up here if someone doesn't speak to them."

"Don't let them give you their daughter," warned his father, "These Elta are always trying to get rid of their unmarriageable daughters." As Derany opened the door they could hear the noise of celebration in the tap room below. "My son, Lords Eldest or no, you were right and I was wrong."

Derany grinned. It was hard having Warany as a father. "Thanks," he said as he disappeared below.

Warany turned to Keré'us, "How do you feel?"

"Still a little breathless."

"Get some sleep and you will feel better." He sighed, "what we both need is a little good red wine, Mundran or

95

Islander, I care not, but I am sick of Elta beer and they think red wine is bad for you."

"I might just have a little in my saddle bags."

Warany brightened. The Quarin poured out some of the fragrant wine for both of them. "It did come straight for me, didn't it?" he asked.

Warany nodded, "I wonder why. The Lord Eldest Gawen is half brother to my Lord of Darkness and his only friend among his Eldest kin."

"I am a sailor and value the Lord Eldest Gawen's luck. I slew the Worm only because it would otherwise have slain me."

"Everyone seems to be changing their allegiance. The world is not as I remember it. It is as if we stand on the edge of a whole new cycle."

"Thank you for the loan of Erindra. Nothing else would have cut those scales."

"How did you know it was Erindra?"

"It had power in it."

"I don't wear it much these days. Magical things grow irksome over the years, but I thought if we are going to war, then I would wear it again for old times' sake. You are the first person that I have met who could tell it was a sword of power by touching it. What power do you have?"

"Only the power of the red earth. I am only a Quarin, the bastard son of Darké'us of Mundra."

"Well," Warany drank the rest of his wine and began to pull his boots off, "I'm glad you are on my side. Hark at the row down there. I'm getting old little Keré'us, sending my son to drink in my place." He rolled into bed and soon was asleep snoring faintly.

CHAPTER ELEVEN

Keré'us could not rest. A feeling of unease had taken hold of him. In any case, Warany's rhythmic snoring was enough to stop anyone sleeping. The Quarin lay on the bed and shut his eyes, only to find that his mind was still racing round in circles. The Worm had ignored Derany and Warany. It had come straight for him. Had the Lord Eldest Gawen sent it after him? If so, what did it mean? Downstairs, despite his relationship to the Worm, Ranhé'us appeared to have joined in the carousing. No one could sleep through his singing.

Into Keré'us' mind suddenly came a thought, which grew into a command, that he must go back down to the lake. He shook his head, telling himself that he was imagining things, but knowing in his heart it was not so. As surely as if he had heard a voice, he heard the command, to go to the lakeside.

He pulled his boots back on and picked up his cloak. Quietly he descended the back stairs and left the inn through the stables to the lakeside. No one saw him.

The embers of the fire glowed dull red. The great body of the Worm lay across the shingle beach and the cruel head where it had rolled. No one had dared touch it in the dark. The Quarin shivered. It was now very cold.

"Whatever you are," said Keré'us to the voice in his mind, "I am here as you commanded me. Show yourself!"

"I am here, mortal."

At the edge of the lake, with the slow ripples lapping about his feet, stood one who could only be the Lord Eldest Gawen.

As Yannya had been terrible and kind, so this Lord Eldest was terrible and unkind. In shape he was like to the André'ans, tall, broad shouldered with long curling dark hair and beard, but still pale faced, like his Eldest kin. His garments were green, not the dark green of the Trumarei, but the bright green of deep waters, worked with pearls and silver. In his dark hair he wore a silver circlet and about his neck hung a green stone set in silver. He took another step towards Keré'us and although sore afraid the Quarin did not run. Instead he knelt, defenceless before the Lord Eldest's wrath.

"Know you who I am?"

Keré'us looked up at him and into the eyes of one of the over-lords of Naru. He saw the power and majesty of the Lords Eldest, their might and cruelty, yet he also saw that kinder part of Gawen that came not from his father Vallior, but from his sea spirit mother. He spoke out boldly. "You are the Lord Eldest Gawen of the Waters, on whom I have been pleased to call in my times of trouble, and who has seen fit to bestow many blessings on me. So many that men have sometimes called me specially blessed by you."

"And in return you killed the Worm, my just punishment for these cold Elta?"

Keré'us stood up. It was difficult to argue from his kneeling position and if, as seemed likely, he was to die, he would rather meet death on his feet. "Lord Gawen, it tried to kill me. Any creature has the right to defend its own life."

Gawen shook his mighty head. "No, for on you rests the curse of the High Queen and that robs you of any rights. I know what the Dark Lord loves before his own life and there are others who love her also. You shall in no wise destroy her. I, Gawen have spoken!"

"The Lady," began Keré'us wildly, following a desperate idea. Instantly he held the attention of the Lord Eldest, "The Lady bade me serve the Lord of Darkness your brother. You cannot touch me while I am bound by her to him for I am under both their protection." The expression on Gawen's face told him he had guessed the truth. He felt the power of the Lady rise up in him, like controlled anger. "You cannot hurt me, so do not pretend to me that you can!"

To his surprise Gawen suddenly smiled, "Surely the Lady has chosen well. So you know you are safe. You were ever one of my favourites, as you guessed. Before she took you from me, I was loath to harm you. But this I must do. Your house must not survive! Hear my words and be mindful of them, for I shall do this whomsoever tries to stand in my path. You shall have but one son, and in the night he is born you shall take him to the southernmost point of André'as, the rock which even now is called the Abard Rock and there you shall lay him, and I shall take him. The Lady Yannya is dearer than all else to me and I can guess the part you will play if your House is to live until the end." He thrust out his hand to Keré'us and clasped the Quarin's hand. It was like shaking hands with a whirlwind. The power of the Lord Eldest was terrifying. Keré'us, protected as he was by the Lady's power, let go as soon as he dared.

"I know you will bring some comfort to my brother in exile. I would not deny him that, so I shall hold my hand over you, until the last." He reached up and unfastened the stone about his neck and held it out to the Quarin. "Take this, little Keré'us. This is the Sea-stone. It holds the half my power that my kinsmen took away from me, for my part in the Diadem wars. Wear it and remember me and all other good I may I shall bring you. Only your son is forfeit to me and if you bring him not to me I shall fetch him and all your remaining life shall be nothing but misfortune. Remember me!"

Then there was only a rushing column of water, which was swiftly gone and nothing remained on that cold shore save the Sea-stone lying heavy in Keré'us hand to tell the truth of the meeting.

The next day the company set off along the lakeside road to Runi, which was a further two days journey away. Warany was uneasy. Things felt wrong. He found himself half expecting an ambush - this in the lands of one of the major lords of the Alliance. But who in their right mind would ambush Warany, his son, the Sea-lord Ranhé'us and a Quarin with a growing reputation for unarmed combat, he asked himself. And what happened to the Quarin last night? The lad had said nothing but suddenly come back from somewhere, cold, somewhat damp and with his mind in another realm. Nothing anyone had said had brought Keré'us out of his silence. It did not seem politic to ask why, but Warany hoped the Quarin would confide in him eventually.

Warany could not see the Sea-stone hanging beneath Keré'us' tunic or feel the weight of the words of the Lord Eldest Gawen upon his mind, but he tried to lighten the mood of the party.

"We'll have to get you some sort of sword soon, Keré'us."

"Must we?" asked Ranhé'us. "I'd much rather he was unarmed. I feel so much safer."

"He can't carry on without a sword, however good he seems to be at unarmed combat. Anyway, I've seen him with a sword. He's even better," said Derany.

"Thanks," Keré'us made an effort to join in the conversation. "I do have a sword. It's just that someone else thinks it's theirs at the moment. It's a family heirloom. I just have to collect it."

Warany's eyes narrowed, "My, we are going to have fun if we ever reach Elen. Does Arno know of your claims to Aren?"

"I don't know. However, I understand he was the one who asked the Maren-Ra to have me killed. That argues a degree of knowledge."

"It's very confusing," said Warany, "so many Lords Eldest, mortals, Quaren and Alliance, and half mortals seem to be mixed up with your life. If only we knew who was in which camp it might at least allow us to guess who will make an attempt on your life next.

"You know," he continued, "I had wondered which sword you would bear, since all the swords of power are taken, as it were. Besides which, they are too long for you to manage comfortably. That wretched rhyme keeps buzzing round my head, *Why now together are four swords to make or mar and Aren the darkest far, master of evil?* I think something will happen when all four swords are met with Aren. But that has happened before and no magic has been set in train. However, with the exception of myself, all the sword bearers are now only part mortal. When I die and Derany takes Erindra all four swords of power will be held by part mortals for my wife Nanenethen was one of the Youngest, like Hara who is Selin's uncle.

Ranhé'us is grandson of the Lord Eldest Gawen and of course our dear Dark Lord is Lord Eldest on his father, Vallior's, side and his mother was Mara, High Queen of Ungarit, a domain in the stars, and he still has her wild magic even if his Eldest strength has been taken away." He sighed, "And here you are, mortal as me."

"And even more confused!"

Warany laughed, "What would you be doing if you were still in the courts of Mundra but trying to survive the plots at court? The board is bigger, the game is the same."

The board, thought Keré'us, was even bigger than Warany could imagine.

As evening began to draw in they reached the small village of Eloruna. The sky had clouded over and it looked as if it would begin to rain at any moment. There was no Trumaré post in the village but there was an inn. Warany thought the matter over, his joints ached with the damp and another night spent sleeping in the poor protection of a hedge with his saddle as a pillow was not much of a prospect. No one attacked us at the last village, he thought, but then, they did not have to, the Worm did. Very unlikely sides seemed to be colluding. Risk it, Warany told himself. At least you can afford a decent room!

He led the company into the inn and arranged matters, then went upstairs with the gear while the three young men went into the tap room, to order dinner, beer and wine. Although Eloruna was a small village, its position on the main road filled the inn with travellers. A Trumaré, clad in the dark green uniform of his order, saw the two tall men, Derany in uniform, and cornered them. Within moments they were deep in Trumaré talk, leaving Keré'us to feel unwanted. A Quarinya serving girl, branded a slave, came up to him and spoke to him, but she only spoke the classical tongue and he could not make out much that she said so he just smiled at her until the landlord called her away to serve someone else. Then an Elta came up to him, dressed in grey livery.

"This is the man!" he called over his shoulder to another Elta. "This is our escaped Quarin slave!"

Keré'us sprang to his feet, hand to his broken sword. Several men in the same grey livery were converging on him, all with drawn swords. Everyone else was moving out of the way.

"I'm no slave!" cried Keré'us indignantly. "I am Keré'us, son of the Lord Darké'us of Mundra."

"Liar," cried the leading Elta, "these Quaren are all the same. Quick, help me secure him!"

Keré'us drew his knife and backed away until he felt a bench behind his knees and could go no further. "Hey, Derany," he called, "tell these Elta who I am!" There was no answer. He looked to where he had last seen his friends but they had vanished. "I am here with the Lord Warany. He is upstairs. Go and ask him!"

The Elta laughed in their cold fashion. Keré'us knew he was trapped. Whatever had happened to his friends, they seemed unlikely to help him now. He was on his own again.

He stepped backwards on to the bench and then on to the table out of the way of the long glinting swords. The customers seated at the table hastily removed themselves elsewhere. Keré'us wondered if the Elta had orders to kill him or merely capture him, but the matter was probably academic.

The Elta moved in, swords outstretched. Keré'us sent a brief prayer to the Lady Yannya on the lines of forgiveness for any presumption of protection and wondering exactly how she intended to get him out of this, because he did not think he was going to manage it by himself.

"Come down," said the leading Elta, "we'd rather take you alive."

"If Arno wants me alive I think I'd just as soon be dead," said Keré'us making a calculated guess.

"I think you're probably right," agreed the Elta, "but that does not change my orders."

Well, that answered that. Keré'us looked about him. The table was about four paces long and standing in the middle he was covered by all six swords. However, he had a chance, or half a chance if he could get outside where the darkness would hide him. He calculated the paces to the main doors, backed carefully to the end of the table then swiftly raced back down it and leapt off the other end covering another good four paces with his jump. The Elta, taken by surprise, took a moment to collect themselves before they rushed after him. He would have gained the night had not a tall man in Trumaré gear been that moment entering. Keré'us ran straight into him. The Trumaré looked to the Elta whilst maintaining a grip on Keré'us arm.

"Yours?" he asked with a slight flicker of an eyebrow.

"Yes lord, one of Arno's slaves who has run away."

The man looked at Keré'us. His face was dark, even darker than the Quarin's, but his long hair curled loosely like Warany's and was not raven black but dark brown. His eyes were a surprising bright green-gold. He was at least as tall as Warany and broad of chest. His face was weather beaten and stern, but there was something of amusement in his eyes.

"It's not true!" shouted Keré'us and tried to push the man away. He might as well have tried to push a mountain.

The man pulled Keré'us' left coat sleeve up. "He does not appear to be branded a slave," he said logically.

"I am not a slave, I am Keré'us, son of Darké'us, Lord of Mundra!"

"He is a slave," said the Elta, "we have been pursuing him these four days out of Elen."

The Trumaré looked at Keré'us, "Your turn?"

"You do not have to take my word," said Keré'us, "but go upstairs and find Warany, Prince of the Warny and First Lord of the Alliance and he will tell you I am no slave."

"Give him back to me, you will find no Lord Warany here."

The Trumaré looked keenly at the Elta, "You do not seem to be able to prove he is Arno's slave," he said in reasonable tones.

"Hand him over or it will be the worst for you!" The Elta threatened the other with his sword.

"I do not think so," said the Trumaré slowly and transferred his hold on Keré'us from his left to his right hand so he might draw his sword, for he, like Keré'us was left handed. The Elta lunged at him and he drew and parried the blow in as much time, whilst pushing Keré'us behind him to the door.

"Get round the back and find what has happened to that fool Warany and tell him to hurry!"

Keré'us fled to the yard where he could hear a regular thunder on a door. Someone, it seemed, was shut in a cellar. There was a key hanging by the door and Keré'us unlocked and opened it, much to the detriment of Ranhé'us who was hurling his bear-like frame against it at the time and fell at Keré'us' feet.

"Trouble in the tap room!" the Quarin shouted and was nearly mown down as the others rushed past him back to the inn, drawing their swords as they went and, in Ranhé'us' case, uttering dire war cries.

Pausing only to pick up a likely looking billet of wood, Keré'us followed them back to the main doors where he surveyed the fray. No one shuts the Prince of the Warny, his son and the High Lord of the Sea-kingdoms of André'as in a cellar and hopes to escape unscathed. The Trumaré was sitting on a stool, drinking a cup of wine. He indicated the seat on his right and poured Keré'us a cup and they sat there together watching the fight.

"I have seen fights in inns and fights out of inns," said the stranger, "and as fights go, this is one of the better ones, but they are going to run out of opponents soon. They should have known better that to have left you on your own," he added.

"I don't think they meant to. It seemed to be well planned," said Keré'us.

Ranhé'us disposed of the last Elta and came and slumped in a chair next to them. There was an abandoned tankard of beer that he claimed and drank straight down.

"Hé! Thirsty work that," he said as he liberated another.

Warany came over, picking his way carefully through the broken pots and wood. He sat down and a cup of wine was placed by his hand by the stranger. They looked at each other, eyes smiling.

CHAPTER TWELVE

"Ouch!" said Warany.

"You are getting old," said the Trumaré, adding the mild reproof, "do you know how hard it is to fight Elta and not kill them?"

"I suppose I must introduce you." Warany looked at Keré'us and then at the Trumaré.

"I think we have more or less guessed who we are," smiled the Dark Lord.

Keré'us nodded, "I feared this meeting Lord, but with no reason."

The Dark Lord said, "I feared it too." His eyes shone with amusement, "but you are not so very terrible."

Servant and master looked at the other: the yellow eyed, red haired, slight Quarin, young and merry and the tall, dark, sternly handsome fallen Lord Eldest, with the doom of mortal man upon him. Light and dark, hope and despair. The one for Yannya and the Quaren, the other for the Lords Eldest and the Alliance. But both doughty warriors with skill in the use of any weapon. Neither of them had a home or roof over their heads, nor kin to acknowledge them save perhaps, curiously, a half brother.

Warany looked at the pair and they brought gladness to his heart. The Quarin *will* be his friend, he thought. I can

let go now, and find my rest. For all the Sorceress is his
enemy she has given him a true friend who will serve him
as I do…did. This last battle I shall serve him and then I
shall retire to the Grey Halls and dandle my grandchildren
upon my knee and grow old by the fireside. If I marry
Anya to Ranhé'us I can always go down to the Sea-
kingdoms when I get bored.

The Dark Lord pulled a ring from his hand which he
had been wearing on his little finger. "Here Keré'us, this I
think is yours as much as anyone's. I had Mildur make it
for that red witch. After she betrayed me she gave it to her
women, the High Queens, whom she loved so much. I took
it back after the fall of Nenaterian. It was not fit that any
other should wear it. However, you are in their direct line,
although you will be the first man to wear it." He placed
the ring in Keré'us palm and the Quarin looked at it. It
seemed a poor thing at first sight. It was made of two
intertwined rings, one of iron for the Lord Malcarious and
one of copper for the Lady Yannya. Both metals were dull
and it had no stone or bezel, but Keré'us knew that it was
one of the most prized relics of the High Queens, second
only to Hiruéven. He slipped it on his second finger and, as
when the Lady Yannya blessed him, he felt the power of
the ring multiplying his own power.

"Heaven help us all when he has Aren as well," said
Warany.

"I think I shall be relieved," said the Dark Lord. "I was
ever anxious about Arno bearing it, although I had never
thought to be glad to see it back into the hands of the
Quarenyos Queens, or at least, their descendants. Now
tell me all of you, how did you come to be locked in a
cellar? I never believed I should see such a day!"

Derany looked rather sheepish. "We were talking to a
Trumaré," he explained, "and he said his horse had the

beginnings of a swollen fetlock and would we look at it for him since the Elta have absolutely no knowledge about horses, but as we reached the stables someone dropped a sack over our heads and threw us into the cellar."

"Then the landlord called me," continued Warany, "and said that there was some trouble outside and would I come and help Keré'us, but he directed me to the cellar and I ended there as well. It was fortunate you arrived when you did."

"Actually, I think I got in his way. He was managing quite well without me."

"He always does," said Ranhé'us grudgingly.

"But why are you here? I thought we were meeting at Runi?" asked Warany.

"We were, but last night, as I waited at the gates of Runi to see if you were coming, I heard one gate ward say to the other that if Warany should come with a Quarin, they were to be let in however late the hour and a message sent to the captain of the guard. It seemed to me that we might do as well to avoid Runi so I set out to find you. I think tomorrow we had better go north and cross the Lee'ma Ra by the old ford to the east of Runi."

"I suppose all this trouble is being caused by Arno?" asked Warany.

"I suppose so. Arno must have realised from the moment the priestess spoke to me at Mara-lei that Keré'us was a threat to him holding Aren."

"I thought there was no way Arno could have known about Keré'us before that meeting," mused Warany, "yet in the space of three hours after it he has a Trumaré on the way to Mundra with instructions to have Keré'us killed. Not only that but he has men all over the place to get him if that fails, and where the Halucias and the Worm come into it I do not know. If Arno knew before me and you, who told him?" Despite his best efforts, he yawned. "I'm to bed. We've paid for them so we may as well use them."

Ranhé'us and Derany rose to follow him, the Sea-lord picking up a huge pie from the bar in lieu of dinner and breaking off portions for Warany and Derany. Keré'us looked to the Dark Lord who nodded. "One of you watch until we return. Keré'us and I have other matters to discuss." He stood up, "Come Keré'us, we shall find a spot outside where we stand less chance of being overheard." He picked up a lamp from the table and led the way outside where it was now raining hard.

They found a small shed mostly containing firewood. The Dark Lord stood the lamp on a shelf whence it shone a small circle of light about them.

On the flood of his fate Keré'us spoke before the Dark Lord had framed his first question. "You want to know about the Lady?" It was a good guess.

The other laughed, "Yes, I want to know about the red sorceress. Does she find her imprisonment irksome?"

"She did not say, Lord."

"Is she chastened, or is she as full of devious mischief as ever?"

"I cannot say, Lord, I met her but the once in the full of the two moons."

"She doubtless impressed you with her charm and beauty?"

"She was very lovely."

"And what did she tell you?"

"That I was to serve you, as my grandmother had promised, that it was my destiny and neither she nor you, nor I could alter this, but she would give me the powers she once gave to my fore-mothers and whatever other aid she could."

"Your mind is still full of her brightness and gladness, is it not, Keré'us? Beware of her, I too loved her once and look at me. I was one of the Lords Eldest. In the place of my father Vallior I should wear the Diadem of the High Lord Eldest. Now I am without any power, condemned to live as a mortal without home and kin, a wanderer doomed to wander until I die. Beware of her, beware her gifts and beware her love. Once the Eldest called her Herénya, Lady of Gladness, but now they call her the Betrayer."

"Lord, I shall serve you as she commanded me, to the best of my ability, but by serving you well I shall also serve her. This is a paradox I do not intend to resolve, but which, if you want me as servant, you must accept."

"A true Quarin, with a mind that thinks in circles. I knew your father well and have missed his devious mind on occasions. Warny are very well, and good loyal friends, but not much endowed with imagination. I shall be pleased to take you as my servant, but more pleased to have you as my friend."

They clasped arms in the Quaren manner. As they did so, the movement brought the Sea-stone swinging out from Keré'us' coat. The Dark Lord stopped abruptly, caught the stone and pulled it so Keré'us had to look straight into his strange eyes. "What means this? Does Gawen too have power over you?"

"He gave it to me after I killed the Worm at Tal Elen."

"This is the dearest thing he has. After the wars of the Diadem he was punished by having half his power taken away and trapped in the Sea-stone. They made him wear it to remind him of his doom. What is happening here?"

Keré'us looked down to avoid the all-compelling eyes. "He gave it to me to remind me that he holds the life of my first born son forfeit for killing the Worm."

"He? Surely he would have been amused by your valour, I know my brother. He would not do such a thing!"

"Yet I hold the Sea-stone. You can hardly think I stole it."

"No, I do not think that." The Dark Lord looked puzzled. He let the stone go and Keré'us tucked it back inside his tunic.

"You must ask the Lord Gawen for his reasons. Lord, I know them not."

"I shall, and fear him not. If you and your house serve me, then can I find the means to protect you, though I may need to call on some unlikely allies. And now, shall we find somewhat to eat before we go to bed? Warany will snore all through the first watch, so you will lose no sleep!" He picked up the lamp and led the way back to the inn.

After an early breakfast they set out the next day towards Runi, but left the road once they were out of sight of the village and took off across country in a north easterly direction. The rain had stopped and the morning sun was warm. Some of the lands they passed through were cultivated, brown sod waiting the seedling grain to burst through. The rest was pasture, great green open plains starred with wild flowers. Riding with his friends Keré'us felt comfortable and cheerful. It was almost like coming home, except, even when he lived in Mundra it had not seemed so much like home. The Dark Lord rode at his side, with Warany on his right hand and although not much was said, the companionship was unlike anything the Quarin had experienced before. These men he could depend upon. He did not have to keep alert all the time to outwit them or avoid a dagger in the back. These men would, the odd distraction apart, fight with him and for him and they were the cream of the Alliance. And they took him seriously, which was more than he could.

The Dark Lord caught his eye. He must have known what Keré'us was thinking, for he grinned at him. This fallen Lord Eldest was a puzzle. Keré'us had expected him to be grim and vengeful, but apart from matters concerning the Lady, the Quarin had the impression that his new master viewed most of what was happening in the mortal world with faint amusement.

That night they camped in the open, the Dark Lord watching the night by the low embers of a fire while the mortals slept. His Eldest kin may have taken his Eldest powers away, but he was by no means human. Keré'us sat with him for part of the first watch, huddled in his cloak. The stars spread across the sky like great jewels, the air was still. Over the vast plain nothing stirred, not even the long grasses.

"There is no need to watch," said the Dark Lord, "I do not need sleep as you do."

The Quarin poked the fire and the sparks flew upwards. "I just wanted to ask you a few questions, if you will excuse my curiosity."

"You may be sure I shall not answer any question I do not like."

"I hope I shall not ask anything you don't like. I was merely curious. You said to Warany something about it being hard to fight Elta and not kill them?"

"Fallen I may be, but I am still one of the Lords Eldest and I am forbidden to kill mortals. Similarly I am forbidden to sleep with mortal women, although I have to say that in that respect I have yet to be tempted. Imagine a woman you love who grows old before you do. That was why Nanenethen, Warany's wife, had to take mortality before she married him, but they cheated her. Mind you, it stretched

the Old Man to be faithful even for that handful of years."
He sighed, "Women, they have a lot to answer for. And it is
female kind, not mortal, nor Lady Youngest nor Lady Eldest.
Thus do they all. You have no woman?"

"No, I have had my fancies, but I remain unbound."

The Dark Lord laughed, "Wise man! Would that I had
been so sensible."

"When we come to Elen, which I suppose we shall,
what shall I do about Arno? Is he as fell a sorcerer as they
say?"

"All that and more, if you ask me. His ambitions do not
always run with those of the rest of the Alliance. The
Elorianen has that effect on most people."

"If he is only mortal and has the Star-stone, why have
the Eldest not tried to take it from him?"

"They like watching games and they have a timescale
you cannot comprehend. Like the stars from which they
came, the Eldest move very slowly. This generation or the
next, what matters to them is that they have the power to
keep it when they take it."

"So if I take Aren, they will start to watch me instead of
Arno?"

"Yes, but you have the red witch and me to protect you,
and now my brother Gawen. You may only be a pawn, but
there are powerful pieces which have you under their
protection. Moreover, to prevent the Elorianen from falling
into the hands of another faction, some of the Eldest will
protect you. Not necessarily the same ones all the time.
Like the stars in the great dance, they change position -
and partners."

"You don't encourage me."

The Dark Lord smiled again, "I did not intend to, but I
have to point out that even if you went back home now,

your fate would pursue you. Better stay with me and Warany. You will at least get fed that way."

"I like this life of wandering. I was a sailor. I don't like to stay in one place a long time. If I had wanted the responsibility of a kingdom I would have taken the kingship Melin offered at the Gate."

"I know what you mean. I too enjoy the wandering life. I am only responsible for you and Warany, not the whole of the Lords Eldest. There are worse things than exile and harder punishments than mortality." He sighed all the same. "Now take your sleep little Keré'us."

They crossed the Lee'ma Ra the next day by the causeway to Nenaterian, then striking out west through the plains, followed the river on a rough track until they came to a wide paved road, broad and white, which had crossed the bridge at Runi and now ran on the north side of the river. From there it was two comfortable days' travel along the north side of lake Vanda to Elen, the Silver City, nestled in the foothills of the Neros Yannyos, the mountains of fire.

As they approached it, Elen seemed to hover on the green hills, the tall white walls supported by many crenellated towers. Unlike Quaren cities, it was not entered by massive gates at each point of the compass, but by one solitary small gate. Most of the white stone used in the city's construction had come from fallen Nenaterian. It had been built by Arno using Quaren enslaved after the wars. Work was still going on, even now, and scaffolding and engines became visible on the walls as they approached nearer to the city.

CHAPTER THIRTEEN

As daylight died they reached the tiny gate and left their horses at the livery stable provided outside the city, then came on to the gate wards who saluted them courteously enough, but demanded their business since the gate was already closed.

The Dark Lord was impatient, not with them as much as their officiousness, in which they obviously were delighting. They knew who the party were. They were just being obstructive in the way of Elta.

"Tell your Lord Arno that the Prince of the Warny, his eldest son, the High Lord of the Sea-kingdoms, the Lord of the House of Abard and the Lord of Darkness wait the pleasure of his gate wards!"

"I beg pardon lord, but after dark we can let no one in unless we have permission from the Hall."

"Very proper. Now let us in!"

"As I know you all, save your slave here, I may let you into the guard room, but without permission I can let you come no further."

The Dark Lord put a reassuring hand on Keré'us shoulder. "This is the Lord of the House of Abard," he said, "no slave, but the son of Lord Darké'us of Mundra. Be certain you let your Lord Arno know that."

Warany laughed; the Dark Lord smiled.

"Thank you," said Keré'us.

"We may as well give Arno as hard a time as he seems to be determined to give us," said Warany and sat down on a wooden bench in the gate house where neither fire nor comfort was offered. Eventually a panting messenger arrived to escort them to see the Lord. They followed him through the narrow streets. The Elta, originally from the marshlands in the north, had always built their wooden houses on stilts to avoid flooding. Now, although halfway up a mountain and building in stone, the lower part of the dwellings were storage areas in between the stone pillars on which the houses were built. It gave the city a strange appearance with only the residue of human life visible, the washing, the wood store and the odds and ends, except in places where some had been made into shops.

Arno's Halls were set on the top of the small hill on which the city was built. Surrounding the cluster of buildings was a wide open space which was used as the gathering place for the Elta. It also offered an exposed area all around the Halls that in times of trouble could be commanded by archers on the roof. In the centre was a large white stone fountain. The Halls were large, made of white stone in a simple style that somehow lacked any of the normal beauty of functional objects. The Elta were a graceless people. The Halls were, however, well fortified and guarded. In the entrance there were again gate wards. This time they demanded that the party should surrender their arms, following Arno's recent decree, that none should bear arms in his presence.

"Does he want us to get rid of the Halucias for him or not?" demanded Warany angrily. "He'll be asking for my Troth-stone next!"

"Since it's my only chance of a meal and a bed for the night, I'll do as the man says," said Ranhé'us.

He unfastened his sword belt and gave Garenmegra to the guard. The Dark Lord took off his shabby baldric and surrendered Yadra.

"I'm not adding Erindra to that heap," said Warany, "Three of the four swords of power are too much temptation for anyone."

"They will be well protected in Arno's treasury," promised the guard.

"I don't care," said Warany. "You may tell Arno that if he wants Warany and the Warny it will be at the price of his silly rules! Erindra does not leave my side."

The others looked faintly embarrassed.

"Go on with you!" the Warny lord sat down on a chest and pulled his cloak about him. "No one tells *me* when and when not to wear Erindra."

"The rest of you go," said Keré'us, "I'll wait here with him." The Dark Lord shook his head and strode off with Ranhé'us and Derany to meet Arno.

"Thanks," said Warany to Keré'us.

"Not really," said the Quarin, "I get the feeling that Arno is as anxious to meet me as I am not to meet him." He could feel the enmity radiating from deep in the Halls. His forearms pricked with it and his ring throbbed with it.

"I doubt we shall have to wait long," said Warany.

He was right. Another Elta appeared shortly. He was tall, grey haired and dressed all in grey, but wearing trousers instead of the kilts of the other soldiers. He was perhaps in his sixties and had a very soldierly bearing. He was obviously a privileged person, since he wore a sword and had just come from Arno's presence.

"Warany, you old reprobate," he cried, "my master has

decreed that in view of your advanced years, he will permit you to enter his presence bearing a sword."

"Hraldor, Arno surely knows how to hurt a man." Warany made a face. "Keré'us, this is Hraldor, Lord of Hosts of Elen. We travelled a long way together in the wars. Hraldor, this is Keré'us, servant to my Lord of Darkness. I should be very upset if anything happened to him, and so should others."

Hraldor appraised Keré'us with his shrewd grey eyes, but said nothing and led the way into the Halls. As Keré'us went to follow them the gate ward stopped him, and demanded his sword. The Quarin laughed, drew it and threw the useless hilt to the floor. "May it do you more good than it does me," he said and strolled off behind Warany to Arno's audience chamber.

The audience chamber was a vast room with stone walls and a high stone ceiling, supported on round arches by squat pillars. There were no hangings or paintings to enliven it, no banners and only grey flagstones underfoot. It was lit by high windows just under the ceiling, but now, since night had fallen, great wax candles as thick as a man's arm had been lit about Arno's white stone throne which was set on a dais at the far end of the hall. The other men in the chamber were mere shadows. Only Arno was lit by the candles and in their pool of yellow light Keré'us could see an old, tall, silver fair man, his long hair mingling with his exceedingly long beard. He was clad in a robe of grey silk which shone softly in the candle light. On his knees lay unsheathed the grey bladed sword. Aren.

Keré'us' heart leapt. The gilded hilt seemed so familiar. On his hand the ring acknowledged the power of the Star-stone.

Arno's pale eyes flickered toward the Quarin for a brief moment. Until this moment he had believed that he alone of all mortals could control the Star-stone, that his magic was stronger than that of any mortal who lived in Avenya. Now he saw the Quarin, not as mortals saw him, but in the twilight world of sorcery. A man with the golden radiance of the Lady Yannya behind him, the Sea-stone like a great wheel of green fire on his breast and his own power, the red earth of the Quarenyos Queens.

Arno put a hand on Aren and felt the Star-stone twist against his power. He was old and a great sorcerer, yet it took him all his power to control it. Like a snake tasting with its tongue he put forth his mind to brush against Keré'us' mind, and not liking what he felt, withdrew immediately. There was time enough to deal with the Quarin as he had dealt with all others who had desired the stone set in the hilt of Aren. Now there were more important matters to be discussed. He stood up, sheathed the sword and walked forward to greet Warany. "I am sorry my Lord Warany that you felt my new rule about bearing arms was unreasonable. I had meant no insult. I am grateful that you are here, for surely we have great need of you."

"I am the High Lord of the Alliance of the Free Peoples and needs must be humoured," said Warany.

Arno inclined his head, "Then shall we say no more of it. I am glad to see you all. The Halucias have made it quite clear that they are not going to return within their allotted bounds and are gathering a great force to the east of the ruins of Nenaterian. It will not be long before they attack Elen and we must hope that the forces you promise have arrived before they make their play."

"I still cannot see what they gain." said Warany, "What do they want with cities?"

"They have told me that they want to destroy Elen, for it is built on land which was theirs and sacred to them," said Arno. "I have given up trying to make them see sense."

"Perhaps the Dark Lord and I will have one last attempt," said Warany. "Even the first of our forces will not be here for many days and it will be as good a use of our time as any."

"Then go to them tomorrow with my blessing. But now, old friend, you must be weary and hungry." He put his hand on Warany's shoulder, "Come to the refectory and we shall dine together."

The refectory boasted a fire, but that was the only comfort. The tables and benches were of scrubbed wood except for that on the dais reserved for the Lord and his friends, which was covered by a cloth. Arno's daughter, the Lady Elwyn, was already eating there and the party was introduced to her. She was a tall blond woman of about thirty summers. By most standards she would have been neither accomplished nor attractive, but amongst the Elta she was considered to be a great beauty. As Keré'us went to take his place at the Dark Lord's side she said, "Slaves do not eat at this board!"

"He is the Lord of the House of Abard and son of Darké'us, Lord of Mundra," said the Dark Lord calmly, "and my friend."

"I am sorry," said Elwyn in tones that belied her words, "but all the Quaren in Elen are slaves. I thought he must be too."

Keré'us look about him. It was true, the only Quaren visible were serving the tall silver haired Elta. "No matter," he said. "You are not the first to make the mistake. Why, only at Eloruna some of your father's men were certain that I was an escaped slave. It was a good thing I had the Dark Lord to vouch for me."

Warany spluttered into his wine, Ranhé'us and Derany looked embarrassed and the Dark Lord just smiled.

Arno ignored the remark. He was beginning to discover what an unusual adversary he had in the Quarin. He desired greatly to see if Keré'us had learned to control and use the power he had at his command, but to do this would bring the wrath of the Dark Lord on him and at present he needed the assistance of the Dark Lord and his friends. He would be patient, and watch.

After the meal the friends were shown to their chambers. Ranhé'us and Derany had one small room and Warany, the Dark Lord and Keré'us shared a larger room which boasted a fireplace with a lighted fire. The floors and walls were unadorned stone and lit only by tiny, high, unglazed windows, the big beds spartanly supplied with two blankets each. The whole party crowded into Warany's room, the main attraction being the fire.

"It's colder here than it is in André'as," said Ranhé'us, warming his hands.

"It's no warmer than Arno's welcome," laughed Warany. "By the Lords Eldest, what have we let ourselves in for? I can think of no one whose kingdom I care less about," he sighed, "but rules are rules. How many days have we got until the van of our men reach us?"

"Six at the least," said Derany.

"Then we might as well use the time going to see the Halucias. Perhaps the Gerhart will listen to sense. You youngsters can stay here, then if anyone gets here before we return you can get them organised. You can do that, Derany." His son nodded. "Besides, it would be tactless to remind the Gerhart that I have several sons and his lordship will pass to a son-in-law."

"But we take Keré'us," said the Dark Lord quickly, "for if we leave him, we shall be lucky if he is still here when we return. Arno is thirsting to try his skills against the Quarin."

"So I noticed," said Keré'us.

"Well, this old man is to bed," said Warany. "*My advanced years!* Arno is far older than me. He was old when I first knew him. The man has some impudence."

"He is a sorcerer and he has the Elorianen, but nothing lasts forever" said the Dark Lord. There will come a reckoning and payment will be demanded in full. The Quarin's grandmother may have cursed me rather than Arno, but she knew where her words would take matters. She was a clever woman with some very devious friends."

Warany pulled off his boots and lay down in the big bed, adding both his cloak and Keré'us' to the covers. Ranhé'us and Derany forsook the fire for their own bed.

"Come on Keré'us, I need you to keep me warm," said Warany.

"There has to be a first time for everything," said the Dark Lord. He blew out the candles and sat down on a chest by the fire to watch the night.

CHAPTER FOURTEEN

It was a cold night and Keré'us slept fitfully. Arno's power was all about him and he dreamed uneasy dreams. In the morning he was glad to get up and break his fast early. They did not see Arno, but Warany spoke with Hraldor who organised supplies for them and they left the Halls of Arno for the stable at the city gate. Here they collected their horses and rode back along the way to Runi, leaving it at mid-day to follow a track which led to the new forested lands where the old city of Nenaterian had once stood. The weather had changed again. It was cold and windy with occasional fierce showers of driving rain and hail. Warany's bones ached and made him morose, the Dark Lord was gloomy and Keré'us almost wished he had stayed behind and taken his chances with Arno. They made bad time and evening was on them before they were anywhere near the Halucias camp.

"Damn," said Warany as the invisible sun dropped below the mountains. "We must camp somewhere soon. I do not want to be anywhere the Halucias will find us in the dark."

"We are not far from the ruins of Nenaterian," said the Dark Lord, "there must be some shelter there and the Halucias would never venture into a ruined city at night."

"Well, if you're not scared of the ruins, then I certainly

am not," said Warany, "and Keré'us will almost be at home."

"So be it." The Dark Lord led the way off the path until dark ruins could just be seen in the now driving rain. They passed between broken and overgrown gate towers and up the main triumphal road to the jumble of old stones which was all that remained of the heart of the city. Most of the stone had been taken away to build Elen's walls. Keré'us was disappointed, he had hoped to see at least the Temple still standing. He wondered what it had been like when it was alive and bright with people.

Warany felt a little of his disappointment. "Once I walked these streets," he said, "with Nanenethen, when it was a city without any thought of war, when the name Warany meant nothing and I was an outlaw, had they known, returning from exile. Then I wore Erindra proudly, for it was the first time I had borne it and I the first mortal to be given a sword of power. And Nanu, fair Nanu; I had rescued her from the Necromancer of the Vadré Dru, Vas Beren that was, and I had fallen in love with her. Never was fairer maid than Nanenethen, Lady of the beech trees. Many women I have had, before her and after her, yet she alone I have loved. It hurts me even now. If I had not been so greedy for her she would still be living and the beeches of the Erueth would not drop their leaves in winter."

"The choice was hers and she alone could make it," said the Dark Lord. "Would you have her still young and beautiful at your board and in your bed? Could she have lived to see you grow old? Not if she loved you. Be glad Old Man, be glad she loved you. She bore you children and she died for you. Some of us have not chosen so well!"

"Ay," said Warany softly, "and now she lies in the cold earth overlooking the sea at the Grey Halls, and every spring I promise her to lie at her side again, but the beech tree I planted at her head grows taller and I grow older."

125

"We still need you, Old Man, we still need you," said the Dark Lord.

"It would not be bad to rest," mused Warany, "be it in the Green Fields of Heaven or the cold earth at her side."

They found a place to camp where a couple of walls and a few beams covered with rubble cut out the worst of the weather. Keré'us lit a fire more for cheer than anything else and the Dark Lord settled down by it to watch while the mortals slept. In the morning they set out again, but not before his friends had taken Keré'us to see the blackened remains of the burnt-out Temple. There was little to see, only a jumble of fire blackened pillars marked the spot where Keré'us' and the Dark Lord's fates had been joined together by the High Queen in the moments before Arno killed her. The three men stood for a moment, each considering how the death of the Queen had bound their disparate characters together. Then the Dark Lord said, "Come, we must find the Halucias," and they followed him out of the city and back along the trail to the Halucias camp.

The new forest which had sprung up about the fallen city soon thinned out and on the edge of it, conveniently placed for collecting fire wood, was the Halucias camp. It appeared to be unguarded, but Keré'us caught glimpses of men armed with bows in the woods and knew that their arrival had been noted. They passed through the untidy tangle of yurts and open camp fires. Children ran amongst the tents, women were at work kneading and tanning hides, and goats on tethers resolutely ate their way through undergrowth, doing their own small part towards the deforestation of the area. Keré'us had never seen the Halucias at close quarters before and had never realised how similar they were to the

Quaren. They were slightly built, their skins golden and their eyes slightly slanted brown, their hair dark brown or black. They were clad mostly in animal skins and if they had a cloth shirt or a metal knife, it had come from trade, for they neither farmed nor smithied.

Warany strode confidently to the centre of the camp where there was an open circle of land used by the Halucias for their councils. Word of their arrival had already reached the head of the tribe, for he awaited them, seated in a chair of wood, with a seat and back of woven leather. Young men of his family gathered behind him and his favourite wife and a granddaughter stood at his left hand.

The Gerhart was old, his hair long and grey mingling with his moustaches and beard. He wore leather trousers and a coat trimmed with wolf fur, the totem animal of his tribe. In his grey hair was a silver circlet to mark his leadership of all the tribes.

Warany strode forwards. The Dark Lord put out a hand to hold Keré'us back. "They will respect the Old Man more on his own," he explained. "Besides, we must count the number of tribes here and the men, if we can." Keré'us nodded.

"Lord of the Tribes," said Warany, "may the Lords Eldest bless you, may they send many children to your tents and many young to your flocks. May the rain fall and the grass not fail." He bowed.

The old man on the throne nodded too. "May you too be blessed, may your women have many sons and your herds multiply," he said. "Now tell me, Lord Warany, what brings you to my tents? It is not often that such a fell leader lowers himself to be my guest."

"I come to speak with you, Lord Gerhart, as one lord of men to another."

"And as such I shall answer you. What business would you have with me?"

"I come at the Elta Lord Arno's behest. You have overrun your bounds and refuse to return. You tell him it is because Elen is built on your land, yet both you and I were there when the Tribes and the Alliance agreed what land was to be yours and what ours. Your bounds were set to the north of the river Telga and east of a line from Mara Keltior, to Mara-set in the north. You have crossed not only the Telga, but I myself have met men of the Grey Wolves who were ravaging the land south of the Lee'ma Ra. You will know this, for they did not all return."

The Lord Gerhart rose to his feet. "Lord Warany," he said with mockery in his voice, "you say we agreed which land was to be ours and which to be yours, but should it not be said rather that you gave us that which you did not want and took all that you desired for your friends?"

"That is not true. Small help you gave us against the Quaren, yet all the land north of the Telga to the slopes of the Erinyos mountains is yours. Far more than the Quaren let you graze in the old days, and you know full well that the Lord Warond desired some of that land, but we made him forbear and take only that to the west where the Telga turns north to the Erinyos mountains where it is born. Of the lands given to the Lord Arno you claimed none at all."

The Gerhart shrugged, "But now we want it. It is ours."

Warany could see the matter descending into a vulgar slanging match and knew he had to put a stop to it. "Know this, Gerhart, the Alliance of the Free Peoples keeps its word. Unless you go back to your agreed boundaries we shall drive you back by force. Already many men are gathering at Elen. We are still prepared to sue for peace, but unless we have word from you I shall return at the head of an army and force you back to your lands. You may call up all the tribes, but they will have to be a mighty army to defeat Warany and the Alliance. Remember we defeated the Quaren with little help from the tribes. So shall we defeat you!"

"I am told," said the Gerhart, smiling the while, "that many do not heed the call and the men who once fought for their own freedom will not fight for Arno's land. I have heard also that your men grow soft and that it will be a collection of farmers, city-dwellers and pirates who come and fight my men. My men learn from their earliest youth to bear arms. We shall see the power of your vaunted army! They will flee from the Tribes in disarray. Take heed of my words. Return to your lands and herds and forget Arno. You are too old to make war any more."

"Then there is no more to be said. We shall meet on the field of battle!" Warany bowed and turned on his heel. The Dark Lord and Keré'us fell in behind him, not without some misgivings on the Quarin's part, for he expected a Halucias spear in his back any moment, but they were allowed to take the Gerhart's message back to Elen.

"The banners of six tribes were set behind the Gerhart," said the Dark Lord.

"They were duplicated in front of the biggest yurts, and five more designs that were not behind the Gerhart," said Keré'us.

The Dark Lord nodded, "That is all the tribes then, all eleven of them. Moreover, there were few young men visible, just women and the old men. The young men must be camped in battle array elsewhere."

Warany sighed, "I knew it would come to this, I just wish I could get rid of the feeling that it has all been managed. Discontent usually growls on for years before anyone does anything. It took me three years to get the Halucias to unite and take sides with the Alliance - now they seem to have done it by themselves in three months. Let us get back to Elen."

The Dark Lord and his friends returned to Elen, making better time and reaching the white city by late evening on the same day. They were depressed by the thought of the battle, which now appeared to be inevitable. The damp had affected more than Warany's bones and he had a return of some fever he had caught long ago in Banéros and had to take to his bed.

By the end of the next day the Warny was running a high temperature and really unwell. The Maren-Ra had arrived at the head of a company of Trumarei and Arno called the Dark Lord and the two younger men to a council of war. Keré'us was not invited in any case, but he chose to stay by his friend, if only to keep the fire going.

Elwyn, daughter of Arno came to see Warany and looked at him through her cold grey eyes. Keré'us felt there was something strange about her demeanour, a secret knowledge that gave her an air of almost gloating.

"He has marsh fever," she told the Quarin. "It could prove fatal but we have a remedy. I shall go and instruct my apothecary to prepare it."

Warany had a lucid moment, "I am not drinking anything she prepares," he said firmly, "it probably would prove fatal. All I need is luén and rahilya steeped in good red wine and mulled. Any of the Quarenyos women in the kitchens will be able to make it. Go down there and ask them for some. They know all about marsh fever. It first came from their lands. Don't stint on the wine. Mundran if possible."

"Of course," Keré'us stood up, "and the kitchens are?"

"Downstairs, far down as you can get and to the rear."

130

Keré'us followed these vague instructions to the best of his ability but it was not difficult. Arno had the right over his people to bake bread, and the smell of the ovens laid a trail though the palace which was easy enough to follow. The kitchens were situated in a long low building to the rear. Guards stood either side of the door, which Keré'us thought was strange, since they let him in without demur. Then however, he realised that the entire kitchen staff was made up of Quaren slaves, mostly women. Tables stretched away before him on which women were mixing and kneading bread. At the far end of the room there was a vast oven fired from below and a continual noise as faggots were thrown on the fire and blown with bellows and the great sheets of bread and rolls were slid into the ovens and pulled out. Over open fires beasts were roasting and great pots of the inevitable Elta stew were bubbling.

An older woman wearing the brown dress of an overseer came over to him. Like all of the others she was branded with the slave brand of Arno.

"Lord?" she asked.

"I come from the Lord Warany who is sick of marsh fever. He begs me ask you to prepare a remedy for him, herbs steeped in wine." He was aware of every one turning to look at him and a faint ripple of sound caused by the movement of their bodies and an intake of breath. Perhaps fifty pairs of brown and yellow eyes were bent on him and then swiftly returned to their work. The hair began to rise on his arms. There was some sort of magic here. Not the cold of Arno's power but the warmth of the Lady Yannya. The oldest of these women had served his grandmother at Nenaterian, the youngest were born in captivity but still hoped - and was hope false? He wondered what he had walked into.

"Nenya will attend to that," the overseer beckoned to another woman who was standing close by, obviously waiting for the instruction. The two women exchanged significant glances.

Nenya was about forty, with brown hair tied back and yellow eyes. Her golden heart shaped face was pale through lack of sun in the kitchens. She was a handsome woman with an air of command about her that did not sit well with her slave brand. She looked at Keré'us, calmly assessing him. She was obviously pleased with what she saw because she smiled. "Luén and rahilya steeped in Mundran wine and don't stint on the wine?"

It was like a password. Keré'us smiled at her, "Something like that," he agreed, wondering how she had come to know Warany.

"Perhaps you would care to sit and have a cup of wine and some honey cakes while I attend to it? The Old Man has marsh fever again I suppose?"

"Yes. The Lord Arno's daughter promised him medicine, but the Lord Warany prefers this remedy."

Nenya laughed and went to prepare the herbs. The overseer came with a tray of cakes and wine. She looked hard into Keré'us eyes and he saw how old she was. She would have known his grandmother. "Lord, I served the Queen at Nenaterian and was at her side when she died. Is it sooth that you are her daughter's son?"

"Yes lady, my father is Darké'us of Mundra."

"Then you are the Chosen of the Goddess?" Her hand flashed out and caught Keré'us' hand to look at the ring the Dark Lord had given him. "Then hope is not false!" She stood up straight and in defiance of her Elta Lord spoke out loudly across the kitchen. "Keré'us, Chosen of the Goddess, Lord, we salute you!" And like corn in the wind the women in the kitchens bowed before him. The overseer knelt and touched her head to the ground.

"Lord, will the day come that we are free?"

"Surely the goddess will not let them hold you captive for ever," he said, and in his heart he desired greatly to set these sad women free from their cold overlords. The ring throbbed on his hand and on impulse he stretched out his arms to them.

"May the Lady Yannya bless you," he said with all the power he had. He meant to bring comfort to them but he set a flame to a fire long awaiting him.

Suddenly one of the older women began to sing. It was a recitative on one note, but others quickly took the antiphon and the sound grew like a living thing. The kitchens began to vibrate with the music of the long dead Queens.

"Behold the Chosen of the Goddess."

"The gates are open, the bronze doors have turned and welcomed the Chosen One."

"Behold your Lord!"

"Surely we shall go up to the Temple and give thanks to the Goddess."

It was twenty five years since they had sung those words last, twenty five years of cruel slavery, but now they knew their goddess had not forsaken them. They poured the magic of their souls into their singing and the very walls trembled.

CHAPTER FIFTEEN

Arno in his audience hall heard the singing and felt the
foundations of his power shaken by the music. He put his
hands over his ears and cried out to the Dark Lord. "Your
servant has set all my slaves in revolt! Come swiftly, lest
this magic sweep my city and destroy it!" Robes flowing,
he ran towards the kitchens, closely followed by the Dark
Lord. By now the singing resonated throughout the whole
palace. As they reached the kitchens the music stopped
them like a solid wall. There were several people there,
guards and servants, none knowing what to do and none
daring to go further. Only the Dark Lord could face the
sound and he strode to the doors of the kitchen and threw
them open. He asked gently, "Keré'us, can you stop this?"

Keré'us turned to him with an air of desperation.
"How?"

"Ask them. Use your mind as well."

The Quarin held out his arms again. "Stop," he ordered,
with mind and voice. "Now is not the time, nor the hour of
my coming. My power has not yet come to me. Aren is not
yet mine."

The music ebbed slowly away. The women looked at
each other confusedly, as if they had awoken from a dream.
Arno, black with rage, strode into the kitchens, screaming

at the overseers. "I shall have every woman here flogged and the ringleaders killed!"

Keré'us looked at Arno and held those cold grey eyes with his. The magic in the singing of the women had added to his power and he knew he could defeat the Elta lord at this moment. "You will not do this, lord Arno."

"By Aren I shall!" said Arno angrily.

"By Aren you shall not! They did not mean any of this to happen. It was not intended."

"Who are you to give me, Arno, bearer of Aren, orders in my own house?"

"I am Keré'us, grandson of the Quarinya Queen. I am Lord of the House of Abard and Chosen of the Goddess. Moreover, both the Lord Eldest Gawen and the Lord of Darkness hold their hands over me. Therefore, if I say you shall not hurt any of these my people in bondage, you shall not!"

Arno gazed upon the slight Quarin with his bright face and the terrifying fire of the earth magic behind him. He longed to take issue with him and destroy him, but he feared to do so yet. He needed the Dark Lord and Warany, for the moment, so he must not come into open conflict with them - yet. He promised himself pleasure in the destroying of the Quarin when the time came. The Dark Lord put his hand on Keré'us' shoulder and his shadow fell over the brightness of the earth magic. He looked at Arno but said nothing.

"Very well, the Quarin meddled in things he did not understand. This time I shall be merciful, but should it happen again…" he marched off angrily, pulling his robes about him.

Everything became normal again. The women were back at their stations and the cup of wine and herbs was pushed into Keré'us' hand by the overseer who had started everything. Keré'us noticed that Nenya had vanished, and wondered why.

"Well," said the Dark Lord, as they walked back along the corridors, "that was certainly a surprise for Arno."

"It was a bit of a surprise for me," said Keré'us plaintively, "I didn't mean any of that to happen."

"No, but I suspect that red sorceress was meddling again. Now, I have three things to say to you. The first is, they were singing the hymn of presentation and Quaren kings do not usually live long. The second is that I recognised one of the women there. Nenya she is called, or at least was when I last saw her as one of the Five, the priestesses of the red sorceress based in the Yana Temple in Banéros. She is no slave, despite her brand, and is usually at the centre of trouble. Lastly, if you mention again in front of Arno that you have not got the Elorianen yet, I do not think you will have to worry about becoming the king." He gave up all effort to keep a straight face and laughed. "I have never seen any emotion on Arno's face for the past thirty years - he thought you were about to take his whole kingdom away!"

Keré'us joined his mirth. "He was worried - I thought they were going to sacrifice me then and there!"

"This will really cheer up the Old Man! He never did like Arno!"

"How wise!"

The next day Warany was a little better, the herbs and discomfiture of Arno both contributing to his improved health, as probably did Keré'us' careful disposal of Elwyn's apothecary's cure. The Dark Lord stayed with him that day and Keré'us rode out with Ranhé'us and Derany to meet the first of the Alliance forces which would reach the city of Elen that day.

Five hundred mounted men clad in the green and pink livery of King Terué of Mordata marched up the wide road to the white city. Riding at the head of the column, with the banner Terué had carried against the Quaren, were his twin sons, Terué and Morda. The proud flag bore their images, two pink baby boys on a green ground. When Terué had sworn on his sons that he would give them a kingdom to be heir to, the banner had been a matter of pride, but now it faintly embarrassed the two men of thirty who rode beneath their babyhood portraits.

The sight of the bear-like Lord of the Sea-kingdoms did nothing to improve their humour.

"By the Lords Eldest, if it's not the Pirate!" exclaimed one.

"By my Grandfather, if it's not the two fat babies!" cried Ranhé'us, a smile curling in the luxuriant growth on his face. He rode on the pair, shouting hideous war cries. He was not over fond of Mordata, since he knew they were trying to annex Loré'as, a small kingdom on the eastern boundary of his kingdoms, which he too would like to include in his lands. He had also heard Warany say that their father had asked him for the hand of his daughter Anya in marriage for one or other of the twins. However, at least they were not Elta. They were men with the same southern accent as he, and there was much back slapping and general bonhomie, the Twins telling Keré'us that if he was a friend of Ranhé'us, he was likely to be an enemy of theirs, matters being somewhat complicated when the Lord of the Sea-kingdoms explained that Keré'us had been the son of Darké'us who had captured him.

"Whose side are you on?" asked Terué.

"My own," said Keré'us, and in a cheerful mood they all rode on to Elen.

That evening the Dark Lord and Keré'us were sitting with Warany in his room waiting for dinner to be brought up. The Warny Lord had recovered considerably from his fever, but he and his friends were using it as an excuse not to sit at board with Arno. There came a knock on the door which Keré'us answered to find the woman Nenya standing there with a tray. A tall jug of spiced, mulled wine breathed warmth into the room.

"The overseer sent me up with your food, lest you send *him* to collect it," she said to the Dark Lord, who looked at her hard.

She returned him a basilisk stare and set her tray down on a chest. The food sent up from the kitchens was vastly different from that served in the refectory, good white, wheaten rolls, succulent cuts of meat and the jug of wine. She poured a cup for Warany and put it into his hands. "Do you feel better now?"

He put the wine down and opened his arms. "Just the sight of you would warm anyone's heart." He embraced her with what was best described as great enthusiasm.

"If I were you, I should start my dinner," said the Dark Lord to Keré'us, "it will get cold if you wait for him to put her down."

"They certainly appear to be old friends," said the Quarin.

Warany reluctantly released the woman, "Nenya, dear friend, tell me, what are you doing here and why are you branded a slave? The Dark Lord said he had seen you yesterday in the kitchens."

"What I am doing here is risking my life, and anyway, it was not you I really had to see, but your Lord of Darkness."

"But he doesn't like mortal women!"

"Hush, old friend, I am deadly serious. I had to come to ask that you do not betray me to Arno."

"And why should we not tell Arno that one of the Five who rule the Yannya temple in Banéros is a slave in his kitchens?" asked the Dark Lord.

"Lord, your Lady…"

"She is no Lady of mine!"

"The Lady Yannya bade me come here to unite the slaves in hope and stand shield between Arno and the Lord Keré'us. Aren belongs truly to Keré'us but he will need all the help he may to take it."

"You think I should not tell Arno that his slaves are plotting to rebel, led by one of the Yanai?"

"Arno is no friend to the Alliance!"

"Strange you should say that," said Warany. "Lord, when you overheard the guard at Runi saying to let me in if I had the Quarin with me, and then you came on Arno's men trying to take him prisoner, did you think it was because of Aren he was doing this?"

"I did not know what to think. At first I assumed that it was only Keré'us he was after because of the threat to Aren, but now, now there is something in his attitude. He seems to be waiting for something… I do not know what, but I shall watch him closely. I am uneasy. I can say no more than that."

Warany nodded, "That is the way I feel too. As you say, there is nothing to which I can attribute the unease, but it is there."

"Gentlemen," said Nenya, "I beg you, give me the benefit of your doubt. Speak not to Arno of me."

The three men looked at each other. "I will take the responsibility on myself," said Keré'us, "she is one of my people. She is here to protect me."

The Dark Lord nodded, "So be it."

Nenya bowed to him and Warany and then knelt at Keré'us' feet and touched her head to the ground.

"Lady," said Keré'us, "take care."

When Nenya had gone the Dark Lord said, "I do not like this."

"From where I am," said Warany with a smile, "things have suddenly improved."

"I feel hemmed in," said the Dark Lord, and he paced across the floor. "Why do I think I can only see half of the game? Why does that red witch have Nenya here? All right, I know that she seeks to keep the Elorianen in the hands of a friend lest an enemy takes it and unmakes her. That much makes sense, but others will want it just for its power. They will not care about her. Her pieces are set with such skill on this board of Avenya - look how well placed they are about Keré'us…yet, yet Keré'us protects us to a degree. He is my servant."

"By serving you I serve her. I said it was a paradox," said Keré'us.

"And no one understands where the Halucias come into this," said Warany. "Not even Arno, if he is to be believed. My head is spinning."

"That's probably because you drank most of the wine," said Keré'us. "We shall find out what is going on. Someone is bound to jump us sooner rather than later."

"I just have this curious desire to know over which shoulder I should be looking," said the Dark Lord.

CHAPTER SIXTEEN

Three days passed, the red moon waned and Warany recovered. On the morning of the fourth day Kéré'us arose early as was his wont. There seemed to be unusual excitement in the Halls. A slave told him that the Warny forces had been sighted outside the city so in the gladness of the bright dawn he went down to the gate tower on the city wall and there, as the morning star dimmed, he saw the Warny from the Grey Halls riding out of the mists of morning, the dawn wind blowing the tattered blue silk banner which the Alliance had followed to victory those long years before.

Soldiers and a few Elta were gathered on the tower together with a handful of slaves including Nenya. She inclined her head but said nothing. Kéré'us ignored her and watched the Warny, tall, blue-eyed men from the Grey Halls riding the great horses of the upper plains. They had no uniform, but were mostly clad in leather, blue, brown or Trumaré green and all wore chains and jewels of silver, their horses' harnesses glinting and ringing with that metal. Leading them was Derany's younger brother, Terany and at his side rode Anya, Warany's only daughter by Nanenethen. Fair she was, almost as tall as a man, with thick black braided hair, clad in men's clothes and with a sword at her side.

"Fair indeed are the sons of the Morning Star," said Nenya softly at his side.

"Fair men and loyal friends."

"Fairer and truer than the Silver Folk."

"So you say. Tell me, am I on the Dark Lord's side or is he on mine?"

"That depends on which side of the mirror you are standing."

Illusion: it was all an illusion as he had suspected. "But..." he began, but she had gone. He too ran back down the stairs, to tell Warany that his family had arrived. Unfortunately the words of Nenya so puzzled him, for he could see they could mean so many things, that he failed to look where he was going and collided with a party of Elta. This included none other than the Lady Elwyn, to whom he had to apologise fulsomely, for the lady was very angry. Eventually he escaped and brought the news to Warany and the Dark Lord. Whilst Warany dressed he went to tell Ranhé'us and Derany the news.

"Is there a girl with them?" demanded Ranhé'us.

"Do you mean the Lady Anya?"

"Yes you fool, black hair, blue eyes and a face to die for."

"There was a girl in men's clothes…"

"Of course she'll be there," said Derany, "nobody, not even Father has ever been able to leave her out of a fight, and Terany is no match for her at all."

"Is she there?" demanded the André'an, grabbing him by the throat. Kéré'us nodded. Ranhé'us dropped him and ransacked his saddlebags, shaking his belongings out onto the floor. From these he rescued a copper mirror and comb with which he beat his unruly hair, which he normally wore tied back, into some sort of order, plaiting his two side locks. Then he pulled on a crumpled but clean coat of dark blue wool over his dirty tunic. It bore red and green embroidered flowers on the cuffs. He ran out of the room with Kéré'us close on his heels. The twins joined them as they reached the courtyard and together they sped to the gate where Warany and the Dark Lord were already greeting the Warny. Arno and his daughter were there as well, making formal gestures of welcome and Hraldor was busy sorting out the arrangements for accommodation. Once the Elta Lord returned to his halls the House of Wargarny was reunited with much hugging and kissing.

The Dark Lord and Keré'us stood to one side, aware that they did not belong. The Dark Lord put an arm round the Quarin's shoulder. "What need have we of kith and kin, Keré'us? We have each other."

The Quarin looked up into his strange eyes and saw a sadness there equal to his own. "I miss only my half brother Darké'us. He was all the family I ever had."

"Likewise I miss my half brother Gawen. Despite his tendency to spend a lot of time as a black bear, he was…is… good company."

Warany glanced back and saw them standing apart. He called his children over to meet Keré'us. His second son, Terany, was like, yet unlike Derany, shorter and thicker built, taking himself more seriously than the rest of the family. Anya, beautiful, headstrong and glad was the most like their father. Warany's other son Nareneth did not live at the Grey Halls, but had taken their mother's place amongst the Erueth, living with their uncle Kaerhoieneth. He was one of the Lords Youngest, as were his Erueth kin and would not go to battle against men.

Anya said to the Dark Lord, "You've not been looking after Father properly. He looks quite ill. You must remember that he is an old man now."

"Nonsense," said Warany, "I had marsh fever again, but it's gone now. That reminds me, warn Terany that he may notice someone amongst the kitchen slaves whom he might recognise. We've promised not to tell Arno for the moment."

"You mean Nenya? By the Lady Yannya, things are going to be more fun here than I thought!"

The Dark Lord half lifted a hand to her, "Do not swear by that red sorceress."

Anya looked at him, her blue eyes level and firm, "I swear by whom I choose." Then she turned away to the other men. "Come!" she called. "The women must pitch the kitchen tent. We need as many strong men as we can find!"

Ranhé'us ran eagerly to her side, narrowly beating Terué, the elder of the twins, and it was on the Sea-lord's arm that Anya walked back to the baggage lines.

That evening Arno's refectory rang to the sound of the house of Wargarny and their friends. Anya sat between Ranhé'us and Terué, and most of the men there watched her, for she put the pallid beauties of the Elta to shame, even Arno's daughter.

There was much talk of the Halucias, and much optimism, for the armies were now beginning to be a reality, a thousand men from the Grey Halls, five hundred Mordatans, and the muster had only just started. News had come that Pelélorné had crossed the bridge at Runi and three thousand Trumarei waited outside the walls. Arno had about five thousand infantry even now gathering from the villages and once Selin, king of Kindath arrived with his men and Danhé'us rode up from the furthest south with Ranhé'us' men there would be more men than the Halucias could muster, and most mounted like the Halucias.

Warany let the talk flow over him. He knew that he was no longer the maker or breaker of battles. He had grown old and young men had taken his place. He sat and watched the animated conversations. Ranhé'us driven by his love of Anya to behave like a love sick youth. Terué, knowing that he had money which Ranhé'us did not, lording it over the rest.

Strange, I love my daughter. She is still a little girl to me, but to these men she is as Nanenethen was to me, a burning desire. They will kill for her if necessary. She is strong. She sets them one against the other, but does she realise how they want her? Something will break. Ranhé'us would make the better husband. He is the stronger man. I pity Terué, she will play him like a fish on an ever tighter line if he wins her. But all this is of no moment. Why? Why the Halucias? Why Arno? Why Nenya? What is there I cannot see? Oh that I could speak to the Lady of the Red Moon - she would tell me. She moves us more surely across the board than the Lords Eldest move the rest of Avenya. Look how she guards Keré'us, and with him our dear Dark Lord! Nenya says Arno is playing traitor. She is usually right. Ah, Nenya, what a time we had in Banéros. Never mind politics and strategy, I can remember the firmness of your body under my hands and the strength of our desire. When all is said and done, what matters more? But I want my sons to rule and I want my daughter to be queen and mother of kings- if they have some little Eldest blood in them so much the better. The Eldest may not be kind, but they are strong. So I must fight on to keep for my children that which I had to take by force.

Is that Nenya I see in the shadow by the door? By the Lords Eldest, this lot will talk all night, but I am an old man and need my sleep. Be still my unruly member - we shall take our pleasure soon. Just one moment to take my leave and then thou shalt be set free!

He stood up. "I am tired. I shall retire," he said, "my fever still has not left me."

"I think the fever that afflicts him is not marsh fever," said the Dark Lord to Keré'us in a low voice as Warany departed, "I thought I caught a glimpse of that Yana priestess. The trouble with Warany is that because I am celibate he seems to think he must do duty for both of us."

"The chance to break such a fast," said Keré'us, "would be a fine thing."

Ranhé'us sat in a window seat, his cloak wrapped round him, gloomily watching the main square. Keré'us saw the Sea-lord and joined him, wondering what was causing the gloom, but on looking out of the window he saw Anya laughing with the twins one of whom, presumably Terué, had an arm round her. "Have you actually asked Warany for her?"

"No, because I already owe him fifteen thousand bathens on my own account and a thousand my father borrowed. She's not the sort of girl you can just buy with a couple of cows. He would want ten thousand for her just as a matter of form. Keré'us, in a bad winter in the Sea-kingdoms we all starve. Warany won't let his precious daughter starve. We don't rob your father's grain ships just for the fun of it! Well, not just for the fun. Damn it all! It would not have been so bad if she had just gone off with someone else and I had heard the news in André'as, but to have to watch that fool Terué with her! I've known her for years. I used to pull her pigtails when she was a little girl… first girl I ever kissed, and got thrashed by Warany for it. Hé, I wish Warany had let your father hang me."

"You are managing to make me feel quite guilty about that."

Ranhé'us smiled and gave him a gentle clout, or what

the André'an thought was a gentle clout, "Hé Keré'us, what shall I do?"

"Ask Warany, anyway. If I was the Lord of the Warny, bearer of a sword of power, I should want my daughter to marry one of the other lords of the swords of power. You *are* the grandson of one of the Lords Eldest. Terué has no immortal blood. Warany will have to send a good dowry with her but with you he won't have to part with any money. He can just knock it off your debt."

Ranhé'us had not seen it in this light before. He brightened, "You're right, I'll ask him."

"Now?"

"I might wait until morning."

"No, ask him now while you still believe you can."

Ranhé'us ambled off to find Warany. The Dark Lord took his place, leaning against the window embrasure.

"Woman trouble?" he asked.

Keré'us nodded. "I sent him off to ask Warany for her."

"That is a pity, for I just saw Warany and his sons ride off to greet Selin, whose men are a day from Elen. They will not be back until tonight."

"By which time Ranhé'us will have lost his nerve. Women, they are more trouble than they are worth!"

"Verily," said the Dark Lord.

In the evening, as the sun set behind the mountains, men rode to Elen bearing the banner of the Kindathen, bright blue as the sky at noon, with a swan in flight across it. Selin led his men riding on a white horse. He was a man of about thirty summers, slender, with an Elta look about him although his hair was not silver fair but grey, with a white lock which fell on his forehead. With him rode

Warany and the sons of Warany, all his dear friends, and behind him rode some two thousands of the stalwart knights of Kindath.

That night at table the four lords who bore the swords of power sat together with Arno who held Aren and they were a splendid sight, bringing hope to all who were present. For surely the Halucias could not match the cunning of Warany, the strength of Ranhé'us, the wisdom of Selin or the knowledge of the Dark Lord? Nor could any match the magic power of Arno.

Selin looked to where Aren lay on the table before Arno. His own sword Kaeordra lay in Arno's treasury with the others and he felt uncomfortable without it. "Have you heard," he asked, "the words that have set all Avenya puzzling?"

"Words?" asked the Dark Lord.

"You know of them, for the high priestess spoke them when she came to us at Mara-lei, *Why now together are four swords to make or mar and Aren the darkest far, Master of Evil?*"

"If indeed they mean anything," said the Dark Lord.

"My uncle was very troubled by them," said Selin, "he fears they signal great change."

"Nonsense, a mere plot from the Pleorine hills," said Arno. " Those Yanai have nothing better to do."

"My uncle thinks not."

"And where did your uncle hear them?" asked the Dark Lord, his polite tone not quite masking a note of rising anger.

"They are abroad everywhere," said Selin, realising too late that he might just be getting into the matter too deep.

"Tell me," continued the Dark Lord unkindly, "what does that red witch make of them?"

Selin looked wildly about him. Arno was smiling, Ranhé'us was waiting for an explosion and Warany already had his hand on the hilt of Erindra. "I know not Lord," he lied. In a desperate effort to change the subject, he cast about him and saw Keré'us' red curly hair glowing amongst the dark heads of Warany's family at a lower table. "Tell me, who is the Quarin with Anya and Derany?

"The Lord of the House of Abard," said Warany.

"I thought I knew every Lord in Avenya, but he is a stranger to me. Whence does he hail?"

"Mundra."

Selin frowned and then realised who Keré'us must be. "The servant that the High Queen promised the Dark Lord at Nenaterian. No wonder he has such a feel of power about him. I could not understand, so much magic. Does he wear a sword of power ... no, of course, they are all accounted for...strange."

"He has no sword," said Warany and because he liked living on the edge he added, "yet." He had the satisfaction of seeing the smile on Arno's face fade as he looked anxiously at Aren set before him. But it was a foolish thing to do.

Arno's revenge was swift. "Selin tells me that his uncle Hara, prince of the Merédur, together with Lara and Tarca will be coming to aid us in this battle..." The rest of his words were lost in the sound of the Dark Lord dropping his goblet of wine. Even Warany paled for an instant. Arno smiled at him. The wine ran cross the board like blood and a slave rushed to mop it up. "The Merédur have never once come to the aid of mortal men in their battles. They are safe on the Hélans Dru, why do they now choose to come to battle? We have not called for their aid!" The Dark Lord's voice was cold.

"My uncle bore a sword of power and fought in the wars of the Diadem," said Selin angrily, "and for you! Can you not see it, smell it? The whole world is changing. We are coming to the end of a cycle. The Merédur know they must change or perish. My kinsmen first served the guardian spirit of Naru, the Shining One, the Lady Zarazinnya who held the Elorianen. When your Lord Eldest kinsmen murdered her and took it a cycle ended. The Merédur were sworn servants of the Elorianen and they followed the Lady Yannya while she was yet its guardian. But now she lies imprisoned under Yakré'a and the Elorianen moves on. It is to serve the Star-stone that my uncle comes. The four and the one come together again as they did in the days of the Diadem wars and all things change."

"They will be traitors to us," said the Dark Lord, "as ever their Lady was to me."

"Their gift of flight could be useful to us," said Warany.

"If any fault there is, it is mine," said Arno, "for I summoned them. We need all the help we may."

CHAPTER SEVENTEEN

In the morning of the next day the Merédur came to Elen. Like three great birds they hovered over the silver city and like falcons they stooped to rest in the main courtyard before Arno's Halls. The city was set afire with curiosity, for these fabled creatures were not often seen in the lands of men and many came to watch Arno and his pale daughter welcome them. Their leader was Hara their prince, white winged, dark skinned and splendid with a silver circlet set in his white curling hair. He had brought his uncle Lara, lord of the eagle kind, who had tawny wings and their friend, Tarca, lord of the raven kind with jet black hair and wings. They were so beautiful, their voices so melodious and their manner so gentle that Keré'us could not understand why the Dark Lord hated them so. Hara asked for him, but he had vanished.

Warany took Keré'us to one side, "Go and find him," he said. "I know that he thinks Hara is that red witch's lover, but that is no excuse to be so rude. We have to maintain a united front, especially for the men. Petty grievances over women must be put to one side. Talk to him, humour him, promise him anything but get him back here. I do not know what possessed Arno to invite them, but having done so, did they have to bring Hara? Are not the enemy outside the gate enough? By the Lords Eldest, had Yatior himself done this it would have been well done!"

The Dark Lord was sitting on the parapet wall of the gate tower, gazing with unseeing eyes north to the mountains of fire where the woman he had once loved was imprisoned.

"Lord," said Keré'us.

The Dark Lord started and his hand slid to his absent sword. "I suppose Warany sent you?"

"Yes Lord."

"And I suppose he wants me to be civil to our dear flying friends?"

"In a word, yes. Fallen and exiled you may be, but you are still one of the Lords Eldest and it does not become you to hide and sulk like a woman."

"Fallen and exiled I may be, but you will do well to keep a civil tongue in your head, mortal!" He made as if to clout Keré'us but the blow did not fall. He sighed. "You are right, little Keré'us, if I show them I am hurt, I have lost and they have won. It is just I hate their gentleness and kindness and shining faces."

"But did they not fight with you against your brother?"

"Yes, but since my father had murdered his father, there was always a certain coolness between me and Hara. It was the red witch whom he served." He sighed again, "Yet we all fought together to try and defeat my brother and win back the Diadem. Hara, Gawen, Amunrhoieneth, myself. The four and the one. But that was long ago. Enough even of thinking about it. Let me smile and do as the Old Man says."

"I'd not show my teeth so much if I smiled," said Keré'us.

As they returned to the Hall they met not the Merédur, but Ranhé'us and the sons of Terué. Neither Ranhé'us or the Mordatans actually saw them, since they were in the middle of a fight, but Keré'us said good day cordially enough to them and would have gone on. However, the Dark Lord turned to him and said, "We cannot have this, fighting over women, as you have told me, is bad for discipline. Come little Keré'us, the twin in the blue coat first I think!"

Keré'us grinned and they bundled first one and then the other twin into the fountain in the middle of the square. As an after thought they threw Ranhé'us in as well, but he put up more of a struggle. Warany was walking across the square with Derany at the time. "It makes me feel old," he said, "to see a brawl to which I have not been invited."

"You are," said his son and went to give the final push that sent Ranhé'us to join the Mordatans.

In the afternoon, Tarca, Merédur lord of the raven-kind came to Warany's room where the Dark Lord and Keré'us were sitting in the window embrasure playing Ra-malcron. Warany was sitting on the bed oiling his boots with loving care.

"Lord Eldest Malcarious," began Tarca, "my prince wishes to speak with you on a matter personal to you both."

"It is unfortunate then that I have no wish to speak with him. My cousin Tritellior informs me that your prince often visits the red witch. I care not why, but I care that he has any truck with a traitor and a condemned prisoner. His loyalty to the Alliance is suspect."

"It is unreasonable to condemn my prince without a hearing."

"I dare say, but that is my privilege."

"Whatever you think, I can assure you that my prince is

not her lover - mayhap he would be pleased to be, but so would all the Eldest Lords from Mérior to Gawen, including that evil young man Tritellior. He only tells you these things to taunt you because he knows you cannot travel on the High Roads to discover the truth."

The Dark Lord carefully put down his piece representing the high priestess which he had been holding in his hand the while. "She holds you in check," he said to Keré'us.

"I think not," said Keré'us, moving his archer sideways to take the priestess.

The Dark Lord smiled his sardonic smile and moved his high priest to take the archer and to check mate.

"Lord Malcarious," said Tarca urgently.

"I have no name, it has been taken away."

"By the Lady Zarazinnya, Lord of Darkness, we serve the Elorianen, we serve you and we serve the truth. The truth is that Lord Arno is not with you. He has called all the Alliance here to destroy them. He is a fell necromancer and serves your brother Yatior who even now has men gathering in the mines to aid the Halucias and Arno and forces from Belia."

"The lady Nenya warned us of this," said Warany, "but you will forgive me if I point out that you are all on the same side, as it were. If the sorceress wants Keré'us to take Aren, how better should she do it than getting her friends to discredit Arno before us all?"

"Can you not see," said Tarca urgently, "you are caught like rats in a trap! All the swords of power are in Arno's treasury save Erindra. You have no magic, no power. Only what the Lady Yannya can give Keré'us. Now will you be at peace with my prince?"

The truth of the matter could not be ignored. The Dark Lord looked at Warany, "We have been feeling uneasy, have we not? All those loyal to the Alliance are gathered here and beyond are Arno's muster, the muster from Belia and the Halucias - and men from the mines you say?" He moved the pieces on the board, setting the white ones outside the small grouping of black ones.

"We watch the mines from the Hélans Dru, Lord of Darkness. There has been much activity of late. Your brother the Lord Eldest Yatior plots some mischief. He likes not the order you have brought to Avenya and he desires to control the Elorianen again. He finds it easier to control Arno than he will a son of the Quarenyos Queens. My prince has indeed spoken to the Lady about this, but he has also taken counsel with your brother the Lord Eldest Gawen."

"I cannot believe you without proof, and I cannot seek out my brother to ask him, not while the doom of mortal man is on me. The High Roads are closed to me and speed is of the essence," said the Dark Lord, almost apologetically.

"You shall have proof soon enough," said Tarca, "but by then it will be too late! How shall you escape?"

"So how do we find the truth of this?" Warany looked from the Merédur to the Dark Lord.

"We have a little time, Pelélorné and André'as are not here yet. If Arno does plot ill, then he will want to trap them all. There is one who would know, one within reach. He is a prisoner in Belia, so I should have to go to him."

"And if, as I fear, it is sooth, then what do we do?" asked Warany. "Where do we find the men to defeat your brother in battle? We had enough trouble calling up this many!"

"I might get four or five thousands," said Keré'us, "but they would have to be under my command. They probably would not take orders from you."

"Do you mean the slaves here?" asked Warany. "It is worth considering, but we really need trained men."

"I had not thought of the Quaren slaves," said Keré'us. "No, these are soldiers, probably the most highly trained soldiers in Avenya."

Warany frowned. He thought he knew the fighting strength of every force in Avenya. "Whence?" he demanded.

"The Gate."

"Long live the King," said the Dark Lord quietly.

"Melin," asked Warany, "will give you his men to fight *with* the Alliance?"

"If news is ill in Belia, we can ride on to the Gate and ask their help. There will be conditions - you will have to take the price off Felanin's head and give those free Quaren the right to own land."

"Done!" said Warany and shook hands on it.

Tarca said, "You will go to Belia then Lord? But how shall you escape without Arno knowing?"

"I know not, for Keré'us will need food and fodder for his horse, at least to Belia. The Yana Nenya may help us there. It will take us the best part of eight days to get to Belia and the same to return if you Merédur are mistaken." Tarca shook his head. The Dark Lord continued with his calculations, "So then another six days to the Gate and nine or so back to Elen. Give us sixteen days and then assume the worst, because either we shall have been killed getting to Belia, or we are on the way to the Gate. Send a Merédur down to the Gate to warn Melin and ask for help anyway. He respects you. Under no circumstances believe any message, dream or vision from anyone, Lords Eldest to the red witch."

Warany was amused. "How shall I know it is you when you get back?" he asked.

The Dark Lord cuffed him on the ear in a friendly fashion. "I shall have Keré'us with me."

"I am relieved to hear it," said Keré'us.

In the evening when they sat down to dinner, Ranhé'us went to sit next to Anya, but Terué managed to get there just ahead of him. The Sea-lord would have accepted this in the spirit of friendly rivalry, but Terué said, "The Lady Anya is to be my woman, let me not see you near her again!"

"Since when?" demanded Ranhé'us.

"Since I asked for her this afternoon," said Terué.

"I have not said yes," Anya tossed her head haughtily and her blue eyes flashed angrily.

"But you will," said Terué.

Ranhé'us gave a roar, "She is not woman to you. She will never accept you. She shall not marry a fat Mordatan with no manners and little family. Just because you have money you think you can buy the daughter of Warany. Pay her court, buy her fine jewels, but there is more to marriage than a dowry and a bride price. Do not order me around because I am poor and a pirate, for I bring as many men as you to this battle. I bear Garenmegra and I am the grandson of the Lord Eldest Gawen!"

"You are a fool," said Terué, "for all you prate of your Lord Eldest ancestor. In Mordata it is said that your grandmother's lover was as mortal as the rest of us and the story of the Lord Eldest Gawen was put about to hide her shame!"

Ranhé'us roared like an angry bear. Derany, Keré'us and Selin caught hold of him and hung on desperately.

"Challenge him!" cried Derany, who knew they would not be able to hold on much longer.

"Yes, challenge him," agreed Keré'us, feeling the stitching of the sleeve he grasped slowly giving way.

"Very well," Ranhé'us shook himself and the three were thrown off. "I, Ranhé'us, son of Ruén, son of the Lord Eldest Gawen challenge you Terué, son of Terué of Mordata, for you have provoked me beyond bearing."

"My pleasure," said Terué, "Trumaré rules, long swords and as soon as we may. And do not forget that you may not use your sword, for it is a sword of power."

"He can borrow mine," offered Derany.

"Who is your second?" asked Ranhé'us.

"My brother. And yours?"

"I'll have the Quarin."

After some initial complaint from Arno, it was agreed that the match would be held the following day, as soon as the seconds judged there would be enough light. It being a private matter they agreed to fight in Arno's great hall. When they had finished their dinner, Morda and Keré'us went to pace out the main fighting area and once it was measured to their mutual satisfaction, they left the hall, Morda to go to his bed and Keré'us nominally to fetch Derany's sword from the treasury.

Anya and her brothers had been watching the measuring with Ranhé'us and Terué, but when Terué offered her his arm she laughed at him. "Whether you win or lose tomorrow, I shall never marry you. I would rather die a virgin than marry a man I despise." Then she hugged the great bulk of the Sea-lord and kissed him on the mouth, much to his surprise and pleasure, and left the hall with Derany.

Ranhé'us went from the hall singing.

Terué vowed to kill him on the morrow.

The Quarin's route to the treasury went via the kitchens. Here he found Nenya. "I need provisions for a journey of eight days, and fodder for my horse - can you arrange it?"

"Your horse is at the gate stables?"

"Yes, it's a little grey mare. My saddle is the only Mundran one there. It should be over the stall."

"I think it can be arranged - how soon?"

"Tomorrow. Ranhé'us fights a duel at dawn and then we hope to escape unnoticed."

"I've heard about that. All Anya wants to do is marry Ranhé'us, but he is too poor to make Warany an offer. Personally I would not feel comfortable with a man whose grandfather spends as much of his time looking like a bear as a man, but Anya says that in Ranhé'us' case it's hard to tell the difference anyway."

"You know the family well?"

Nenya's lips quirked, "Some better than others. But not all the House of Wargarny are opposed to the Lady Yannya. Anya's grandfather on her mother's side was Amunrhoieneth and he fought with the Lady Yannya in the Wars of the Diadem. Nanenethen was a friend of the Lady, of long standing. But it is foolish to talk thus even here. Depend on me, for the Lady bade me come here to serve you. My thoughts will be with you and Anya tomorrow."

"Look after my people. If it comes to a battle we might need them."

"Yes lord." She bowed deeply and Keré'us went on his way to the treasury.

159

CHAPTER EIGHTEEN

The morning was grey and Arno's great hall ill lit. Keré'us watched the growing light doubly anxious. First the fight and then the flight. The Dark Lord sat in a chair. Like many of the others he was cloaked against the cold morning air and his hood shaded his face, lost deep in thought, his mind travelling the miles to Belia, calculating how fast they could go and whether Ranhé'us' men would be in Elen before they got back and where they might be ambushed.

A crowd began to gather and the light strengthened. Ranhé'us had put rosin on his boots to grip the stone floor better. He made a few practice strokes with Derany's sword, his boots squeaking protest. The twins whispered together. Anya was nowhere to be seen.

Morda came to Keré'us as the light grew and they agreed that it was now good enough. The two competitors went to their respective corners and the seconds inspected the swords to make certain that Ranhé'us did not have Garenmegra. The basic rule of fighting by the Trumaré rules was that the fight took place within a square and if a combatant stepped out of the square he was disqualified. Sometimes the square was marked with pegs or ropes. On this occasion it was chalked on the grey stone floor.

Then Anya came in, leaning on her father's arm. She looked pale, for she truly loved Ranhé'us and feared not for his skill but treachery from the twins. Arno followed them and took up his position on his throne with Aren unsheathed before him on a grey velvet covered table, to remind these lords of the swords of power who was king here. Elwyn stood next to him and since she out ranked Anya in her father's halls, to her went the privilege of starting the fight.

The two men saluted her by holding their swords in both hands before them and touching their foreheads to the blades. Then they returned to their corners and came back into the centre with swords outstretched to touch in the centre of the square. Elwyn smiled, first raised then dropped her hand.

The two men touched swords and the fight began. They had fought against each other many times before in the hard school of the Trumarei. Each knew the other's strengths and weaknesses and knew it would be a hard fight. They cautiously thrust and parried, Ranhé'us growling all the while. Terué was much the calmer. The Mordatan made some good strokes. Ranhé'us nearly made the fatal error of stepping out of the square. He fought back. Terué landed a blow on the arm which drew blood. Ranhé'us hit back angrily and wildly. He caught Terué's shirt and the fabric slit from waist to shoulder. The twin stepped back. Now he was caught between the invisible wall of the square and the bright blade. Keré'us moved behind him to check that he stayed in the square. The Mordatan ducked and thrust back. Ranhé'us took the advantage and pressed the attack home. Terué tried to regain the initiative, but Ranhé'us had the edge on him and a score to settle. Suddenly the Mordatan's blade spun up into the air and Terué was left clasping his wrist in a dazed fashion as it skidded and rang across the floor almost to his brother's feet. Ranhé'us grinned, his anger gone, and held out his hand to his foe, but in that moment Morda seized his brother's sword from before him and leapt on the victor. His first blow knocked Ranhé'us' sword from his hand and the next would have run him through had not Keré'us with great presence of mind snatched up the only other sword there and disarmed the twin.

That was the plain fact of what happened, but from the moment his hand clasped the worn hilt of Aren Keré'us found himself in a whirlwind of confusion. He heard the metallic blow as he disarmed the twin, but he did not see it. Either the iron blade caught the light of the morning sun or white light lit from the blade itself. It dazzled the crowd and while he held it and stood in Arno's Halls, it seemed to Keré'us that he stood elsewhere in a great open space, a wind blowing on his face and a light shining from him. The sky was full of the great northern stars, and two crescent moons were bright silver over the horizon.

They came, they came and doom was come. Five Lords Eldest with murder in their eyes. Now was the end but the trap would be shut forever. The Lords Eldest Yatior and Tritellior, golden haired and gloriously fair, the Lord Eldest Mérior, silver fair like the Elta and Vallior, golden haired, magnificent and terrible, clad for war, whose haughty mien and stern face made him a lord even of those lords. Then they parted to let through an old man with grey hair whose power was immense and was the most terrible of them all.

This was what they had worked for, this was the sacrifice so gladly given. Now unto the Elorianen I commend my spirit! A woman's voice cried out. The white light became incandescent but redness engulfed Keré'us. He could not see, nor hear, nor breathe.

The ground was blessedly cool under him and the sky was blue over his head. The face of the Dark Lord hovered on the edge of vision. His heart surged with fear - one of the Eldest! "They killed me."

"Not a traditional opening," said the Dark Lord. "Do you not want to know where you are?"

"It would be a start to know who I was," said Keré'us. He struggled up into a sitting position and rubbed his eyes and yawned. "What happened?"

"You picked up Aren and used it to disarm Morda, but fainted before Arno had used enough magic on you to kill you. In the ensuing chaos I picked you up, collected our horses, which some Yana had very thoughtfully provisioned, slung you over my saddle bow and got the hell out of Elen. Eventually you showed some signs of wishing to live so I stopped and let you recover."

"They killed me, you know, the five Lords Eldest came and they...I don't know what I'm talking about," he shook his head. A thought struck him, how can I use Aren if it does that to me?

The Dark Lord was professionally interested. "What did it do?"

"It showed me pictures, picture of four Lords Eldest... I knew their names. The Lords Eldest Yatior, Mérior, Vallior and Tritellior. Then they parted to let an old man through, and his power killed me...at least, I think he killed me, it all went red."

"Arno was using his power too. Perhaps he took power from the Elorianen to turn on you. The red witch would not have given the keeping of it to you if she did not think you

could control it. I have wielded Hiruéven and used the power in the Star-stone, but it never showed me visions. We must proceed. Arno will notice we are not in Elen sooner or later."
He held out his hand and Keré'us took it thankfully and struggled to his feet. They were some way from Elen, out of sight of the city in a hollow. His little grey mare and S'elrashen were patiently cropping the grass. The Dark Lord lifted him on to his horse and they continued their journey east.

When Keré'us had recovered enough that he did not have to concentrate all his efforts to stay on his horse he began to wonder about what he had seen and try and sort it out in his mind. "To whom did the Star-stone belong before it belonged to the Lords Eldest?"

"My mother owned it, and she sent it to the Shining Ones who gave it to Zarazinnya," said the Dark Lord shortly.

"What was Zarazinnya?"

"I do not know properly, I was but a child then, I remember my father going out clad for war, to end her rule. They have always called her one of the Shining Ones."

"What had she done?"

"She stood in the way of the Eldest." He spoke carefully as though he had always been told this and now that he was telling Keré'us he realised how foolish it sounded."

"She must have been very powerful if it took five of the Lords Eldest to defeat her. Are there other Shining Ones - yes, for you said she was one of them. How is it that we do not see them?"

"The Shining Ones dwell in the stars. The Lords Eldest dwell here." The Dark Lord was obviously uncomfortable.

"But why?"

"I do not wish to discuss this matter further."

"Very well, perhaps I shall ask the Lady some time."

"Do that, let her tell tales on the Eldest, but she will

know little of the truth. She was not made then. She will only be repeating gossip heard from Mildur or the Merédur. It was far later that Yatior made her to be his concubine and I doubt that he ever wasted time talking to her about such things."

Such a vehement answer silenced Keré'us.

They rode hard, stopping at midday to rest the horses and eat, then they went on, halting only for the dark. They did not dare light a fire and Keré'us slept while the Dark Lord watched, a darker shadow in the night.

In the morning they rode on at first light, pressing hard all day, until they came to the point where the road turned sharply south to cross the Lee'ma Ra. Here the Dark Lord dismounted and looked down on the small town of Runi on the far side of the river.

"What do you think?" he asked.

"They were waiting for us there last time."

"My own feeling exactly. We had better take the causeway. That means we cannot change your horse, but we at least have good provender for her. We had better get on, I have a feeling that they will come looking for us if we do not turn up as expected."

"I thought I might walk for a bit. Give the horse a rest."

The Dark Lord followed his example and they strode on into the growing twilight.

In the indigo mists of early night they rested, until the silver moon rose and they could see to go on. The rolling scrub lands were shrouded in fog but far off they caught the sound of harness jingling.

"If we can hear them, they will hear us," whispered the Dark Lord, "I think we are going to have to abandon the horses and travel on foot. It will be much quieter and not much slower. I shall send S'elrashen and your mare straight to the causeway while we travel by a more circuitous route. Get some food and water, but only enough food for yourself. I can do without."

As silently as he could Keré'us took a bag of food from his saddle. The Dark Lord slung it over his shoulder and spoke in a low whisper to his horse which moved off slowly south with Keré'us' mare. Then the men turned north, up a low hill away from the river and on, away from the sounds of horsemen behind them. The Dark Lord found and followed a limestone escarpment and in some caves they spent the rest of the night.

Keré'us slept well and was alarmed by the height of the sun when he awoke the next day, but the Dark Lord shook his head. "We shall not travel until the evening. While you slept I walked the land about and I have seen Arno's men looking for us to the south. You may as well sleep."

"I'll have something to eat and drink first. It will save time later," said Keré'us unpacking his food. Unthinkingly he offered some to the Dark Lord who shook his head.

"You want some water though?"

"I drank from a stream earlier. Save it for yourself."

"But you do need water?"

"All creatures in creation need water. Warany was always fascinated by my needing no sleep or food. What is it with you mortals? Am I so strange to you?"

"Like but unlike," yawned Keré'us. "I thought the Lords Eldest were immortal, but the Star-stone showed me you were not. You must be to us as we men appear to animals. Think how a cat sees the farmer's wife. From kittenhood to death the farmer's wife changes but little. She is always there to bestow blessings like cream, to heal wounds and give favourites a warm place by the fire. And does not the cat bow before her and worship her for this?"

"And how did the Elorianen show you this?" asked the Dark Lord warily.

"By showing me three generations of Lords Eldest together so I could see how they grew old."

The Dark Lord turned away from him, looking over the rough lands, which led down to where the river curved like a silver snake along the horizon. "What did she choose you for?" he asked, as much to himself than of Keré'us.

"I don't know. Do I scare you as much as I scare me?"

The Dark Lord laughed, "I think one of us should have drowned you when you were a kitten."

"I thought people were still trying to," said the Quarin.

"No more questions. Go back to sleep. You will get none tonight."

As the sun began to set they set off again, the Dark Lord letting Keré'us set the pace and they covered good ground until the silver moon set and the stars were too faint to travel by. Then they rested until dawn, when they set off again. It took them the best part of three days to reach the causeway, where in a secret valley to the north the horses were waiting, grazing unconcernedly. Keré'us looked up at the proud arching neck of the Dark Lord's beast and thought that anyone seeing S'elrashen would know exactly to whom he belonged. On the other hand, no one was likely to steal him. The Dark Lord spoke soft words to S'elrashen and the horse whinnied back. "They are ahead of us on the road, going to the Gate. I hoped that would be so."

Now they pressed on, Keré'us changing horses at the Trumaré posts, safe in the knowledge that Arno's men could not catch them. In five days they were at Belia.

Belia was not quite like any other city in Avenya. To begin

with it smelt more, even more than Furah in a hot summer, and this was not only due to the drains. The government of Belia prided itself on being rotten to the core. It had been founded in the days of the Queens but had never been under their control like Banéros and Furah. No massive temples to the Lady or the Eldest could be found here. The only gods they worshipped were profits. The city had grown up where the Lee'ma Ra met the Evénfel and most of the bulky trade from Elen and earlier from Nenaterian was carried by the Lee'ma Ra, whilst copper ore from Hordé came on narrow boats down the Evénfel to join the Lee'ma Ra and go on to Banéros. The massive walls about Belia were built, it was said, not to keep anyone out, but to make sure that they stayed in until they had paid the tolls. This was, of course, the cause of a great deal of enmity from the river-men, who plied their trade on the two rivers, but worried Belia not a jot.

The population of the city seemed to consist largely of rogues and thieves, ladies and gentlemen of ill repute and the occasional necromancer. There may have been honest folk living there but no one has ever mentioned them.

Keré'us looked up at the massive wall of grey stones that towered above them, supported by a wide range of variously crenellated towers. He had never seen any of the great cities before and compared to Belia both Mundra and Elen were mere villages.

At the gate they managed to find enough money between them for the toll. They passed the gate-wards and entered the darkening city. Tall wood and stone buildings overhung the streets cutting out the remaining light and hiding the stars. The smell, after so long in the fresh air of the open road, was overpowering. People pushed past them. Empty carts from the closed markets rumbled and bounced over the cobbles, rushing to get out of the city before the gates closed for the night. S'elrashen looked pained, and Keré'us' skewbald post horse looked uneasy.

"Where are we going?" asked Keré'us.

The Dark Lord gave one of his rare grins, "I am going to the dungeons of the Haughty Lord of Belia and I suppose I had better take you with me, since it is remotely possible that you will be safer with me than in a tavern on your own. But first we must stable the horses. There is an inn up here called the Black Hawk where we can get a room for the night and leave them."

"I am not anxious to be left on my own, but I find your choice of destination curious. Are we such friends of the Haughty Lord of Belia that we must save him trouble and incarcerate ourselves?"

"To discover the truth of the Merédur's words I go to speak with a ...a creature. The Quaren called him one of the Old Ones. You might call him a spirit. He is not like the Lords Youngest, the Merédur or the Erueth. He is of the earth ... or in this case of the water. He was a faithful servant to Zarazinnya and after her execution was imprisoned here under the hill on which Belia was built. The Haughty Lord of Belia, of course, had need of dungeons and later made use of the other caves about him."

"If this person is in prison, how can he help us. How will he know what is happening?"

"The Leehréma Ra rises in the mines under the mountains."

This utterance left Keré'us none the wiser.

They stabled the horses at the Black Hawk, which bore a curious resemblance to a Trumaré post, had such establishments not been banned by the Haughty Lord. Here they ate a hasty supper and then set out across the city.

The Quarin trotted beside his friend, trying to keep pace as he strode through the gathering night.

"How do we get into the dungeons?" he asked as they reached the windowless curtain wall of the castle. "I assume that we do not take the obvious course of picking an argument with the castle guard?"

"No, there is an easier and less permanent way." The Dark Lord followed a now deserted alley which ran in front of shuttered shops built hard against the castle wall, until they came to a point where the old external wall of the west side of the city cut the river Lee'ma Ra. Because there was now a new wall and new gates some quarter of an hour's journey west, the old river gates had been permitted to decay and hung open, rotting in the green slimy water. Night had fallen and the traffic on this part of the river had ceased. The Dark Lord led the way down some decaying stone steps to the water's edge, where several small boats were moored.

"We shall borrow one. I would not ask you to swim a Belian river." He untied a boat.

At this moment Keré'us made what he felt was an important discovery. The Dark Lord was unarmed. All the time they had travelled his long cloak had hidden the fact, but now he removed it to make it easier to scull, the Quarin realised that the long scabbard of Yadra was no longer slung over his back. "Where's your sword?" he asked in a voice which he hoped did not betray his anxiety.

"In Arno's treasury, I trust. I could not draw attention to us by trying to get it back. It is of no matter."

Keré'us rolled his eyes heavenward. So neither of them were armed and it was of no matter. He sat in the prow of the boat and sent up a quiet prayer to the Lady as the Dark Lord took it slowly out into the main stream, ripples breaking round them in the oily water. It stank. Keré'us gritted his teeth. They passed under the rotting gates and into the dark beneath the bridge beyond.

CHAPTER NINETEEN

To their right the high wall of the palace was a black shadow in the night. Neither the waxing silver moon nor the dying red were visible. The only light came from torches born by occasional parties on the riverbank or the guards on the palace walls.

The Dark Lord dug his sweep in vertically. The evil smelling water swirled as the boat turned sharply, slipping through a gate that was little more than a culvert. It was velvet black beyond. Water dripped and plashed. The walls were close and he quanted the boat along, needing only the feel of the oar on the walls to direct him. Suddenly there was light. He put his finger to his lips and poled the boat as silently as he could. The light came from a torch burning by a stone landing stage. A flight of steps led from this dank spot into the upper castle. Not surprisingly it was deserted.

They drifted on into the dark again.

"How much further?" asked Keré'us in a low voice.

"Not far now."

Then there was a force about them. Keré'us gasped. His breath was knocked out of his body, as if he had dived into deep water. The Dark Lord put a hand on his shoulder. "That was the gate. It should not harm mortals." Keré'us was too winded to argue.

There was light again and the whole nature of the tunnel changed. The roof was high above their heads and torches burned brightly on distant walls, lighting the ceiling and the wide pavements of stone stretching either side of the water. The stream flowed on for another hundred yards or so, where it entered a great black pool and beyond the pool was the further wall of this vast cavern. On the left was a stone table on which stood plates and a pitcher. On the right was set a grey stone chair which would have dwarfed even the Dark Lord.

The Dark Lord caught a bronze ring set into the wall by a set of steps and tied up the boat. Then he disembarked and held out his hand to Keré'us. When they had both gained the quay he called quietly.

"Hréma!"

"Who calls?" came a voice, deep and dark, reverberating as if it came from the depths of the water.

"I call, I, the son of Vallior and Mara."

"Have you no name?" queried the voice, still echoing strangely.

Keré'us was very aware of a presence, although he could not locate the source of the voice. He moved closer to the Dark Lord. The voice scared him. It was so old, so malevolent.

"Does not the Leehréma Ra flow from the mines? Has it not heard how my name was taken away?" asked the Dark Lord angrily.

"I have, but would hear it from your own lips," came the voice, deeply amused. There was a heaving and bubbling in the waters and suddenly a creature rose out of them. He was big and repulsive, remotely similar to a gross man, clad in what appeared to be long strands of slime which flapped about his body. His face too was grossly fat, with but a little semblance of humanity, his eyes and lips the same sickening grey-green as his putty like face. He laughed and waddled over the stone floor to the chair, squelching into it, water flowing from him back to the river in noisome rivulets.

"Who is the mortal?" he demanded. "No, say not, let me guess. There is a glory on him. Surely he has been with the Lady, the sweet Lady. Hé, and you come here with *him* to see *me*? They took your wits as well as your name. One or other of us will destroy you.

"Now, why have you demeaned yourself to see Hréma? What is it that Hréma knows and you do not?" The creature half closed its eyes, giving the Dark Lord a cunning look.

"Listen, oh noisesome lord of the Leehréma Ra," said the Dark Lord, "while you decompose here in a pool of stagnant water, things stir above. The Alliance makes war on the Halucias. Arno has called up the Alliance, but the Merédur tell us it is a trap set by my brother Yatior and that Arno is in league with him. You know what happens on every inch of your river. You know what is happening in the mines!"

"And what if I do?"

"Then, fool, I must know. Many lives are at stake, lives of men. In the name of your Shining One help them if you will not help me! Do you wish to see them enslaved by my brother and the whole of Avenya his kingdom?"

"La la!" rumbled Hréma. "Does this last spawned Lord Eldest concern himself with men? Did any of the Lords Eldest look to men to be anything but slaves? Mérior or Yatior, they are both the same. I see the gift of mortality has sharpened your wits, Lord of Darkness. Mayhap mankind have found a champion at last - but stay, was that not the Lady Yannya, and have you not imprisoned her?"

"Tell me," demanded the Dark Lord coldly, "has my brother aided Arno to trap the Alliance and destroy them?"

Hréma looked to Keré'us, "Well mortal, shall I tell him what he wants to know? Tell one of those murdering Eldest Lords, who bound me under this city, what is plotted by another of their kind? Will it aid men, little mortal?"

"Lord of the River, we need to know what Arno plots. It pleases no man to be a slave and if what the Merédur say is sooth, then the Lord Eldest Yatior through Arno will have us all enslaved."

"Hé, Lord of the River is it? This man chooses words well, Lord of Darkness, but how is it he serves you, for I can smell in his blood the blood of the Quarenyos Queens." There came a strange hungry look in his eyes as he mentioned blood. The Dark Lord tried to move unobtrusively between Keré'us and Hréma.

"Then I shall tell you, little mortal. Yes indeed does Arno side with Yatior and even now the Haughty Lord of Belia prepares his men to march on Elen after the last of the Alliance men have crossed the bridge at Runi. Men will come from the mines too. I have heard them forging their weapons of war." He laughed a deep gurgling laugh. "Belia, the mines, the Halucias, Arno's own men. What shall you do?" He heaved himself up from the stone chair and meandered back to the water. The oily river closed over his repulsive body until only his bloated face was visible.

"Hréma gave you knowledge, small one, so perhaps you can tell him something in exchange. Tell me, there is a feeling, an unspoken word: change. Things are moving, things that are good but bad, bad but good. You have seen the sweet Lady. She knows all. Has she told you what is happening?"

"Lord of the River, you must know the Lady. She says nothing, but the Merédur say there is an end to one cycle and a beginning of the next."

A long fingered webbed hand crawled over the stone edge towards Keré'us. Hréma watched it almost in surprise, but at a motion from the Dark Lord withdrew it and sank instantly, his gurgled farewell reverberating about the chamber.

"Come," said the Dark Lord, and with indecent haste he made Keré'us get into the boat and began to retrace their steps. As they left the chamber laughter suddenly reverberated about their ears. The barrier slammed shut behind them and Keré'us began to feel a little safer.

"The Gate it is then, little Keré'us."

"Are we sure he spoke the truth?"

"Yes, it pleased him the more to tell me of my impending doom. Yet I wonder. His laughter disturbs me. What has he not told me that I should know?"

They reached the torch lit landing stage they had passed on the way in. The Dark Lord was no longer cautious, only anxious to be as far away from Belia as he could get. Keré'us glanced at it expecting it to be as empty as when they came, but at the foot of the stair stood an old man. His long straggling hair and beard mingled with his robes, all grey as dust. Over this robe he wore a sleeveless coat of purple silk which gleamed with hidden lights. On his hand glowed a ring set with an amethyst. "Greetings, Lord of Darkness."

The Dark Lord started, his mind had been far away. He tried to arrest the progress of the boat but it had drifted too far out of the tunnel.

"Come to me." said the old man. Keré'us could feel his power.

The Dark Lord tried to get the boat into the safety of the next part of the tunnel. "I said, come to me!"

"I think not," said Keré'us under his breath.

In anger the old man thrust both his arms forward as if he was throwing something at the two men and purple light sprang from his hands. The colour and light brought with it a great shock of pain. It doubled Keré'us up and stole his breath. The Dark Lord put himself in front of the Quarin. "You have no argument with the mortal."

"Next time it will kill him," said the sorcerer, "now will you come with me?"

Keré'us looked to the Dark Lord for guidance. He nodded slightly, "This is Dar Regan," he said, "sorcerer and servant of my brother Yatior. I doubt not that Arno warned him of our coming. For the present I fear we must do as he says." He got out of the boat and helped Keré'us out, trying all the while to stand between the Quarin and the sorcerer.

Dar Regan smiled. He was pleased to have one of the Lords Eldest fearing him.

"Arno spoke to me mind to mind and told me of your flight from Elen. I did not dream it was to me you came. However, at my gates you are always welcome; it will be my pleasure to accommodate you - for a little while. You will walk ahead of me up the stairs."

The Dark Lord pushed Keré'us ahead of him and Dar Regan followed hard on the Dark Lord's heels. Keré'us was still shaken from the power unleashed on him and the strength of the Dark Lord's arm was all that kept him going. As they climbed the Dark Lord was thinking fast and weighing up their chances of escape, which seemed very slender. He was regretting leaving Yadra in Elen and knew this information must have been passed to Dar Regan.

The stairs seemed to lead upward forever through the levels of the dungeons, then through the castle and still on, up and up into the night until they reached Dar Regan's tower, where he dwelt like a spider spinning his webs of intrigue and evil.

He made them sit down, while he stood before them and considered them thoughtfully.

"Lord of Darkness and Lord of the House of Abard, what good fortune has brought you into my hands in my moment of need?" he laughed. It was a dry, crumbling sound.

Keré'us looked at the Dark Lord whose anxious face told him all he needed to know. "Your brother, the Lord Eldest Yatior will doubtless reward me suitably when I send you to him, nameless one. This time I am sure he will guard you better. He will not make the same mistake twice. Besides, the Dalines hate you now, for you have imprisoned the Lady.

"And this little lordling, this Chosen One, oh you are wanted by so many, such a price I could get for you, but I think I shall keep you for my own amusement. Arno grows anxious about you, while you live you are the greatest threat to his power and I would increase his fears. I like not the way his thought turns to ruling all Avenya. And the Starstone looks for you, it seeks you and what power I should hold if I held the Elorianen! What price that Elta upstart then?" He smiled and rubbed his hands, the purple stone in his ring shone with its own light.

"Now I must go, I have many arrangements to make. Nameless one, look well on the dawning for you shall not see the sun again." He bowed and went out of the room. The substantial oak door slammed shut behind him and there came a faint murmur as Dar Regan said some words over it.

Keré'us stood up and wandered around the room, looking at the strange instruments and books which lay in heaps on the floor. The Dark Lord tried the door. At his touch there was a flash of purple light and he pulled his hand away hastily and rubbed it. "Not that way. But we must do something before we are separated."

Keré'us looked out of the wide windows. There were four, one in each of the four walls of the tower giving a panoramic view of the whole city. Far, far below, the lights of night time Belia burned. "Not that way, either," he said.

"Can you do anything with the door - no, do not touch it! With your mind I meant."

Keré'us came over to look at the door. "She gave you the power of the red earth. You have her ring. The Queens had power. I thought mayhap you could use it too."

"I have never tried."

"But you did, with the women in the kitchens. Think back, you spoke to them with your mind and when you faced up to Arno the whole of your magic was bright about you. He did not dare take issue with you."

The Quarin stood, a little unwillingly before the door and raised his hands. He could feel Dar Regan's magic in the spell on the door and somehow he pulled his own magic together, shutting his eyes to concentrate better. He felt the power grow and opened his eyes again to see a shining globe of red gold light between his hands. He carefully directed this at the door with his mind. The wood shimmered. He could see the stair faint beyond and then the door snapped back, thick oak bound with iron. Keré'us hung his head wearily. The magic had all but drained him.

The Dark Lord sighed. "If only I had a way of using my wild magic from my mother's kin. The Eldest could not take that away from me, but without my Eldest strength I could not focus it and it would like as not kill us. It would be a pity to assist Dar Regan."

Then a picture floated into Keré'us' mind. It was alien, another's thought. He said rather uncertainly, "This picture has come into my mind, of the Lady and Hiruéven. She holds it hilt and blade to focus her power, then you stand behind her and put your hands over hers and the light becomes a full rainbow..."

"And we drive back Yatior... yes, I had forgotten, but we do not have Aren."

"But I have the Sea-Stone!" The Quarin fumbled inside his jerkin and pulled out the silver and green jewel. As it lay in the palm of his hand he thought he could hear the faint thunder of the breakers, the ever moving green depths full of storm. He had never before realised how much power it held. And Gawen had promised him his life.

There was hope suddenly in the Dark Lord's eyes.

"There is Eldest strength enough in the Sea-Stone to hold my wild magic. Try on your own first though. My magic must be a last resort. Try the door!"

Keré'us stood square before the door again and took a deep breath. Then he turned his mind through the green sea-deeps of the stone and thought about the door opening. This time green light countered the purple spells and the door began to fade. The Dark Lord stepped forward into the door arch and passed through it, then slowly Keré'us, concentrating hard, followed him. The door snapped back across the arch behind him. He was utterly drained. He dropped the Sea-stone and leaned against the wall.

"We cannot stop here," the Dark Lord pointed out reasonably. Keré'us stumbled after him down the stairs. When they reached the castle proper he followed the Dark Lord down a corridor and found an empty chamber, throwing himself on the bed. "I must rest," he said.

"Yes, rest and I shall watch, but we cannot spare much time. Dar Regan will soon discover that we are free." He pulled the door to until there was a mere crack through which he could watch, pressed against the wall to surprise any who dared enter.

Eventually Keré'us stood up, reasonably in command of his body. "I think I can go on now."

"While you rested I was thinking. You are more important than me, Melin will give his army to no other, so should it happen that I have to field an attack so that you can escape, do not waste time looking for me, but get to the south western section of the new city wall. There is an establishment, called the Red Moon, built on the wall itself. It is the Yanai priestesses' equivalent of the Black Hawk. They will help you. Especially if you mention Warany's name," he added with his sardonic grin.

"Oh, that sort of establishment," said Keré'us smiling.

"I believe they are more profitable than the Black Hawk. Now shall we go, I can think of nothing else but to find the gate court and hope for the improbable."

They walked silently through the sleeping castle and found another stair which led down towards the gate court. It must have been past midnight and although there were still lights and sounds of revelry coming from the main hall they only saw one patrol and were able to hide from them. Most of the soldiers of the Haughty Lord of Belia were abed in comfortable bunkhouses, gathering their strength for the day of bullying ahead.

"There must be guards on the gate. How are we going to get past them and open the gate?" whispered Keré'us as he trotted, desperately trying to keep pace, at the Dark Lord's side.

"I have to say, the way our luck is holding the main gate

is as good an idea as any. I know no other way save the way we came in."

"That was what I was afraid of."

"Well, if you have a better idea I should be delighted to hear it."

"We're mad," said Keré'us, "there is no way the Haughty Lord of Belia's men are going to let us out in the middle of the night through the main gate!" He laughed. The whole thing was hilarious. The Dark Lord joined in. For sheer idiocy it was glorious. Like two late night revellers they strode across the courtyard to the main gate, laughing and clinging to each other as if they were drunk. They were within hailing distance of the gate wards when Dar Regan stood before them again.

"Damn," said Keré'us.

"Knew our luck was not that good," said the Dark Lord. "Now when I put my power through the Sea-stone do not attempt to do anything but focus it on Dar Regan."

Dar Regan stretched out his hand. He knew he could call on greater strength than the Sea-stone wielded by Keré'us' power. The Quarin held out the stone and looked into the stormy depths, holding it with both hands. Then the Dark Lord closed his great hands over Keré'us wrists and his madness rushed through Keré'us' mind in a great surge of power. The stone seemed to explode in light, green, gold and blue. Keré'us and the Dark Lord were in a maelstrom of madness, power and light. Dar Regan shuddered and staggered backwards, gasping as he fell. The Dark Lord released Keré'us wrists and caught the Quarin as he too fell, throwing him over his shoulder and running for the gates.

Bad new spreads fast. The guards on the gates had melted into the night by the time the pair reached them.

They had even thoughtfully opened the gates a crack, secure in their reasoning that whomsoever these people were who had just defeated Dar Regan, they were safer out of the castle than in.

As the Dark Lord made his way across the cobbles outside the castle he heard the gates slam shut behind them.

CHAPTER TWENTY

The Dark Lord dropped the Quarin on the road. "I can carry you no further."

"Thanks anyway," Keré'us yawned, "I could sleep for a week. Did we kill him?"

"Sorcerers are notoriously hard to kill. We certainly slowed him down a little. I still think we should get out of this city as soon as we may." The Dark Lord led the way through the cobbled streets to the edge of the city where the city wall overshadowed all else, black against the midnight blue sky. Lights shone from the shops and houses built against the wall, lanterns shone in the hands of the many revellers who were tasting the exotic fruits of the theatre, the renowned eating houses and those darker delights Belia offered to the discerning libertine. A torch burned on the wall of a house, lighting the sign of the Red Moon.

They stepped through the curtained door into the subtly lit and heavily perfumed vestibule. Keré'us suddenly felt his forearms prick with an awareness of magic. He put his hand out to the Dark Lord. He could do no more tonight.

"It is all right, little Keré'us, it is ours, or should I say, yours?"

A scantily dressed girl came up to them, "The Red Moon

is at your services sirs, if you will come with me and tell me your desires..."

"Our business is urgent," said the Dark Lord. "If Nenya has told you of Keré'us, then know he stands at my side and needs your help. If not, look on him, smell him. Is he not the Chosen of your Goddess?"

The girl's kohl darkened eyes widened. She took Keré'us' hand and led him up the stairs to the rear and up to the third floor of the establishment. Here she flung open a door and indicated that he should enter. He did so rather reluctantly as the magic he had felt emanated from this room.

A woman sat in a chair, a queenly woman who was attended by four girls in the brown and orange uniform of the Yanai. She was in her mid fifties. Her underdress was of heavy brown silk and her coat of cloth of gold. About her neck was a pectoral of gold set with topaz and carnelian. Her greying hair had been red. Her eyes were still bright brown, set in her heart-shaped face. She stood up and bowed. "All hail Keré'us, Chosen of the Goddess." Then she sank to her knees and touched her forehead to the ground, her women following her.

Keré'us looked round desperately for the Dark Lord. He had suffered all that it was in his capacity to suffer that night and could face no more. He motioned the women to resume their seats.

"I dare not ask," said the Dark Lord, "what you are doing here, madam priestess, but for the moment it does not serve us ill. Keré'us and I must leave the city unseen and I wanted to use that facility so often offered to Warany, that of a rope over the city wall and our horses brought to us."

The priestess' eyes twinkled, "I believe that was not

the only facility usually offered to Warany. However, we shall be delighted to serve the Chosen One. He looks very weary."

"He needs food and sleep. He has done more magic this night than any other I have ever seen, save the red witch your mistress, and had it not been for him I would even now be on my way to a terrible death in the mines under the mountains. But now he needs your protection, for he can do no more magic tonight and should any come against us, we shall need your power. I am helpless without him."

The High Priestess clapped her hands and sent her women for food and wines and to prepare baths and beds. Keré'us sat and ate an exotic meal from one of the best eating houses in Belia and scarcely noticed its quality. He drank exquisite wines and knew only that they made his head heavier still and he fell asleep in his bath. He could not remember going to bed, only the Dark Lord awakening him at first light.

They ate breakfast and then went up to the roof from which they could reach the wall. There was a spot here which could not be seen by either adjacent watch tower and down this section of the wall both men were lowered on ropes.

The dawn was grey, the sun rising in wreaths of mist; they waited against the wall in a huddle of mud huts which hung like swallows' nests on the solid masonry. Then suddenly they heard the great bell of Belia which was rung morning and night to signal the opening and closing of the gates. In a little while one of the girls appeared from the direction of the West Gate, leading their horses.

"We've checked," she said. "There were men on every gate looking for you, so Dar Regan is still alive. She indicated

S'elrashen, "We had to be a bit unkind to him and he did not like it, but we were scared of being questioned as it was. If Lanya, the other girl, had not stayed to chat with the guards we would never have got through. They were questioning everybody."

S'elrashen was smarting under a heavy load and a quantity of mud, his mane was tangled and his tail looked as if it had been hewn with an axe.

"They still asked me where I got him from," she said, "but they believed Lanya when she said he was a present from a grateful Trumaré." As she spoke she was stripping the panniers from both horses, taking the saddles from one and blankets from another. "If they had searched us that would have been the end. Come on, help me with these things. You must be away fast! We've put some provisions in the bags for you."

The dwellers in the mud huts watched with fascination as the men saddled up.

"You haven't seen them," said the girl. "If you tell the Haughty Lord's men the Lady Yannya will blight your crops, blast your houses and give your goats the staggers!"

The morning sun lit her face and her orange robe fluttered beneath her dark cloak; for a moment she had the power of the Lady, but then it was gone, swift as the shadow of a cloud and she was just a girl of doubtful calling helping two men escape from Belia. Not an unusual occurrence.

They followed the dusty unpaved way through the corn-lands where the winter wheat was already tall. This part of the Belian hinterland was a patchwork of small strips, won at high cost from the old forests of the Upper Plains. Small farmhouses of yellow limestone thatched with straw huddled behind windbreaks of pine.

Eventually the farmland turned to scrub and the land began to rise. Even now in the far distance they could see the grey bulk of the mountains. Then these vanished behind low cloud scudding in from the east. They did not speak. Keré'us was exhausted, the Dark Lord brooded on the fortunes of the Alliance, while S'elrashen, dispirited by the treatment of his tail, maundered on.

They rode all that day, pausing only briefly for food, rested for the now shortening night and were away at dawn. The Dark Lord seemed to expect pursuit from Belia. Keré'us hardly cared. All he wanted was a good night's sleep.

It was when they paused on a high ridge to rest the horses and eat a hunk of bread and cheese that the Dark Lord pointed to what looked like a cloud of dust far away on the road. It could only be a large body of mounted men. "They must have spare horses," he said, "they could not hope to catch us otherwise. This is going to be difficult. I had expected this journey to take us six days, but when we left Elen I had not expected that our enemies would feel so confident as to openly attack us. The war has begun, little Keré'us. My brother shows his hand at last and I do not know how long we shall be able to hold him off. Not long enough to get to the Gate, that is for sure. Now even I could wish to see the Merédur, but preferably not Hara," he added honestly.

Keré'us laughed, "I won't even start mentioning your sword still in Elen. And don't tell me you couldn't use it. You could still have lent it to me!"

The Dark Lord smiled. "Come, we must go on. We shall ride another day, then your horse will be too weary and you shall ride S'elrashen and I shall walk."

The day was hot and dusty, the up-hill going did not

please the tired horses and the soldiers grew closer. Keré'us thought there were about twenty men, distinctly heroic odds. They rode on into the twilight, stopped for Keré'us and his horse to rest and as soon as the first thin crescent of the red moon gave light enough to see they pressed on until it set. Then they rested until dawn broke. The Dark Lord watched and weighed up their chances. By the dawn he had made his mind up. He could see that Keré'us and his horse had obviously reached the limits of their strength but for the sake of a few more miles he drove them on until they reached a stream and the horses paused to drink. "We shall leave your horse here Keré'us, unload him but do not bother with your gear, S'elrashen carries the few provisions we have left."

Keré'us nodded. "How far do you reckon to the Gate?"

"Too far."

It was a good enough answer. Keré'us stripped his horse of its gear and left it cheerfully cropping grass, then he mounted S'elrashen and the Dark Lord walked on at his side, his long legs swinging in an easy pace which kept them yet ahead of the soldiers. They rested again and it seemed no sooner had Keré'us closed his eyes than the Dark Lord was shaking his arm to wake him to go on. The gap narrowed. The soldiers pressed on. They were gaining, but even with spare mounts they too were weary.

"Tomorrow they will catch us," said the Dark Lord. "When that happens I mean to send you on with S'elrashen, but even he is weary. I know not how this will end. Rest, in any case. They too will rest, they will not ride through the night, they can see they will have us tomorrow."

He woke Keré'us from the dreamless sleep of the exhausted to the dawn of another day. They broke their fast and then Keré'us mounted a now reproachful

S'elrashen. The ground here was very uneven, with great rocks thrust through the thin soil of the foot hills. Only the old Quarin road cut through the land with an easy gradient and that had begun to zigzag up the side of the first major hill. The Dark Lord looked about him for a place to make a stand and with ease borne of long practice selected an outcrop of rock facing the oncoming soldiers.

"Time you were going, little Keré'us."

"You're not going to stop twenty men?"

The Dark Lord shrugged.

"No, Lord, look, they will catch me anyway in hours, whatever you do. You can't kill them. Servant and friend we said, that gives me the right to stay."

The Dark Lord smiled his rare smile. "I keep wondering how *she* is going to get you out of this," he said.

"Not as much as I do." Keré'us drew the knife he used for dinner.

The Dark Lord laughed at the absurdity of it all. "This is going to be nearly as funny as our escape from Belia."

"And just as likely!" Keré'us wished he was not so tired. "I suppose we cannot use magic on ordinary men?"

"No, it would not be a fair fight."

"You will excuse me, but this does not look like a very fair fight anyway. The odds are ten to one."

The soldiers were nearly in range now. Keré'us hurled a rock at them. The men hesitated. The wall of rock behind their victims meant that they would have to dismount to attack them.

The Dark Lord was busy looking at a speck in the sky, "I think the odds may just be turning in our favour."

Keré'us was looking at the soldiers, who, swords drawn, were advancing on them.

"Not the way I'm looking!"

Then there were suddenly shouts and the sound of horses. The Belians' expressions changed from those about to win a fight to those who would think themselves lucky if they escaped with their lives. Orange and brown clad mounted soldiers from the Gate were everywhere and the Belians were putting up a half hearted fight.

"I think we shall just keep out of the way," said the Dark Lord and helped Keré'us up on to a rock from which they could safely watch the rout.

In a little while it was all over. Felanin came striding over to them, wiping his sword on someone's cloak as he came. "Not bad," he called up to them. "They had some good horses. We're always short of horses at the Gate. You were lucky though, another half an hour and we would have been too late." His men were rounding up the horses and stripping the surrendered Belians of their armour. "We got a message from the Merédur. Someone in Belia said you were in trouble, so we came as fast as we could. I do feel, however, you might have joined in, just for the show of the thing."

"With what?" asked Keré'us, indicating his dinner knife. "Neither of us were armed!"

Felanin rolled his eyes in horror.

Felanin found a new mount for Keré'us and while his men were burying the dead they set off to the Gate in a more leisurely fashion than they had started out. It took just over two days to reach the fortress where Tarca and Melin were waiting for them.

"Yet again you escape," said Melin as he embraced Keré'us. "Surely you will become our leader now?"

"No Lord Melin, yet I come to ask a great favour of you."

191

Melin put an arm round Keré'us shoulder, "I can guess what that is," he said. "Shall we speak in private?"

"As long as it includes Felanin, the Merédur and the Dark Lord!"

Melin nodded and led them to his study. "I hate to do this while the dust of your journey is on you, but I fear we are getting short of time."

"I fear so too," said Keré'us, "but our enemies wait for no one, nor can we." He looked to the Dark Lord, but knew that this was his responsibility and took a deep breath. "Lord Melin, once you offered me men to take back the Quarin throne. Would you offer them to me to save the Alliance from sorcerers and the Lord Eldest Yatior?"

"We are not of the Alliance, what is it to us?"

"I have agreed with Warany that you would be granted the right again to own land, and the price would be taken from Felanin's head. The Gate will not last long without the Alliance and you know this. Once before you were defeated by magic, should the Lord Eldest Yatior put out his hand to you there will be no returning."

"But it is hard to side with our enemies."

"Then do this for me, take arms against Belia. We know that they will march to join Arno once the last of the Alliance armies have crossed the Lee'ma Ra, following behind them to trap them between the Halucias and Elen. Take your men to cut Belia off at Runi. With the aid of the Merédur you can time it just so."

Tarca nodded at this.

Melin looked thoughtful, he glanced at Felanin. "What think you, brother?"

"Our men will do much for the privilege of owning land and that will solve some of our problems here. I am sorry about the price on my head, though. I was hoping to get it up to a million bathens one day."

"I am sure that could be arranged," said the Dark Lord.

Melin laughed, "It is a strange step to take, but take it we shall. By the Lady, the Quaren are at war again! We have mouldered too long here at the Gate arguing over tolls. We are soldiers and we have a few scores to settle with Belia!"

"Then I will away to tell Warany what has happened," said Tarca, "and return as soon as I may."

"It might be helpful if you came back via Belia," said the Dark Lord.

"The Yanai will keep us appraised of matters in Belia..." Tarca suddenly realised what he was saying, "Lord Malcarious, you know the Lady watches though her mirror in Yakré'a. She guards Keré'us and is advising us all the time of events. Why must you torment me thus?"

The Dark Lord was smiling, "I was fairly certain but I needed to know. It is a new experience for me to be on the same side as her, however briefly."

"We all have to make new allies now and then," muttered Melin.

"I shall mobilise our men," said Felanin. "You must excuse me. Not a moment is to be lost." He saluted and left the room. Tarca flexed his wings. The Merédur were never comfortable in enclosed spaces and he wanted to be away.

"Go you," said the Dark Lord to him, "and tell her I may perhaps be in her debt, a trifle."

"Your life is but the merest trifle to her," said Tarca, with a smile, and he left.

"And now baths, I think, and good food, for you must be weary beyond imagining," said Melin.

But the Dark Lord did not look weary. There was a new buoyancy about him and Keré'us realised that the exchange with Tarca had cheered him beyond all measure of the words.

For a short time they remained in the haven of the Gate. The last part of the Alliance armies, those of the Sea-kingdoms, five hundred men, passed through the Gate. Keré'us and the Dark Lord went down to speak with Danhé'us, a cheerful bear-like man who was Ranhé'us' lord of hosts. With him rode Herumanus, lord of the tiny kingdom of Loré'as, who had brought a spare one hundred men.

"I have brought all I could," he told the Dark Lord. "I might have brought six more, but they had to stay for the haymaking. If this crew of pirates and those Mordatans had not come I would not have dared send any to the battle. As it is, I know I have to get back before them to keep control of my city."

Danhe'us grinned. "It has such a splendid harbour."

Herumanus winced.

CHAPTER TWENTY ONE

On the twentieth day before the red moon was full, Melin's forces from the Gate set out cross-country for Runi. Keré'us and the Dark Lord rode with them for two days and then went their own way, crossing the Nenaterian causeway and reaching Elen within eleven days, without any of the problems that had beset their outward journey.

It was late in the afternoon of that eleventh day that they were reunited with the others who bore the swords of power in Warany's room. Warany was more than glad to see them. "You would be amazed at the various fates which were rumoured to have overtaken you."

"A few people chased us," said the Dark Lord, "but no one of importance caught us."

"Did the Merédur tell you that the Halucias want to fight on the full of the red moon?" asked Warany.

"Yes, that is what Tarca said. My brother Yatior learned to harness the power of the red moon after he was exiled, to free himself on that one night, but whether he will chance his personal might against us I know not. It is against the tenets of the Eldest to kill, or use Eldest magic on mortals, yet he may argue that some of you are not full mortal. I am sure he will consider me fair game!"

"I had hoped," said Warany, "that if we could remove

Arno, the Halucias and Belians will choose not to fight us."

"Which of us can remove Arno from power?" asked Ranhé'us. "None of us have enough magic."

"Perhaps the four of us," said Selin. "Our swords hold a great deal of power, if only we knew how to release it." He looked to the Dark Lord, "Do you know how we should do it?"

"While Warany yet holds Erindra you will not be able to release their power," said the Dark Lord. "Besides which, they are still in Arno's treasury."

"But we are agreed that Arno is a traitor to the Alliance and must be removed?" asked Warany

Selin said, "I know it is unconstitutional not to try him, but I do not believe there is any other course open to us. He is too dangerous to be made a prisoner. On the other hand it has to be said that Arno has not lifted a finger against any of us yet. Do we plot a murder? And if we do, are we any better that Arno?"

"Well, do we let him destroy our armies and then kill him?" demanded Warany.

Derany and Ranhé'us had the grace to look uncomfortable. It was a very difficult decision.

"Of course," said Selin, his honest face clearing, "there is one amongst us with a legitimate grievance against Arno." They all followed his eyes and looked at Keré'us.

"After all he did murder your grandmother," said Warany.

"You mean you were not intending to murder her?" asked Keré'us.

"Judicial execution," said Warany. "Entirely different."

"I never even knew my grandmother!"

"What I meant," explained Selin, "was that Arno holds Aren in which is set the Star-stone, which is the property of Keré'us."

"Only if I wear a skirt!" said Keré'us. He was very aware how small he was compared to these Warny and André'ans who were now crowding round him. "Look, I've done my bit. I fought with Dar Regan. No one should be asked to fight two sorcerers in one lifetime!"

"That lets me out!" said Warany.

"I am not allowed to," said the Dark Lord.

"And we aren't important enough to," said Derany, for his generation.

"I can't do it," said Keré'us.

"The Elorianen will fight for you," said the Dark Lord.

"And will you be behind me?" asked Keré'us.

"You will not need me," said the Dark Lord. "You have the red witch."

The Quarin looked at his friends, the four bearers of the swords of power - a king, two high kings and one of the Lords Eldest. All forcing his hand. Yet he knew that what they said was true. He had far more magic power than they. It was a time of turning, a time for great speeches, but he just looked hard at them all and said, "Shall we go?"

The corridors were empty, for everyone was at their evening meal in the refectory. Keré'us wondered where Nenya was and if the women would have power to help him. And the Lady, the sweet Lady, would she aid him? He sent a frantic prayer to her and in answer remembered her words *by birth, by the power of your grandmother's curse and by my own power the Elorianen belongs to you...* The stone floor rang under his feet and echoed; his heart was as cold as the stone and sick with fear. Yet, there was a feeling of propriety. The Star-stone set in Aren was his and the right to take it was his.

They came to the doors of the refectory. Keré'us knew

that Arno was aware of him. He smelt the faint odour of evil, as thin and bitter as that of tarnished silver and read Arno's arrogance underlined with fear. The Elta had never lost a battle. Perhaps his fellow sorcerer Dar Regan had been defeated by the Quarin, but no matter, then the Quarin had used the Dark Lord's wild magic. Now, since he walked into this at his own risk, the Dark Lord could not aid him.

With the Dark Lord at his left hand and the other kings behind him, Keré'us strode through the doors. The lords and ladies of Arno's court stopped chattering and looked in surprise at their grim faces.

"So you have returned," said Arno. "That was foolish."

Keré'us walked forwards. There was absolute silence. "I have returned, I, Keré'us, Lord of the House of Abard, even I have returned to take that which is mine." As he spoke his fears vanished. Allowing himself to be swept on by the flood of his destiny he could feel power building up behind him, the power of the red earth, the power of the women in the kitchens and the power of the Lady Yannya. Like a mighty wind it began to press against his back and from his outstretched hands began to glow an orange red light. The stone set in the pommel of the sword, Aren, lying on the table before Arno, began to glow with white light in reply.

Arno lay a hand on the sword. It was warm to his touch and he knew that he could never control it as the Quarin could. In anger he put forth his might and subdued it, so that he could pick it up. He walked round the table to come directly before Keré'us, holding the sword in front of him in both hands, hilt and blade. The white light faltered as the sorcerer twisted it against Keré'us.

"If they have told you that your power is greater than mine, they have lied," he said. "Behind me stands the Lord Eldest Yatior, greatest of all the Eldest."

Keré'us held out his hands, "Give me Aren, for the Star-stone is mine, and calls to me!" For it did, he could hear it, feel it.

"So I shall die first," said Arno and he lifted the iron blade. His magic, like the mist over a frozen lake, took form about him, and his mind spoke to Keré'us of all things cold, of the south of the world where only the white bear reigns in the twilight amongst the cold ice.

The glow of red light swelled between the Quarin's hands and burned bright as he told Arno of the gladness of life and hope, of the glory of sunrise on a summer's morning, and the joy of warm days and warmth of friendship. Behind him he could feel power growing as the slaves in the kitchens began to sing a gloria to the Lady Yannya.

But now another mind, an alien mind, took control, channelling its power through Arno. It spoke of the blackness of deep space where no stars are, of blood shed and bodies cold, of death and the dark, the dark. Keré'us' mind closed in. The darkness was all about him. He could not see although his eyes were open. Panic took hold of him. He cried out to the Lady. He could not fight one of the Lords Eldest on his own. Then the singing swelled and the dark became red, and he could see the bright light from the Star-stone, although Arno was misty as wood smoke in the strange world that threatened to engulf him. The shining might of the Elorianen was slowly lifted against him. He put up an arm to protect himself as Arno brought the blade down. There was pain. Blood flowed down his arm and trying to stop the sword he clawed along the blade to find the hilt. And as his hand touched the stone in the pommel, so blinding white light leapt from it, destroying the darkness, burning the alien mind, lighting the whole refectory with its power. Then Aren was safe in his hands and he slew Arno.

The light dimmed as the power waned and the singing died. Keré'us was aware of the Dark Lord with Erindra in his hand, the blue stone already glowing bright, ready to do battle on the Quarin's behalf if his brother had prevailed. In the half light they caught each other's eyes and knew the loyalty each had to the other. Warany put out a hand to support the Quarin who was swaying, exhausted but exhilarated, clutching his bleeding right arm. Selin found a napkin to bind round the arm. For a moment time stood still until the magic faded. Then came a terrible scream. The lady Elwyn had realised what had happened. She cried out to the guards to take Keré'us prisoner, but Warany stepped forward.

"No," he said, "Arno was a traitor to the Alliance. By force of arms this city belongs to the Alliance now and Keré'us is king. Kneel, kneel before your king!"

The Elta looked at the Warny Lord, at the other kings and princes who stood so grimly on either side of the Quarin and knelt. Hraldor, captain of the guard looked at Warany, who nodded, then knelt before Keré'us.

Elwyn became incoherent with rage, screaming and shouting.

"Get her out of here," Keré'us told Hraldor, who signalled to two of his guard. Then he looked at his assembled people. The power and the gladness of the Star-stone flowed through him.

"You will all leave the hall quietly," he told them, "and on the morrow go about your accustomed business. Now here I stand, by chance your king and, should you dispute that chance, you may challenge me and win the kingship as did I!"

No one moved lest it be taken as a challenge.

"The guard will take Arno's body to the square and there it shall remain for three days, that all may see he is dead and know that he was a sorcerer, and remember that thus will the Alliance deal with all who serve the Lord Eldest Yatior!"

Hraldor's men did as they were bid. As they left the refectory, Nenya entered, her eyes full of gladness, her bearing triumphant. She sank to her knees and touched her head to the ground before Keré'us. "Lord, thou who hast come into thine own, we praise thee, we serve thee and are glad. The sea may ebb, the fire dim, but we the Quarenyos shall remain thy servants."

Keré'us said, "Go, Nenya, tell them in the kitchens, in the stables and in the fields, the time has now come. The Lord of the House of Abard has come into his inheritance. Now he is lord in Elen the Quaren, his people, shall be slaves no more - but I must ask one thing of them, they must remain in their places until after we have fought the Halucias. For eleven days I ask your patience."

"Eleven days is nothing to those who have waited a generation."

"Then shall we eat, lady, for these lords my friends have not eaten tonight, and you shall make us a feast - setting a place, of course, for yourself, for I now give you your freedom! If such be necessary."

Nenya's face lit with a smile, "Lord, it shall be our pleasure to do your will." She rose to her feet and positively skipped out of the hall to give orders, returning shortly with water and bandages to attend to his arm.

So the friends and their allies ate a sumptuous meal, cooked with great skill in the Quarin fashion and many of those who had already eaten found excuse to join them and they laughed and were glad and many times passed round the red wine and the white, toasting Keré'us and wishing equal luck on all else the Alliance set its hand to.

And as they made merry, Teno the sister-son of Arno came to them and bowed low to Keré'us.

"Lord Keré'us," he said, "I beg you believe that I had nothing to do with my uncle's plots against the Alliance and that my cousin Elwyn is equally guiltless."

"My anger was directed only at Arno," said Keré'us.

"Then lord, please hear me. I am here on behalf of the lady Elwyn whom you orphaned this night. The lady apologises for her outburst earlier, but she loved her father, whatever his faults. The lady does not dispute your right to do as you did, but in one stroke you robbed her of father, house, fortune and country. She begs you remember the laws of the Alliance, that he who robs a woman of her protector must in turn become her guardian."

"I shall grant her a pension, if that is what she wants," offered Keré'us.

"She was the highest lady in the land," said Teno, "now she is no more than the slaves in the kitchens."

Keré'us saw Nenya whisper something apposite to Warany and Anya and they all laughed. He wondered what to do. Most of his friends were not exactly sober and he did not think that they were going to be much help to him.

"Teno, you must wait until after the battle with the Halucias, if indeed it will happen now. I cannot make any decision until then."

"By your leave, lord Keré'us, no, for if you are killed in battle Elen will be thrown into anarchy. She asked that you marry her."

Keré'us had no answer for that. Warany choked into his wine and Nenya and the Dark Lord both cried, "No!"

"Tell her," said Keré'us, "I cannot speak of this now, I shall see her tomorrow."

Teno bowed and left. The Quarin looked at his friends.

"The woman has a good point," said Warany, "and what is worse, a legal claim."

"She cannot make you do it," said the Dark Lord.

"She can," said Selin, "it is the law, and it is custom."

"Damn the law," said Nenya. The Alliance as a man turned and scowled at her.

"And damn custom!" added Anya.

"Come the morning, come wisdom," said Hara. "Tomorrow will be long and we shall all have much to do. You mortals and we Merédur must sleep the night." He looked sternly at Warany who was much too old to blush.

Hraldor saluted before Keré'us, "Lord, it was the custom of the late lord to have a bodyguard at his door all night. I personally will stand guard over you, should you desire it."

"No," said Keré'us yawning, "just show me to his chamber. The Dark Lord will give you all a good night's sleep, but you may send someone to bring in a brazier of hot coals to warm it."

The party dispersed. Keré'us and the Dark Lord followed Hraldor to Arno's suite. Here, as a sop to the silken covers the Dark Lord removed his boots and lay on top of the wide bed, hands behind his head. Keré'us snuggled down into the goose feathers.

"You should have demanded Nenya," said the Dark Lord, "I could have sat outside all night."

"I wouldn't deprive Warany," said Keré'us yawning again, "besides, I'm too tired and she is a lot older than me!"

"But very talented, or so I hear," muttered the Dark Lord sotto voce, but Keré'us was asleep.

The Dark Lord woke Keré'us from his sleep at dawn. His arm was a bit stiff, but not too painful. "We need an early start, we must get the Elta organised and then go to the Halucias and see if we can stop the battle at this late stage. I think we can trust Hraldor, for he was with us in the Quaren wars, but I cannot guess how far the rot from Arno has travelled through his people."

"I've seen it all in Mundra. Arno wanted to control people. He won't have given anyone much power. I should think that most of his officers will be capable but not ambitious. Let's have breakfast in the kitchens and then I shall hold a council meeting."

So they broke their fast and then Keré'us held a meeting in the great hall. All his friends joined him. He sent for Hraldor. "Hraldor, you knelt to me last night, will you accept me as your lawful king and continue to serve me as lord of hosts of Elen and the lands of Arno?"

"My allegiance is given to the Star-stone, set in Aren, and I shall serve you as long as you hold it. My men will obey me and all the muster that Arno called up will also follow me. I have always been a man of the Alliance, Warany will vouch for me."

"You had your chance last night to depose me if you wanted to, I do not need Warany's word when your own is proven sooth."

Hraldor bowed. "Now go, and see to your men, we must be ready if the Halucias persist in their demand for battle."

Hraldor departed and Keré'us sent for the chancellor. This appeared to cause a few difficulties. It seemed that Alden the chancellor had been imprisoned. He arrived with soiled clothes and a manacle still on his left wrist. He made a bow to Keré'us.

"What means all this?" demanded the Quarin. "Why did your lord imprison you? Had you been embezzling his gold?"

Alden looked at the young man before him and made a decision. "No more than I required to maintain my style of life," he said. His accent was very well bred. It was a strange contrast to his dress.

"And for this you were incarcerated?"

Alden laughed depreciatingly, "My life style is very modest. No, I was fool enough to ask him where an amount of gold in the treasury had come from."

"That sounds tactless to me."

"I realised that afterwards. Happily he could not execute me while you lords were here, for which I thank you."

"And do you know where the gold came from and why?"

"Much of it was shining new bathens. The gold was good, but the die was an inferior copy. All bagged in hundreds and sealed with the seal of the mines under the mountains. Of course, he did not realise I knew what the seal meant - I pretended ignorance. It was marginally safer. The gold still awaits your disposal. I took the liberty of checking before I attended you." He held out a key to his new lord, "In token of my good will I surrender my personal key to the treasury. The one the lord Arno did not know I had."

Keré'us took the key. He understood Alden and Alden understood him. They were both men who had survived, although one by the merest hairsbreadth, the rigours of court life.

CHAPTER TWENTY TWO

"I do not believe this," said Ranhé'us, "how does he do it? He kills a sorcerer and not only becomes king, we can all do that, but first he claims the most magic sword in Avenya and then he has a treasury overflowing with gold. And he does not even like gold!"

Warany looked concerned. "Dare I ask how much? I assume it was payment for the Halucias, Belia and Elta to destroy the Alliance?"

"That was the conclusion I came to," replied Alden. "The amount - I made it somewhere in the region of five hundred thousand bathens."

Ranhé'us had to be controlled by Selin and Derany. Warany put a hand over his face to hide his smile.

"You will bow to me and be my chancellor?" asked Keré'us.

In answer Alden bowed his knee.

"Then once you have lost your bracelet and found some more suitable clothes, I have my first mission for you. I owe the Lord Ranhé'us nineteen thousand, nine hundred and fifty bathens. I want you to repay him." He held out the key, "You will need this - unless it has a brother hidden somewhere."

Alden shook his head.

"Thank the Eldest!" cried Warany. "Now perhaps that fool Sea-lord'll ask me for my daughter!"

Then Keré'us sent for Elwyn, his heart sinking. She entered the hall clad in blue, the Elta colour of mourning. She inclined her head to him for she could not bring herself to bow.

"Lady Elwyn, I shall be frank with you. I do not want to marry you. However, I understand that it is your concern for the people of Elen which makes you anxious to secure the succession. Now, it was never my intention to become lord of this city, indeed, it is the second kingship I have been offered and I am only continuing as lord because the city cannot run itself. After the battle I hope to make other arrangements, for I do not wish to be tied here. I should then consider passing the lordship back to yourself."

"I cannot have you die without a direct legal heir," said Elwyn. "I do not want to marry you, but it is the only solution. If there had been another way I should have found it."

"Would it be easy to dissolve our marriage after the battle?" asked Keré'us of his friends.

"If there are no children, under Elta law it can be done with the mutual consent of both parties," said Selin.

"Very well, I say this to you lady Elwyn, we are going today to the Halucias in the hopes that they will see the wisdom of returning home, now the forces they expected from Elen will not be there to help them. When I return, if they still insist on having a battle, I will marry you, and after the battle, you will either be a very rich widow or I shall divorce you and give you the lordship of Elen. Save in one thing, I shall free all the Quaren slaves and if they want it, give them land."

Elwyn looked at him. His yellow eyes scared her. He knew what he was doing, this strange Quarin. He knew she was party to her father's plans. But with luck he would get killed in the battle - it might even be possible to arrange it. She forced herself to smile. "That is fair and agreeable to me, lord, you have dealt with me most justly." She bowed and left.

The Dark Lord looked after her departing figure and frowned, "She must have known what her father plotted. What a good thing you have so many friends to watch your back for you. I am concerned about the gold, though. This was all most carefully planned and we had no inkling of it."

"Look on the bright side," said Keré'us. "At least Ranhé'us will be bearable now!"

That afternoon the four and the one set off along the now familiar road for the Halucias camp. Reaching it late the next day, they faced the tribes. Warany again acted as their spokesman, but with Keré'us standing at his side, Aren drawn. The Warney wasted no time in politeness. "Lords of the Halucias, Arno is dead and in his place stands this Quarin lord who now bears Aren. We know that Arno enticed you with promises of gold from the mines, but he is gone and you may honourably depart to your own lands. Go back to the north where the sun is warm, back to your herds and your wide lands, for you will not take ours."

The Gerhart stood up, "Lord Warany, we did not serve Arno. Say rather that we and Arno served the same master. Think you that you can overcome the might of the Lord Eldest Yatior? He has promised us much iron and the very land you graze when he rules Avenya. All we desire shall be ours when the Lord Eldest Yatior is lord in Avenya. It is not too late. You too could serve him and protect your people. Two nights ago he spoke to us through our shaman.

He said we stand on the cusp of a cycle, that the Star-stone passes from one hand to the next and that it will be his to rule over us all in the next cycle."

"He lies," said the Dark Lord suddenly.

Keré'us was surprised. His friend did not usually involve himself in matters like these.

"He lies, the cycle ends, but the Elorianen has already changed hands. It shall not be his, for between the Lord Eldest Yatior and the Star-stone I stand, and others with me."

The Gerhart laughed, "You may choose your Eldest Lord, Warany, for me it is the might of the Lord Eldest Yatior - think you this fallen fool can stand guardian between you and the Eldest might of Yatior?" He looked at the Dark Lord and his lip curled with scorn.

Warany looked the Gerhart firmly in the eye. "Beware the battle," he said, "for those words I shall slay you myself!" He turned to his friends, "Come, the Halucias understand only force, as any baseborn man may do."

They left and returned to Elen. When they reached that city again only eight days remained until the full of the red moon. The Merédur reported the movements of Belia's troops and that the men from the Gate were almost in position.

That night, at supper in the refectory, Keré'us announced his forthcoming marriage to Elwyn, which was to take place the following evening, since he had to be on the road the day after that to keep his promise to join Melin and the forces from the Gate to lead them against Belia.

Also that evening Ranhé'us and Anya plighted their troth and the marriage contracts were signed and witnessed.

The next day was spent in working out the defence of Elen, for being now in enemy hands, the Lord Eldest Yatior would probably want to retake it to use it as he had originally planned, as his base against the Alliance. There were not enough men from the Alliance to protect the city and make war on the Halucias, as they had not expected to have to defend it. They were going to have to rely on the freed Quaren and the Elta muster defending their own. This was not a happy combination but the chance had to be taken, since the Lord Eldest Yatior might not risk his men on a siege when a weakened Alliance could be destroyed immediately. There were no certainties, only probabilities.

In the end Keré'us, with the assent of his friends, appointed Anya and Nenya joint wardens of the city with Hraldor in command of the fighting men.

That evening after the meal, Keré'us and Elwyn exchanged marriage contracts. She promised to obey him. He promised that she and the heirs she might bear him should inherit Elen. The Elta had no fixed form of marriage and merely signing a piece of paper seemed unsatisfactory.

His friends saw them both to bed with the customary ribald jokes, but in the privacy of their chamber he offered not to touch the lady. However, she demanded that the marriage be consummated to fulfil the terms of the contract.

In the morning Keré'us rose early and joined Warany and the Dark Lord for breakfast. Warany would not be taking the men of the Alliance from Elen until two days before the day appointed for the battle, and he might not see the Dark Lord again until then, for he rode with Keré'us. The Merédur were also there. Lara had returned from a night's flight down the east side of the Neros Yannyos.

"Matters grow graver, Lord," said Hara, "listen to Lara."

"I saw armed men marching forth from one of the small east gates of the mines," Lara told them, "perhaps six thousand, and their objective appeared to be Elen. They will be here in six days, perhaps sooner. I understand that Minrod of the One Hand is leading them and he drives his men hard."

"It was fortunate that you thought to look down the east side of the mountains," said the Dark Lord, "I trust that while you were recognising Minrod no one noticed you." Then he softened, "Let the red witch watch for you. I do not want to lose you now, when you are so vital to our cause. It looks as if we shall be fighting three battles at much the same time. You know how we shall need you, so take greatest care. Warany, speak to the women and Hraldor. Warn them, they have to hold off my brother's men while we defeat the Belians and the Halucias. If Elen can hold out that long, we can save her. In six days much can be done to protect the city." He stood up, "Come Keré'us, our road is long and we must be away!"

The Quarin gulped down his last mouthful of yeast pancakes with honey and cream and followed his friend.

Two days later they crossed the Lee'ma Ra by the bridge at Runi (for the first time) and rode on east towards Belia, meeting Melin and Felanin late in the evening. The red moon, almost full, lit the land copper. Camp fires dotted the landscape. They left their horses with the sentries and were escorted to Melin's tent. As Melin and Felanin came out to greet them, Keré'us drew Aren in salute and white light lit from the blade. Both men knelt.

Keré'us motioned them to their feet.

"Lord Keré'us," said Melin, "full glad I am to see you

have indeed taken Aren, and great will be the joy of our men when they find the grandson of the Quarenyos Queens now bears the iron sword reforged in the hilt of Hiruéven. I shall have them called together so you may show them Aren and speak to them." He shouted orders at his aides and they rushed to do his bidding.

Felanin asked, "You do have armour?"

Keré'us shook his head. "I was a sailor. Armour just got in the way."

"These are Belians you are fighting, not André'ans. I'll find you at least a leather cuirass with some hefty brass studs." He sent a messenger who eventually returned with a well studded leather jacket and laced Keré'us into it. Felanin's own armour was shining bronze.

When the men had gathered, Keré'us looked on rank upon rank of small, slight golden skinned men, mostly with brown curly hair, all clad in the brown and orange livery of the Gate. His own people. They all looked at him expectantly.

Melin said, "This is Keré'us, Lord of the House of Abard, King of Elen, grandson of the last Queen and he who bears Aren, the sword that was remade from Hiruéven!"

The men cheered.

Keré'us held out his hands for quiet. Then addressed them as he would have done his pirate catching crew on the *Kemikae*. "Lads," he said, "I am Keré'us, son of the daughter of the last Quarinya Queen and for that reason some of you might think I have the right to call you to battle, even though it is the Belians we are fighting, on the side of the Alliance.

"I'm not quite sure how we ended up on the side of the Alliance, but we have, and that is a good thing because with this battle you are buying your freedom. The freedom to leave the Gate when you retire, the right to buy land, buy that little farm or tavern you have been dreaming about and settle down and raise children. Remember that tomorrow, it is not for me you are fighting, but yourselves!

"Remember also, should we lose, we shall all become slaves of the Lord Eldest Yatior. The Gate is not so far that he cannot destroy it. But we shall not lose! The Great Lady Yannya is with us! I am her Chosen One and I am the bearer of the Star-stone set in the iron sword, Aren!" He drew the sword, the white light dazzled the company and they all cheered.

"Behold, the Alliance may have the Four, but we have the One. May the luck of the Goddess go with you all!" As they cheered again, he bowed and returned to Melin's tent.

The night seemed long and he slept little. The Dark Lord paced up and down outside, wrestling with the problems of the Alliance, trying to guess how his brother intended to fight. Finally in the grey dreamtime of dawn Keré'us rose and joined his friend.

"Little Keré'us, as you know, I am forbidden to shed the blood of mortal men. Therefore, my road lies back to Warany, not forward with you. I pray your red witch guards you well and we shall meet again." They embraced and the Dark Lord set off again towards Elen.

To the sound of drums, foot soldiers marched out, led by Melin on a white horse. At his side rode the standard bearer, carrying the banner of the Gate. It was new, made of bright orange silk, and embroidered in gold with the letter 'Ya', the sign of the Lady Yannya. It was not the banner the Gate had fought under in the old wars, but a new one Melin had adopted. Keré'us was both scared and glad to see it, for he knew it was chosen for him and the reflection that he could now command all the land from the Gate to the river Telga along the western side of Avenya terrified him. Melin's son, Alrin, took the cavalry on the left flank, with Ranin the captain of horse, and their flag was a white horse on an orange ground. On the right flank rode Felanin under his banner of the red fox, with Keré'us at his side.

They marched for an hour, until the sun was over the horizon and then broke their fasts. They were within a mile of the Belians by then.

"This is it," said Felanin to Keré'us, he was grinning. Keré'us could not even smile. He wondered even if he could face the enemy but reminded himself he had faced the André'ans many times at sea. He touched the hilt of Aren and felt the cold, hard Star-stone in the pommel and prayed without words to his Lady.

The trumpets sounded. Into battle marched the Quaren of the Gate against the Quaren of Belia. The morning sun was bright on their harness, their spears and swords glinted in the early light and their banners streamed out on the wind.

They met the Belians head on. This was no duel of tactics and skill but sheer force against force. While the foot soldiers strove, the horse encircled them and took issue with the knights of Belia.

The Haughty Lord of Belia had not marched with his men, but his lord of hosts, Méanden had known the Quaren were coming and had been prepared to meet them. However, his knights were courtiers, dilettantes, ministers who had bought their posts, mostly men who had expected to do little fighting, and a certain amount of looting. They were no match for the horsemen of the Gate.

But they had brought Dar Regan, thirsting for revenge

and he brought his fell magic to bear on Felanin's men. He struck fear into them and their mounts, and they might have fled but Keré'us, drawing Aren, called them on. When Dar Regan saw him, the wheel of the Sea-stone bright about his neck and the absolute power of the Star-stone joining that of the sacred ring and Keré'us own power, he hesitated, then called upon the power of the Lord Eldest Yatior. Yatior's power was split in several ways. He watched the Halucias; he watched Elen; he had to be aware of the Dark Lord and the Lady Yannya and his uncle Mérior, who would be glad to see some diminution of his power. Dar Regan had already failed him once and while Keré'us held the Elorianen and the Sea-stone there was no way Dar Regan could defeat him. It was time to let go.

The sorcerer tried to fling his power at Keré'us and the light drained from his hands. In that moment he knew he had been abandoned. He turned tail and fled the battle.

Seeing Dar Regan fly, many of the knights followed him and Méanden, seeing that they could not prevail, surrendered to save his men. He came to Melin and offered his sword, but Melin said, "Take it to the King" so Méanden offered it to Keré'us.

Keré'us bent from his saddle to take the blade. "Your men remaining are the true soldiers. It saddens me to see you surrender when others whose loyalty should have been stronger flee the field."

"Aye lord, and I beg mercy for these my men."

Keré'us leaned back in his saddle and looked to Melin.

Melin looked impressed. "They are all good Quaren soldiers. Nicely trained some of them."

Keré'us knew they had no facilities to deal with a surrendered army. He thought of the gold in his treasury. "Are you mercenaries, or loyal Belians?"

"Neither, for the Haughty Lord has not paid us for three months. We came out in hopes of plunder."

"Then if I were to offer you real gold for your services you might agree to fight for me?" Out of the corner of his eyes he saw Melin smiling quietly.

Méanden looked at him thoughtfully. His city's survival might depend on his choice now and it was hard to be certain which course to take. But he had started life as a freebooter and knew that a chance never comes twice. Moreover, since the ignominious flight of Dar Regan, the Haughty Lord might even be grateful if he changed sides now. "I should have to speak to my captains first."

"Tell them I shall give them their back pay and a bonus, in gold, if they fight for me. Of course, this is subject to our winning, but I shall pay the widows or dependants of those who die."

Méanden bowed again and went off to speak with his men.

"You do realise," said Felanin to Keré'us, "that we could leave the Alliance to deal with the Halucias, sweep east with these combined armies and take Banéros, and by the time the Alliance caught up with us we would have rallied every Quarin in Avenya and you would be King on the Golden Throne. They would have to sue for peace, for we should be stronger than they."

Keré'us laughed, "I want a quiet life. I don't want to have to look over my shoulder for the rest of my days. It's bad enough being lord of Elen!"

CHAPTER TWENTY THREE

As he had expected, the Belians chose to fight for Keré'us, so with an army two thousand greater than he had brought to the battle, he took his men west to the battle ground agreed with the Halucias.

Tarca the Merédur came to them at evening to find how their battle went, and was surprised to find them already on the road. When he learned what had happened he laughed, "I have known many men, of great valour and might, but you are the only man I have ever met with such a talent for the unexpected. It was well for Warany that you were not leading the Quaren in the Alliance Wars for I fear the Quaren would have won."

"You may tell Warany that I have ignored their blandishments to abandon the Alliance and go east to Banéros. But it is always an option."

"That should certainly amuse him," smiled Tarca, and took his leave.

In Elen the Alliance spent what time there was left to them building up the unfinished walls and making what defences they could. The army of Minrod of the One Hand burnt and destroyed as it advanced and the farmers in the outlying districts were driven before them like so many cattle to the shelter and comparative safety of Elen. Supplies were going to be a severe problem, even though the city was well provisioned.

Warany, bound by his own obligations, led out the mounted men of the Alliance who were to meet up with the Trumarei forces on the battlefield. He had sent four thousand of Arno's muster ahead on foot, leaving a scarce thousand to help defend the city since there was nowhere inside the wall to accommodate more men.

With feverish activity the fletchers made arrows and the freed slaves collected stones but this was no Quarin city with high, broad walls and men trained in defence. Arno had never thought to have to defend himself with his lip service to the Alliance, his sorcerer's powers and the Lord Eldest Yatior behind him.

"I shall be back in a few days," said Warany to his troubled womenfolk.

It was no comfort. Anya, with all she loved now going to battle, would have been in tears had she not been Warany's daughter. "Take care," she said kissing her father and hugging him, smiling like winter sunshine. Ranhé'us she kissed long and lovingly; her brothers she hit and warned not to come back without their father.

Nenya had already bidden Warany adieu. She had other matters on her mind. She could see that the fate of Elen was of no importance to any of the lords of the Alliance or the immortals. Even the Lady had to make a judgement, had to keep the Elorianen safe before all else. But that too was Nenya's mission. Keep the Star-stone safe - at whatever cost.

In the evening of the day after the alliance left, terrified folk came fleeing to the gate of Elen, with the tale that

Minrod's army was just behind them. They were carrying what few belongings they could scrape together. As night fell Nenya, Anya and Hraldor went up on to the gate tower roof to see the fires of an army encamped to the south.

Hraldor looked at the two women and could see that they knew as did he that the Alliance could not attend to Elen before it had dealt with the Halucias. "Our job is to hold out," he told them. "Keep them tied up here until the others get back. What we must not do is let them follow behind the Alliance and attack them from the rear."

"We have arrows enough for perhaps two days," said Anya. "They have run out of the materials to make them."

"Then we shall throw stones," said Hraldor.

"They are bound to want to treat first," said Nenya. "We should be able to make that take a long time. A little feminine indecisiveness will go a long way. After all, Anya, Warany only needs us to occupy Minrod until the Alliance army can turn back to Elen. We only have to gain them a breathing space."

Warany sat in his tent alone with his thoughts. Oh Lady, my heart hurts for my little Anya and for Nenya, yet what other course have I? We do not even know that the Lord Eldest Yatior will attack Elen. Minrod may just turn north east and come up behind us. But in my bones I know the timing is wrong. Had Arno still held Elen, that is what he would have done, but he should have turned east a day earlier to catch up with us. And if he holds Elen, what does he do? Hold the city against us knowing that as soon as we have dealt with the Halucias we shall deal with him? He shook his head.

The Dark Lord came into the tent. He too was frowning, burdened by the lack of certainty.

"If we could but guess," said Warany, "I fear nothing I can see, only this uncertainty."

"We forced Yatior's hand when Keré'us took Aren and killed Arno but the stakes are too high for him to withdraw. He does not have sufficient men now he has lost both Arno's men and the men from Belia. Therefore, he must rely on trickery. If he is to control this cycle he must have the Elorianen in his or a servant's hands. He has but a few brief days to the full of red moon when he can walk abroad. And still those words go round in my head: *Why now together are four swords to make or mar and Aren the darkest far, master of evil?* The four are here. The one rides to our aid at the head of a Quarin army. I remember the high priestess and I wonder. It is all a ploy, the quickness of the hand deceiving the eye, but who is doing what to whom and why?"

"It is all some great magic," said Warany morosely. "Yet how will it all end? I must not deceive myself. I know how it will end. This is my last battle for the power of the four is not tuned to mortal blood and not until my son Derany holds Erindra will the magic flow. Still, it will not be bad now to rest again at Nanenethen's side. I grow weary of life. Shall I grow old by my own hearth until I am half blind and needs must be led? Shall I be ministered to by my daughter-in-law Garnya, showing the world how generous she is to her father-in-law?"

"Nay, say not so old friend, you are not old." The Dark Lord looked at Warany with new eyes. It was true that the seventies were no age for a Warny, but Warany had begun to look old. He had never known anyone who grew old and the whole matter was terrifying, mostly because he loved Warany and partly because he too was growing old. He had always been the youngest of the Lords Eldest, last born, in deep space, before they made planet-fall on Naru, but now his older cousin Tritellior looked younger than he. To the end that Warany was fast reaching he himself must come and within the span of but a few mortal lives.

"No one lives for ever," said Warany, "I would rather die in battle than in bed, even Nenya's bed, so shall I concern myself with naught but tomorrow and the battle. We must get into position and I must speak with all these petty lords and convince each that they are my mightiest warrior. Erindra shall speak of death one more time in my hand, for did I not promise the Gerhart I should slay him?"

To the gate of Elen came Minrod of the One Hand, bastard son of the Lord Eldest Yatior. He was half Daline, small and of a swarthy appearance. His right arm was a bound stump. The Lord Eldest Malcarious had cut off his hand in the wars of the Diadem during his desperate effort to escape from the mines after Yannya had betrayed him. Minrod stood before the gate tower with his herald and his standard bearer, who carried the burning serpent banner of the mines. His herald blew a fanfare on his brazen trumpet. "People of Elen," called Minrod, "you who have dared rebel against the servant of the Lord Eldest Yatior, hear his words through me and surrender this city to him!"

Anya, Nenya and Hraldor came to the gate and passed through to stand before it to speak with their enemy. They were a splendid sight: Nenya was clad in the red and gold of one of the Five of the ruling Yanai, with a circlet of gold in her brown hair. Anya, tall and magnificent, was clad in a dress of midnight blue sewn with silver and pearls, her black hair unbraided and tamed only with a narrow silver crown. Hraldor, silver grey, was clad in a steel corselet which rang as he moved. His hand hovered over his sword ready for

221

any treachery. The wind stirred their hair and garments, their faces were firm and Minrod knew there would be no surrender.

Nenya glanced at the others. Hraldor nodded. She had the most authority for in Banéros she ruled the Yannya temple. "Lord Minrod," she said, "have you not heard, there is another Lord in Arno's lands, the Lord of the House of Abard and we hold this city for him. There is no way we shall surrender until we are too few to defend it. We hold it for he who bears Aren!"

"It will fall ill for you when we do capture it," said Minrod, "and for you lady." He nodded to Anya. "And as for the noble Hraldor, much trust your master put in you and well it has been repaid!"

"I swore on Aren to serve Aren," said Haldor, "and still I do. If your Lord Eldest Yatior held it, then I would serve him, but until that time I serve its present master, whether it please you or no."

"Will you think again?" said Minrod.

"Come," said Nenya, "what can we say? Give us until sunset, we must speak one with another, then we shall answer you. What terms do you offer us?"

"What kind of fool do you take me for?" asked Minrod. "Give me an answer now, yea or nay."

"Then the answer is nay," said Nenya. "So go your way!" She turned and followed by Anya and Hraldor walked away through the solitary gate. They watched as Hraldor's men piled bags of earth and sand against the timber gate to secure it from attack.

"What now?" asked Anya.

"We wait. We gain nothing by wasting our ammunition on them," said Hraldor. "Let us see what they have to throw at us and act accordingly, but set a watch on the roofs. They are mostly thatch in the lower town and dangerous."

The day before the battle with the Halucias dawned clear. The Quaren, led by Méanden's Belians, crossed the bridge at Runi and their van reached the battle ground by mid-day. The Belians were at the head of the army because it was possible that the Halucias had not heard of their defeat and there was a chance they might be mistaken for friends. By the evening all the Quaren were in position to the south and east of the field. Across the scrubby ground of the battle field they could see the camp fires of the Alliance and the Halucias. Tarca came as twilight dimmed with Warany's final orders.

"How fares Elen?" asked Keré'us. He cared nothing for the city but a great deal for Nenya and Anya.

Tarca's face fell, "The men of the Lord Eldest Yatior are encamped about the city. The lady Anya and the lady Nenya are still full of hope, but I cannot see how they can stand against Minrod."

"Two days and we can be at Elen," said Keré'us.

"Two days will be too late." The Merédur bowed and set off back to Warany.

"What do they do?" asked Anya, frowning into the twilight from the roof of the gate tower.

"I am not sure," said Hraldor, "we drove off their first efforts to mine the walls. I do not see what they can do at this distance.

"It looks as if they are bringing up a catapult," said Nenya, "but we can cope with a few stones and a little fire. I have set a watch on the thatch in the lower city."

"Will they attack tonight?" asked Anya.

"We are ready if they do," said Hraldor.

"How still the air is," said Nenya, "and how bright the Lady's moon, yet I am knowing fear for the first time since Arno died."

There came a flash of white wings and Hara dropped out of the sky. "Warany bade me come and watch the night with you."

"I am glad," said Nenya, "for I fear this night. They must surely attack us tonight."

Hara took her hand, "Lady Nenya, the Lord Warany bade me especially remind you that he thinks of you." Then he turned to Anya, "Lady of the House of Wargarny, the Lord Ranhé'us bade me tell you that he also thinks of you. He muttered much else that I did not understand, the burden of which was that he hoped you would be safe without him to look after you."

Anya laughed, "Him, look after me?"

"What," asked Hraldor, "no message of love for me?"

"No, only your death promised if either of these ladies should come to harm."

Hraldor laughed.

"The catapult!" cried Nenya. They all turned to look as a great bolt of fire flew through the air into the city, but instead of the minor fire they expected from it, there came a terrible explosion and fire raced through the thatched roofs. More bolts flew, each exploding with a deafening thunder, setting the buildings ablaze.

"Back to the Hall," cried Hraldor, shepherding them off the roof, "we cannot stop this fire. Get the people into the Hall. The slate roof will hold. It is the only place they will be safe.

"The city is crowded," cried Nenya, "with all the people from the villages. How can we keep them all safe?"

"Women and children in the Hall," said Hraldor, "the old men will be safe enough in the square. The rest are already at their stations. Nenya, organise a watch on the

Hall roof. The rafters are wood and will burn well enough if a fire takes hold. The men on the walls can do little. The enemy are too far for us to reach with arrow or stone."

When they reached the Hall they found that Alden the Chancellor had already organised the people who were fleeing from the fire in the lower town.

"We can stand little more of this," he told them. "We shall be burnt alive!"

"It is that or slavery in the mines," said Nenya.

In the main square Anya was organising bucket chains to put out those fires that might threaten the Hall. There was nothing else that could be done. The lower town was ablaze.

Keré'us went to the tent which had been set up for him and Felanin, but could not sleep. Outside the red moon glowed in the sky, too bright to let any creature sleep. Felanin had spent some time with Melin, but returned and had a goblet of wine with Keré'us. He could not sleep either, so they tried to play Ra-malcron and found it impossible to concentrate.

"Is it always like this before a battle?"

"I don't know," said Felanin yawning, "the only other real battle I was involved with was not like this. When the Alliance attacked us at least we had proper beds." He lay down on his camp bed. Keré'us, still restless, went outside to watch the clear sky dominated by the red moon. He prayed to the Lady that he might acquit himself well and that the Halucias might return to their lands. When he had finished he would have returned to the tent, but he heard the sound of hooves drumming across the turf. His hand strayed to Aren, but he need not have been concerned, for it was only the Dark Lord.

225

"Come on up," he called, "Warany wants to see you!" He reached down and pulled Keré'us up to sit before him and then S'elrashen almost flew over the wastelands to the Alliance camp. It was an exhilarating ride. Keré'us had never travelled so fast in all his life. The wind blew cold in his face and drummed about his ears. In a very little while they were at Warany's side.

All the other lords of the swords of power were there, with Derany. Warany reached up to help the Quarin down from the horse.

"Come and drink with us, Keré'us, for it may be the last time we do and I would not like to leave the world without bidding you farewell, especially as you have put us in the position where the Alliance will be most likely to win tomorrow." The Warny was clad not in his old green Trumaré gear but in dark blue, the sapphire of his Troth-stone glowing on his breast, an answering blue shining from Erindra at his side. In his greying hair shone the crown of the Warny princes, silver set with sapphires. His cloak of blue velvet, lined with grey silk, was embroidered with silver and his heavily quilted coat, which was all the armour he wore, was also traced with silver and sewn with pearls and sapphires.

Keré'us looked at this noble old man and tears came into his eyes. Warany had been as a father to him. They clasped each other and kissed, for the love between them was great, beyond words to tell.

Warany said, "Keré'us I know not what the future shall bring, but if your house and mine walk hand in hand through the years, then the Alliance shall be at peace with the Quaren."

Derany took Keré'us' hand, "Father, there shall be peace. I pledge it!"

Then Warany took a goblet of wine and handed it to Keré'us saying, "Master of the One, shall you and we who bear the Four drink to our success?"

And they drank, the Lord of the House of Abard, The Lord of the House of Wargarny, the Lords of the Houses of Ruén and Kindathen and the Lord Malcarious, Lord of the House of Alvious, High Lord by right of birth of the Lords Eldest: they pledged their faith in the Four and the One, but all knew Warany was bidding them farewell and setting Keré'us in his place. Then the others each bade each other farewell, for none knew what the morrow would bring and departed to their men. But Warany took Keré'us to one side, "Look after the Dark Lord for me, you know as well as I that he is as vulnerable as a kitten. There is no other Lord Eldest I would say this of, but he is true as steel. His kin hate him for he is a threat to them all, but I have loved him. A better friend no man has ever had."

"You know the Lady has commanded me to guard him, and never was a command more willingly obeyed."

"Ah yes, the Lady, if he hated her less I would think he cared less for her. I do not know what is in her mind, but keep him safe for me, Keré'us, that I may go to my last long sleep in peace."

"Friend," said Keré'us, "speak not so."

CHAPTER TWENTY FOUR

As he turned to look for the Dark Lord, Keré'us happened to glance to the west, towards Elen and saw the glow of fire in the sky. He pointed to the orange light and the faces of his friends grew grim.

"Who of the Merédur is at Elen?" asked the Dark Lord.

"Hara."

"And he is not back yet?"

Warany shook his head. They waited a little while, but there came no white bird from the sky, so Keré'us mounted up before the Dark Lord again and rode back to the Quaren.

His camp was quiet, the men fitfully sleeping, the horses shifting uneasily, the red light of the watch fires glowing on the columns of smoke that rose in the still night air. He pulled his cloak about him, for he was cold. "I shall not see you tomorrow?"

"Who can tell?" asked the Dark Lord. He leaned over from the saddle and held out his hand, "Good go with you, little Keré'us."

The Quarin took his hand, "And with you, Lord."

As the false dawn began to cast shadowed light on the devastated city of Elen, there came two explosions that made the very foundations tremble. Anya and Nenya rushed to the Hall roof to find out what had happened only to discover that a section of the wall had crumbled into dust and the men of the Lord Eldest Yatior were already scrambling through the debris.

"Oh Great Lady," cried Nenya, "what shall we do?"

"Surrender," said Anya, "we have no hope here. They will just kill all our people. The Alliance will be able to deal with them when they return."

"There will be terrible slaughter if you do not surrender," said Hara, who was already on the roof, waiting to see what would befall before he took his leave.

Hraldor joined them. "We have no option," he said. "Let us hope they will still accept surrender." He thought to himself that Minrod would be a fool to do so, for the city lay open for the taking. "I shall send the herald to blow the call for parley and we shall all have to go down to the breach."

"I shall take my leave then," said Hara.

"Stay!" commanded Nenya. "Do not tell them that Elen has fallen until after they have fought with the Halucias. I want nothing else on their minds!"

"Then I shall wait a little longer, for I find it hard to lie, even to mortals," sighed the Merédur.

On the field of battle the Halucias made their first error in assuming the purple clad Belian army was still on their side. (A mistake people often made.) They found the Trumarei on their right pressing down from the north behind them to close with a very doughty Quaren force on their left. Before them was the Alliance. They began to draw together rather than stand and fight where they had space.

As they joined the Trumarei in a pincer movement, throwing the Halucias on towards the main Alliance force,

Felanin was heard to mutter that he hoped someone had told the Trumarei that the Quaren were on their side this time. The Fox banner and the Trumaré banner of dark green with the silver nine-pointed star rode side by side, tall Trumarei on their big black horses and the slight Quaren on their ponies and light horse.

Keré'us crossed his own lines to speak with the Trumaré leader of that flank. "What are they doing? Do you know?"

"Not the least idea," said the Trumaré cheerfully. "Hoped the buggers would have stopped to fight. There won't be any room for it in the middle. I was wondering if we should move apart again, give 'em an escape route. No point in killing more than we need!"

"Warany will open up an escape route to the north west for them, between your other flank and the Warny. We just keep jogging along and compressing them. We shall see fighting enough for anyone if they try to break out through our lines."

The Trumaré nodded. Keré'us rode back to Melin, "I'm going to headquarters. See what they want to do. You hold the line with the Trumarei!"

"This is easier than I expected," said Melin. "We certainly need news of what is happening elsewhere."

Keré'us broke into a gallop and rode south round the field of battle, behind the Alliance lines until he reached the battle headquarters. Only the Dark Lord was there with Hara. The other lords were with their men. One look at the Merédur's face told the Quarin all he needed to know about Elen. "The city has fallen. They destroyed the wall with some fell magic and the ladies surrendered to prevent the carnage that would have otherwise ensued. But worse than that, Minrod has bound the ladies and leaving only a token force at Elen has driven on towards this battle with his men."

"Hostages?"

"That was what he sought all along," said the Dark Lord. "And we may guess the price he will want for them. I suppose we had better go and tell Warany, and Ranhé'us."

"Nenya bade me not to tell the Alliance lords, lest they failed to give of their best in battle for worrying about them."

"I think this will concentrate their minds considerably," said the Dark Lord. "What problem did you have, Keré'us?"

"The Halucias are running before us. We have joined with the Trumarei with hardly a loss and are just proceeding at a slow pace west. We did not expect this."

"Hara, go see what the shape of the battle is and tell Melin. He and Felanin will know what to do," ordered the Dark Lord. Hara bowed and flew away. "Keré'us, you and I shall go and find Warany."

The two men rode north east, soon entering the fray. Warany had, of course, ridden out at the head of his people, but when they reached the Warny van, only Derany and Terany were there. Warany, it appeared, had gone to find the Gerhart and kill him as he had promised.

"He is trying to get himself killed," said Derany. "He is sure he will die today."

"At this rate he will," said Keré'us. "Come Lord, we had better see if we can find him." They threw themselves into the mêlée, the Dark Lord even now hitting out with his right hand and using Yadra only to ward off blows. Keré'us followed him, Aren bright in his hand.

They found Warany, uninjured, surrounded by a mass of Halucias who had cut him off from the Alliance. He waved cheerfully as he cut down yet another tribesman. "I killed him!"

"Come here!" shouted the Dark Lord.

Warany cut his way back to them. "Derany can handle everything!"

"Not this," said the Dark Lord, ducking as a spear slid over his shoulder. "Elen has fallen and the women are hostages. Minrod marches to this battle as fast as he may."

Warany's cheerfulness vanished, "That was why they detoured to Elen. We were fools not to have seen it. My little Anya... but the battle is now. They cannot reach us until the evening. By then we shall be the victors. Does Ranhé'us know?"

"Not yet. We tell him next. He is somewhere to the south!"

"I'll come with you," Warany looked about him. They were still cut off and surrounded by a circle of dead and injured. Keré'us had already received several slashes to his right leg, for Aren was too short to defend himself comfortably on horse back against the Halucias with their long curved swords. The Alliance van had nearly reached them and they fought their way back to it, all of them cut and bleeding by the time they reached safety. They paused at the headquarters where a Warny woman bound the more serious of Keré'us' wounds and he and Warany snatched a bite to eat. Tarca was there and reported that the Quaren and Trumarei were holding the back line and the Halucias had begun to move north west, to the escape route planned for them.

The Dark Lord, with Warany and Keré'us then set off to the south, to find Ranhé'us. The Sea-lord was leading all the men from André'as, driving the Halucias hard to the north. They were by now not fighting but running. He left Selin to continue the onslaught and came to speak with his friends.

"Elen?" he guessed.

"Yes, they threw down the walls and took the women hostage. They are marching on us now, as fast as they may. They will be here in a few hours. About sunset Hara reckons. They lead a great beast and he thought it was for the Lord Eldest Yatior who cannot leave the mines until the red moon rises."

"We had better finish this now then," said Ranhé'us. "I'll bring my men west to headquarters as soon as I can." He turned savagely back to the fray.

As Keré'us and his friends turned back to headquarters, the field began to clear. The Halucias galloped for their own lands and safety. A few small fights continued, but the battle was certainly over.

"Their hearts were not in it," said Warany, almost sadly. "We gave them so many chances to go back. They must have really feared the Lord Eldest Yatior if they had to fight."

"They were seventeen thousand men short," said the Dark Lord. "They had no chance. All they could do was occupy us this day and keep us from defending Elen. It matters not now who won this battle. Our true battle is to come, for we must stand before my brother tonight and defend the Elorianen."

When they reached the headquarters, Keré'us felt so weary that he borrowed Warany's tent and lay down on the camp bed and soon fell asleep.

He awoke with a start. It was grey now, twilight. He must have slept for some time. He sat up and to his surprise saw someone standing in the entrance to the tent. The figure was clad in a flowing black cloak, with a great hood that overshadowed the face. He rubbed his eyes and stared puzzled, until the hood was pushed back to reveal the radiant glory of the Lady Yannya. The Quarin sprang off his bed and knelt to her.

"Keré'us!" she held out her arms to him. He came to her as a child goes to its mother, and laid his head on her breast. She kissed his forehead and his weariness fell from him and the tight ache of his wounds faded. Then she stood him away from her and looked at him. "You have done well Keré'us. I gave you the power and you have indeed used it." She paused for a moment and then asked, "Would you give me Aren?"

Keré'us did not question her. He drew the sword and held the hilt out to her. She took it, hilt in her right hand, blade in her left and held it horizontally before her.

"Stand back," she commanded. The blade began to glow with light, red at first, growing in intensity, then orange and yellow. As she shrugged her cloak back, her bright hair mingled with the light, her whole body began to glow and then shone until Keré'us could not look on her. Then slowly the light ebbed away. She pulled the cloak back round her and as the last light faded she brought the hilt up vertically before her, kissed the Star-stone and gave it back to Keré'us.

"The choice I made was mine alone to make," she said, almost to herself, "yet there was no other choice."

In that moment there came the sound of someone running and the Dark Lord entered the tent, Yadra in his hand. He stopped as if struck. The air had suddenly become electric. Between the two ran a power terrifying in its intensity. This was no place for a mere mortal and Keré'us would have fled, except they stood between him and the entrance.

"What do you do here, woman?" demanded the Dark Lord.

THE LADY OF THE RED MOON

"It is my night, the night of the red moon. I told you long ago that none of your kin can bind me on this night."

"I care not what night it is," said the Dark Lord, "you may go." He menaced her with Yadra but she laughed low.

"Will you make me go Lord?" she asked as she pushed the shining blade away to stand close before him.

Her perfume was sweet in his nostrils, she was peerlessly beautiful and strong, and he needed her, not her body - although that would have been sweet - but her mind. How was he to defend Aren and the Star-stone? She would have been at his right hand once, but now he was alone with his brother riding to destroy him and take the Elorianen, what could he do?

"Long ago," she said, reading the fear in his mind, "long ago I gave you the Four to fight with my One. They are still with you, still in the hands of friends. Have faith in men." Then she reached up her arms about his neck and brushed her lips against his, intending to drive him away, for she had matters to discuss with Keré'us. In anger or desire, and he knew not which, the Dark Lord caught her against him and kissed her savagely on the mouth, then let her go and fled the tent.

She stood there for a moment and touched her mouth, almost wonderingly, then regained her grave manner. At that moment, Warany, who had seen the Dark Lord rushing angrily from the tent, came in. He saw the golden woman and threw up his arm to cover his eyes, but it was too late. He had looked into her eyes and the Lords Eldest had decreed that it was death for mortal man to look into Yannya's eyes save the House of Abard. So, having seen his death, he looked on her again, for she was the loveliest woman he had ever seen and she brought warmth to the winter of his heart. And she too smiled, for she saw not an old man but the Warny prince Nanenethen had loved when all the world was young. He took her hand, bowed over it and kissed it. "Lady, sweet lady,"

With love and laughter in her voice she answered him, "Warany, dear friend, I have never thanked you for sparing my women when you failed to sack my temple under the Pleorine hills."

Warany smiled, "You know I did not wish it razed. After all, I had worshipped there in my own fashion so many times!"

They were both laughing.

"So tonight Warany dies?"

"Tonight he returns to Nanu."

"And what then? Shall Anya live?"

"I cannot tell, nor would I if I could."

"Aye lady, but I crave knowledge of that world that I shall not now know."

"Do we not all?" she asked. "Would we not give anything to know the future? The future that neither I nor the Lords Eldest can do any more than guess at."

Warany nodded, "Then I must bid you farewell Lady, for I have matters to arrange, although it breaks my heart to leave your presence for truly you are the brightest and fairest of all womankind. I would I had met you when I was younger..."

"Would I have dared?" asked the Lady, much amused. "But before you go I have matters which I too must arrange with you and Keré'us. Tonight Yatior will come and try to take Aren. His power is great in the full red moon, but so is mine and I am with you. There will come a time tonight, a time of making and breaking - you will know it when it comes. In that moment call upon the power in your swords, speak the rune words and release the power. Warany, you must make sure Derany is at hand. If you can free the power in the Four and then the One the doom of mortality will be lifted from the Dark Lord and he will keep the Star-stone safe."

"And he shall have all his Eldest strength again?" asked Warany eagerly.

"No, not straight away. Some shall return and when I see he grows no longer old, then I shall put the last magic in motion that will free him."

Warany's keen eyes gazed into hers. He saw what she did not say, guessed the price of the Dark Lord's freedom and remembered the price his own dear wife had paid for his love. "Now I must go. Many of my people call to me from the battle field. I must go to bring death to the dying and sleep to the injured."

Warany still held her hand, he put his other hand on her waist, "Sweet Lady, might I kiss you farewell?"

"Did Warany ever need to ask?" she said smiling. He embraced her hard and kissed her with enthusiasm on the lips, then he let her go and left the tent.

Keré'us asked, "Shall I go with you a little way?" She held out her hand and he took it and they walked together.

"Lady, what do you do this night? Why is the air oppressed with magic? What is this night?"

She turned her calm face to him, "A new cycle begins, the cycle of your House if all goes well.

"How can that be when my only son is forfeit to the Lord Eldest Gawen?"

She stopped and there was alarm in her face, the fear of a player who has just seen a most unexpected piece lying in ambush and threatening the king. "Tell me!" she commanded. He drew the Sea-stone out of his jerkin and told her the story in a few words.

As he spoke the fear in her face died and by the time he had finished she was smiling confidently again, as if something had occurred to her and she knew whatever plans she had made were still safe. "Fear not, my hand is over you. He will not dare harm you or your line."

They had reached the battlefield. Men lay dead or dying in the lurid light of the red moon. Keré'us turned his face away for he knew he had killed.

"Go," she said, "you are a man. To you goes the breaking; to us the making and mending."

So Keré'us turned back to his place by the side of the Dark Lord and Yannya pulled her dark hood over her glorious hair and thus sombre walked slowly into the night.

Warany called together all the unhurt horsemen he could muster and formed them up into companies. Led by the Four and the One, banners streaming out bravely in the wind, they took the road west towards the men of the Lord Eldest Yatior. The red moon was bright and the Dark Lord, riding at Keré'us' left, was grim. On Keré'us' right rode Warany, stern and terrible, and then Selin, calm, unable to guess what would come and so making no judgement yet. On the Dark Lord's left rode Ranhé'us, his face set as he scarcely controlled his anger.

CHAPTER TWENTY FIVE

They had travelled several miles up the road when they met a party, mostly on foot, led by Minrod of the One Hand. Further west they could see the dark mass of Yatior's encamped army. Warany reined in his horse and told the trumpeters to signal a halt. Then he and the leaders drew forwards and waited for the heralds to treat. One of them called: "This is our lord Minrod of the One Hand who has come to parley on behalf of our master the Lord Eldest Yatior."

"Tell him to come forward," said Warany. "We hurt no heralds, whomsoever they serve."

Minrod walked forward. The red moon gleamed on his harness and showed him to be unarmed. "I have a message from the Lord Eldest Yatior, my father."

"We shall hear you out."

"The Lord Eldest Yatior, Lord of the Mountains, says, *I would speak to the Lord Eldest Malcarious my brother, if he be among your rabble. Also to the self-styled Lord of the House of Abard.*"

The Dark Lord and Keré'us moved their horses forward, their harness jingling in the quietness. "I am here," said the Dark Lord. "What is it that my brother wants?"

"The Lord Eldest Yatior says, *I would speak to my brother and the Quarin alone, to which end I offer my son Minrod as hostage*'"

Warany pushed his horse forward, "Lord, do not go!"

The Dark Lord looked at Keré'us, "What think you?" he asked.

"We have business with him this night for he holds Anya and Nenya prisoner and we must redeem them. But this is a night of great magic and we only have one magic, that of the Four and the One. We must stay together. The Lady bade you have faith in men, Lord. Trust us now and take all of us with you."

"My sword waits your command," said Selin.

Ranhé'us dismounted from his horse and there came the sound of metal on metal as he drew Garenmegra. "By my Grandfather," he swore, "I shall free Anya or die in the trying!"

"Very well," said the Dark Lord and dismounted. "Hara, guard Minrod well for me." He threw his dark cloak over the saddle bow and unsheathed Yadra.

"Verily," Hara stared hard at Minrod who drew back.

"Fear not," said the Dark Lord, "Hara is the noblest of the Lords Youngest. He would never harm you while you are my hostage, whatever old scores he has to settle." Both he and Hara smiled, but neither smile was kind.

So they left Minrod and, with swords unsheathed, walked up the road to where the Lord Eldest Yatior had set up his throne. Behind them Derany was following as his father had instructed him, but hesitantly, not certain quite what to do and how close to be, when someone came to his side clad in a great black cloak with a deep hood over their face. "Derany, make haste, you must be with them. Take my hand and I shall guide you, but look me not in the eyes or you shall see your death even as your father did." The Lady's slender hand drew him towards her so that she might throw part of her cloak over him to hide him. "Now we are hidden unless he looks hard for us and his mind is on other things. Your father has told you that you must take Erindra when he lets it go?"

"Yes, lady." The radiance of her shining power was almost too much for him. He did not dare look at her but her hand kept him safe.

The Four and the One stood before the Lord Eldest Yatior, the single most powerful of all the Lords Eldest. He who had rebelled against his kin and stolen the Diadem from his uncle Mérior. He was beautiful. His fair hair softly curling, restrained by a wide gold circlet, was the perfect foil for his pale face and straight set blue eyes. His robes were of richest crimson and across his knees lay a sword. He was a true born Lord Eldest of the ruling house, not like his brothers. He was no half breed like Gawen or powerless prisoner like Malcarious. He was the Lord Eldest Yatior and his power numbed them all.

His blue eyes found Keré'us and the Quarin felt his terrible surge of lust for the Star-stone. He had held it once, when he had made Yannya out of a copper statue and it had given her life. This time he would keep it and be Lord of all his kin. Fear stole through the Quarin but the Elorianen shone adamant in his mind like a star. He held hard to it.

"Greetings, self-styled Lord of the House of Abard. Your party is larger than I had anticipated but I dare say we can accommodate you all." Yatior's voice had a dangerous, persuasive quality.

"Greetings, Lord Eldest Yatior," said Keré'us.

"Nay Keré'us, be not so cold. You have the Star-stone, which in truth is mine and I beg you return it before any more harm is done. Then we shall say no more and these ladies shall be returned to you." His men brought forward Anya and Nenya, tightly bound. Despite their bonds they stood there proudly ignoring their captors. Ranhé'us made a faint noise of pain. Warany gripped his sword tightly. Keré'us looked alarmed at his friends.

"The Elorianen is not yours, brother. Keré'us holds it by right of conquest, nor will he deliver it to you!" cried the Dark Lord.

The Lord Eldest Yatior looked at the Quarin, looked with his bright blue, numbing eyes. "Give me the Star-stone now or I shall weight my demand with a greater forfeit."

"Aren is mine and if I gave it to anyone, it would be to the Lady who first gave it to my mother's house. But to none other shall I surrender it for it is my weird, my destiny."

Yatior bent his gaze upon Warany, "Well, Lord of the Alliance, what think you? You have never concerned yourself with matters of the Eldest. You are Lord here, Warany, just say the word and he will give me Aren."

"And the forfeit?"

"A mere trifle. I would have my brother, this lord of darkness, for nothing. A small price to pay for peace in Avenya and the return of your daughter." He laughed at their pain. "Come, I shall not wait long." He picked up his sword, stood up and walked over to the women. "A small price for Warany's daughter and one of the Five."

"To avoid a little pain now would doubtless bring us much pain in the future," said Warany. He looked to the Sea-lord, "I am sorry Ranhé'us."

"If my ransom was such a burden to me, what burden would this ransom be to the Alliance?" asked Ranhé'us.

"Our answer is no," said Warany firmly.

"Are you quite sure?" asked Yatior. He took hold of Nenya's hair and pulled her face to look in his. "Tell them how death feels, Nenya, when it is so close."

"I fear it not!" she cried proudly, her head high.

"Then die!" cried Yatior and stabbed her through the heart. The sight and smell of her blood sickened them, though they had not long since been in the thick of battle. Anya paled and might have fainted, but she was Warany's daughter and with that knowledge she fought the darkness and held her head yet higher.

"Are you still sure?" asked Yatior as he caught hold of Anya. "She is very beautiful, is she not, Ranhé'us. And not wholly mortal. Perhaps I shall not kill her, not yet, perhaps I shall take her back to the mines and tame her. She might be worth the taming!" He laughed at them, poor little mortals. They has so much power in their swords and they could not touch it because Warany was full mortal. The Star-stone was almost back in his grasp. It was all so simple. He would kill Anya for the pleasure, and then he would kill Keré'us. The fools were still waiting for him to make the first move. Did they know nothing? He brought up his sword and brought it down on Anya, but as he did so Warany was there to take the blow.

"Old fool!" cried Yatior, and ran him through. But that bought Ranhé'us the moment of time he needed to cut Anya's bonds and Keré'us and the Dark Lord to spring to their protection. Ranhé'us thrust his long knife into Anya's eager hand. The Star-stone in Aren began to burn white as the four faced Yatior who took a step backwards. Then the Sea-stone began to glow green about Keré'us' neck.

Ranhé'us remembered what he had been told and spoke the rune words on his sword, *Mildur made me,*

Garenmegra, Sea-lord I, the man slayer! Green light leapt from the hilt stone. The night began to take on a strange aspect in the green and white light. While Yatior's full attention was taken by this, Selin bent over the body of Warany to pick up Erindra and toss it across to the Lady. The blue stone began to glow in the field of her power. She nodded to Selin and he spoke the words on Kaeordra, *I Kaeordra, made for the Merédur, windswift sun's light, I the slayer!"* Yellow light from the hilt joined the rest. Yatior, aware now of this new threat, was still able to knock Aren from the Quarin's hand and bent to pick it up. But the Dark Lord was there before him and snatched up Aren and threw it back to Keré'us.

"Speak the words Lord," said Keré'us. Suddenly the Dark Lord understood: *I Yadra fire am, woman's lord and master's bane.*

Red light burnt from the hilt.

Yatior summoned all his power. He stood back and thrust his sword in the ground before him and held his arms outstretched. Darkness and fear began to flow from his hands. He spread his fingers wide and the darkness descended like a cloud on a mountain. The bright stones dimmed, even the Sea-stone faltered.

"Now," said Yannya quietly and placed Warany's sword in his son's hand. Derany held aloft Erindra and spake the words engraved on the blade. *"I Erindra for Erueth made, peace comes in the even but morn brings the blade!"* Blue light leapt forth, proudly at first and then falling away before the darkness of the Lord Eldest Yatior's might.

Then appeared another Lord Eldest, the mightiest and most terrible High Lord Mérior. His brightness put the darkness to flight. "Nephew, I have ordained this. Cease your meddling."

Yatior looked at his uncle, "On your own head be it." He bowed and the darkness began to ebb away.

Keré'us was aware that the Lady had used the moment while Yatior was taken off guard by Mérior to move round behind him.

She shrugged off her dark cloak and put first her left hand to the hilt of Aren over his, and then her right hand took his so they both held the blade. "Now speak the words on Aren."

"I Aren am, fire born of death, destruction's child!"

From Aren, from the Star-stone, light began to flow, burning through the night until that and the red moon made it light as day.

"Now say the binding words," commanded the Lady.

The Lord Eldest Yatior cried out, "Speak not the binding words for they will bring all the Lords Eldest to their doom, yea, even this fallen fool whom you serve. Give no power to the Elorianen for it will destroy us all!"

But Mérior said, "Speak them!"

And by the side of the Lady the Dark Lord said, "Speak the words, there is nothing I love to my destruction."

For a moment Keré'us did not know what words they meant, but then he understood and spoke out loudly. *"Why now together are four swords to make or mar and Aren the darkest far, master of evil?"*

Light exploded all about them, and the ground shuddered under their feet. They were in the centre of an elemental storm which tore and smashed at the very ground on which they stood. Lightning and thunder smote the sky. The earth was not firm. The only thing that was true for Keré'us was the Lady behind him, shining bright gold, her hands still over his. Then she spoke. "Enough. It has begun."

The lights dimmed in the jewelled swords, and the Star-

245

stone faded into darkness. The Lord Eldest Yatior looked at the Lady Yannya, his eyes full of impotent anger. She smiled and he vanished from the sight of the men, returning to his palace in the mines by the High Roads, beyond human sight or understanding, leaving his men to fend for themselves. The Lord Eldest Mérior inclined his head to the Lady, and departed.

The Lady stood back from Keré'us and bowed to the lords of the Four and the One. "Fare thee well, dear friends," she said, and she too vanished on the High Roads.

The Dark Lord stood apart, aware of some change in his body, the return of a little of his Eldest power, which he could not understand. He looked about him and found Keré'us who stood with the others about the body of Warany. Anya was crying silently and Derany too had tears running down his cheeks.

"What means this all?" asked the Dark Lord, but Keré'us understood no more than he. The Lord Eldest could not look on the dead face of Warany. Instead he knelt at Nenya's side. He cut her bonds and then carried the slight body back to the Alliance lines.

CHAPTER TWENTY SIX

Drums throbbed dim in the distance. In the half light of evening, neither day nor night, the Warny, with torches spluttering in the rain, walked behind their lord on his last long journey, from which there could be no returning. Draped in blue and cloth of silver Warany lay at rest, his grey hair smoothed, his face peaceful. One hand lay on the Troth-stone gleaming blue on his breast, the other on the hilt of Erindra. His four friends walked before the bier, swords unsheathed as was the Warny custom. His daughter and second son, Terany, walked with the body with their brother Nareth the Eruéth and uncle Kaerhoieth, brother of Nanenethen. Of Derany there was no sign and many thought him to be dead after the fight with the Lord Eldest Yatior. Terany had taken over the stewardship of the Prince of the Warny, until Derany returned or it was established that he was dead.

A tomb had been built in the Warny fashion, walled with stone, roofed with great timbers and covered with a mound, outside Elen. For despite Anya's pleas that her father should be buried by the side of her mother as he had always wished, Terany had decreed that his father should be buried close to his last battle. Many there felt the same, for there were men enough to build the tomb and dig the great earthwork.

Thus Warany, High Lord of the Alliance, would be honoured as he should be, before all those who had fought with him.

They laid Warany's body in the cold stone chamber and the lords of the swords of power bade him a last farewell. Keré'us shivered as they left, for he had loved Warany and liked not to leave his friend's body in such a comfortless place.

The Dark Lord caught hold of Keré'us' hand for the warmth of another's touch and shook his head heavy with grief. "Even in death the Alliance forces him to break his word to Nanenethen."

"And Erindra," whispered Selin, "how can we leave Erindra here, captive, where it can never be drawn again? Who can guess where and when we shall need it?"

"More important, "said the Dark Lord, "Where is Derany? What happened to him after the fight? I saw him at his father's side, then Keré'us and I went back to our people with Nenya's body. We have not seen him since."

"He muttered something which I did not catch, and went," said Ranhé'us.

"His father made him make an arrangement which was not correct by Warny law," said Selin. "That is why he had to go. The Warny would have made him Prince and he had promised his father not to take that title. But come, this is no place to speak of the future."

They left the tomb and the oak doors were shut by Keré'us. He locked them with a great iron key. At the door of the tomb the next Warny Prince should have been proclaimed, but in the absence of his brother, the Warny High Council proclaimed Terany Steward Prince until Derany's return, and never again have the Warny been ruled by a true Prince. Then in the dark rainy night they returned to Elen, hearts heavy. The next day the doors of the tomb were due to be closed forever and stones and earth would be piled over them.

They gathered together in the room Warany had once shared with Keré'us and the Dark Lord, the three lords, Anya, Nareth and Kaerhoiethen. Terany was not there because the Warny Council were having their first sitting for half a year. Keré'us looked round the room, empty of Warany's gear, but still half expecting to see the old man. "I suppose it is all over," he said. "The Quaren are burned, the Alliance buried and even Warany gone, in that cold tomb."

Anya was crying, not intentionally, but the tears were spilling from her eyes and she could do nothing to stop them. "Why would they not listen to me?" she asked. "How long ago was it he first said he would be buried at our mother's side?"

The Dark Lord sat beside her on the bed and put an arm round her. "The day he and I buried her," he said, "I promised him he should lie there one day." Even his eyes were suspiciously bright. "Keré'us and I spoke to Terany. We argued long and got nowhere. Your brother, lady, is a fool. Where is Derany, why is he not here?"

"Never mind Derany," said Selin, "we have all seen what the Four swords and the One can do. The Alliance needs the protection of those swords. How can we let Erindra be buried? Will not the Lord Eldest Yatior be laughing at us? We cannot let it be buried and with your leave Keré'us, I shall go and get it. Nareth here must take it if there is no other."

"Not I," said Nareth. He was hardly more than a youth, for he was younger than Keré'us, a mere child in the eyes of his Erueth kin.

"I shall take it into my guardianship if it will help," said Kaerhoieneth. "The house of Wargarny is a noble line, one will come forth who can bear Erindra with honour. It was made for my father but I cannot wield it, it has passed beyond the control of the Lords Youngest."

"Then shall we now to our tomb robbing? It is late enough and they carouse in the refectory remembering the good that was Warany," asked Selin. "Shall we seize the chance?"

The Dark Lord suddenly sprang to his feet. There was gladness in his face for the first time since Warany died. "Wait!" he cried. "Not just Erindra! I am going to bury Warany, as I promised him long ago, where he wanted to be buried. I know it matters not where the body is laid. All that was Warany has long since gone from it, but he loved Nanenethen and he was unfaithful enough to her in life without breaking his word in death. Many were the promises he broke to her for the sake of the Alliance and even now they take him from her. No one will know if the tomb is empty. Keré'us holds the key, and the body is embalmed."

Anya's tears dried and her face lit up. "And I shall ride with you," she said. "But I have an idea. Last night a Warny died from his wounds in the hospital. He was not a man from the Grey Halls, but an exile, Gerany of Heru, who killed Therany in a brawl long years ago. He came with Herumanus. He was of an age with my father and much like him, for the House of Heru is related to us on my grandmother's side. We could change the bodies. No one cares about Gerany. They would just think someone else had buried him. There is nothing to stop us. This is our last chance to honour my father's wishes. Tomorrow will be too late!" She turned to her betrothed, "Ranhé'us, you will come with us, will you not?"

"And I," said Keré'us, "I owe him at least that. Just give me an hour to sort matters out with Hraldor and Alden."

"I shall just go and give Danhé'us my orders," said Ranhé'us. "If he goes off at dawn no one will guess I am not with them."

"We were leaving at first light tomorrow any way," said Kaerhoieneth. "It would lighten my heart to accompany you."

"I shall now to my captains," said Selin.

"In an hour then," said the Dark Lord. "I shall go to see to the horses and provisions and bring them to the tomb to wait for you."

So one by one they went their ways and later Keré'us met Selin and they took charge of Gerany's body, Selin saying that Herumanus had left him responsible for the man, since the king of Loré'as had already left Elen. They took the body on a rough stretcher down to the gate where only Hraldor saw them pass and made their way to the tomb on the hillside. Here the Dark Lord waited and another at his side. "Derany!" cried Keré'us, and hugged his friend. "Where have you been?"

"Following my father's instructions," said Derany. "He told me that when I took Erindra it was a sword of great power and I would be bound to it, even as he was. He said it was too much responsibility for the Prince of the Warny to carry, and I must keep in hiding until the Warny went home and let them proclaim my brother Prince. I gave my word on this, but in the battle, after the Lord Eldest Yatior was defeated, I let drop Erindra, for to me it was still my father's sword. I went away to think about matters and how best to follow my father's orders. I was waiting to see the funeral procession to the Grey Halls. I intended to join it and take back Erindra when he was buried, giving him my sword in its place, but now I find Terany has disobeyed his instructions and has made this tomb for him. I came to pay my last respects and take Erindra, but it is locked, and I knew not what to do. I did not want to be seen in Elen."

"Fear not," said Keré'us, "it will give us all great pleasure to put Erindra in your hands where it belongs. Selin has been most worried about it."

At this moment Anya and Ranhé'us arrived and there was more hugging and explanations. Then the two Erueth arrived and the party was complete. Keré'us unlocked the doors of the tomb, lit a torch and by its flickering fire they entered the chill room where Derany laid his hand on Erindra, and the blue stone shone faintly in welcome. He laid his own sword under his father's hand and sheathed the sword of power. They acted swiftly to wrap Warany's body and lay that of Gerany in its place. They composed his body to look as Warany's had done and Derany took off his blue stone he wore in imitation of his father and placed it around Gerany's neck. Then with Warany's body securely wrapped in many layers of cloth and hide and bound to the rough framework of a travois the Dark Lord had fashioned, they harnessed the frame to two ponies. Keré'us locked the gates of the tomb and as swiftly as they could they rode off into the night. They travelled by night, but travelled hard. By the second dawn they had gained the bridge at Runi and here Keré'us threw the key into the Lee'ma Ra that Hréma might guard it until the world ended.

During the day they rested out of sight and at night they rode on trails only the Dark Lord and Warany had known, eastward to the sunsrising and Warany's old love. And for all their dismal burden, they were merry and the miles sped under their horses' hooves. They skirted Belia, crossing the Evénfel high above that city and by the time the red moon was half dark they came to the Grey Halls, that stone city of granite on high cliffs by the sea that the Warny call home. The day caught them, dawning pink behind the strong towers and Derany grieved a little, for his house had dwelt there as Princes since the time when the Warny sailed out of the dawn mists from a land whose name they had forgotten. Now it was forbidden him, who should have been its lord.

The Dark Lord led them up into the beech forest on the hills behind the Grey Halls and there on the edge, where two trees stood together apart from the rest, a beech and an oak, they dug a shallow grave for Warany under the oak tree. They buried him at the side of his long dead wife, piling turfs and stones over the grave.

Then Keré'us said, "Farewell friend, safe journey and a glad meeting," and they wept, for never again would they see their friend by sun's light or moons' light. They looked out over the sea where the bright sun was rising and the Dark Lord remembered how they had buried Nanenethen and thought of all that the years had brought and he too wept with the mortals. "Thus ends the greatest son of the morning star," he said, "for we shall not see his like again."

Anya cried out. She could not bear her grief, but the Dark Lord put his arm round her and spoke gently to her, "Sister, that part of your life is over. You go on to a new life in André'as. Do not forget him, nor remember him always. He was one of many who died for the Alliance."

"All ways lead to new beginnings," said Derany. "Was it only spring when we first met, Keré'us? The world has ended and begun again since then. Now I am a wanderer indeed, for I dare not go back to the Trumarei."

"A new cycle," mused Selin, "what does it all mean?"

Then suddenly, sitting on a boulder where there had only been shadows a moment before, was the Lord Eldest Gawen. Ranhé'us knelt, the others followed him, even the Erueth, but Keré'us did no obeisance. The Dark Lord cried out and with arms outstretched ran to embrace his brother who out of the great love they bore each other had come to comfort him in his hour of need.

"I thought now you could travel the High Roads you might want to spend a while in my halls," said Gawen. "Leave these mortals to make their own mistakes for a space and come and tell me how you defeated our beloved brother Yatior."

"I had a little help from my friends."

"So I hear. There are other plots afoot as well which might interest you."

"Anya and I go south," said Ranhé'us. "The landless rabble are welcome to come with me and I'll find them some land. I could use a good privateer who understands Mundran grain ships."

"Thanks," said Keré'us, "but I have a divorce to organise and I must make sure my Quaren are still free. Then I have to arrange something for the Gate. I promised them land and I must supervise that." He looked to the Dark Lord, "Will we see you again?"

"Eldest time does not run as mortal time." The Dark Lord hugged the Quarin. "Good go with you, little Keré'us. Call me should you need me and I shall be there." Then he took the High Roads. For a moment his image hovered in the air and then it was gone. The Lord Eldest Gawen turned to Keré'us. "Do not think, Keré'us, that because you have some little magic power of your own now I shall not require your son of you. Because of the magic the Four and the One started in the full of the red moon it is impossible to permit your line to continue. I shall have your first born and only son and you shall not deny me his life!" Then he too vanished.

The mortals mounted up and left the new grave and the old under the two trees.

The Erueth rode south east across the mountains to their land. Selin was travelling with Ranhé'us as far as the Gate which took them south west. Keré'us realised that he would be alone on his western road, expecting Derany to go with Ranhé'us.

Derany looked at the others, all with homes to go to and then looked at the Quarin, "Do you want any help?"

"All the help you can give."

And so Warany's son rode with the son of the daughter of the last Quarinya Queen, on to Elen and then the rest of the world.

"I've just realised," mused Derany, "I am about to be related to the Dark Lord, because my sister is about to become the wife of his brother's grandson, which I think makes her his great niece in law. The Old Man would have enjoyed that!"

CHAPTER TWENTY SEVEN

Derany and Keré'us rode back to Elen. It was an uneventful journey.

"Say what you like," said the Quarin, "it was more interesting when people were trying to kill me all the time. The most exciting moment we have had so far was when I argued over the tariff at the inn before last. The innkeeper tried to set his men on me and then they discovered you were with me."

"And then they wouldn't even fight! I haven't drawn Erindra yet in anger."

"Mind you, I am sure that when we get back my lady wife will be intending to liven things up."

"Hraldor and Alden will guard you well though. They don't want to be ruled by a woman."

"We shall see."

After many days they reached Elen and to Keré'us surprise his two councillors welcomed him enthusiastically. Alden was already preparing the manumissions for the Quaren. Elwyn had tried to delay this and they were truly glad to have their lord back.

That night, after dinner, Keré'us sent for Elwyn. She entered his room and bowed before him, but there was something smug about her gestures.

"Lady," said Keré'us, "now I have returned we shall work out the divorce we agreed when we were married."

"I think not lord," said Elwyn.

"Why not?" he demanded. "Is it not written in Elta law that a childless couple may be divorced on the agreement of each party?"

"A childless couple," said Elwyn and smiled. Keré'us knew that the fates had outwitted him.

"No!"

"It pleases me no more than it pleases you, but the fact remains, I believe I am pregnant and until we can be certain there can be no divorce. And if I am to bear your child, your legal heir, you will find me very hard to cast off."

"I did not intend to remain in Elen for long," said Keré'us, "but I see now it will be longer than I expected. I intended to pass the lordship of Elen to you, for I have no wish to rule the Elta. Now I shall pass it to our child, and you shall be regent for it."

"As usual lord, you are fair and proper," Elwyn said and bowed, but these were not the thoughts in her heart.

Keré'us put a hand to the Sea-stone, remembering the Lord Eldest Gawen. "It may not be possible," he said to himself. "We shall see."

One morning when he came down to break his fast in the refectory, Keré'us' heart leapt to see a familiar dark clad figure sitting at a lower table, before him a goblet of wine and a plate of yeast pancakes with honey and cream.

"Lord! Thrice welcome back!" Keré'us rushed to his friend's side and sat down with him.

"I stayed with my brother until we went to Mangawen for Ranhé'us and Anya's wedding. We did not know, because Anya had unaccountably failed to tell any of us, that her brother Terany was seeking to annul the betrothal because he wanted her to marry one of the fat babies. The man is a total fool! That was why she went to André'as with Ranhé'us. I thought it strange that they did not marry at the Grey Halls. I stood in Warany's place for her, as her father." He smiled, he had always liked Anya and had always reckoned that out of Warany's children she was the one most like her father.

"And now you come to put up with us mere mortals again?"

"I find peace unaccountably dull. Keeping the peace, now that is more fun."

"I know what you mean. Well, be the first of our little circle of friends, save Derany, to congratulate me. My wife is pregnant."

The Dark Lord made a face. "Difficult."

"So now I must remain here until she has the child, so that I can then bestow the lordship of Elen on it."

"And if it is a boy?"

"You said you would speak to your brother about that."

"Yes, I have done so, but there is something going on, some reason why he does not want your house to continue. It is to do with the Elorianen. Have you asked the red witch about this? My brother will do anything for her. He imagines he loves her dearly."

"I spoke to her on the night of the red moon, before the magic and she was most concerned, but then said she would protect me."

"I myself may speak to her about it if the need arises - it might well be a girl. Your line usually has first born girls."

"That won't please the fond mama."

"How are they treating you? The Elta generally? I did not think they would want a Quarin in their midst, but they seem to be unworried."

"Alden reduced taxes. I could afford to do so with all that money from the mines. Then we freed the Quaren slaves, and are now paying them wages whether I owned them or not. Most of them were mine, not many households had slaves. The Elta are not generally a slave owning society. They seem to think that self-reliance is akin to morality. They are proud to do unpleasant tasks themselves"

"Pity they are not easier to love."

"There are some plots floating around, but the general opinion seems to be that they want Elwyn less than they want me. And I have Aren."

"Difficult to argue with," said the Dark Lord.

At this moment Derany joined them, delighted to see his father's old friend. "Thank goodness you are back Lord. I was very nearly dying of boredom. These Elta are the most boring people on earth. They neither dance, nor sing nor get drunk, except on beer, which I do not count. And Keré'us has all the fun running the place while I do not know what to do. I thought of going to the Trumarei and joining as a ranker, but someone would be sure to recognise me and then all hell would be let loose."

"I keep telling him to be patient," said Keré'us, "but he wants instant results."

"Some result of any sort would be nice," said Derany.

"I know just how you feel," said the Dark Lord.

"What you could do," said Keré'us, "both of you, if you have nothing better to do, is help me allocate land for the men from the Gate and Belia. I have not been able to get round to that yet and it worries me. When we have eaten, come back to my room and we can look at the maps and see where it would be best to go."

After breakfast they repaired to Arno's tower, which now

belonged to Keré'us'. They spread maps over the table amongst all Arno's strange devices and looked at the land Keré'us owned. "The S'afel here in the north is the boundary, which then runs down the old road to Nenaterian and from Nenaterian to the Gate. All the land to the west."

Derany whistled, "How did Arno lay claim to all that?"

"I certainly felt it was more than he deserved," said Keré'us. "Which is why I have no compunction about granting men from the Gate and any of my freed Quaren slaves some land."

"Where the Wyre joins the Telga looks good. As I remember it, it is good plains land with some forests. It could be well farmed," said Derany.

"But there is no protection," said the Dark Lord, "you are miles away from anywhere. It would be six days to Elen, five to Mara-lei."

"Well, let's build a city to protect the farmland!" cried Keré'us.

"Let me build the city," said Derany, "my father did everything else by all accounts, but he never founded a city!"

"Derany City-founder, sounds a good name to me," said Keré'us. "Look, why don't you take some of my master masons and ride up to the meeting of the rivers and find a good site for a city, see how the farmlands lie and survey the area?" He pointed to the map, "There is even an old ruined Quarin city nearby. You can take the dressed stone from there to build your new city. If you go now you can spend the winter working out how you will do it and in the spring we can build the first new city on the plains since Belia. I don't want to be lord here in Elen, but to be lord of my Quaren people in this new city would be good, where all people are equal, men from the Gate and Belia..."

"Trumarei who want to settle down, second and third sons with no inheritance," cried Derany.

"Even the Yanai, their temples are always full of women and children who need homes. There would be women glad to take on a pioneering man for his protection of their children. We all owe Nenya a debt," said the Dark Lord. The two mortals looked at him hard.

"Your father had a great fondness for the Yanai," he said to Derany, a touch defiantly.

"There is a vulgar answer to that," said Derany, "but I shall not make it."

"That's a relief," said Keré'us. "You see what I mean, I dare not leave Elen, but you two can do this for me. It will work. I leave the arrangements to you Derany. Anything you want you may have."

So within two days Derany and the Dark Lord, together with two master masons, rode north. Keré'us wished with all his heart he could go with them, but he was tied to Elen. Elwyn grew great and the high ranking Elta watched him, trying to guess what he intended to do, wondering if he would in the end decide to stay in Elen. Alden and Hraldor were both interested in the city founding project. Both had separately come to Keré'us and told him they would like to go to that city when it was built, if he was intending to go himself. The Quarin was much cheered by what was either their loyalty, or their fears of what revenge Elwyn would take when she ruled Elen.

The Dark Lord and Derany returned to Elen with the master masons and a great handful of plans surveying the land. Their eyes were full of wide vistas on which a golden walled city had been built in their imaginations and peopled by the landless from all Avenya. Their hearts were full of hope and the master masons, glad of the chance to build a city how they thought it should be built and not following Elta commands, were overflowing with enthusiasm. Keré'us felt angry that he had had to remain in Elen, but he was sensible enough to recognise his anger for what it was and not grudge his friends their freedom. It was arranged that in the spring, as soon as the roads were passable, they would go and set out the city, with a view to beginning to build it as soon as they could. Derany drew up terms of grants of land that were circulated to the Gate and Belia.

That year winter followed hard on the heels of autumn. The frosts were early and the snow earlier still. Soon the white city was truly white, and the roads deep in snow became impassable, even those to Mara-lei and Runi. There were no travellers to bring news and no hope of getting supplies. The stone hall, cold in summer, was abandoned as everyone gathered in the kitchens, nursing the supply of wood to serve the bakery for the whole city.

The Quaren celebrated the Year-turning in one festive day of plenty, but the Elta had no such ceremony and watched in scorn. Elwyn grew nearer her time and was obviously plotting something. Why, Keré'us could not understand, for he was determined to leave Elen as soon as he could.

In late winter a party of Trumarei dared the snows and came to the gate of Elen. Their plight was even greater than that of the people of Elen, for the Trumarei were not farmers and much of their winter supply of grain had not reached them because of the early snow. They brought deer with them, thin but still fresh meat, and Keré'us gave them some of his dwindling supplies of corn. They rested the night and then went back, not daring to stay longer lest the path they had cut closed behind them.

About a week before the new year dawned, when the snows had thawed, men began to arrive at Elen on their way to Mara-lei. Ranhé'us and Selin rode in together, full of humour and glad to see the others of the swords of power again. Selin's wife had borne him his first child, a son, and Anya was pregnant. It was hard for Keré'us to expect them to sympathise with his unwanted wife and child. They had several nights of carousing before they could be persuaded to go on. Derany and the Dark Lord would ride with them, for all the Four were to go, even Derany, since Selin brought word that his brother Terany would not be going.

Keré'us went down to the stables to see them off and the Dark Lord suddenly realised that he was not going with them.

"Has no one told you," he asked, "that Arno always had a seat there, although he was not a member of the brotherhood. The Four and the One sit at the High Table. Besides which, Derany and I need you to help us sell the idea of the new city. Mara-lei is well situated to assist our defence, should we need to call on outside forces, and they may find our corn lands of use, we shall be much closer than Belia, from where they normally get their supplies."

"But if I leave Elen again, it may not be mine when I get back."

"With the Four at your side I am sure you will have no problem, and in any case, did you really want Elen that much?"

"I need the gold in the treasury for my new city and I must keep my Quaren safe."

The Dark Lord sent the others on ahead and waited for

Keré'us while he made arrangements with Alden and Hraldor. Alden instantly grasped the strategic importance of Mara-lei to the new city. "You must go, lord," he said. "It is of great importance for them to meet you and know you. Take my advice as a married man, the lady Elwyn is so great with child that she will be unable to think of anything else for the next few weeks. We can hold the city for you."

So Keré'us belted on Aren and taking the little grey mare from the stables he set off again, to the city of his grandmother's enemies. "It seems strange to me," he said to his friend as they rode the muddy track to Mara-lei. "This time last year they were asking for my death. Now I am mentioned in the same breath as Warany."

"Then a new cycle has truly begun," said the Dark Lord. "I suppose this will be a peaceful meeting, if our friends are any measure. Just congratulations on a battle well won and the large amount of breeding that seems to be going on."

"It's depressing, is it not?" asked Keré'us. "Connubial bliss I mean. They all have their futures mapped out, their blood lines for the swords, kingdoms rock firm. And here are we, me with a wife I don't want and a child about to be born. If it is a boy I must sacrifice him to your brother and if it is a girl I shall have to stay in Elen to protect her from her mother! And you have found that keeping the peace is more fun than peace. You did not stay long with your brother."

"No, I find someone who turns into a black bear and smashes up the board every time you beat him at Ra-malcron makes me yearn for the company of men. Do you know, I never once saw Warany lose his temper, nor you, I have to say."

"I should repay the compliment," said Keré'us. "I have seen you angry, but never out of control."

"Save perhaps once. She tricked me even then, I realise that now. She had to make me leave so she could tell you how to use the Four and the One."

"She did not look displeased with your reaction," said Keré'us slyly, looking sideways at his friend. The Dark Lord's lips softened a little into the ghost of a smile, and he changed the subject.

They stayed at a Trumaré post that evening and caught up with their friends. The next day they continued on to the ninth city. Mara-lei was the old Quarin city of Mara Malac, repaired and renewed by the Alliance and their own Trumarei warriors. It was set high in the mountains and there was still snow on the ground. The bas-reliefs on the bronze doors were etched in snow. Green clad men welcomed them and took them to the palace of the Maren-Ra where they were feasted by him as the most honoured guests.

CHAPTER TWENTY EIGHT

On the first day of spring they sat at the high table, swords before them, but no one took Warany's chair as high lord of the Alliance. Many looked to Derany, but he shook his head, "Nay, for I have promised my father that I would not take any position of power while I bear Erindra. Besides which I am young. You need a man of experience to command the Alliance."

The Maren-Ra looked at his fellow priests, "Then today I shall take the chair," he said and sat down.

The business was boring as such business always is. Taxes, battle casualties, small insurrections put down, and all with a slight air of self-congratulation. Then the Maren-Ra said, "The Halucias have sued for peace and to that end I have permitted the current Gerhart to approach us and present their case, if I have your authority?"

"Wake up," whispered the Dark Lord to Keré'us. "This might be interesting."

"It's Ranhé'us who is snoring, not me!"

The lords of the Halucias walked into the great hall. They were clad in rich furs and skins, wearing gold about their necks. Dwarfed by the mighty pillars and by the tall green clad men who stood there, they came before the high table and bowed deeply.

"Lords," said the Gerhart, "we come in humility to beg you for peace, that we may trade with you once again for iron and bronze. To this end we bring many gifts." He bowed and signalled his servants to bring forward bales of rich furs and wonderfully worked leather. Then he laid one hide on the floor and poured a bag of uncut stones from the bed of the river Telga on to it. He clapped his hands and a girl was brought forward. She was about sixteen, small and very delicate with serpentine black hair and green eyes.

"This is interesting," said the Dark Lord to Keré'us, "he brings a girl like that into a city of celibates. To whom does he think he will give her?"

"This is Eri my niece. I brought her as a bond slave for the lord Warany."

"Warany is dead, did you not know?" demanded the Maren-Ra.

Keré'us thought, how strange he does not know the thing that is most important to all of us.

The Gerhart was thrown. He paused and doubt spread across his face. The Dark Lord saw this, "Little Keré'us, if the Gerhart looses face and we humiliate him in front of both his lords and his enemies, we shall have lost all we fought for." He stood up. "It is most generous of you to give your niece as bond slave to the high lord of the Alliance. It is true that Warany has died, as must all men, yet there is a new lord who will honour your gift. He who is mightier than the Four, he who defeated not only Arno and Dar Regan, but the Lord Eldest Yatior himself. The Lord of the House of Abard, Keré'us, the bearer of Aren, lord of Elen."

"Thank you," muttered Keré'us under his breath, then he stood up, knowing there was nothing else the Dark Lord could have done. Treaties hung on the marriages of Ranhé'us and Selin, Derany was still nominally a Trumaré and the Dark Lord forbidden mortal women. As usual it was up to the Quarin to save their hides. "Lord of the Tribes, it is not right that we should be at war. Peace is the greatest blessing a leader can bring to his people. I speak for all these lords behind me when I thank you for your gifts and hand extended in good will."

His friends all nodded, in thankful agreement.

Keré'us walked round the high table to stand before the Gerhart and the girl. "This is Eri to be your bond slave."

Eri looked at the great lord to whom she was given. Among all that gathering of mighty lords he only was light and bright, he only was small like her and his eyes were yellow, but friendly. She had been scared, but now she knew this man would be kind to her. They had promised her Warany, the old lord, but the younger looked to be much preferred.

Keré'us could see how scared the girl was. He held out his hand. She knelt to him and kissed it.

"Truly," said Keré'us, "of all your gifts this is the most precious and the most fair."

The Gerhart was the same height at Keré'us. They could look each other in the eye. The Gerhart knew that Keré'us had saved face for him. He held out his hand and Keré'us took it, then they hugged each other in the Halucias fashion. "Now must I call you brother," said Keré'us, "for we two and your people and the Alliance are at peace."

"If it be your will, it is our will, lord."

Keré'us looked back at his friends, "Is this the will of all the Alliance?"

They roared, "Yes!" and stamped their feet.

Then the whole gathering took up the cry, "Peace be between the Tribes and the Alliance!" Keré'us held their clasped hands above their heads so all could see, then took the hands of the Kemikae, the second most important lord, and held them up. The Trumarei shouted and stamped their feet again. The Maren-Ra descended from the high table to give the Halucias the kiss of peace, followed by the Four who did likewise.

"I shall get my own back on you," the Quarin muttered in a low voice to the Dark Lord.

"I look forward to that," the Dark Lord replied smiling. "The immortal equivalent of Eri will be most interesting!"

So they feasted the Halucias and after the feasting Keré'us found himself going to bed again with a woman he had neither chosen nor particularly wanted, but with whom he was going to be obliged to make love in order to save face for both the Halucias and the Alliance. Halucias women were not allowed at feasts so someone had directed her to his room hours before. She had lit a candle, gone to bed and was curled up like a kitten, sound asleep. Since it was a very narrow bed (it was after all the Trumarei headquarters) there was nothing Keré'us could do but wrap himself in his cloak and sleep on the floor.

In the morning he awoke to someone tickling him. It took some little time for him to recall the previous day's events and realise that he was in the bastion of male chastity with a girl who had been ordered to do her duty by her entire tribe and, interestingly enough, did not seem in the least bit shy about this. "Lord, I am disgraced, you slept on the floor and let me have the bed. Did you not want me?"

"I was drunk, tired and the bed was too small for two of us. Since you had it, I thought I would let you keep it. For the time being."

"But you have got cold," she said, "should I let my lord get cold? Come, my uncle gave me this bearskin to keep me warm, come into bed with me."

The bearskin was glossy and black, and she was naked under it, her hair the same colour as the pelt, her body white. He began to see his duty as Warany would have seen it, a substantial pleasure. He took off his own clothes, "We shall need every inch we can find in that narrow bed," he said as he slid into it. She giggled and joined him, pulling the bearskin chastely over them both, but not for long.

"You look," said the Dark Lord when they next met, considerably later that day, "as if your revenge on me will be infinitely more pleasurable than I had dared hope."

Keré'us growled. They had to return to Elen the next day for Elwyn's child was due any moment and he had to be there. "My revenge will be getting you to explain Eri to Elwyn!"

The Dark Lord shrugged his shoulders, "You are lord in Elen. Your word is law. Did not your father have anything up to fifteen women in his harem at one time? However, Derany and I were thinking of asking you for a house in Elen of our own. Eri could live there with us until Elwyn has her child, then everything can be arranged properly."

When they returned to Elen a servant was waiting to greet Keré'us and tell him Elwyn was in labour. He went to see her as she lay in her bed.

"Go away," she said, "this is woman's work."

"I was not intending to stay."

"And when my son is born I shall rule Elen as Regent for him."

"And if it is a girl?"

"Then I shall have her drowned!"

It was a girl. The women brought him a mewling red haired daughter with a scowl just like her mother's. His friends were with him. The Dark Lord looked at the crinkled red faced creature, bawling lustily, with distaste. "I can understand her mother's desire to drown her," he said.

Derany took the baby away from him protectively and stroked her soft red hair, "They'll be pleased in the kitchens," he said.

Keré'us laughed, "She shall be called Nenya," he said.

"That is well chosen lord," said one of the women, a Quarinya.

"Is she being put out to nurse?"

"Yes lord. The lady Elwyn will have nothing to do with her."

"Then she is to have a Quarinya wet nurse and it is not to be forgotten that her great grandmother was the High Queen of the Quaren."

"You are stirring up trouble for the future," said Derany, little realising for whom.

Keré'us took his daughter back from Derany and held her up before the fire. "Great Lady," he said, "this is my daughter, thy servant, and although she was conceived in hatred and born in anger, I beg you bless her, that she shall grow to be beautiful, merry and wise."

The fire flared up as Keré'us stepped away. He gave the baby back to the women. They took her away, but as they passed the Dark Lord he put out his hand and touched her soft little head and said, "Peace and joy, little sister."

So Keré'us, now bound to stay in Elen to protect his daughter, bestowed a house on her where she lived with her nurse and serving women, Derany, the Dark Lord and Eri. Through the spring days they made their plans to build the new city and in the evenings they all played with the red haired baby who gurgled and laughed.

At the end of late spring some visitors came to see the daughter of Keré'us. First came two of the Yanai from Banéros, bringing such gifts that they needed an armed guard of the Lord over Banéros' men. It seemed that when word had reached the cities of the birth of a red haired daughter in direct line from the old Queens, all those who had any reason for hoping that the Quaren would once again take power had sent tokens of that hope. Keré'us, the Dark Lord and Derany met them in the great hall and they had brought such bolts of rich fabrics, such jewels, precious woods and perfumes, that the floor of the hall was covered. Even the poor had sent gifts, for such had always been the custom in the days of the Queens, that every person who could sent a gift to the new born queen. The men looked at the piles of precious things and the other gifts, of no intrinsic value but rich in love and Derany asked, "When are you going to overthrow the Alliance?"

There was no answer Keré'us dared make to that before the priestesses. He sent for Alden who gleefully valued and catalogued each gift. The value of that from the Lord over Banéros alone was five thousand bathens.

And this was only a beginning. The Haughty Lord of Belia sent a goblet of solid gold that was rumoured to have been stolen from a temple at Banéros and served ill all those who used it. He was anxious to get rid of it. From Furah came gifts brought by other Yanai. Even the Hill, that last temple of Yannya which Warany had failed to destroy, sent some women under a flag of truce to give the little Queen all they could from their dwindling store of treasure. Unknown to his friends, Keré'us sent them back with a gift of gold equal in worth, in the name of his goddess and theirs, for he would not have their generosity prove their defeat.

And the high priestess, whom he had met that time in Belia, bowed before Nenya and touched her head to the ground, thus acknowledging her as the true Queen.

Even Melin and Felanin came to pay homage to the new Queen, bearing gifts of great worth from the treasuries of the Gate. They too knelt before her and touched their heads to the ground. Melin drew his sword and offered it to her, saying, "Long ago I offered this sword in service of your great grandmother. Now I offer it to you, in the hope of a new age when the Alliance and the Quaren live together like brothers." Nenya laughed and tried to touch the hilt. Then Felanin showed her all the toys the men at the Gate had carved for her, and the clothes which the women had embroidered and gave her father the gold.

"There is one other thing," said Melin. He picked up an old leather trunk with a round lid. It was not very big, but battered.

The Dark Lord stiffened. He knew what it contained. "I wondered where that was."

Melin looked embarrassed, "Shall we say it was left in my care? I have thought long and hard about it and I think that it actually belongs to Nenya. At least it will be as safe with her as it will with anyone, and probably cause less trouble. The Hill do not know I have it." He thrust the box into Keré'us' hands as if he were glad to get rid of it.

Keré'us opened it carefully, wondering what it could possibly contain. It was filled with blackened linen wrappings, but once these were removed he found it contained the crown, pectoral and bracelets of the Quarenyos Queens. He looked at Melin reproachfully. With Hiruévén, which had now been remade as Aren, these were the most precious relics of the Quaren. The great copper crown with its strange mask was black with age.

"What did they deliver to Warany?" the Dark Lord asked.

"Copies made when these were considered too sacred to be worn."

"How old are they?"

"It is said the Lady had Mildur make them for the first Queen, Helya."

"There is something missing," said Keré'us pointing to a small space in the moulded packing next to the bracelets, "Should there have been a ring?"

"You are wearing it," said the Dark Lord with patience, "and Aren would have fitted along the bottom when it was Hiruéven with a shorter blade."

"Anyway, now they are your problem," said Melin.

"Thank you so much," said Keré'us. It was strange to think that he, so recently a penniless fugitive, now held all the sacred relics of the Quaren and this made him the most powerful Quarin in all Avenya. Moreover, he had more wealth than most of the other lords of the Alliance.

So they feasted Melin and Felanin and the two Quaren lords returned to the Gate with the terms of the grants of land for the new city.

Elwyn had had nothing to do with Keré'us since the birth of her daughter, but now she came to him. "Lord, what are you about? I hear so many rumours of a new city, or that you are leaving for André'as, I know not what is happening."

"You should ask me. After all you are legally my wife."

"True, but you have never come to my bed, save the once."

"Would you have welcomed me if I did?"

"It was not part of the bargain you made before you set out for war."

"Then what is your problem? You will not acknowledge our daughter, who is my true heiress. How can I make you regent for her if you will not accept her?"

"The Elta are not ruled by women. Though I was Arno's daughter, what ever happened I would not have been queen. My husband would have been lord. Only by remaining unmarried could I have followed my father as ruler of the Elta. Divorce me now and part from me so that I might be queen.

"But as you say, matters have changed, I have a daughter whom I love dearly and she is my heir and rightful ruler of Elen after me." He looked at the silver fair woman before him and shook his head, "How can you not love our daughter?" Then he relented, "It is true that Derany and the Dark Lord are seeking a site for a city to protect the farmland I promised the Quaren from Belia and the Gate when they fought for the Alliance and not against it as your father wished. When that city is built I shall go and live there with Nenya. The Quaren of Elen will come with me and all the wealth your father took from the Lord Eldest Yatior to betray the Alliance. But if you are reasonable, then I shall make you regent of Elen."

"A city without resources, gold, or slaves?"

"You know your people prefer working for themselves. If gold has such a hold on you I will divide that which I own in the treasury between us before I leave for my new city."

"But you have spent it all on freeing slaves and gifts."

"No, ask Alden. He will tell you there is enough left for a fair divorce settlement."

She bowed and he gave her leave to go, but wondered

exactly what she was intending to do. He did not trust her. Only the fact that he did not really want Elen stopped him caring about what she intended to do. He did wonder if she had an Elta lord who wanted to marry her so he would become king, but that could not be while he and his daughter lived. Perhaps he should take care.

He went to Derany and the Dark Lord. "My lady wife is getting restless. Can you arrange to take the master masons and lay out the city? I want to get the walls started this summer. Melin tells me there are many men from the Gate who will come and work for us in exchange for land and most of the freed slaves here could go to help you. The work on the fields is almost done. They will not have to be back until harvest."

So Derany and the Dark Lord proceeded with the master masons and those Quaren who could be spared. They set out a great city on the slopes of the Wyre hills which ran down to the place where the Wyre river joined the Telga, with walls and palaces, squares and market places, small houses and shops for craftsmen. Men came from the Gate and Mara-lei and some women, mostly Yanai, turned up from Banéros and worked as hard as ever did the men, weaving ropes, mending clothes, cooking and hauling stones when the need arose. As each worked they earned land both within and without the city.

Meanwhile Keré'us waited in Elen, with Eri and the Quarenyos women guarding his daughter. Elwyn had said nothing about the Halucias girl and he had been circumspect in his relationship with her. Elta generally only had one wife but they did not seem to resent his one discreet concubine.

The months sped by. Summer became harvest and all the freed Quaren from Elen were obliged to return to gather the harvest, but the men from the Gate and the erstwhile Trumarei laboured on. They built their own temporary huts and intended to spend the winter there. Derany had already arranged supplies of corn from Belia to see them through the winter and great stacks of wood were made from the trees they had had to fell.

In early autumn the Dark Lord rode back to Elen. "I am instructed to summon you to the city founding. All the foundations of the walls are marked and the stones have been cut for them. The master mason tells me to tell you that until the foundation stone for the great gates is placed, nothing else can be done. This is not true. There are several thousand things that could be accomplished, but the master mason claims that if it is not built in accordance with the rules laid out by Ya Pharen, who forty generations ago built Banéros, it will be unlucky. As I remember, Ya Pharen said, *Boys, I'm not dragging that dammed stone an inch further. We'll have to build the gates here*, but who am I to spoil a good legend."

Keré'us laughed, "I'm glad to see you Lord. Every time I see Elwyn my shoulder blades get itchy and I need your moral support. How soon will it be before we can move into the city?"

"At the end of next summer it should be far enough advanced for you to have a house of sorts to move your family into. I am afraid you will have to suffer the lady Elwyn until then. After the founding the men will be off clearing their own fields in advance of the winter. They have to do that so they can cultivate them next year. The two things have to run together."

Kere'us looked serious. "Let's hope I survive that long then."

CHAPTER TWENTY NINE

Keré'us called all his Quaren people together and told them of the city founding. Not many would be able to go, for few could ride and the distance was so great, but some who had been allocated land set out on the road to the new city, intending to remain there. Elwyn and her people stayed behind. Alden volunteered to remain behind as well, but Hraldor eagerly joined the party. He had a house in the city allocated and many acres of land which he was anxious to see. They were merry as they travelled the new track which had been beaten into the earth by all those who had made a straight way to the new city. The weather was fine and it was a holiday for them all.

Eventually, they came across the valley of the river Wyre and saw the city on the Wyre hills. The site Derany had chosen looked out eastward across the valley of the Telga to the hill where the old ruined city of the Quaren stood. It was from here that a large amount of the dressed stone was being brought although there was a quarry on the west side of the river as well.

It was warm, rich country, and the earth was red where it had been dug. Across the hills and down into the valley, fields had been measured and pegged out, although few were yet ploughed.

Derany was waiting to welcome his friends and showed Keré'us where his estates were to be. He also pointed out those of the House of Abard, and where he had planned the country houses and where their halls were to be inside the city. Hraldor was much impressed by the estates he had been awarded and so eager to decide where to site his country house that they had to force him to enter the city. Here the great lords were gathered: Melin, Felanin, Méanden, dark clad Trumarei, the Maren-Ra and brown clad Yanai, even the High Priestess. Keré'us stood before the gates of his city, holding his red haired daughter in his arms and thanked the Lady Yannya for her bounty in his friends.

The Dark Lord stood by him and put an arm on his shoulder. "This has done more to unite the races of Avenya than ever Warany did fighting the Quaren."

"The fighting had to be done first," said Keré'us, "All of us, you, Derany and I have merely built on those foundations."

"Then I have to say," said the Dark Lord, "that I heartily concur with Ya Pharen's sentiments."

The morning of the city founding dawned clear, with just a hint of early frost in the air. The master masons rushed round panicking, checking their engines for the last time. People from Elen, Mara-lei, Belia and the Gate gathered on the hillside outside the walls and when all the various lords were assembled, the massive founding stone was lowered into place on the left side of the great gate. The Master Mason, Lord of the Guild, who had come from Banéros to perform this honour, poured a libation on the stone and called upon the ghost of Ya Pharen to protect the city. Then he called out in a clear voice, "Lords, what name has this city?"

Derany looked at Keré'us and they both looked to the Dark Lord. They had never called it anything but "the city".

The Lord Eldest spoke in his clear, beautiful voice and all the assembled masses heard him. "This city shall be named Ebrinen, city of good fortune, for it has been built in gladness and joy, hope and hard labour."

The Master Mason cut the name upon the foundation stone. Then the Maren-Ra came forth and blessed it, in the name of the Eldest, and the Quaren looked to the High Priestess, but she beckoned Keré'us. The Lord of the House of Abard, with his small daughter on one arm, put his hand on the foundation stone and felt his power flow into the stone and from it too. "Lady Yannya, hear me, let this stone stand that it might never fail; let this city stand and may she never fail and let her be a monument to the House of Derany Cityfounder and the House of Abard, the Warny and the Quaren, that they shall always be friends and Ebrinen shall be their home."

Then he and Derany kissed, for they were full of gladness. The people shouted, for it seemed to all of them that a new age had begun when men could walk in friendship, one race with another. Some laughed and some wept.

And then the singing began. The Yanai started it, singing the song of safe harvest. They joined hands and the freed Quaren slaves joined with them and a slow dance around the city began. More and more people joined in. The High Priestess took the Maren-Ra's hand and he took Hraldor's. Eri slipped her hand inside Keré'us' arm holding Nenya and caught Derany's hand with her other. The Dark Lord took Keré'us' other hand and that of a dark cloaked Yana priestess on his right. The mass of assembled people joined hands and danced round the city and the magic mounted until all could feel it.

Who shall call up the corn in spring, they sang, *and who shall dance in the fall?*

Round the city they circled. Keré'us saw that on the right of the Dark Lord's Yana was Hara and to his right, the Lord Eldest Gawen. They were all dancing.

Three times they danced round the city and by the end the blue stone in Erindra, the red in Yadra, the Sea-stone and Star-stone in Aren were all glowing, so much magic was in the air.

The dancing broke up and wine and bread were distributed to the masses. The Dark Lord, still holding the Yana's hand, his brother and the Merédur stood apart. Keré'us, Eri and Derany went over to them. Hara held out his arms for Nenya. The red haired baby giggled at him.

"She will be fairer than you, that is for sure," said the Lord Eldest Gawen to Keré'us.

"She's beautiful," said Hara and stroked her red hair. He held her up to the Yana, "Lady, is she not exquisite?"

The Lady took the little girl and kissed her soft head. "Little sister, you have all my blessings," she said. In a sudden movement, she pulled her hood over her face to hide her eyes from Derany and handed the baby to the Dark Lord. "Lord, thank you for this brief moment. I shall not trespass on your good humour any longer." She vanished, her image hovering for a moment in the air.

"I too must go," said Gawen and vanished. Hara spread his wings, bowed to the Dark Lord and took flight.

"Gawen begged me free her for just this moment of time," said the Dark Lord to Keré'us, "She was too proud to ask me herself. A gift much desired from the wrong donor can be very irksome, so I thought it a kind act to allow her to be present." He smiled.

Eri put her hand in Keré'us', "They are dancing still.

Would you join them?" Keré'us nodded and followed her to the dance. Derany and the Dark Lord both watched them go with sadness tinged with envy.

The Warny turned to little Nenya, who held out her arms and twinkled her brown eyes at him. "I'll marry you," he said, "when you're a bit bigger."

She went off into fits of laughter, which was more than the Dark Lord did. "I would be careful what you say if I were you, in this crazy atmosphere of magic!"

"When I am the age my father was when he got married, she will be about twenty five. I think that is quite reasonable. In the mean time I think I shall also join in the dancing, if Nenya is happy to stay with you."

The baby gave the Dark Lord a dazzling smile.

"Little sister," said the Dark Lord, "if you smile at every man like that, Derany will be in for a hard time when you grow up." But the baby only hiccupped and tried to pull the gold earring from his ear.

Keré'us, his family and the Dark Lord rode back to Elen. He wondered what Elwyn had done during his absence, but no one barred the gate to him and all seemed as it had before he left.

Alden was very glad to see both his lord and Hraldor return and quickly took them aside for a very private conference. "Lord, in your absence I am sure the lady Elwyn is plotting with several of the Elta lords and plans to kill you and Nenya. They have not involved me, so I am not certain of the details. What I have been able to do is protect the gold in the treasury. I have parcelled it up into lots that will fit on a mule and just outside the city, in the hands of some men I could trust, I have been accumulating mules. Should we need to make a speedy retreat to the new city, it will not take long to secure your treasure. You will need that to pay for corn this winter. If you will give me leave of absence, I shall go and visit my lands by this new city now and mayhap my family will also go with me and my servants, and we shall take as much of your gold as I can hide."

"You will excuse me," said Hraldor, "but how do we know we can trust you?"

"You don't," said Alden, "but that's your problem, not mine. I will, however, remind you that the Lord Keré'us saved my life."

"He's right," said Keré'us, "I don't have any option, but I did save his life. I might, if I were foolhardy, wonder about your loyalty, but no one who has gone so dewy-eyed over his estates at Ebrinen could possibly be thinking of betraying me."

"Is the land that good?" asked Alden.

"Amazing, rich, fertile red earth, just waiting the plough. Hunting - deer, hare, wild boar. I didn't want to come back, but I think it will not be for long."

"How long do you think we have?" asked Keré'us.

"I think she will try and lull you into a sense of false security. I also think she was waiting to see which of your friends you brought back with you. She would not wish to kill Derany as she does not want trouble with the Alliance and she could not kill the Dark Lord without magical help."

"That gives us perhaps a week. Hraldor, we need to turn back all those who have not yet returned. Send men out you can trust to make them go back to Ebrinen. Get them to ride escort. Then we must secure all the horses. When we go we must take them all with us. We cannot chance Elwyn riding my people down. There are many Quaren here who want to live in Ebrinen who will have to travel on foot. They must be sent on ahead."

"I'll organise the horses now," said Hraldor, "but if you send the Quaren on ahead she will know what you are up to."

"You're right, we shall have to wait a couple of days before we do that. I need a messenger to send to Melin as well, to secure more corn and one to go to Derany. I need men I can trust. I cannot let these messages fall into Elwyn's hands."

"Most of my men are loyal. I can trust all those who hope to get land at Ebrinen."

"Then get to it. Alden, You set out with as much of my treasure as you can, and all that you wish to take to Ebrinen of your own family and goods."

Alden smiled suddenly, "I am sure that my mother-in-law will not wish to ride all that way out just to see a half built city but will remain behind to bully the servants," he said. "Every cloud has a silver lining."

Keré'us found the Dark Lord and told him what was happening.

"Do not underestimate Elwyn," he warned. "She is Arno's daughter. She may even have learned some of his magic."

"I am more concerned as to how we shall over-winter in Ebrinen and how we shall stop Elwyn's men from overtaking the Quaren and slaughtering them. I have told Hraldor to secure all the horses, but strong well armed Elta, even on foot, will soon overtake the laden Quaren."

"Then we shall stop them leaving Elen," said the Dark Lord. "There is only one gate. The damage to the walls that Minrod caused has long since been repaired. Stop the gate and that might give us a few days, enough of a start to get most of the Quaren safely to Ebrinen."

Alden and his family moved swiftly and in two days he left Elen to go to visit his lands in Ebrinen. Hraldor's most loyal men drove carts out of the city and loaded the contents on Alden's mules. Elwyn knew something was happening, but she was not sure what. That night both the lady and most of the high ranking Elta were absent from the refectory.

"Tomorrow," said Hraldor.

"Tomorrow," agreed the Dark Lord.

"I shall secure the gate tonight," said Hraldor. "Those we do not trust I shall imprison in the gate house, together with those who may wish to remain here. There are some such and I would not have them blamed."

After the meal Keré'us went down to the kitchens and called together the overseers "I want you to tell every Quarin to be ready to leave the city tomorrow morning at first light with everything they can carry, but warn them, they are going to Ebrinen and the journey will be long and hard. They have the choice. They can stay here, but Elwyn will enslave them again. And let them not breathe a word to the Elta. Here in the city we are outnumbered and if Elwyn finds out, we shall all be slaughtered."

It was getting late. "Get a few hours sleep while you can," said the Dark Lord. "I shall watch."

"No," said Keré'us, "I must stay here in the Hall, but someone must protect Eri and Nenya. They know nothing yet. Go to them and get the household ready to flee. They are the most precious things I have. I should like to get them out tonight with you as guardian."

"The night is cloudy. There is no light. They cannot travel in the dark. I shall go to them in an hour or so and promise you they shall be the first through the gate, but then you will need me. We have to close the gate when all have left, and you will need me for that. Hraldor's men will protect Nenya and Eri until we can join them."

Keré'us yawned. "Wake me when you return." He threw himself on his bed, fully clothed, and knew nothing until the Dark Lord shook him awake. The room was light, but it was the moons' light. The sky had cleared.

"Your women are already through the gate with Hraldor's family and his best men as protection. Some of the Quaren are already on the road. They waited all night for the moons and were off as soon as they could see. Now it wants only an hour to dawn."

Keré'us looked out of the window to see the whole city stirring. A dark silent tide of people moved through the city. Hraldor knocked on the door and joined them. "One of the Elta lords sent the men of his household out to stop the Quaren. There was some fighting, but we convinced them to go back home. We still have the problem of stopping up the gate. I don't see how we can do that. It's designed to be barred from behind. We could use sand bags, but a couple of men over the walls would soon sort that. Even if we take all the horses, the Elta foot soldiers would soon catch the Quaren."

"Your lord Keré'us and I will deal with that. How long do you think it will take to get everyone out?"

"Most are through already. My men are waiting to follow behind as some sort of protection."

"They sky grows light in the east," said the Dark Lord. "Come Keré'us, we have one last task before we can leave the city."

"Task?"

"In Arno's room of seeing are many instruments which I should not like to fall into another sorcerer's hands. We shall destroy them."

Keré'us followed his friend to the tower. He had often wondered what Arno's instruments were for, but never enough to try them out.

The Dark Lord picked up an iron bar and smashed the strange devices of glass and metal. "That is well done," he said and they descended the stairs to the Hall.

"I think I have started running again," said Keré'us with a smile.

The Dark Lord smiled back at him, "We might even get a fight."

"It feels good to be my own master again."

There were soldiers already fighting at the main doors of the Hall. Hraldor's men had been waiting for their lord and Elwyn's men had attacked them.

"All present?" called Hraldor.

"Yes! Now go!" cried Keré'us and Hraldor's men parted from the fight to run to the gate, followed by Keré'us and the Dark Lord. A party of Elwyn's men tried to stop them, but were soon routed. The Dark Lord did not even bother to draw Yadra. Then last of all they passed through the gate. Hraldor's men were standing by with sand bags and rocks.

"Go on, protect the rest. Do not bother with the gate," the Dark Lord told them. Even now Hraldor hesitated.

"Go!" commanded Keré'us. Hraldor was holding the bridles of their horses. He reluctantly let go and mounted his own.

The Dark Lord pushed his sleeves up, "You remember what the red witch did before Yatior? What we did in Belia? We shall use the magic of the Elorianen to close the gate." As Keré'us drew Aren, light flashed. He held it in both hands, hilt and blade and the Dark Lord put his hands over

Keré'us' and grasped them firmly.

"Now tell the gate to shut, never to open, with your mind."

The Quarin found his power flowing through the sword and with it the power of the Dark Lord. He braced himself for the terrible maelstrom of the Dark Lord's magic, but this time it was more controlled. Since the meeting of the Four and the One he had indeed changed. The Star-stone glowed with white light that slowly became green, blue and purple. The bright, male power of the Elder god poured through him and he ordered the gate to shut and remain so.

CHAPTER THIRTY

It took them eight days to get all the Quaren to Ebrinen. As soon as Alden's mules had been unloaded were they sent back to the rear of the Quaren and ferried the weakest back. All the mounts from Ebrinen were used in this way, from Derany's thoroughbred to the least donkey. The ground was too rough for carts until they reached the old road that led from Nenaterian to Mara-mer, but many were sent out from Ebrinen to ferry them the last part of the way. S'elrashen made the journey to Nentaterian and back many times, day and night, the Dark Lord leading him, with four or five small children in panniers on his back each time.

The master masons and Derany met with Keré'us and Hraldor to decide what to do. They were not sure if Elwyn would pursue them, or if she would just count herself fortunate and take over the lordship of Elen. There were other pressing matters as well. Where would they all over-winter? There were no houses, just the huts for the men, but now they had pregnant women and small children to consider. At least Melin would be sending some grain to feed them and the hunting was such that they would not want for game. Derany had already ordered extra supplies from Belia and these were on the way.

The walls of the city stood about the height of a man in stone on either side of the main gateway and one stone high for the whole circumference. There were no gates.

"We have to decide," said Derany, "do we use our man power to get the walls high enough to defend or do we use it to build huts to house everyone? It cannot be long before Elwyn gets here, if she is coming."

"Housing is the most important thing," Keré'us told them. "Although the winters here will not be as hard as those at Elen or Mara-lei, we must still have shelter. Our families must be protected."

"Suppose," suggested one of the masons, "that we continue with the walls and the rest of you make wattle and daub huts within the city. Those men who were expecting to over winter here have already made provision for themselves. They can still help us. At present you have perhaps five hundred adults without shelter. Get them busy. Even the children can weave panels for the houses or gather the branches to build them. You have a vast labour force that only needs organising."

"We are used to a communal kitchen," said Keré'us, "I shall appoint the kitchen overseers to organise that. It will save much time if food is prepared centrally, and make rationing easier. Then the other able bodied people must build huts. The grandmas can look after the children to free up the young mothers. Then if the masons need extra manpower to pull a stone in position, they can call up the other men for an hour or so."

So all of them, from Alden to the smallest child who could mix mud, helped to make the wattle panels and cover them with daub. By the time Elwyn and her army came in great array to Ebrinen, they were all housed in some fashion and the walls stood the height of a man around the whole city. The gates were make-shift, but they were closed.

Elwyn was clad in white, wearing magnificent armour like a man and riding a white horse. Her lords with her were also mounted and boldly accoutred, but her forces, some three thousand strong, were on foot. The lords of Ebrinen were scruffy, mud stained and weary. They came onto the battlements of the main gate and Derany spoke to her. "Greetings, lady Elwyn."

"Greetings, lord Derany."

"What do you want of us?" asked the Warny.

"I want Keré'us my husband and his Halucias whore. The rest of this rabble is of no concern to me. They will die in the snow or come crawling back to us in Elen to beg a crust in return for their life's service, but Keré'us I shall have, and kill him now!"

"If he does not want to come, as seems possible," said Derany, "what do you propose to do?"

"We shall starve you out. Whence come your promised supplies? The Gate? Belia? They cannot pass us. Are your wells dug yet? You will never get past us to the river. We can wait, we can wait for ever!"

"We shall not hand over the least of our people," said Derany, "and certainly not the lord Keré'us."

"Then you will die a cold and hungry death."

In the great round thatched hut that was acting as Keré'us' halls the lords talked. It was one thing to put on a brave front, another to make their people suffer the realities of starvation.

Keré'us said, "We shall have to leave. There is no other option. Eri and I will go tonight and make our way to the mountains and along them to the Gate."

"That is madness," said Derany. "You have seen those mountains in winter. Besides, I thought Eri was pregnant?"

"She only thinks she might be," said Keré'us, "and there

is no other way out. Have I led my people out of captivity to deliver them back to Elwyn just to save my life? No, I shall run, as I always have. Ranhé'us wanted me to live with him in André'as. I shall go there."

"What of Nenya?" asked the Dark Lord.

"She did not ask for Nenya. I shall leave her here. Derany will look after her."

"You will die on the mountains if you do not die at Elwyn's hands," said Derany, desperate not to let his friend go to what could only be certain death.

"I shall go with them," said the Dark Lord. "After all, I have had it comfortable here in Ebrinen too long."

They all laughed. The Dark Lord's clothes and boots were caked in mud, his face was smudged with it and he had not taken off his clothes, let alone changed them, for he had worked without ceasing, day and night, since he had left Elen. His words greatly cheered Keré'us.

"Keré'us must leave us," said Hraldor. "Elwyn will destroy us otherwise."

"We do not need to let Elwyn know of this immediately" said Alden. "We can buy you a few days' grace."

"So be it," said Keré'us. "Hraldor, get me two horses provisioned and S'elrashen ready. We go tonight."

The old soldier bowed and left the room.

Derany held out his arms to Keré'us, "You have given me so much, yet I have robbed you of everything to keep it." They hugged each other.

Keré'us shrugged, "What are friends for? Look after my daughter. You know how much I love her."

"Always," promised the Warny. "Give my love to my sister when you see her in André'as."

That night three horses, with hooves muffled, carefully

picked their way through the rear gate of the city which led to the mountains and into the night, while Quaren archers stood at the ready to kill any ambush.

They hurried away and travelled while the moons were in the sky, then rested until dawn and rode on again, following the pattern of flight which was now too familiar to Keré'us. But Elwyn was not stupid. By that same dawn she had men circling the city who picked up their tracks. She then sent her foot soldiers back to Elen and with her mounted lords she followed the trail.

By the end of the third day, the land became so rough on the mountainsides that it was obvious they would soon have to walk and lead their horses. Eri's strength was now their only concern. A Halucias on foot is no match for an Elta.

In the dark watches of the fourth night, the Dark Lord sat and turned over the possibilities in his mind. He was beginning to think that there was only one way to save them, but it was not a way he wished to take. As the silver moon rose he woke Keré'us.

"Tomorrow, if we continue on foot, they will be on us and you will die and Eri with you. I can see no hope. There is no Warany to rescue you here, no Merédur to take sword against the Elta, no Gate. No chance. You cannot use my magic or that of the Lord Eldest Gawen against mortals and I think there must be about twenty of them."

"I am aware of that," said Keré'us, his heart going cold at the thought, "but I have done my part, I have led them away from Ebrinen. At least I have kept my word to the Quaren slaves and the men of Belia and the Gate."

"There is one way Elwyn and her men cannot take. One way I swore I would never walk again." The Dark Lord pointed at the mountains beyond them, the Neros

Yannyos, snow lying on the lower slopes of the black smoking peaks which lit the western sky dull red. "There are many roads that lie under the mountains. By tomorrow we could be at the Mara-mer gate. I do not say that we shall not die if we walk that road. I say only that we shall put off the hour of our deaths."

"Then that road we must take," said Keré'us, "I do not want Eri to die." He looked again at his friend and realised what he had said. "Lord, you said *we* and not *you*. I would not ask you to take any unnecessary risks for us."

"I have it in mind to take a hostage to secure our safe conduct," said the Dark Lord, but the matter obviously worried him. However, he had made up his mind, "Come, if we die, there is an end to it. If we do not we have no cause to worry. Wake the woman."

They set off again, leaving the two mortal horses, the Dark Lord leading Eri perched up on S'elrashen's back. By morning they had reached a wall of black rocks with many cracks and fissures in them. They soared above their heads like cliffs, but here were no stormy seas to breast, only the sighing pinewoods which lapped about their feet.

There was a narrow deer track that led along the cliffs. The Dark Lord lifted Eri down from his horse to follow it. In the misty dawn the noise of the armed Elta rang behind them, although they could not be seen. "Quickly," ordered the Dark Lord and they followed him up the track to a large opening in the cliff wall. "Get inside, go right to the back!"

"But there is nothing here, only a blank wall!" cried Keré'us.

"You are going to have to wait here," said the Dark Lord, "I have to take my hostage before we attempt this road. It will not take long, for as I told you, time does not run for we Eldest as it runs for you. Give me Aren, for I need the Elorianen and you take Yadra. Fear not, I shall return as soon as I may!"

Keré'us handed over Aren and received the unfamiliar hilt of Yadra. The Dark Lord, much to Eri's astonishment, vanished. Eri slid her hand in Keré'us'.

"He won't abandon us," said Keré'us as reassuringly as he could. She clung to him and he held on to her. The sound of the pursuit grew louder.

"Get in the shadow!" They pressed themselves against the wall of the cave, deep in the gloom, and waited, hearts pounding, trying to breathe silently and watching the opening.

They saw an Elta, silhouetted giant-like against the bright opening. He found the cave and gave tongue.

The Dark Lord took the High Roads to Yakré'a and materialised in the room of seeing. It was empty so he ran though the corridors to find the Lady's sitting room, lit by a deep shaft in the rocks that let in the bright morning. She was there giving orders to her Daline people, a quiet domestic scene into which he stormed, his travel stained clothes muddying the deep pale carpet, his face full of desperate anger, Aren bright in his hand.

She leapt to her feet. Her Dalines drew their ready swords and turned on him. He had downed two of them before she could cry, "Stop!"

The Dalines obeyed and retreated.

Eyes blazing, she approached him. "What means all this?"

"You will come with me!"

"Will I indeed?"

He caught hold of her arm and held Aren at her throat. This was serious. Even the blade gliding over her skin drew blood. All she had ever worked for hung in the balance now. All her power was needed, but what to do?

He twisted her arm behind her back. "You will come with me!"

"I think not!"

He twisted the arm harder. Pain jagged through it and a bright bead of blood rolled down the iron blade of Aren. "We go to the Mara-mer gate! Now, woman!"

"I shall do no such thing!" But enough of his Eldest power was returned for him to tear her through time and space to stand before the Mara-mer gate.

Still holding her, he spoke the word to open the gate. Keré'us, fighting with the long sword and Eri with a knife, saw the back of the cave roll open to reveal a lighted corridor. The Dark Lord called them and they ran to the gap to join him. Again he spoke and the doors rolled shut behind them. Keré'us looked aghast at the sight of his bright Lady, blood dripping from a fine line on her throat, her eyes furious. The Dark Lord pulled on her arm again to stop her struggling. For the first time, Keré'us feared him.

"Silly me," said the Lady, "I thought I was going to be murdered, but it would seem we are to have some other fun first. Why are these mortals in the mines?"

"It happens to be safer than the outside world at the moment," growled the Dark Lord.

"Then the outside world must have changed since I last saw it."

"Lady, Elwyn's men would have killed us," said Keré'us.

"And you think the Lord Eldest Yatior will not? What do you have in mind?"

"We travel a little way south," said the Dark Lord.

"Well, I suggest that you get moving. It is not safe to stand still in the mines, even in these distant corridors Yatior may yet see you."

"Go then!" The Dark Lord pushed her savagely forward. She dug her heels in.

"You know the way. What do you need me for?"

"I do not know the mines as well as you do, and besides, should we meet with my brother, you may prove a useful hostage."

"He does not want me. He has outgrown my charms."

He whispered softly into her ear, "Did you think I meant alive?"

Eri gripped Keré'us' hand and he held it hard. The Quarin was horrified. In the year he had known the Dark Lord, he had never believed he could act like this.

"So to this end you hurt two of my people and kidnapped me?"

"You were unlikely to come willingly!" He changed his grip on her, for she had ceased to struggle and in that moment she took her chance, dug an elbow back into his stomach, bit his hand and kicked his shin. He lost his balance for a fraction of a second, for she was strong and angry. She wriggled free, again biting the hand that held Aren and wrenching it from him.

She stood before him holding the hilt and blade, threatening him with all her power, her yellow eyes blazing. So strong was she that he stepped backward, his face full of the realisation that he had probably cost them all their lives.

She laughed bitterly and threw the sword at Keré'us' feet.

"Shall we start again, my lord?" she asked. "You had but to ask and I would have helped you for the sake of

Keré'us and his woman. You Eldest think that violence answers every case!"

The Dark Lord stood before her, blood dripping from his bitten hand, surprised by her words that she would willingly go with them, risking her life as he would risk his. He had not for one moment considered this.

"If you would go with Keré'us, would I do any less?" she demanded scornfully. "Keré'us is my chosen servant and I shall give him all the aid I may, even if that means I must help you also. I am not one of your merciless Eldest women. Now shall we go?"

She haughtily led the way along a corridor of grey slate. Bright lights shone from the ceiling and the path was smooth. They soon joined a tunnel broad enough for two files of men to pass, where the walls were covered with cream tiles and at junctions mosaic pictures appeared on all the walls, presumably showing their destinations. Eri quietly touched the Dark Lord's injured hand and offered him her kerchief. He wrapped it round the wound on his hand and the smile he bent on her was so gentle that Keré'us knew his friend was as true as he had ever been. No one, Keré'us reflected, can annoy us as much as the women we love and I think my dear Dark Lord has more than a little affection left for the Lady, and she for him.

The Lady Yannya led the way fearlessly, bright in her dress of purple and gold, her stormy hair glinting copper under the endless globes of light that hung from the tunnel roof. It was an alien environment. There were no smells, no sound of the wind, only the occasional echo of their feet on the hard stone and dripping water. Sometimes a stream ran in a drain along one wall or the other, only to vanish from sight through a culvert. Eri began to falter. They had had no rest the previous evening and she was already weary from their flight.

"Slow down," said the Dark Lord, "the girl is worn out. We walk these roads with two mortal Quaren and you stride on as if it were Warany we had with us."

"Oh that we did," she sighed, her eyes mocking him, but slowed her pace. "It is urgent," she explained, "that we drop a few levels. We are bound to be seen on this main road. I want to reach the ninth stair and descend to a lower level. Then you can rest, but not before."

"How much further?"

"Half an hour or so."

"I shall be all right," said Eri. Keré'us took her hand again.

CHAPTER THIRTY ONE

The tunnel suddenly widened into a great circular hall, without floor or ceiling, a mighty flight of stairs that soared above their heads and plunged into the depths. Neither Keré'us nor Eri had ever seen anything to compare with them. The mosaics on the walls recorded the fact that this was the Ninth Stair and they were on the Main Level. There was a sudden noise of harness jingling.

Other tunnels joined at this stair and the Lady pushed them back into the comparative shadow of a narrower one. A party of twenty men marched up the stair, clad in armour and fully armed. She put a finger to her lips. The Dark Lord rested his hand on Yadra. When the stair was silent, they all dared breathe again.

"They are hunting for us," said Yannya, "Did you think you could enter Yakré'a without Yatior knowing? You sprang every alarm in the mines. Well, at least they search the wrong level, but that sort of luck will not last long. Now, we must descend this stair."

Cautiously, they took the downward stair, checking at each level, descending six levels in all. Keré'us and Eri's ears were bursting, their legs ached and neither of them could go much further. The Lady looked at them with compassion, "Not far now and we can rest," she told them.

The passages of the lower sixth level were rough hewn, the lights were far apart and the roof much lower. Eri stumbled and almost fell. Yannya spoke sharply to the Dark Lord. "If you carried the girl, we would travel much faster. She can barely put one foot before the other."

The Dark Lord bent over Eri and lifted her easily. She clasped her arms round his neck and he walked on unfalteringly. Eventually, they turned to the left and, following this new road for a little, they came to a room. It had no door and the only furniture was a stone seat that ran round the three walls and a stone cupboard which held ewers and jars.

"There is water here," said the Lady "and food. Do you have any provisions?"

"Just a little, biscuit and dried meat," said Eri.

"There will be biscuit here and probably dried fruit." She poured some water for them and they sat and ate raisins and dried apricots from summers the mines had never known. When they had eaten, the mortals lay on the floor on their cloaks to sleep. Keré'us held Eri tightly. She smiled at him. She knew there had been no other course they could have taken and did not blame him. At least they were still alive!

The Dark Lord and Yannya sat on the stone seat, he in uneasy silence, she calm and relaxed.

"Where are you taking us?" he asked eventually.

"I have no idea," she answered, unconcerned. "We would stand a greater chance of escaping in the south, for those gates are less heavily guarded, but I think that we would be caught long before then. There are few gates like the one you entered by. Yatior is systematically blocking them. If only you had spoken to me first, mind to mind, instead of using brute force in your usual Eldest manner, we could have been prepared. When we get to the East Gate complex, the whole area is under close watch. What we need is Mildur. He alone can walk from north to south unseen."

"Shall I go and get him?"

"How? He cannot travel the High Roads and any use of your power would be picked up by Yatior in his room of seeing. I tell you, Yatior has these mines so watched that even a mouse might not walk here unseen."

"A mouse may be, but a red witch?"

She laughed softy, "You touch my vanity, lord. Our only weapon is indeed my mind which does not think as you Eldest think. What did you intend to do next?"

"Get out as soon as we may."

"It is winter on the mountains. Eri is pregnant. Even Keré'us is weary. They would be safe with Melin at the Gate, but nowhere nearer. I think we shall go south."

"And the East Gate? My brother's palace?"

"I think we can pass under the palace. Your brother did not make the mines. He merely stole them from the Dalines. Yes, south it is. If you were intending to leave at the next gate, Yatior will expect you to do just that. Why should he expect us to prolong our peril by remaining here a minute longer than we need?"

"But he knows you are with me."

"Does he? You pulled me here by force, using your own power on the High Roads. He will not know that I have left Yakré'a, not yet. I did not use the magic in Aren, I merely threatened you. I have learned to be circumspect in my journeys through the mines." She leaned back against the wall and closed her eyes. He looked at her in the dim light, her long copper eyelashes gleaming on her smooth cheeks, her wonderful stormy hair. He touched a copper curl that had wantonly lain on his dark coat, then closed his own eyes to shut all matters of desire from his sight and from his mind.

When the mortals woke, they set off again, back to the main tunnel and then on. Eri and the Lady walked ahead, for Eri had to set the pace, and the two men walked behind. They rested, sitting in the corridor, their backs to the rough wall, ate and went on. Day and night were nothing but a half remembered dream. They used another rest station, slept and walked on. It was as if life had never been anything but empty passages of grey stone. Then the colour of the rock began to change, and there were more side passages. At the next rest station, the Lady spoke to them. "We are now approaching the East Gate. This is the part of the mines where the Lord Eldest Yatior lives. There are many people here and it is closely watched. I intend to take us deep, into old workings where it is dark and any enemy must carry light. It will be hard and I must ask you to bear with me. I have not often travelled these roads before and I may get lost, so be patient if I have to choose a way I am uncertain of or we have to retrace our steps. Now you must eat and sleep, for although this rest station may lack comfort, in the lower levels you will remember it as luxurious."

The mortals slept. The Dark Lord sat, eyes closed. He had no responsibility here. He could do nothing but offer his strength as protection. She looked at him from hooded eyes and half smiled to herself. Even to be near him was a pleasure. Reluctantly, she turned her mind back to the road they must take, the turns and the dangers.

When the mortals woke again, she led them down a right

turn as soon as she could. "We are now going to find a back stair," she explained, "and go down another four levels to the lowest level of all." She glanced at the Dark Lord, "Even lower than the dungeons, which are all on the ninth level."

"We need not speak of that," said the Dark Lord. "We may see them soon enough and I for one shall not be sorry if I never see them again."

Their narrow passage led to a junction where it crossed a wide passage, brightly lit like the main road they had travelled above. Dalines, with tools over their shoulders, marched southward. The Lady pushed the others back out of sight, but she was not quick enough to hide herself. The leading Daline stopped. She walked forward to speak with him and the others moved quietly back.

The Daline bowed, "Great Lady, you should not be walking these roads. Word is out that the Lord Eldest Malcarious walks the Mines with Aren. He has come surely to kill you. Lord Eldest Yatior seeks him hard, and if Lord Yatior should find you, or Lord Malcarious find you, things will not be good for you."

"I do not fear either Lord Eldest, but thank you for your warning, Nandur." She bowed to him, "I would not ask you to put your people at risk, but it would help me if you did not mention that you had seen me."

Nandur bowed to her, "The people of the Dalines know in whom they put their trust, Great Lady and were we of Mildur's people, free in Yakré'a, we would not betray you. Yet we are not free, we work for the Lord Eldest Yatior's gain, not our own pleasure. It may be we have to tell, to save Dalines from hurt."

"Then you must tell."

"But not until asked." Nandur bowed again and ran off

to join the rest of his party. The Lady rejoined the others. "He is so scared of Yatior that he will tell of seeing me, but only if asked. The punishment your brother inflicted on them when he found out a Daline woman had freed you will be with them for ever.

"Should I have stayed there then?" asked the Dark Lord.

"I personally wish you had!" she retorted, for she was trying to puzzle out the route and balance the Dalines' affection for her against their fear of Yatior. She led them across the main road and followed the small tunnel until they reached a stair, a narrow spiral cut out of the rock that led down into darkness. Each level they passed was dimmer than the last and the fourth, where the stair stopped, was in pitch darkness. All they could see was the faint nimbus of light that glowed about the Lady.

"There are lamps in a cupboard at the bottom of the stair," she said, finding them and lighting one, which she gave to Eri, then she took a spare bottle of oil. "I dare not take more. It might be noticed. There is always some movement in the amounts, for they are taken from one stair to another, but few people come to level ten for any reason."

Three passages led away from the foot of the stair. The Lady hesitated and then took the most westerly tunnel, turning left at the next two forks to bring them back further onto the road she wanted . She grinned at the Dark Lord, "That should confuse things a little," she said.

"Why aren't these tunnels lit?" Keré'us asked her as they walked on.

"They are not meant as roads. They are worked out seams of ore. There is no point in lighting them and it is because of the lack of light that I am using them. The Lord Eldest Yatior will not be able to find us here and any enemy must bear light. It gives us a slender chance."

The tunnel narrowed. Eri stumbled on the rough floor, so the Lady led them, followed by Keré'us with the lamp, then Eri and the Dark Lord behind them. There was no room here to draw Yadra and fight, but he held a dagger in his hand.

There were many turnings and junctions. Yannya hesitated often in the maze and more than once they had to retrace their steps. The silence in the roots of the world smote on their ears. Occasionally, a stone would be kicked and skidded along the floor, bouncing off the walls. The Dark Lord hated these tunnels. He kept close to the others. He was a creature of the wind and sky and had surely risked the mines as a last resort.

They rested, ate and went on. Keré'us felt like a child again. In these alien surroundings he could not make any useful contribution. The Lord and Lady were at home in their adult world, speaking of things neither he nor Eri could understand. Even Aren, that he had killed for, he knew would be taken from him if the need arose and wielded by the Lady, to whom the Star-stone truly belonged. Again, they were being told to sleep. Eri was desperately tired. He put his arms round her and kissed her in the darkness that fell as the Lady put out the lamp to save oil. The Dark Lord sat by her, as close as he could be to the only light, the faint glow about her.

"By my reckoning we are going south west."

"Yes, we have to avoid the main gates and I have had an idea to shorten our journey. It may not work, but it will be worth trying."

"The mortals will not stand much more of this."

"I know, but what else can we do?"

"Things are too quiet," he brooded. "My brother must surely know where we are, so why is he doing nothing?"

"He is probably waiting for us to come up to a more convenient level where there is light. It would waste a lot of man power to pursue us here."

"Yes, but we would be so much easier to kill down here. What does he do?"

"He plays us like a cat plays a mouse."

He nodded, "You may well be right. In that case I shall cease to worry. Trouble will doubtless find us soon enough and even I need rest."

She laid a shining hand on his, "Then rest, Lord, we shall need all your strength when the fighting starts." She shut her eyes and in the gloom, he glanced at her. It was long since he had spent so much time with her and the old power she had once held over him was still strong. He would have to be on his guard.

When Eri woke, they continued the journey. After about an hour, there came a short exclamation from the Lady. The passage was wider here and they could all join her to see what the matter was. Water lapped against the stone floor and the lamp light glistened on it as far ahead as they could see.

"Well done," said the Dark Lord.

The Lady turned on him. She had already realised the implications of this flood and his sarcasm was too much for her. "I should like to have seen you do better."

"Well, I could not have done worse!"

"Can we wade through?" asked Keré'us.

"Not here, it is moving, rising. This is no normal flood such as we might get when the snow thaws. This is engineered. My guess is that Yatior is flooding the lower levels and will have men posted on all the stairs to capture us, or else we remain here and drown. Either way, he achieves his aim. They must be running the waters of the mere on level seven into these workings." She frowned, "There is a stair due west of here. We had better try to make for it. There is a chance it is not guarded or we can fight through. I fear we shall have to pass through the water to reach it, but not through this tunnel. Come, hurry! Every moment counts now!" She led them swiftly back to another turn, but this too was flooded. They retraced their steps, tried another way and again that was filled with the dark, swiftly rising water.

"There is nothing for it. We must get through. We shall have to wade! Leave your gear. Nothing else matters now except speed!" She hitched up her skirts and waded boldly into the water. Eri followed her, abandoning her bundle. Water pushed against them. It foamed and churned in the light of the lamp the Dark Lord still held in the rear. They fought their way down the tunnel, passed a side tunnel through which the water raced and were soon onto dry land.

"That was a near thing," said the Dark Lord.

"It will be if you stand there talking. Come on!" Yannya led the way at a run, the others hard on her heels. On higher ground, they paused to catch their breath.

"It surged suddenly and is rising faster," called the Dark Lord from the rear. They ran on.

Suddenly, the Lady put out her hand to stop them, and whispered. "We shall soon be at the stair. Let us hope that it is not guarded." They advanced a hundred yards more before they could see the faint light from the stair well. She put her finger to her lips and walked back to the Dark Lord. "Would you go and see if it is guarded? my light will show," she asked quietly. He nodded and silently made his way up the tunnel. Then, in the dark between the stair and the

Lady's faint glow, he stumbled over rocks which had sometime fallen from the roof.

At the sound a voice shouted, "Lights!" The tunnel was flooded with light from the stair well. After so long in the dark, it burned their eyes and for precious seconds they had to fight to see again. Several thunderous reports rang out, echoing around the tunnels.

"Back! Back, they are armed!" called Yannya. She caught Eri's arm and pulled her back down the tunnel, pushing her and Keré'us down the first turning they came to. "Get down there! Never mind the water!" Then she returned to find the Dark Lord. Within moments, she was back, dragging him behind her. Keré'us now led the way through the rising flood.

The current in the water was pushing them south, which meant that as long as they could keep ahead, they were safe, but it was soon waist high and rising faster than ever. They had lost the lamp in the confusion and now they only had Yannya's light, although it seemed brighter than it had before. Keré'us looked back to the Dark Lord and saw that he had blood on his coat.

"Get on," said the Dark Lord, "waste no time!"

They struggled on. The waters rose and the roof of the tunnel dropped, so that the Dark Lord had to walk bent. Then the thing which Keré'us most feared happened. The waters reached the roof.

"We cannot go back," said the Lady. "Come, take my hand Keré'us and we shall find a way through." Keré'us took her hand, breathed deeply and swallowed, half swimming, half walking, through the drowned tunnel. His lungs felt that they would burst. He tried to surface to see if there was any air, but cracked his head on the stone roof. She pulled him down and on, and then suddenly there was air on his face and he could breathe freely. He struggled through the water onto dry land and leaned against the wall, gulping in air.

Yannya brought Eri to him, closely followed by the Dark Lord. They scrambled up a slope in the tunnel and found somewhere to rest, safe from the water.

The Lady asked, "Were you hit Lord?"

The Dark Lord looked at his arm and moved it experimentally. "Nothing much," he said. "They need more than that to hurt one of the Eldest."

"Is it still in there? If it is I had better get it out." She opened his coat, made him slide his arm out and looked at the wound. "Only a flesh wound. Give me your knife." In her faint light she worked on it, while he grumbled at her when she hurt him. It did not take long. Keré'us was curious to see what had hit him, but the thing she showed the Dark Lord looked like no bolt he had ever seen. He was suddenly aware of the gulf of understanding between them.

She stood up and went back to look at the water. "It has slowed," she told them. "We must rest now and think what to do. We have to go up, but they are watching every stair. But not every stair... I know one they will not watch." She looked at the two exhausted mortals and the Dark Lord with his injured arm. "I know a way, but I doubt that you could travel it, any of you."

CHAPTER THIRTY TWO

Despite their soaking wet clothes, the mortals slept huddled together. The Lord and Lady sat a little apart from them, heads bowed in weariness.

Yannya asked suddenly, "How long will it take your arm to heal?"

"Perhaps a day. I still heal slowly. You did it no good poking it around. At least it was me they hit, not one of them."

"Will you be able to climb with it in about twelve hours?"

"Probably."

"And help Eri?"

The Dark Lord made a face, "I doubt it, and she is our weak link. We are only as strong as she is." He sighed, "I shall do what I can, but I fear I know the route you are intending to take and doubt that any mortal could make it. It is the Daline Stair you have in mind?"

"Yes. How do you know of it?

"I have travelled it."

"When you escaped?"

"I cannot say."

"But you know how desperate our plight is."

"I knew that anyway. Think you I would have chosen the mines if another way was open?" He sounded weary and close to defeat.

"But we are not done yet," said Yannya. "We yet live and if we make the stair we stand a chance!"

"If we both know it, surely my brother Yatior knows it?"

"I learned of it from Mildur. He would die before he told another, especially Yatior."

"His daughter freed me. If she knew, then others may know too."

"It is possible," mused the Lady, but a faint smile curved on her lips. None was more aware that only she, Mildur and the Dark Lord knew of the stair.

Keré'us awoke, stiff and cold. Darkness pressed in on him and only the faint glow from the Lady told him that he was not blind. "Has the water risen?"

"No. If anything it has fallen a little, but we are still trapped on this level. When Eri wakes we must go on."

"I am awake," said the Halucias girl. She looked at her damp clothes and shook her head. "The sooner we are on the road the sooner our things will dry."

"Well, one thing is for sure," said Keré'us, "there's no breakfast." He looked to the Dark Lord, "Is this road we must take so hard?"

"It is bad, but I have done it before."

"What about your arm?"

The Dark Lord was surprised by the question, "It will soon heal. My body heals much faster that yours." He held out his hand, "See, the bite marks the Lady gave me have already gone."

"I can always make them again," she said.

They set off again. The lower levels were warm and once they got moving their clothes began to dry, although Keré'us thought his boots would never be the same again. After about two hours they came to a place where the ore workings turned back into proper tunnels and widened out. The Lady stopped them. "This is going to be the part which makes or breaks us. We are about to enter a huge cavern. This was the Meeting Hall of the Dalines, before Yatior enslaved them, and most of the tunnels on this level run into it. We are coming in from the south. The north end will still be under water. At that end there is a straight stair which will be guarded. It is the only known stair and leads to the eighth level, for it rises two levels. We, however, will leave by the Daline Stair which rises three levels and will bring us out above the level at which the guards are probably set.

"Once we are in the cavern, we must not speak for we would be heard easily, so I shall explain it all to you here. The stair is made in the first part of a series of metal pegs set in the rock wall, hidden from sight by a waterfall. I am afraid we shall get wet again. The second stage is a narrow ledge that zigzags up the cavern wall. It changes direction four times in all. I shall travel with you each in turn, for you will need my light. I shall take Keré'us first, then Eri and then the Dark Lord." She bent and tore strips from the rich fabric of her overdress. "Wrap these round your hands, for the metal pegs will cut them. Now follow me and remember there will be guards at the other end of the cavern at the top of the straight stair, but there will be water between them and us. My light must go out, so hold hands. You will know when we get there by the sound of the waterfall."

Her faint glimmer died. Keré'us took her hand and Eri's, the Dark Lord her other and she savoured the brief contact and laughed in her heart at the firmness of his grip. Carefully she led them, keeping in her mind all the time an exact picture of the cavern. She knew it well, for in the days when she was first made to be Yatior's concubine, he had held feasts here for all his kin and she had danced for them.

There was the smell of wet rock, the sound of the stream that fell from the eighth level and then the plashing of droplets on her face. She took Eri's hand and placed it in the Dark Lord's, then took Keré'us' and put them over the first pegs. Hidden by the waterfall she allowed a little light to show and by this he began to climb. He began well, but weariness soon overtook him. He clung to the pegs and caught his breath. Then he drove himself on. The pegs were set for Dalines, a head shorter than him and were at the wrong intervals. Once he nearly fell, but her hand was there to hold him. Then the pegs stopped. For a moment he panicked, but she spoke soft into his ear, "Ledge on your left, pegs as hand holds but set low."

He shuffled along. The ledge was only just wide enough for his feet. He could not see it and knew that it would stop and change direction after a while. He was terrified of falling. The pegs bit into his hands and tore them, he was cold and tired. Then the ledge failed. For a moment his foot hung in nothing, but the Lady had her hand firmly clasped round his wrist and pulled him back. She breathed in his ear, "Two pegs up and then the next ledge is to your right."

There were three more changes in direction and on the last he could see a faint glow of light. It sped his feet and at the top of the stair he scrambled through a culvert into a lit corridor. Exhausted, he lay on the floor and closed his eyes.

The Lady had not wasted time with words but vanished back down the stair. At the foot she set Eri before her and laid her hands on the pegs. The Dark Lord touched her shoulder and whispered softly in her ear, "Follow now. Save time." She smiled. He obviously feared she would not come back for him.

Eri was strong from the outside life of a woman of the Halucias. Half a year with Keré'us had not changed her habits much and she was still strong, but the early days of her pregnancy, lack of food and sleep had taken their toll. The Dark Lord had to leave Yannya to guide her up the second part of the climb, for he knew that he too would need help since the hand holds were set much too low for him to use. When the Lady returned, he clasped her hand eagerly. She smiled to herself, then led the way, showing him holds he could use. Slowly, they made the climb up the ledges and were on the top one when disaster struck. Light flooded the cavern. The Dark Lord, blinded again, slipped. Somehow she caught his arm and for a moment took all his weight as his feet found a hold and she pulled him back up. Shaken he leaned against the wall.

"Come on!" she whispered. "They watch the tunnel we left, but it is only a matter of time before they look up!" They scrambled the final stretch of the climb and at last all were safe in the tunnel.

"We must get to level six and find a rest station," said the Lady apologetically. "We cannot rest here."

"I'll carry Eri in a little while," said the Dark Lord, "but I cannot yet."

The stair was not far and they clambered up it to level six. The Dark Lord now carried Eri and the Lady held Keré'us hand, urging him on to the comparative shelter of the rest station, but as they reached the room a party of Dalines leapt to their feet and drew strange weapons from their belts. The Dark Lord did not bother with Yadra. He dropped Eri and put himself between the Dalines and the mortals.

"No!" cried Yannya and pushed the Dark Lord back, her tired mind refusing to work as fast as she needed it to.

"Mildur," she said and whether she addressed the Dark Lord or the Daline even she was not sure. The Dalines advanced, weapons at the ready, for they had last seen the Dark Lord kidnapping her with the apparent intention of murdering her.

"No, do not hurt him."

They reluctantly lowered their weapons.

"Let me sit down you fools," she said. Even her great strength was ebbing away. She had brought them thus far on her will alone and now she needed rest.

The Dark Lord caught her and gently guided her to the benches. He took a cup from Mildur and pressed it into her hands. "Drink," he commanded.

She obeyed him and with the red wine, strength flowed back into her. "Look to the mortals," she said, but the Dalines were already offering them food and drink. "How was it you found us?" she asked Mildur.

"Great Lady, when Lord Eldest took you Dalines watched from your room of seeing. Then Nandur sent messages. Many many messages of tunnels flooded. Guessed you would use stair, only way out. Came fast on upper levels without rest. Lord Eldest Yatior looking for mortals and Lord Eldest Malcarious, not Dalines."

"Mildur, never was I so glad to see you."

"Rest, Lady. We watch."

She looked to Keré'us and Eri, already asleep on blankets the Dalines had brought and then to the Dark Lord, silent in his weariness, his head drooping as he fought sleep.

"Mildur will always watch for Great Lady."

She smiled at them. The Dark Lord, finally overcome by sleep, slipped until his head leaned against hers. Mildur would have moved him away, but she shook her head and put an arm about him, resting her face against his, and slept.

She needed but an hour to recover and woke first. "Tell me what you learned from my mirror?"

"He seeks the Elorianen, but has not picked up any trace if it."

"I did well to keep my temper and not use it."

"Great Lady, he is sure you are with mortals but cannot trace you. If you not use magic you are safe."

"He can still track me with his mind."

"Great Lady, you learned to hide from his mind long ago."

"He may still find me. Now you and your people must go. I would have you safe in Yakré'a. I do not yet know what I may have to do to keep Keré'us and his woman safe and I would not have you put at risk as well. As it is, it will take you several days to return.

Mildur bowed, "Lady, we go, not willingly."

"Go," she said firmly.

The chief of the Dalines called his men to order. They formed up and marched out of the chamber, north back to their home. The Lady thought longingly of the safety she enjoyed in Yakré'a, then looked at the Dark Lord, still drowsy, leaning on her shoulder. Perhaps there were compensations.

The mortals slept for about four hours, and when they had awoken and eaten they went on. It was a comfort to be walking in lit passages in clothes that by now were dry, except his boots, which, Keré'us thought, would probably never be dry again.

The Lady was more cautious now and tenser, as if she was straining to hear or feel something. Suddenly she stopped, "We must change levels. We must go back to that last turn, quickly. Yatior has found me! There will be soldiers on our trail! Yatior's palace is sealed so that you cannot get into it from this part of this level, and likewise they cannot get out, but we must lead as obscure a trail as we may."

She turned back and quickened her pace. The new tunnel was wider than the previous one, with black walls and a well beaten unpaved floor. As they travelled it, they noticed several doorways that had been blocked with stone.

"This runs around the outside of the palace of Yatior," explained Yannya. "He has made sure no one can enter without him knowing."

The tunnel swept round in a curve, obviously round the perimeter of the Lord Eldest Yatior's palace. The furthermost part was hidden to their view, but as they rounded the curve they saw Minrod of the One Hand waiting for them at the head of a considerable number of men.

"Back!" called the Dark Lord, who had been leading. He unsheathed Yadra.

Keré'us drew Aren and grasping Eri by the hand turned and ran. "Where do we go? There were no turnings for miles."

"There was a blocked door. Could we unblock it?" asked Eri.

"I do not know, but I am going to try," said the Lady as they reached the archway in the wall filled with regular blocks of stone. "You watch the rear," she ordered the Dark Lord, as she stood before the arch, considering it.

"I have a feeling that this may be unwise," she said, then she held out her hands and spoke one word. There was a flash of light and a thunder as the stones fell in. The tunnel behind was black. "Get down it!" she cried. Keré'us and Eri scrambled over the stones and ran boldly into the dark. The Lady stood still in the entrance to get her bearings. Outside, they could hear the pounding as Minrod and his men caught up with them. Yannya called out, "Is there a bronze ladder at the end of the passage?"

Keré'us called back, "Yes!"

"Get up it and watch your ears!"

Minrod had already reached the entrance. The Dark Lord defended it. The sound of their swords rang in the tunnel.

"Get back, Lord. I shall close this door," the Lady shouted.

The Dark Lord vaulted the heap of stones and joined her. She spoke one word again and there was a great boom. The ladder on which Keré'us and Eri still stood trembled, the walls shook and the entrance collapsed behind them. The Dark Lord, hair, eyebrows and beard grey with dust, grinned. "Well done."

"Yes," said the Lady. "I have just sealed us inside Yatior's palace."

They caught up with the mortals.

"We are now inside the palace of the Lord Eldest Yatior," the Lady explained. "We are on the domestic level, store rooms and the like. There will be Dalines here who will ignore you and men who most certainly will not. The Lord and I face another problem. We are now close enough to Yatior to..." She sought for words which could be understood. "...for him to hear our thoughts. If he finds us in this way, I shall know. If that happens, the Lord will take you on and I shall go a different way to confuse Yatior. When I was first made, I lived here and I know every part of the palace. But," she looked sternly at Keré'us, "do not use Aren except as a last resort. He will instantly pick up the Elorianen if you use it. Let the Dark Lord do the fighting."

They set off at a fair speed through the stores and cellars. In some, Dalines were working, who did not even look at them, not wishing to draw attention to the Lady.

She led the way unerringly though the maze of rooms and passages and for a little while Keré'us wondered if they would perhaps get through this dangerous area into the safer ways beyond. Then Yatior found her. She had forgotten how hard it was to resist his mind. She put her hands to her head as if to wrench the alien mind from hers and cried out to the Dark Lord. "Go, Lord, swiftly!"

"No woman, we cannot leave you."

"Fool, was this not why you brought me? Keep the Elorianen safe and I am safe. Now get you gone!" She turned back and the Dark Lord ran on with Eri and Keré'us. They scattered a party of Dalines, turned left and by pure luck found themselves on Main Stair Three. They ran down two levels and then on, south west as fast as they might. When they had struggled on for an hour or so, they rested, too exhausted to do anything but slump on the stone floor. The Dark Lord sat next to them, leaning against the tunnel wall, Yadra unsheathed on his knees.

"Will she be all right?" asked Keré'us.

"You heard her. Keep Aren safe and she is safe. My brother may catch her, but if he gives her but a moment she will escape. As the Elorianen gave her life, so it only can kill her. I tell you, it takes all the power of the Lords Eldest to keep her in Yakré'a and then she can get out when her moon is full. Moreover, they only imprisoned her because they had not the means to kill her, or they would have done so. Rest. I have never known her to be worsted." A faint smile curled his lip as a memory came to him.

CHAPTER THIRTY THREE

Yannya knew exactly where Yatior was and instead of flying from him, she went to meet him, reckoning that while she held his attention in his room of seeing, he would not be thinking about the others and they could get to a place where he would not find them easily. She dropped from the High Roads and materialised before him. It was a long time since she had been in Yatior's palace and she was not prepared for the vast room with its array of mirrors with which he watched the mines. Nor had she expected to see any other than Yatior, her erstwhile lord and master.

Yatior was seated with another at a table discussing something, presumably the mortals' progress through the mines. He rose to greet her. "Lady Yannya!" he cried, a smile spreading across his face. "How kind of you to visit me. I thought I was going to have to use force to bring you back to my domain. I trust you did not get too wet."

There was something wrong. She heard it in his voice and saw it in his demeanour. He knew they were not equally matched and in a fight she could get the better of him, especially if he was trying to watch the others at the same time. But his voice was glad, triumphant!

Then the other man stood up. "Sweet Yannya, dear Lady, what an unexpected pleasure!" The Lord Highest Eldest

Mérior, oldest and most terrible of all the Eldest, bestowed on her the most sparkling of smiles and she knew she was doomed. Without the power of the Elorianen she could not defeat the two of them and she was sure they both wanted her dead. But Aren only can kill me, she told herself, only the Elorianen can unmake me. I have started the magic and that will protect me until it comes to its proper end. Whatever they plan, they cannot destroy me. Hold hard to that! Hold hard to the knowledge of the Elorianen, the bright stone set in white platinum, hold hard to that last night of the red moon when I sent Yatior flying with it. But I dare not touch its magic here or they will find Keré'us and with him my dear lord."

She bent a dazzling smile on him. "Lord Eldest Mérior, what a pleasure. I have not seen you since we made a certain arrangement last year." If she could remind Yatior's of the plot between them, the latent jealousy of all Eldest might work for her. From his actions on the night when the magic to free Malcarious had begun she knew that Yatior had not wanted her to set it in train.

The mighty lord of all the Eldest, usurping uncle of Malcarious' throne, smiled at her. "Alas Yannya, that you would not do me the honour of being my queen."

"I told you not to let her set that magic going at the time!" said Yatior, a little sulkily. "And you ignored me!"

"Peace, nephew Fear not. She will die."

"But not here," said Yannya.

Yatior looked at his uncle, "The Elorianen stands between us all."

"Nothing will come between me and thee. I told you I was only securing her death against your brother's life, bound with magic of the Four and the One."

"And do you not understand what will happen when the Elorianen takes her soul?" demanded Yatior.

"But she has no soul. She is a copper statue given life. She is nothing. You concern yourself unnecessarily."

"By Deep Space, uncle, you have set things in motion that none of us will be able to repair."

"I do hope so," smiled Yannya.

"Fear not, nephew," said Mérior. "We shall gain breathing space to look into this further. You have forces set about this room that she cannot counter and ones that I can join." He nodded to Yatior and raised his hand. Yatior smiled and also raised a hand. The Lady was aware of the power between them, some power she had not met before. It was visible only as disturbances of the air shimmering about them and then about her. It drained her power so she could not use the High Roads, so that she could not move nor use any power of her own. Power that drained the very essence of her existence away into nothing. She clung to the sharp centre of her being and held fast to the Elorianen in her mind, but without its power she could not defeat nor flee them and she dare not risk exposing the mortals and her Lord.

"Send her to limbo," said Yatior, "until we can find a way to mend things."

"Nephew," agreed Mérior, "that suits me well, for if she breaks the agreement we have made Malcarious' life is forfeit, and imprisoned in limbo she cannot help but break it."

He raised both hands and Yannya knew only a mighty rushing wind, the burning cold and the darkness. But still she held in her mind the sharp, adamantine light that was the Elorianen.

When the mortals had recovered, the Dark Lord led them forward confidently. He was now in part of the palace he knew from days long gone, before his brother had been in open rebellion against their uncle Mérior.

At last they came to a gate which would lead them outside the palace. It was just an archway in the rock and Keré'us would have passed it without a thought.

"Wait, the gate is watched. We must not get any closer or they will see us. If both of you walk with your knees bent, trying to look like Dalines, and I change my shape a little, we may not rouse their interest, especially as the Lady is doubtless creating havoc in the main part of the palace. She must be else she would be here annoying us."

They watched, amazed, as his shape shivered slightly and seemed to shrink. Both his form and his garments changed until, instead of the tall dark haired, dark skinned Warny, he became a medium height Quarin half-breed with light brown hair and a pale skin, clad in bright fish-scale mail over a brown livery. "It is the skin tone that is hardest," he mused, "but hopefully that will not matter."

They marched boldly down the corridor, Keré'us feeling foolish. He felt a band of power, like that that had held Hréma, across the archway, but kept his mind blank and it relaxed to let them all through. They continued walking thus until they found a stair to drop to level seven. This was a poor tunnel. Many of the few lights were out and the floor was uneven. A stream ran down the side of the tunnel and they were all glad to drink from it.

"The Lady *will* find us again?" asked Eri. She had been silent most of the while, conserving her energy.

"She is as hard to hold as a handful of water," the Dark Lord reassured her. "She will find us." Eri smiled at him. His new shape amused her because he seemed so much more approachable. His whole character seemed to have changed. "Are you remaining in that guise, Lord?"

"I thought it might be useful. To be mistaken for one of my brother's men could help us."

They found a dark cave off the tunnel and hid in it to sleep, but once he did not have to hide his feelings for the mortals, a frown spread across the Dark Lord's face. He *had* expected Yannya to have returned by now.

He thought over her words. She had told him she had "an idea" to save them time, but she had not shared it with him. Which way had she meant to go? They were way south now of the East Gate. He had assumed she was making for the South Gate, but she had insisted on travelling south west and he knew they had left from the south western side of Yatior's palace. Had that only been to confuse Yatior? How could he tell?

Then, suddenly, he heard a noise in the corridor outside. Not a metal shod Daline or man, but something shuffling. He stood up, drew Yadra and walked silently towards the sound. In the dim light he could see something, human in form, staggering and limping like a soul of the unquiet dead. It was garbed in grey rags. He wondered if it was a man escaped from Yatior's dungeons. "What are you?" he demanded, holding Yadra upraised.

The creature stopped, looked about it, puzzled, as if it could not see him.

"What are you?"

"I am the one alone," it said, and its voice was almost like the voice of the Lady.

"Yani?" he said cautiously.

The creature stared at him through black wide eyes. Its hair was grey, its face old. The travesty was horrible. He backed away from it.

"Lord," it said, "I seek my Lord Malcarious. I thought he was here but he is not. Have you seen him?"

"What are you?"

"I remember now, Mildur called me Evénya, the woman of copper, when I was first made, but *they* called me the woman of fire. Yannya, Yannya the Dancer. Who are you? I must find my Lord. He is here but I cannot see him." The creature fell suddenly into a crumpled heap of grey rags. The Dark Lord stood away from it as the creature tried to crawl towards him. Then it shuddered and lay still as if it were dead. He walked towards it, just touched it with his sword and cried out, for power drained from him through the sword into the thing. He snatched his sword back, but it had stolen some of his wild magic. Slowly, as the creature lay on the tunnel floor, a light began to glow about it. The grey hair transmuted to copper. He knelt by her. "Yani!" he called urgently. "Yani!"

She opened her eyes and looked about her as if she still could not see him. "Who are you?" she whispered. Then the Dark Lord caught sight of his pale hand and let his true form flow back over him. She smiled, closed her eyes again and whispered, "Just a little more of your magic."

"As much as you need," he said gently, taking her hand. The surge of wild magic leaving him was like plunging into deep cold water. For a moment he could not breathe, but she was not greedy and took only enough to repair her own. Brightness spread through her body until, apart from her rags, she was her own golden self again.

She sat up and looked at him. "I'm cold."

He slipped off his cloak and wrapped it round her. "Yatior has learned a few things since he and your uncle made peace with each other. I was very lucky to get out of that."

"What happened?"

"I ran a few circles round them to confuse them and then went to his room of seeing, using the High Roads. I thought I would cause as much trouble as possible and take the High Road out again. What I did not realise was that your uncle was there as well as your brother. They nearly killed me."

"But?"

"I knew that only Aren could kill me, but I had a hard time believing it. One or the other I could have dealt with, without the Elorianen, but both came hard. They have a new device, a sort of force-field which drained my power. They tried to send me into limbo, but I was able to hold just enough power back so that when they sent me away into nothing. I could just cling to the centre of my being and hold to the Star-stone. They think I am somewhere in limbo now. They will not worry about you. It was never you they feared. Oh, but you confused me by shape shifting!"

"And now?"

"Now I must sleep. Where are the mortals?"

He showed her the cave and she lay down in the dark, her light all but extinguished. He took off his coat and rolled it up for a pillow.

She smiled, "Beware, lord. Show me no charity lest you come to regret it later."

Keré'us awoke first. When he saw the Lady, he was delighted. The Dark Lord put a finger to his lips, "Hush, she must get some sleep. She needs rest, probably more than we can afford her. When Eri wakes we must go on."

When Eri woke, he shook the Lady into awareness and she looked about her. "Must we go on?" she yawned.

"I am afraid so."

"Then we must, but I must have something to drink."

Keré'us took a goblet the Dalines had left with them and scooped water from the little stream outside the cave and she drank deep. Then, pausing for a moment to get her bearings, she led them on.

They had walked for about an hour and changed direction at several junctions, when they heard a strange rumbling sound, which grew as they walked into a clinking and groaning. They turned into a narrow unlit tunnel and came on a strange sight. By the light of the Lady they could see a huge tunnel through which rolled two lines of metal cars. One line rolled on downhill, filled with ore and the other line, that closest to them, ran uphill, empty. It was an endless chain.

"What is it?" asked Keré'us.

"Our way out. High on the Aré'las lodes, this side of the Gate, the cars are filled with ore. Their weight takes them down hill to the furnaces at the East Gate and pulls the empty ones back to the lodes. It is very simple and we shall just sit in the empty cars and be pulled up to the Aré'las. No one will think to look for us here and we shall leave the cars before they reach their destination. It may be dirty and uncomfortable, but at least we shall not have to walk."

The cars banged and jolted as they moved. They seemed to run on a single rail set in the ground, as no wheels were visible. The part in which they had to sit was triangular in section, suspended from an upright at either end, with a brake to control the tipping. The Dark Lord lifted Eri into one and Keré'us scrambled in after her. Yannya chose her own car, but after some hesitation, the Dark Lord joined her and watched while she and the mortals slept.

At first when they woke, they were glad of the rest, but they had to spend more than a day riding the ore cars. The Dalines had given them food and a flask for water, but even though this was full when they began the journey, it was hardly enough for the two mortals. The Lady and the Dark Lord refused it every time it was offered.

"How much longer?" asked the Dark Lord as the mortals slept again.

"Soon. When we leave the cars we shall have perhaps two marches. I shall take you to a little gate to the west of the South Gate. There is no point in attracting trouble by going to a main gate. You must come back with me to Yakré'a on the High Roads and get clothes and food for them. It will be deep winter outside and very cold. They will have forgotten how cold, for the mines are never cold. I shall get a message to Melin so he sends men out to look for them. I wish I could use the High Roads back to Yakré'a now to do that, but I dare not let them know I am still alive.

"You might ask yourself, when you have the time to give the matter your full consideration, what your uncle is doing in association with your brother."

The Dark Lord smiled, "Clinging desperately to my crown."

"I thought all Eldest wanted to be the Lord Highest."

"Not I, nor Gawen."

"Yet you are the true heir of Vallior. Your mother was High Queen of Ungarit."

"I do not remember my mother, save sometimes in dreams."

"I understand that she was very beautiful. Yatior once told me she had a skin as black as ebony, black eyes and hair as dark as her eyes, but so tightly curled it was like a halo about her head. Mara, queen of Ungarit. Yatior said the Elorianen once belonged to her royal house. If so, in all truth, it belongs to you."

"Fear not, I shall not take it from your little lord of Abard."

CHAPTER THIRTY FOUR

Finally, the lady chose the moment for them to leave the cars. They were all glad to be walking again. She led them to a stair and they began to climb. Seven stairs to reach the main level and then four more. Even the Dark Lord was tired when they gained the upper fourth level and they rested for a while. Then the Lady led them on at a brisk pace for some hours before she let them rest.

"In a few hours," she told them, "you will be out of the mines and I shall be obliged to return to the safety of my prison. The Dark Lord will come back to Yakré'a with me to fetch food and warm clothes for you, for there is thick snow on the mountains outside. We are about to go south, turn east up a tiny stair to a half level, then due east and you will see daylight for the first time in many days. At least, I have no idea whether it will be night or day outside. I lost count long ago."

"It will be night," said the Dark Lord, "your moon will be nearly full."

"I find it hard to believe that there is any world outside the mountains," said Keréus.

"Come, only a few hours more and I shall prove it to you."

So they went on. As they mounted the spiral stair, the quality of the air began to change. It was no longer dry and stale but cold and smelt of frost. They were all eager now and pressed on swiftly.

Then Yannya cried out, "No!"

Before them materialised the Lord Eldest Yatior, bright and glorious. A cruel lord who was just about to accomplish his most desired aim, to take the Elorianen and destroy his brother.

The surprise of seeing Yannya there when he thought she had been imprisoned in limbo gave her moment enough to call, "Keré'us, give me Aren and get you gone swiftly. There are no more turns. The way is straight!"

He gave her the sword but no light came from it, for she was conserving her strength. The Dark Lord, knowing how weak she was, caught hold of her and she leaned against him for a space, then pushed him away to stand straight and proud before her enemy.

The mortals fled down the tunnel. It grew narrower and narrower until they had to bend double. Then they saw a patch of moon light which marked the end of the mines. They squeezed through a hole and dropped several feet into a great drift of snow. All the sights and smells of the real world smote their senses. The mountains were silver wrapped in snow and the cold like a physical barrier. They laughed and were glad and threw great handfuls of snow at each other like children, for they were free!

But in the mines the Lord Eldest Yatior, not caring about the mortals, for they no longer had anything he wanted, faced his recalcitrant concubine and thought that even though she had tricked him and his uncle and returned to the world, she was too weak to defeat him now. Even though she held Aren, with the Elorianen bright in the hilt, he would send her back to limbo and end the chaos he had so unwittingly begun when he had used it to give her life. But he had reckoned without his brother. His fallen brother whom he had imprisoned and tortured in these very mines.

Lord and Lady, sworn enemies now, but with him as common foe.

The Lady lifted Aren, holding hilt and blade, and the Dark Lord put his hands over hers in a move that was almost a caress. She leaned against him, for she was weak, but he stood firm and supported her. His wild magic flowed through her and with what little remained of her power, she turned it against Yatior. Malcarious' strength gave her strength. The tunnel glowed with red and orange, green and purple light. The whole spectrum of their power burnt out from the Elorianen towards Yatior and with their minds they bade him be gone.

He could not counter them. It was as it had been on the night of the red moon but worse. This was no little magic of mortal men, but the whole of his brother's wild magic directed by the creature he had created and learned to fear. He took the High Roads back to his fastness by the East Gate.

The Dark Lord gathered the Lady in his arms and took her back to her palace-prison of Yakré'a, where she gave him the goods she had promised the mortals and put Aren into his hands. Then he should have gone, but he lingered and said, "Farewell Lady, I would you had always treated me as fairly." And he took her hand and kissed it.

But she looked at him with eyes which could not be read and said, "You may yet be sorry."

By sheer good fortune, or perhaps Mildur had warned him, Hara the prince of the Merédur was flying along the mountains, and saw the mortals and the Dark Lord struggling in the snow. He joined them swiftly. "Melin waits you at the Eldraede falls. I thought perhaps the mortals would welcome a flight with me, especially the maid."

"Not so much maid as mother," said Eri, her spirits returning, "but if you would carry me I should be more than grateful"

"I shall fly low, so fear not," said Hara, and lifted her. She clasped her arms about his neck and they flew to Melin's camp. Then Hara returned for Keré'us. Of all the things Keré'us had done in the last few years, flying with Hara was the most thrilling. He was sorry when it was over. Never again would he see the moonlit mountains under snow from such a vantage point. When he reached Melin's camp, the Dark Lord was already there. Melin welcomed Keré'us as he would his son, and they travelled on to the Gate on the small, hardy horses that the Quaren used, the Dark Lord on foot until S'elrashen appeared to serve him. At the Gate they over-wintered and it seemed to Keré'us that after so long running, he would at last have a chance to rest.

At the end of the year, the Dark Lord went north, to take news to Derany and attend the Spring Meeting of the Trumarei. Keré'us waited a little longer, but on the first day of early spring he set out on a journey he hoped would be his last until it was safe to return to his little daughter in Ebrinen. Melin loaded him with gifts and Eri, plump in pregnancy, followed her lord south, first to see Selin in Kindarth and then on to André'as.

Selin was delighted to see them. He had heard of the city's foundation already from a letter Derany sent him, but wanted to hear all Keré'us had to tell about it. He showed Keré'us his kingdom, with its two cities, and his blond wife and blond son, now a sturdy youngster. Then he accompanied Keré'us as he rode on to Loréas, to see Herumanus. It was hardly more than a city state, for it comprised only the magnificent natural harbour surrounded by a city well fortified against the rest of André'as, who desired it so much. It was long since Keré'us had smelt the sea and with the joy of a man coming home, he watched the ships and wondered if, when he reached Ranhé'us, the Sea-lord would really expect him to lead an expedition against his father's ships. He might have been half Quarinya queen, but the rest of him was pure Darké'us and the idea sounded amusing. Herumanus joined them to go south through André'as.

The days ran by. Moons waxed and waned. The grass was green, covered with drifts of yellow and purple crocuses on the downlands, which changed to daffodils and narcissi in yellow and white clouds as they reached the little lakes and hills of the borders of Ranhé'us' own kingdom.

Here Ranhé'us, Anya and their first born son Marcé'us were waiting to greet them and there were great celebrations spoilt only by the absence of the Dark Lord and Derany.

Eventually, Selin and Herumanus excused themselves on the grounds that kingdoms do not run themselves and Keré'us and Eri followed Ranhé'us south, through the increasingly rugged landscape.

It was on the first day of early summer that they entered Mangawen, and the city was hung with flags to welcome their king back. Ranhé'us rode into his little town with as much pride as the Lord over Banéros had of his city. He waved to his subjects, calling after them, for he knew all their names, and they waved and shouted back. The grey walled town closed round Keré'us as might the arms of his mother. It welcomed him as if it had waited long for him. The houses of cobble and brick, decked with window boxes of flowers, seemed to be all the home a man ever needed. The smell of the sea and fish was omnipresent and reminded him, however briefly, of Mundra and his own ship. For a wild moment he almost regretted his loss, but he glanced at Eri and thought of Nenya, safe with Derany, and knew that had come home. It was farewell to the Dark Lord, farewell to Four and the One, no more wealth or kingdoms. He would be a farmer fisherman, as was Ranhé'us, with perhaps a little piracy on the side.

Ranhé'us gave them rooms in his palace until the title of the lands he intended to give Keré'us could be transferred, but Keré'us spent his time in the harbour, looking at the tall Eye-ships, the fast Sea-kingdom ships which have painted eyes on the bows, that they may see their way. It was not long before he had a deck moving under his feet again and although he feared the loss of his craft, once he and Ranhé'us had the *Dolphin*, Ranhé'us' flagship, under way, it was as if he had never left the sea. There was a reasonable north-easterly wind, so they took the *Dolphin* to the furthermost south of André'as, a long grey rock which ran out from Mangawen.

"The rock of Hope," shouted Ranhé'us over the noise of the ship, "the Abard Rock they call it. They say if you see it as you round the point, there is hope you will get into Mangawen. If you don't see it you are probably about to founder on it!"

Keré'us made no answer, for in that moment it was brought home to him that the Lord Eldest Gawen had demanded his son be sacrificed to him there, on that rock.

He remembered the Lady, what seemed a lifetime ago, promising him but one son. And Eri so close to her time.

"What's the matter?" asked Ranhé'us, looking at him in alarm.

"Nothing you can help me with," said Keré'us, "but you have reminded me of something I am bound to do against my will. Turn the ship about and let us go back."

That night as he lay in bed and the limbs of his unborn child kicked against him, Keré'us thought over and over again of the Lord Eldest Gawen and prayed to the Lady that she might somehow take this burden from him. But no answer came to him.

Summer came, and Eri's time was almost on her. Keré'us had still had no word from the Lady Yannya or the Dark Lord and he knew not what to do. This was one burden he could not share with Eri. How could he tell his woman that one of the Eldest required he should murder their unborn child?

In the evening of the ninth day of summer, Eri was brought to bed and Anya sent her midwife to her and sat with the girl herself. Keré'us talked to Eri for a little, but he was in the way of the women and they told him it would not be for some little time yet. So Ranhé'us took him out to the nearest tavern and they remained there, amusing themselves as men, do until the landlord made it obvious that he wanted to close and go to bed, but the presence of his lord prevented this.

When they returned to the palace, Eri's room was lit by one sole candle. Anya was still by her bed. "It will be a long time yet," she whispered. "Go to bed, if anything happens I shall wake you. Eri is sleeping."

"Is there anything wrong? Surely it should not take so long?"

"It might have taken three hours, it may take two days, without any harm coming to her. Don't worry Keré'us, she is in good hands."

Keré'us left but he could not sleep; instead he went to the sea shore and walked by the waves. The silver moon was almost full, but the red moon was dark. He felt alone and helpless and he missed the comforting presence of the Dark Lord.

The next day dragged on. They let Keré'us see Eri, but not for long. He thought she was growing weaker, but they tried to quiet his fears. Towards evening, Anya came to him. "As you may have realised, things are not going too well. We have sent for a doctor who lives at Raga. He will be here soon. Go and speak to Eri and comfort her, but do not let her know we are anxious.

So Keré'us followed her back and spoke softly with Eri. She talked a little but he left her when he realised how tired she was. The wind began to build up into a gale that night and in the morning when Keréus woke, there was a terrible storm raging. The sea was lashed into great mountains of water which thrashed the quay. He and Ranhé'us were out all day trying to secure the Eye-ships and by nightfall, exhausted by their efforts, they returned to the palace to be met by Anya, who was about to come to search for them. From her face Keré'us could see that things were bad.

"She's had a boy, Keré'us, but you must come quickly. They think she is dying!"

Her words only confirmed the cold fear in his heart. He dropped the tackle he was carrying and ran after Anya.

Eri lay still and pale on the bed, the swaddled bundle of their son in her arms. She was hardly conscious.

He said, "Eri, Eri," and took her hand. She smiled at him.

"I have borne you a son," she said proudly, "now I must sleep." She gave a deep sigh and closed her eyes. The dark haired baby stirred hungrily. Keré'us lifted him from Eri and her arms fell limply back. Then he realised that she was dead. He looked wildly round him, at the doctor, the midwives, at Ranhé'us and Anya.

"She is dead!" he said and he began to weep, for she had never asked anything of him, only to be with him, and she had given him his son and now even his son must die. He stood up, holding the baby tightly to him, and turned to the door, intending to go back out into the storm. But in the doorway, before them all stood the Dark Lord, grim as death. He held out his arms for the child. "Come," he said, "we are not done with death tonight." He strode out of the room and through the palace, with Keré'us running at his heels. They crossed the town to the harbour and went on westward, along the shore, scrambling and slipping on the wet rocks until they stood on the long grey rock, the Abard Rock. As the Dark Lord gave the child back to Keré'us, it whimpered, a poor creature without even a name.

"My brother waits for you."

"Lord, thank you for all you have done for me. If you see the Lady, thank her as well for me."

"She could not have stopped Eri dying," said the Dark Lord, unexpectedly defending his enemy. "If she could have done, she would, but she can only twist fate, not alter it."

"Goodbye then," said Keré'us. The Dark Lord's keen eyes looked into his, "No," he said, "this is not goodbye, not for you. Now go and do what my brother demands and I shall wait for you."

"Do not wait too long," said Keré'us, and he walked

along the rock until the rising tide reached about his knees and he held the child out over the waters and called out. "Lord Eldest Gawen, as I promised you, so I have come. This is my son, my firstborn son, and such that he is, I give him to you. But one thing I ask, take my life as well. You who are neither merciful, nor kind, show me mercy tonight and take my life as well, for there cannot be any gladness in it ever again."

Then out of the sea, out of the foam and wrack and thundering waves, came the Lord Eldest Gawen, his robes swirling in the wind, his mantle of power bright about him. The child cried and Keré'us hugged it against him, for even now he loved it.

"Keré'us, Lord of the House of Abard, you who shall bring doom to the world. Mighty as I am, there are others mightier still and the Lady has forbidden me to take your son. She says that your House has a part to play that none other can fill, for you alone of all men can bear Aren. Therefore, out of my love for her, I shall not demand this sacrifice of you. Your son shall not die now, but this hold I shall have over your House, you who wear my Sea-stone. When I call you at your life's end, you shall come to me and die here. In return, the power of the Sea-stone is yours. Now let me bless this son of yours and name him, and all others of your line shall also bring their first born sons here to be named. This rock is called the Abard Rock. It was named for your House before you existed and that shall be its name until the world ends.

"Now I name your son Abarté'us, hope, for hope is not false and may he be a good son to you, strong of heart and full of the deep laughter of your people."

The sea rose up into a great wave, which touched Keréus and his son Abarté'us, but harmed them not. Then the swell died away, the sea was empty and the clouds cleared. When the baby cried, Keré'us hugged him closer. The silver moon sailed silent in the sky. He turned and in the north east, over the mountains, the first hair thin crack of the new red moon rose.

The Lord of the House of Abard, carefully holding the second of his line, made his way to the shore where the Dark Lord was waiting.

THIS IS THE END OF THE HISTORY OF
THE FIRST LORD OF THE HOUSE OF ABARD
IT IS NOT THE END OF THE TALE

APPENDICES

The Lords Eldest and Naru

Before the world of Naru was formed the Eldest were. They travelled from world to world, sacking them, taking the female guardian and spirits and goddesses as concubines, murdering the gods, leaving the mortals to fend for themselves. Destroying all. And thus it was that they came to Ungarit on the furthermost arm of their own galaxy.

The guardian spirit of Ungarit was Mara. She was young and strong and she had a talisman, the most powerful magic that anyone had ever known, bound in a white stone, which her world called the Elorianen, the Star-stone, and with it she held the Eldest at bay.

Mara had a brother, Algol. They both realised that if the Eldest were driven away from Ungarit, they would go on to sack other worlds. So Mara sent Algol, with the Elorianen to protect him, across deep space to the next place the Eldest would attack, the galaxy of Acré'on. Here he warned the guardian spirits, the Shining Ones, of the danger of the Lords Eldest to their lower worlds. He gave them the Star-stone on his sister's orders, so that they might protect their lower worlds. The Shining Ones were very grateful for his help and grateful to Mara who had thus sacrificed her life and her world to save theirs. They set up a trap for the Lords Eldest. They made a world to tempt them on the very edge of the galaxy, the world of Naru, and about it set a shield of power with but one gate through which the Eldest would enter. The Elorianen controlled this gate.

The youngest of the Shining Ones, Zarazinnya, the one alone, took on herself the task of guardian spirit of Naru, and others offered her their help. Mildur, Lord Youngest of the Dalinei came with his kin. Mehara the Merédur, came with his wife and children, Hara and S'elora, his brother Lara, his wife and their cousin Tarca, the winged ones. Also came the Lords Youngest Erueth, led by Amunrhoieneth. And that it might seem an ordinary world, there were mortals too, from the lower worlds, many tribes, who came to the Lady Zarazinnya's aid out of love for her and the other Shining Ones. Algol gave Zarazinnya the Elorianen, that she might escape through the gate if the need arose, for alone on Naru there would be no other help for her. Then the Shining Ones made the magic, which bound the world of Naru, so that should misfortune befall Zarazinnya, the trap would shut and the world of Naru close forever with the Eldest bound inside. The Shining Ones were just, they could not punish the Eldest for a crime they had not yet committed, they had to give them the benefit of the doubt before binding them forever.

The Eldest left Ungarit and with them took Mara the queen, to be the Lord Eldest Vallior's concubine. In their ship they set out through deep space to the next world. But Vallior loved Mara, and took her as his legal wife, although she hated him. In deep space she bore him a son, Malcarious, and then she died, for she was far from the world she loved and she grew weaker and weaker as time passed and her world was lost to her forever.

And so, in time, the Eldest came to Naru, and dwelt there, led by Alvious, their High Lord. The Shining Ones saw all was true as Algol said, and the Eldest as wicked as they were reported, and they begged Zarazinnya to leave Naru, but she would not, for she had come to love that world and feared that her absence might warn the Eldest, and the trap might not shut.

The day came when the Eldest could no longer stand her preventing them from doing as they willed to the Lords Youngest and mortals and they went to Zarazinnya to murder her, and when she died the portal shut forever and the rest of the lower worlds were saved.

When Zarazinnya died, Alvious took the Elorianen and would have used it on his kinsmen to subdue them, but his son Vallior slew him and took it. His son Yatior rebelled against him and was exiled to the mines under the mountains in Naru, of which Mildur had been the lord. He compelled Mildur to make all manner of treasures for him and because he was lonely for a woman, he made Mildur make a woman in copper. But try as he would he could not bring her to life and so prevailed upon his father to lend him the Elorianen to use its magic.

Thus Yannya was brought to life, and all the Lords Eldest desired her. Vallior was so enamoured of her he offered Yatior the Star-stone in exchange, but Yatior took it then slew him. Mérior, brother of Vallior and uncle to Yatior, Gawen and Malcarious became lord of the Eldest. However, Yatior was not noticeably punished, nor did he claim the lordship as he might, but he did make the gesture of returning the Elorianen to his uncle to avoid further trouble. This, however, was not the real Star-stone, but a copy. Yatior told Mérior that all the power from the Elorianen had gone into Yannya. At this point in time, since Mérior had never handled the Star-stone and did not know its nature, he believed his nephew.

Malcarious saw Yannya brought to life and fell in love with her, but he kept his love secret because she was his brother's concubine and slave.

Then Yannya rebelled against the way she was used and with the aid of Mildur, took the Elorianen from Yatior and had it forged into a copper sword, Hiruéven. The Eldest spent all their time in internecine wars and the use of any weapon save a sword and magic was forbidden, in order to reduce the casualties, although the Lords Eldest were, in any case, very hard to kill and had marvellous recuperative powers. With the aid of Hiruéven Yannya was able to protect herself and begin to take her place in the politics of Naru. Gawen and Malcarious, together with Hara and Amunrhoieneth came to be her close friends and allies, and Malcarious became her lover, much to the chagrin of the others, especially the Lady Eldest Félanya, who had previously been his lover. Mildur remained with Yannya as her steward, despite her associations with the Lords Eldest.

Then Yatior "stole" the Diadem of the Eldest from Merior. As eldest son of Vallior he had a right to it, although because he had killed his father, most thought he was disqualified and it should belong to Malcarious. (Gawen did not count because his mother had been a minor sea spirit) Malcarious, Amunrhoieneth, Hara and Gawen were tricked by Mérior into trying to get the Diadem back, Yannya joined their side. But Malcarious was captured and in order to save his life Yannya had to appear to be on Yatior's side. With Malcarious safely in prison both Mérior and Yatior offered her marriage to gain the Elorianen and, so they hoped, to use it to escape from Naru. Deviously she agreed with Yatior not to marry Mérior, provided Malcarious was not hurt, although she would have to make it appear that she was on Yatior's side again by branding him with her mark, and agreed with Mérior not to marry Yatior, in exchange for which he would grant her Malcarious' life. Yatior knew she had the real Star-stone, but let her hold it, knowing by now its true nature.

Mérior cheated her and granted her Malcarious' life as a prisoner of Yatior.

Yannya gave Hiruéven to the Quarenyos queens, thus it fell out of the sight of the Lords Eldest, for the Queens could not use its magic powers. Then she shape shifted to appear to be a Daline, calling herself Mildur's daughter and freed the Dark Lord from the mines, managing to bring Yadra his sword with her. Nanenethen, her friend, sent her brother, Kaerhoieneth, to get Warany to look after Malcarious, but the Lords Eldest took him back and tried him and he was condemned to mortality. He wandered the lands of Avenya, now known as the Dark Lord, since his Eldest name has been taken away, growing old, until Yannya made a contract with Mérior, offering her own life in exchange for his. This time she made the agreement with the help of Darké'us and bound it with magic, so that she could not be cheated again. The magic began in the days of the first Lord of the House of Abard, Keré'us and ended in those of the last, Kerin

Warned by Yatior's curious behaviour, Mérior realised something untoward would happen if Yannya died and he did not call on her to fulfil the contract. However, following the terrible injury she received at the hands of the Erueth at the time when Ebrinen fell, she knew her days were numbered and set the final magic in motion that brought about her death and the redemption of Malcarious.

The Tenets of the Eldest

The Eldest had rules by which they were obliged to live and which they kept with a few notable exceptions. It is believed that Zarazinnya bound the Eldest to the tenets when they came to Naru, but they generally adhered to them and might have brought the rules with them.

They might not kill mortals (unless they really had to)

They might not sleep with mortals (Gawen, who was not technically a Lord Eldest had his own arrangements under these rules)

Eldest magic could not harm mortals.

Mortals could not be taken on the High Roads. (The fast invisible paths the Eldest used)

The minds of mortals could not be read, although the Eldest might talk mind to mind with each other.

Those with part mortal blood, generally who were descended from the Lords Youngest, and the Lords Youngest themselves were considered fair game.

Mortal magic could not harm Eldest.

No female child born to the Eldest, save one of full Eldest blood was permitted to survive. Sons of half blood were accepted as equal to sons of full blood, their rank being determined by their mother's rank. Thus Malcarious, whose mother was a goddess, outranked his older half-brother Gawen, whose mother was a mere sea nymph.

The Peoples of Avenya.

Languages

Like many old languages Quarin, and to a degree the common tongue, declined. Thus the plural of Quarin is Quaren (masculine) and Quarinya, Quarenyos (feminine). Trumaré caries the plural Trumarei and feminine is Yana, Yanai. The plural of Daline is Dalines in the common tongue but Dalinei in Classical Quarin.

Because the alphabet for both Quarin and the common tongue is phonetic, some names are difficult to transcribe into English and I have resorted to the é where the e is short, but this is not immediately obvious, as in Banéros and Mérior, and in names where the last e is sounded, Keré'us, Darké'us etc. In the names of the people belonging to a country or city in the plural the s becomes th so the inhabitants of Banéros are Banérothen, singular and plural and of Kindath (previously known as Kindaros), are Kindathen.

The Quaren

The Quaren were an agrarian people, mostly cultivating the vast Avenyan plains. They tended to dwell in cities and very large villages. Their chief city was Banéros the Beautiful and they traded across the seas from there. They were skilled metal workers and masons, great road builders and traders. They were ruled by the Queens, although the cities tended to have a city lord in control, but responsible to the Queen. Towards the end of their dominance over Avenya they overran the lands of many of the other peoples of Avenya, supporting a large standing army to do this. As a people they were cynical, luxurious, mostly out for profit, but not cruel. They did, however, run a well controlled empire, well policed and ruled with a light hand. Their chief crime in the eyes of the Lords Eldest was that they had taken the Lady Yannya as their goddess, not one of the Ladies Eldest, although they did worship other Eldest, particularly Gawen and Mérior.

They were short, slight with brown hair and brown or yellow eyes. Red hair was usually a sign of royal birth. They did not live as long as other races of Avenya and were lucky if they reached sixty.

The Warny
The Warny were not an indigenous people of Avenya. Long ago they had come across the sea and settled on the land where the Aré'las mountains met the coast, and built their Grey Halls, a stone city, as a stronghold against any who would dare threaten them. They slowly took over the lands known as the High Aré'las plains and mostly herded cattle and horses there. They did grow corn, but only as much as they needed and worked their own metals, but it was easier to buy what they needed from the Quaren. They were ruled by a Prince (latterly a Steward Prince) who was descended from Wargarny, their first lord. They were hard men, tall and usually with pale faces, dark hair and blue eyes. The women were beautiful and skilled at all the feminine arts, although they would fight beside their men if called upon.

They lived far longer than the Quaren, many to one hundred or more, and generally had a reputation of being old and sage. They were skilled fighters on horseback. They worshipped the Lords Eldest as far as they worshipped any god. They preferred to think that their own skill and wisdom would protect them. On the far side of the Aré'las the Lords Youngest Erueth lived and these very much influenced the Warny. When Nanenethen, the niece of the ruler of the Erueth, was stolen by a necromancer, it was to the Warny they sent to rescue her.

When the Lords Eldest decided that the Quaren were too powerful, it was via the Erueth that they sent for Warany to form the Alliance and defeat the Quaren, giving him Nanenethen as his bride in reward.

The Elta

The Elta were a tall, silver blond race with grey or blue eyes and very pale skins who originally lived in the marshes of the central plains of Avenya. They wove linen and were famed for the borders they created on their fabrics. Their cooking was terrible, they boiled everything, they drank beer and generally disapproved of everything. More necromancers and sorcerers came from Elta stock than any other. They had a single minded hardness. They preferred justice to mercy.

They were almost as long lived as the Warny. They worshipped the harder Lords and Ladies Eldest.

The André'ans

South of the Aré'las mountain was André'as, a wide variety of small states divided into the Sea-kingdoms and the rest.

The Sea-kingdoms

These made a living by subsistence farming and fishing with a certain amount of piracy on the side. They were famous sailors, and infamous pirates. They looked similar to the Warny, being tall with dark hair, but their eyes were green and brown. The ruling house of the High King, Ruén was descended fro the Lord Eldest Gawen and although they could not turn into a bear when annoyed as Gawen habitually did, they took the black bear as their standard. They were not as long lived as the Warny, but more so than the Quaren. Quick to anger and as quick to forgive, they had been hardened only by the poverty of their land. They worshipped the Lord Eldest Gawen and the women worshipped Yannya, but did not mention it except to each other. The Quaren never conquered them, there was no profit in it, but taxed them heavily on their exports of salt and iron.

The Upper Kingdoms of André'as

There were various kingdoms ranging from Mundra with a continental climate down to Kindath, all warmed by the equivalent of the gulf stream. Mundra was especially attractive to the Quaren as the wine it produced was the best in Avenya (Visualise, or rather, taste a Cote du Rhone fringed by Chateauneuf du Pape). Further south Pelelorne and Mordarta produced the Bourgognes and St Emilions. The Quaren took control of these very early on, expanding the empire through the Gate, driving the great road along the south of the Aré'las and taking all the north eastern lands. There was, consequently, a great deal of unrest amongst in the Upper Kingdoms of André'as. The Quaren had thoughtfully kept the main families of all these lands in power as puppet kings, but when the Warny rebelled, these too rebelled, to keep all the profits for themselves. They were mostly of mongrel race, brown hair with any coloured eyes and longer lived than the Quaren, though not as long as the Warny or Elta. Since none of the Lords Eldest realised wine came from plants, most of the André'ans worshipped local spirits and the Lady Yannya who understood exactly how things worked.

The Halucias

These were tribes who followed their herds, living in yurts. The were very close kin to the Quaren, but had black hair and dark eyes, although they were of the same slight, short lived build. They did not weave, nor smithy, trading beautifully worked skins for these goods. They rode the same stocky ponies as the Quaren, but did not shoe them. There were eleven tribes, all named for animals, of whom the Gerhart, the grey wolves, were the chief. The Quaren left them well alone, since they were very unreliable about borders but Warany persuaded them to join the Alliance to defeat the Quaren. They continued to be unreliable.

Main Houses of Avenya

There are six main Lords of Avenya. The first was the House of Wargarny, ruling house of the Warny. After the death of Warany it split into the Steward Princes, descended through his second son, Terany, and the bearers of Erindra descended through his oldest son, Derany City Founder. Warany, recognising the dangers of power, forbade Derany to take the Princedom. All descendents in the true line are, however, known as the Sons of Warany. All wear a replica of the Troth-stone except the true heir of Warny, who carries Erindra. Their last Lord was Wargos, lord of the Lywarny who dwelt in Irranya when Yannya died.

The House of Deranin was the house of the rulers of Kindath, descended from Hara's sister, S'elorah. They bore the sword of power Kaeordra, and could be recognised by the white lock of hair on their foreheads. They were a scholarly family, interested in law and history for its own sake. The last Lord was Mendas, childless ruler of Irranya at the time when Yannya died.

The House of Ruén was descended from the Lord Eldest Gawen. This was the house of the Sea-kings of André'as. They were mostly pirates. They bore the sword of power, Garenmegra. The last lord was Ranhé'us, who had only a daughter, Anya, to follow him.

The Lords of the House of Abard were responsible only to the Lady Yannya and Lord Eldest Malcarious. In the iron sword, Aren, was set the Elorianen, the most powerful talisman known throughout the universe. This belonged to the Lady Yannya by acquisition and the Lord Malcarious by birth. In the beginning there was a separate Lady of the House of Abard and Lord, descending from Keré'us' daughter Nenya and son Abarté'us. These were amalgamated after the fall of Ebrinen, when the last Lady, Arhoiethenya, bore a daughter to Tarca the Merédur who married the Lord of Abard whom the couple had rescued from the fall of Ebrinen as an infant. The last Lord of the House of Abard was Kerin, Lord of the Keltos, who with the other lords was there when Yannya called in the magic and died to protect the Dark Lord.

The last house was that of Darké'us, variously of Belia and Irranyan Mundra. This descended from Keré'us half brother Darké'us. Timeserver, turncoat, call them what you will, when the chips are down, if they are on your side, you will win. If not, of course, you will not. Dakin was their last son and had the distinction to be the only one who died in bed. They bore a sword made by Mildur, but unlike the swords of power, the blade was steel and it had no magic, but a very sharp edge. From time to time, when something untoward had happened to his own sword, the Lord Eldest Malcarious carried this sword.